"Does this hurt?" Asher asked, bending Jane's foot back a little.

It hurt like hell, but she was pleasantly distracted by his touch. "A little," she said.

He knew exactly how much pressure to apply as he moved her foot around. He moved his hand up her ankle again, probing it. "I don't think anything is broken." He lifted his gaze to hers and for one slender moment, Jane believed she felt a spark between them.

Then again, it seemed that she—silly girl that she was—had imagined it, because Asher looked down and put her foot on the ground. "Let me help you up," he said and stood, reaching his hand out to her. Jane slipped her hand into his; he closed his fingers tightly around hers, put his other hand around her waist, and helped her stand. "What do you think?" he asked as Jane tested her weight on the ankle.

She thought her heart was going to jump right out of her chest. He held her so easily, so securely, and his body was hard against her. The sensation was intoxicating and maddening—what was she doing? "It's okay," she said. "I think I can walk." She needed to step away from him, breathe some air, find her bearings again.

"A heartbreaker of a romance. . . . London's characters continue to be fully crafted and very real."
—*Romantic Times* on *Summer of Two Wishes*

Also by Julia London

Julia London

ONE SEASON *of* SUNSHINE

POCKET BOOKS

New York   London   Toronto   Sydney   New Delhi

Pocket Books
A Division of Simon & Schuster, Inc.
1230 Avenue of the Americas
New York, NY 10020

This book is a work of fiction. Any references to historical events, real people, or real places are used fictitiously. Other names, characters, places, and events are products of the author's imagination, and any resemblance to actual events or places or persons, living or dead, is entirely coincidental.

This Pocket Books paperback edition July 2020

POCKET and colophon are registered trademarks of Simon & Schuster, Inc.

For information about special discounts for bulk purchases, please contact Simon & Schuster Special Sales at 1-866-506-1949 or business@simonandschuster.com.

The Simon & Schuster Speakers Bureau can bring authors to your live event. For more information or to book an event, contact the Simon & Schuster Speakers Bureau at 1-866-248-3049 or visit our website at www.simonspeakers.com.

Manufactured in the United States of America

10 9 8 7 6 5 4 3 2 1

ISBN 978-1-9821-3192-0
ISBN 978-1-4391-6891-2 (ebook)

For Kathleen Givens. She knows why.

ACKNOWLEDGMENTS

I would like to acknowledge the insight and help of Carol Pierce-Davis, Ph.D. I don't think she fully realized she was doing it at the time, but in allowing me to pepper her with questions and a lot of what-ifs, her wisdom and knowledge of psychology helped me to form these characters.

ONE SEASON
of SUNSHINE

PROLOGUE

*C*olors are exploding over Susanna's head, shades of blue and pink and red, splashing around her, on her, in her. A man's hand slides under the hem of her silk dress, the sensation of it warm and slippery, like a snake. "Come on, baby, let's go."

His breath is hot and smells of beer. Who is he— Ash? No, not Ash. Ash is too plain, too dull, too staid. *Boring*. He can't see color like Susanna sees it. He can't see the radiance or the subtle nuances in the sheen of colors. He doesn't know that capturing that on canvas is what makes a good painting really great. Susanna wants to paint *these* colors, the ones swirling around her and splashing inside her, lighting her up, making her glow.

The man's hand inches higher. Susanna pushes it away and slides off her stool, stumbling.

"You're drunk. Let me drive you home."

Stupid, he's so stupid. "I'm not drunk! I'm *alive*! I want to paint this!"

"Paint what?"

"*This,*" she cries impatiently, flinging her arms to the ceiling, twirling around in a shaft of green and yellow and pink.

"Okay, all right, we'll paint," the man says. He grabs

her arm. "Just sit tight and let me see a man about a horse, huh? Then we'll go paint whatever you want to paint, baby. I got a few ideas of my own."

He laughs low. She feels his hand again, sliding up the side of her breast. It sets Susanna on fire, makes her want to take her clothes off here and now and have him touch her everywhere.

Not yet. First, she has to paint. She *must* paint before she forgets this. She picks up her beaded clutch, notices the colors above reflecting back at her in the little crystals of her bag. Paint *now* before she loses it. Susanna walks out of the Rawhide to her car, swaying a little.

She heads toward Highway 16 and turns right, onto a long, two-lane stretch through the Hill Country, gaining speed. The night is clear and cold, but Susanna doesn't feel it; she feels hot. She opens the moonroof of her Mercedes, looks up, and gasps with astonishment. The stars are burning bright over her head, a brilliance of diamond white exploding on velvet black. Just like the ideas in her head, brilliant thoughts and ideas exploding, crowding each other for breath.

She can reach the stars. It is an old cliché, but Susanna believes she can really do it and puts one arm through the moonroof. No, no, not close enough. She kicks off one Christian Louboutin shoe and leans down, wedging it against the gas pedal. When she has it jammed in tight, she maneuvers herself out of the moonroof, steering with her knee while she reaches her arms up overhead.

She cries out at the electrifying thrill star-catching gives her. Her silky black hair streams behind her, her diamond necklace twists around her neck.

Susanna never sees the sports utility vehicle approaching from Black Cow Road. She never sees it turn onto the highway ahead of her. Susanna sees nothing but the stars, feels nothing but the hot thrill sluicing through her veins. She doesn't realize she has quit steering with her knee and her car has drifted into the other lane until a kaleidoscope of fire in vivid color engulfs her.

1

HOUSTON

*W*hen the final bell rang at Bruce Elementary School on a warm May afternoon, Jane Aaron's best friend, Nicole—a teacher, like Jane—helped her carry her things to the car. "Wow," Nicole said, as she wedged a box into Jane's trunk. "This is kind of like the end of an era, isn't it?"

"Not at all," Jane said unconvincingly. She shut the trunk. "It's just a break, Nic. I'll be back next fall." She wrapped her arms around Nicole and gave her a hug. "Okay. Here I go, off to tell them."

Nicole smiled and tucked a curl behind Jane's ear. "Hang in there."

Hang in there, as if Jane had been dangling from the end of a rope, twisting in the wind. Which, when she thought about it, wasn't too far off the mark. "I'll call you later and tell you how it went."

"You better!" Nicole warned her. She looked at her car, parked next to Jane's. "Don't you dare leave without talking to me, Janey," she added, and glanced sidelong at her friend.

"Nic, it's just one summer," Jane assured her. "I'll be talking to you a million times. I'll call you in a little while, okay?"

Nicole smiled again. She had a great smile, a Colgate

smile, and with her dark hair pulled into a ponytail, and her little Bruce Elementary Rocks badge on her shirt, she looked like the poster child for wholesome second-grade teachers everywhere. "Okay. Good luck with the fam," she said, and with a cheery little wave, she walked to her car.

Jane got in her car, too, and made it halfway down the street before she pulled over, put the car in park, and covered her face with her hands. "What am I doing?" she whispered. "Seriously—*what* am I doing?"

Finding yourself, she answered silently and groaned. That sounded so clichéd, such new age crap. But in her case, it was true. She was literally, truly, finding herself—or rather, the woman who'd given her away.

When Jane pulled into the back parking area outside The Garden restaurant that her family had owned and operated for years, she couldn't make herself get out of the car.

They were in there, her family, getting ready for the evening rush. Just imagining them working together, laughing, and playing that stupid game with the creamers gave Jane butterflies of anticipation and dread. She was going to walk into that happy little scene and tell them that after much thought, she'd decided to go and search for her birth family.

She'd actually practiced her speech last night in front of the bathroom mirror. *"My decision did not come lightly,"* she'd said gravely to her mirror, as if she'd been some politician removing herself from office. But it was true: the decision had not been easy to make. Naturally, Jane had wondered who she really was for a long time, but she hadn't realized just how much she'd wondered, how deeply that question had sunk into her marrow, until Jonathan, her boyfriend, had asked her to marry him.

Jonathan's proposal had not been unexpected. It had

been the natural progression of their relationship. Jane had figured it was coming, and she'd figured she'd say yes. But the moment Jonathan had asked her, Jane had been stunned to discover that she hadn't been ready to say yes. She hadn't known why her epiphany had occurred at that inopportune moment; she'd just known that something had felt wrong and even a little raw and she'd not been able to commit fully to Jonathan. Not yet.

Jane would be the first to admit that she could be a little obtuse about her feelings. She wasn't very good at self-examination and preferred to go through life happy and cheerful and looking forward, always forward. But her reluctance to say yes to Jonathan had dredged up a whole lot of emotions she'd realized she'd been feeling for a while. Such as . . . was he really the one? And how could she know who was really the one when she didn't really know who *she* was?

The more she came to understand that knowing the who and why of herself had been questions in her for a long time, the emptier and more uncertain she began to feel. About everything. About marriage, and kids, and family. About her thesis, the one thing she needed to finish in order to get her graduate degree. She couldn't move on with her life, not without answering a very basic and fundamental question about herself: Who *was* she?

Of course Jonathan didn't understand her sudden change of heart, but he was at least trying to. Neither did the people inside this restaurant—they loved Jonathan, and they didn't get Jane's sudden reluctance to make it permanent. It really wasn't like her. She had a great family, a loving family, and she'd never felt anything but completely and totally loved.

Yet she'd never felt like she was one hundred percent one of them, either.

The need to know who she was had, in the last couple of years, begun to gnaw on her, eating away from the inside out, especially after she'd signed up for the national registry and no one had come looking for her. Why hadn't her biological parents kept her? She felt alone, like she was straddling two realities. She felt a little unlovable.

After much thought, I have decided to move to Cedar Springs.

Cedar Springs was a small town west of Austin. She'd been born there, and that was all she knew about her beginnings. And now Jane was going to go into The Garden's kitchen and tell the family who loved her beyond measure that she was moving to Cedar Springs to look for the family who didn't love her quite as much.

Wish me luck!

She'd tried that in her mirror, too, a cheerful and carefree end to her little speech, but it hadn't worked. Jane didn't expect her family to like her decision, but she did expect them to accept it.

God, she was nervous! Why was she so nervous? She checked her reflection in the mirror of the visor, running a hand over the top of her head. "At least one thing is going right," she muttered. Her dark, unruly hair was still in the braid she'd managed this morning. Jane took a breath, closed the visor, and opened the car door.

There was a faux brass monkey and coconut-shaped basket attached to the wall in the kitchen of The Garden, hanging right next to the time clock, where it collected receipts and bills of lading. It reminded Jane of home . . . perhaps because there was an identical monkey and coconut in the kitchen there, as well. When her mom found a bargain, she took advantage.

The rest of the Aarons agreed with Jane: those baskets were hideous.

"I refuse to touch that," Jane's cousin Vicki had vowed when Jane's mother, Terri, had hammered it securely to the wall right next to the time card machine.

Terri, swishing by in her rectangular glasses and colorful apron dotted with artichokes, gave Vicki a friendly little pat on her derriere. "That's a little dramatic, isn't it, sweetie?"

While it was true that Vicki could be dramatic and a little too pointed in her comments at times, she'd had a point. But the Aarons had managed to adapt to the monstrosity by making it the centerpiece of a popular family game. Before the lunch and dinner rushes, before the staff started to trickle in, they liked to toss creamers at the thing from established two-point and three-point lines. Uncle Barry held the record for the most points ever earned in a single game, an astounding eighteen points.

Terri always issued her standard warning when a game began: "If you break that, you better pack your bags for China, because that's where you're going to have to go to replace it!"

Yes, the kitchen at The Garden was just like being at home. As several of the Aarons earned their living there, and one of them was always working, they tended to gather there more than they did anywhere else. This kitchen was a professional one, what with its large ovens, walk-in coolers and freezers, and spotless, stainless prep areas. But it also had the touches of family. The walls were livened up with pictures of the Aarons and some loyal staff through the years. There was a string of Christmas lights scattered through the overhead dome heating lights, which someone had hung one year and never removed.

There was a small desk in the prep area that was

stacked with bills and food orders and travel brochures addressed to Uncle Barry and Aunt Mona, both chefs at The Garden. They seemed always to be planning a trip they could never quite seem to make. Taped to the door of the walk-in freezer were the required Health Department certificates and a pair of crayon drawings that were really pretty good. Barry and Mona's daughter, Vicki, had made them years ago, when the kids had had to troop to the restaurant after school and sit at the bar and do their homework under Uncle Greg's watchful eye.

Uncle Greg had since moved to Dallas, and Vicki was a sous-chef now, having left her art behind for the security of a job that actually paid the rent, but the crayon drawings reminded Jane of pleasant afternoons spent in front of the liquor bottles.

Years ago, Jane's parents, Terri and Jim Aaron, now the majority owners in the restaurant, had knocked out a wall that had separated their small office from the kitchen and turned the area into a general gathering place. Terri, the head chef and bargain hunter, had found a pair of gold couches with big red oak leaves at a garage sale. Suffice it to say that Terri's talent for cooking was vastly superior to her talent for shopping, but those couches, and the scarred, laminate coffee table between them, made a great place to gather before a shift, or to collapse with a glass of wine at the end of a long shift.

That area was always cluttered with the family's things. Jane couldn't count how many times she had tripped over her brother Eric's guitar case, dropped just inside the door. Eric was a floor manager, which gave him the freedom and the cash he needed to pursue music, his true love.

The culinary academy books littering the coffee table belonged to Jane's other brother, Matt. He was the heir apparent to Terri because of his own personal desires and the popular vote of the family. His talent was desserts, and the kitchen usually carried the scent of his latest creation. Apple tarts drenched in heavy cream, red velvet cakes with a rich cream cheese filling, and Jane's personal favorite, Jane's Chocolate Thunderdome, an enormous chocolate brownie from which warm chocolate oozed, developed especially for Jane's sweet tooth.

Jane had no talent for cooking herself, but she'd turned out to be a pretty good hostess, and she'd supplemented her paltry public school teacher salary by hostessing on the weekends.

Over the years, the Aarons had made a habit of having an early dinner together every night before the dinner rush, which is where Jane intended to make her announcement today.

As she walked into the kitchen, a creamer narrowly missed her head and bounced off the door frame. That near miss was met with a masculine chorus of *"Oooh,"* as if they'd just missed a three-point basket in the last second of the NBA play-offs. Jane scooped up the creamer, slid her gym bag under the coffee table, and asked, "What smells so good?"

"Mom's secret recipe eggplant parm," Matt said. "Hey, we're just starting a new round. Are you in?"

"What's the pot?" Jane asked.

"A used Starbucks gift card with an unknown amount still on it."

Jane grinned. "I'm in!"

"Yes! Fresh meat!" Eric exclaimed. He swept by her and tried to tousle Jane's hair, but she was too quick for him, dodging out of the way of his beefy hand. Eric laughed and picked up the waitstaff roster to make the evening's station assignments. Jane's younger brothers were blonde, tall, and athletic. Nicole called them Norse Vikings and proclaimed them hot. There were many times in her life when Jane had wished she'd looked like them—or at least had had their hair. She was shorter than them, with dark, curly, unruly hair. Where Matt and Eric were pale and blue-eyed, her skin had a bit of an olive tint to it. Her eyes were brown, and she had a smattering of freckles across the bridge of her nose.

Eric missed his shot. "Come on, Janey," he said, handing her two creamers. "Put a little English on it."

"I have no idea what that means." She closed one eye, took aim—and sank her first creamer into the basket. "Two points!" she cried, earning another boisterous chorus of *ooohs* from the guys. She was lining up to take another shot when her cousin Vicki walked in. Vicki took one disdainful look at them and shook her head.

Jane threw her creamer at Vicki, hitting her on the shoulder.

"I refuse to play," Vicki said, as if nailing her with the creamer had been an invitation. Vicki had brassy blonde hair, the result of the highlight touch-ups she'd done herself. Today, her hair was knotted high on her head.

"Aw, come on, Vic," Eric said, catching her in his arms and making her dance around a tight little circle with him.

"The game is pointless," Vicki insisted. "And furthermore, no one ever pays up the promised pot."

"Stick in the mud," Eric said with a grin and let her go.

"Your stick in the mud is what other people call mature!" she called over her shoulder as she continued her trek to the office, where Terri and Jim, their heads together, were going over some paperwork.

Matt stood up next on the three-point line.

"He's going for three! The crowd goes wild!" Eric cried, then made a noise like a crowd cheering.

Matt missed and handed his creamer to Uncle Barry. "I'd love to stay and kick butt, but I've got to get the soup going." He bowed out as Terri wandered into their midst, pausing to look sternly at Barry.

"What?" Barry asked innocently. There was no mistaking them for brother and sister. They were both a little round, and they both had blue eyes that crinkled in the corners from a lifetime of smiling and laughing. "Watch this, Terri," Barry challenged her, and whizzed a creamer into the basket from the three-point line. "Champion!" he shouted, throwing his arms in the air. *"Again."*

"High five," Eric said, lifting his hand to his uncle. "And lucky you, it's your Starbucks card."

"When's dinner?" Barry asked.

"As soon as Mona gets here," Terri said. "Janey, I love your hair!" she added, reaching her daughter. She caught Jane by the arms and leaned back, studying her hair with a critical eye. Jane's hair was unmanageable. She could remember the agony of her mother trying to run a brush through it to tame it. She'd tried a new look today, braiding it loosely, but she could now feel a bit of it trying to work its way free of the braid. *"Cute,"* her mom said, nodding her approval. "You always look so cute."

"Mom."

"Okay, I won't gush. Hey, did Jonathan like the shirt I got him?" she asked eagerly.

She'd found western shirts on sale and bought them for all the guys. Alas, Jonathan was not a western-shirt kind of guy. "Am I really supposed to wear this?" he'd asked, bewildered, when Jane had delivered it to him.

"He loved it," Jane assured her mother. "I think he might have worn it to his gig in Galveston tonight." Jonathan was a computer programmer by day and a musician by night. Eric had introduced Jane and Jonathan to each other about four years ago, when he and Jonathan had been playing in the same band. They'd begun dating seriously a couple of years ago, and they were still together, in spite of Jane's clumsy response to his marriage proposal.

"That's so nice," her mother said with delight. "Such a great deal, those shirts—"

"Terri? Terri!" Jane's dad was suddenly standing beside them, papers in hand, reading glasses perched on the end of his nose, and wearing his western shirt. Where Jane's mother was soft and a little rounded with age, her father was tall and thin, with graying blonde hair. He peered at Jane over the rims of his glasses. "Hi, pumpkin," he said, leaning over to kiss her cheek. "Did you do something to your hair?"

"Sort of."

"Terri, I cannot read this," he said sternly to her mother. "Where did you learn to write?"

"Overholser Elementary, same as you," Terri said, snatching the papers out of his hand and squinting at them. "Ten pounds, Jim. It says ten pounds."

"That's not the only thing I can't read. I need you to go over this with me, please."

Jane's father was, hands down, the best dad in all of Houston. He would do anything for anyone, and he especially loved working on the Habitat for Humanity projects. But when it came to running the restaurant, he was completely dependent on his wife. It wasn't that he wasn't capable; he was. But Jane had the sense that they'd been together for so long—high school sweethearts—that their thoughts were almost intertwined. Dad needed Mom to think straight.

"Honey, I've told you a dozen times that you need new reading glasses," Terri said. "Just go down to Walgreens and pick them out. It might cost you all of fifteen dollars."

"Okay, okay, but I have to finish the ordering now, so please come and help me."

"All right," Terri said, and rolled her eyes at Jane. But she was smiling. "Oh, honey," she said, putting her hand on Jane's arm. "We're having egg parm tonight. Would you mind getting a salad together and putting it in the dining room? I'll be in to help in a bit."

It was a running joke in the family that Jane was only allowed to prepare salads. And they came preprepared. She grabbed the salad mix from the chiller and dumped it in a serving bowl. She'd finished adding tomatoes when Aunt Mona arrived, burdened with several Target bags.

"Mona!" the guys called in unison.

Mona, a redhead, was always a little late, and they loved to greet her like a returning warrior. "You won't believe all the great stuff I found!" she trilled, dumping the bags on one of the couches. "Vicki, I found that face cream you like, and it was twenty-five percent off!"

With a smile, Jane picked up the salad and a pair of tongs, sidestepped Uncle Barry, and made her way to the private dining room.

Originally, the restaurant had been a house, and it had been renovated to fit eight tables. Over the years, the family had added to and rebuilt sections of the restaurant, so that now it was a sprawling thing that could seat two hundred people at once. It was in the old part of town and considered by many to be quintessentially Houston.

The private dining room, where the family dined every night, was the original dining room. There was a fireplace they used in the winter and a large picture window that overlooked their kitchen and herb garden. The walls in the dining room were adorned with pictures of the restaurant taken over the years. In one picture, taken in the late thirties, Jane's grandparents stood proudly outside.

In another Uncle Greg stood behind the bar he'd tended. In another one, taken when they were kids, Vicki, Jane, Matt, Eric, and Vicki's brother, Danny, who was in the army now, were sitting on the front porch. And a big picture from the seventies, of Terri, Jim, Barry, and Mona at a ribbon-cutting ceremony for the addition of a new dining room.

There was a stack of plates at one end of the table— Jane's mother insisted on sit-down dinners, served family style, as opposed to having waitstaff serve them. "They aren't here to wait on us," she'd say if anyone whined.

Jane set the salad down and picked up the plates. She had them laid out when her mother swept in with a cheery smile, her hair in a net, and that goofy artichoke apron. Terri Aaron always had a smile on her face; she was the most upbeat, positive person Jane had ever known.

"I was just talking to Mona," her mother said as she gathered silver and began to set the table. "Kohl's is having a big sale this weekend. Mona and Vicki and I are going to go. Wanna go with? I'll buy you some sheets."

"Ah . . ." Jane wasn't quite ready to broach her big news. Her mother wouldn't be surprised by it, exactly, but Jane didn't think she'd particularly like it, either.

Her hesitation caused Terri to look at her. "What's up? Do you and Jonathan already have plans?"

"Ah, no . . . well, sort of." Jane drew a breath. "I was planning on moving to Cedar Springs on Saturday."

Her mother stilled.

"I'm going to do it, Mom," Jane said earnestly, moving closer. "I am going to Cedar Springs." There, she'd said it.

Terri slowly put down the silver she was holding. "Cedar Springs?"

"I've been thinking about it a long time."

"You've been thinking about what? Moving there?" she asked, her voice a little incredulous.

Jane nodded.

Her mother's gaze flicked to the carpet a moment. "Janey, I know you want answers, but . . . to move there? Are you sure this is what you want?"

"I'm sure, Mom. It's really been on my mind, and you know I've been considering it."

"Considering it, yes, but I didn't know you were going to . . . to *do* it."

"I'm going to tell everyone today," Jane said. "You know, so all of Vicki's questions will be answered." She smiled a little ruefully at her joke.

Terri's smile was a little sad. "Okay," she said, nodding. She crossed her arms over her chest like she was suddenly cold. "Okay."

"Mom . . . are you okay with it?"

"Yes!" Terri said, a bit too emphatically. "But it doesn't matter if I or anyone else is okay with it, Jane. *You* have to be okay with it. This is your life and your quest. I just don't want you to get hurt," she said. "That's the only thing, Janey. I want you to be happy, but I can't stand to see you hurt."

Jane walked to where her mother stood and wrapped her arms around her. "They can't hurt me," she said reassuringly. At least, they couldn't hurt her any more than they already had.

Her mother slipped her arms around Jane and held her tightly for a long moment. Jane knew she had reservations. They'd talked about this before, and while her mom had encouraged her, there was always that hint of reluctance, a glimmer of unease in her eyes.

"Well," her mother said, pulling away. "I better get the egg parm before it burns."

During the meal, her mother was unusually quiet. Not that anyone would have noticed, what with the running debate of Matt's love life being waged across the dinner table. Eric thought Matt's current girlfriend, Holly, wasn't his type. "You know who I liked? I liked Jaime. Now that girl was great."

"She was," Matt agreed. "But she didn't think I was so great, remember?"

"Then she must have been an idiot," Mona said firmly.

"You guys have this all wrong," Vicki announced. "Matt's at that age where he likes anything that moves."

"Stop right there, Vicki," Matt said with a playful groan.

"I just don't think we should all guilt him into anything he's not ready for."

"You guys have no clue," Matt said, chuckling. "But if it's okay with the jury here, I like Holly. She's nice. You think so, don't you, Jane?"

"What?" Jane asked, looking up from her plate.

"Holly," Matt said, sketching a female shape in the air with his hands. "Blonde? Hot? Bank teller?"

"Oh. Yeah. She's nice." Jane tried to remember Holly. She'd only met her once, and Matt was a bit of a serial dater.

"What's the matter, pumpkin?" her father asked. "You've hardly said a word tonight."

"Who, me?" Jane looked around at their expectant faces. These were the faces of the people she loved. These were the faces that she could depend on to be with her from beginning to end. Why was it so necessary to find the other faces, the faces that looked like her? She only knew that if she didn't at least try, she'd be stuck in this holding pattern until something broke. "Actually, I have an announcement to make."

"What is it, honey?" her father asked, pushing his reading glasses to the top of his head.

"Okay." Jane put down her fork and braced her hands against the table's edge. "You guys know that I've been trying to find out more about who gave me up for adoption."

"Right," Eric said, nodding.

"Well, it's not . . . it's not working out. I keep running into brick walls. I've looked as far as I can, and I put my name on the national adoption registry, and nothing has come of it. I mean, they obviously aren't looking for me, so I've decided . . ." She paused, took a breath. *After much consideration* . . . "I am moving to Cedar Springs," she blurted.

"Huh?" Eric asked, confused.

"Just for the summer—at least I think it wouldn't be longer than a summer. I'm going to move to Cedar Springs to just . . . just look around and see what I come up with." She shrugged nervously.

Her announcement was met with silence for a moment. Her family all looked around at one another, then at her again.

"Well, well, well," her uncle Barry said. "Well, well."

"Isn't anyone going to say anything besides . . . 'well'?" Jane asked hopefully.

"*Move?*" her dad said, as if he couldn't quite grasp the concept.

"I think it's great," Eric said. "You've been looking for a long time. Go for it, Janey. I hope you find them."

"But find who?" Vicki asked. "What if she finds her birth family and they are a bunch of nutjobs?" Vicki could always be counted on to say what everyone else was thinking but was too polite to say. "They could be certifiable, you never know."

"Have you met my sister?" Matt asked. "I think there is no question there is some nuttiness in them." He winked at Jane. "I'm with Eric. Godspeed and good luck and hurry up and get back here as soon as you can."

"No, seriously—what if they are lunatics or crooks or politicians?" Vicki persisted with a slight shudder. "You could be in for a very rude awakening, Janey." She forked a healthy portion of eggplant into her mouth and pointed her fork at Jane. "I'm only going to say this because I love you, but people always think they want to know. And reality is never really what they imagined."

"Honestly, I don't care if they are lunatics," Jane said. "I just want to know a few things, and then I'm done. I'm not looking for a family or friends, obviously, nothing even close to that. But I would like to have some information about my ancestry, and medical history, and . . . and talents. I want to know what my talents are. I'm only trying to understand." *Only trying to fill this hole in me.*

"What's to understand?" Vicki said. "They gave you up. You're ours now. And even if you find them, *they* can't tell you what your talents are."

"Try and be more supportive, Vicki," Mona said. "This is obviously very important to Jane."

"It's not that I'm not supportive," Vicki protested. "But here's the thing, Janey. You'll go out there and find your birth family, or maybe you won't, in which case you have wasted time you could have used to finish your master's thesis. Or, you find them and they either surprise you or disappoint you, or even worse, they reject you again, 'cuz let's call a dog a dog—they basically rejected you once, right? All I am saying is why put yourself through that? We care about you. *We're* your family."

"Vicki, eat some more pasta," Barry suggested more firmly to his daughter.

"I know you are my family," Jane said. "Nothing will ever change that. But there are things you guys know about yourselves that I don't know about me, and I think I deserve the chance to know."

"If this is what you need to do, Jane, then I think you need to just do it," her mother said firmly. "And when you have found them, know that your real family will be waiting for you to come home where you belong."

"Dad?" Jane asked.

"Janey, whatever your mother said. But do you have to move?"

"I think so," she said quietly.

Vicki sighed. "I'm not trying to piss anyone off, I swear I'm not. You know what they say—be careful what you wish for. But hey, if you're going, I support you one thousand percent."

"Thanks, Vic," Jane said with a smile.

"So when are you going?" Mona asked.

As Jane answered their questions as best she could—when would she go, and for how long, and what about Jonathan—Vicki's warning kept banging around in Jane's head.

Be careful what you wish for.

2

$\mathcal{T}$he alarm on his phone startled Asher Price awake; he bolted upright and blinked, trying to focus and look around, to place where he was.

A hotel room. *What hotel?*

He glanced to his right, groped around the nightstand for the little table tent that urged one to save the environment and not ask for clean sheets. He squinted at it; the language was German.

Munich.

Asher tossed the table tent aside and sank back into the thick goose feather pillows. He stretched his arm across the bed, felt the cool emptiness of it. It was odd, he thought sleepily, that his wife had been dead for a year and a half now—gone longer than that, really—but he'd never gotten used to sleeping alone. He missed the weight of a woman's body in bed, the warmth of skin, the rhythm of her breath to remind him that he was in the present.

He sometimes wondered if he'd ever feel that again. He sometimes wondered if he'd ever really felt it but maybe had just imagined he had. It had been so long since he'd been with a woman who hadn't been angry or just indifferent, and that had been his wife.

Asher yawned and blinked up at the ceiling. *I need to run.* Running cleared his head, helped him focus. He hadn't run in what, three days? Four? He pressed his hand to his abdomen—he was starting to feel a little soft. *What's that?* he wondered, noticing a bulbous thing on the ceiling, marring the pristine white like a wart. Probably some sort of sprinkler head. Once, in a hotel in Hong Kong, he'd been sound asleep when the fire alarms had gone off and the sprinklers had opened up. Not a good way to start the day.

The only really good way for him to start a day was at home, with his kids. Asher wished he was home now, where he knew what all the warts and bumps in the ceiling were, where he had a fancy full body shower, where his kids were waiting for him to make something for breakfast, where he knew all the running trails and how fast he could run them.

Speaking of home . . .

Asher groaned and pushed himself up. He was still fully clothed, and papers and sketches were spread out across his bed. He'd fallen asleep reviewing them. They were the staff work on the BMW America advertising account. He was in Munich to meet his German counterparts, developing a message and look that unified BMW sales around the world. His firm—Green, Sutcliff, Dyer and Price—was on the verge of losing this account if they didn't come up with some creative advertising, something sexy and fast, something that fit BMW's desires and the American market. And if they lost BMW . . .

God, don't think about that now.

Asher shoved the papers aside, swung his legs over the side of the bed, and pressed his fingers to his eyes, trying to wake up. He'd been so busy since he'd arrived in Munich earlier this week that he'd never really caught up on his sleep. He pushed his hand through his hair . . . *something smelled.* He looked up, his gaze landing on the tray that held what was left of his dinner on the table.

"God." He stood up, stretched his back, and wandered over to have a closer look. The grease in the meat loaf had congealed. The beets or cabbage—whatever it was, it wasn't something Asher typically consumed—was limp on the plate. He picked up a cold fry and shoved it in his mouth, then covered the tray and carried it to the door, depositing it outside his room.

He returned to the bed and the bedside table and picked up his phone. It was a quarter to two in the morning. That meant it was almost seven at home in Cedar Springs.

Yawning, Asher glanced at the small, travel-sized dual picture frame he carried with him on all his trips. On one side was a picture of his son, Levi. Levi was grinning in the picture, his smile full of the baby teeth that had started to come out now that he was five. He had a smattering of freckles across his nose, and his dark hair was a mess. Lord, but there was nothing that seemed to tame those cowlicks. Asher had tried everything short of axle grease to get that hair to lie down, and nothing worked. His late wife, Susanna, could do it. If he could see Susanna again, those were the sorts of things he would ask her. *How do you make Levi's hair stay down? Where did you put my Garmin watch? When did you start drinking again?*

On the other side was a picture of his daughter, Riley. She was eleven in that picture, but almost thirteen now, and Asher was reminded again that he needed an updated photo of her. Between saving his listing company and getting his kids off to school and then making sure their homework was done, updated pictures landed way down on his priority list.

Riley's picture was taken shortly before her mother's death. She was staring calmly into the camera, her gold hair combed straight, her bangs clipped just above her eyes. Those bangs had grown long and now served to cover her face from the world.

Beside the picture frame was a smooth rock, polished and buffed by the waters of Lake Del Lago that lapped the shore just below his house. Levi had found it and given it to Asher as a good luck charm to protect him from evil ninjas. Asher picked up the rock now and ran his thumb over its smooth surface, smiling softly. Levi really liked rocks. Maybe he'd be a geologist some day.

He punched the number to home on his phone. Both of his kids had cell phones so they could reach him anytime, anywhere. But when Asher made his nightly call home, he liked the house phone, because he could be talking to one child and hear the other in the background. It was as close to being there as he could get. He'd tried to do video conferencing with them, but the feed was always bad and the kids couldn't sit still that long in front of a computer.

"Hi, Daddy!" Levi chirped into the phone after the first ring. "Guess what we're doing?"

"Hey, buddy," Asher said, already smiling. Nothing could infuse the slog of his work with sunshine like the sound of his children's voices. "I can't guess. What are you doing?"

"We're making cookies. Carla said we could decorate them."

"Carla?" he said, squinting at the drab drapery of his hotel room. Carla was his housekeeper and left promptly at five every day to see after her house and husband. "Carla is still there?"

"Uh-huh."

"Where is Crystal?" he asked, referring to the night nanny he'd hired a month ago when his full-time nanny had decided to go to Los Angeles and pursue an acting career.

"I think she quitted."

Asher's belly knotted. *Not again.* Maybe Levi had it wrong. He would ask Carla, but first he wanted to talk to his son. "So what did you do today?"

"I don't know," Levi said.

"Did you go to school?"

"Yes. Brandon had to go to time-out because he hit Jason with a brick. It was cool!"

"Hitting is not cool, Levi, remember? What else did you do?"

"Watched *SpongeBob* when I got home. Carla said I could. When are you coming home, Daddy?"

That question always slayed him. Unless he was on his way at that moment, there was never a satisfactory answer for it. He gave Levi his stock answer. "I don't know yet, buddy." *I don't know, I don't know.* "As soon as I can."

"Are you coming in a plane?"

"You bet—in the biggest one they make."

"Cool! I have to go now. The cookies are ready."

"Levi, listen," Asher said, catching him before he ran off. "You know I love you, right? I love you all the way to the moon and back."

"I know, Daddy!"

"Listen, I'll call tomorrow. Let me talk to Carla, will you?"

"*Carla!*" Levi shouted, dropping the phone.

Asher stood up and walked to the window. He pushed aside the drapes, stared out at lights blinking sleepily against a dark Munich night.

"Hello, Mr. P," Carla said into the phone a moment later.

"Carla, how are you?"

"Oh, pretty good."

"What's going on? What happened to Crystal?"

"I don't really know," Carla said. "She just quit. Gathered up all her stuff and left, just like that. I'll tell you what,

Mr. P, in my day, people were thankful for jobs. You'd think she'd be pretty thankful, too, given this economy."

"I hear you," Asher said absently. He wondered briefly if Riley had anything to do with her abrupt departure. "I'll call Tara and see if she can't come out—"

"What, tonight? No, that's all right, Mr. P. I called Don and told him I was going to stay the night. Surely the man can warm something up in the microwave one night of his blessed life. And your mother said she'd come get the kids tomorrow. She couldn't get them tonight because she has her bridge club and said she missed it last month."

"Right," Asher said. He let the drapes drop. "I am really sorry, Carla." He meant it, too, and deeply. Carla had been with him for years, through the worst of Susanna's troubles before she died. He couldn't risk losing her—hell, he'd be lost without her.

"It's okay, Mr. P," Carla assured him. "I know you're really busy right now."

Busy seemed like a lame word for it. He and his partners at GSD&P were fighting to hold on to the business in an uncertain economic time. And when Ron Sutcliff, the managing partner, had been diagnosed with pancreatic cancer, everything had begun to nosedive. Asher had been made chief executive officer, effectively doubling his workload. His life, always chaotic, had been turned on its head, and he could hardly keep up with whether he was coming or going. He just knew that he seemed to be halfway around the world from his children more often than he liked, and all he wanted was to see them, to kiss them, to hold them, and make sure everything was all right.

Since Susanna had died suddenly a year and a half ago, the need to protect his children had ballooned in Asher, like some gear kicked into overdrive.

It didn't help that he couldn't find good, reliable help.

"I'll get with Tara tonight, Carla," Asher assured her. "We'll get someone in there as soon as possible." He glanced at his watch. "I very much appreciate you staying."

"It's no problem."

It was a problem, and they both knew it. Carla had her own life. "Is Riley around?" he asked.

"Ah . . . yes, there she is, lurking in the door. Just a moment."

"Hey, Dad," Riley said a moment later.

"Hey, baby girl," Asher said softly. "What's up?"

"Crystal quit. I texted you."

He hadn't received the texts because he had fallen asleep. He winced with a slight pang of guilt. "So what happened, Ri?"

"Don't ask me," Riley said defensively. "I think her boyfriend didn't like her spending the night out here."

Asher pondered that a moment. "Did you say anything?" he asked carefully. Riley was not adjusting to his frequent absences very well. The last nanny had complained that Riley wouldn't do anything she asked.

"Dad! No, I didn't say anything. She had a meltdown all on her own. Anyway, you don't have to worry, because Grandma Cheryl is coming to get us tomorrow. When are you going to be home?"

"I don't know. But as soon as I can. I promise."

"I just wish you'd come home," Riley said softly. "School is out for summer soon, and I don't want to live with Grandma Cheryl. Her house smells weird."

Her house did have a weird, antiseptic smell. "You're not going to live with Grandma. You're not going to live with anyone but me. Don't even think about that. Tell me, how was school today?"

"The same as always," Riley said, not unhappily. "I got a B on my science test."

"A B!" Asher said, sinking back onto the bed. The news elated him in a way nothing in his own life could do any longer. Riley had so much promise, so much talent— but her talent was not math or science, and Asher worried about her grades. "Riley, I am so proud of you! That's excellent news! All that studying paid off after all, huh?"

She giggled. "Calm down, Dad."

The sound of her laugh ran down his spine and warmed him. "Way to go, kiddo. Anything else going on today?"

"No. Oh, I saw this great book in the library, Dad. It's about a wishing well in Spain. People go there and throw some money in, and then whatever they have is cured."

Asher listened to his daughter. She was such a quirky kid. Things like wishing wells in Spain interested her, but not bikes or friends. Riley was a loner. Susanna used to say that Riley was artistic and creative and had a hard time fitting in with the run of the mill. Asher had believed Susanna, but now there were times he believed something a little deeper than that was going on. Something he damn sure couldn't figure out halfway around the world.

Asher glanced at the pile of papers on his bed. He had a meeting in six hours and he still didn't have a clear vision of where they were going. "Maybe one day we'll get to Spain so you can check them out," he suggested when Riley had finished telling him about the wells.

"Yeah, right," Riley scoffed.

Okay, he deserved that. "Never say never," he said as cheerfully as he could. "Okay, Ri, I've gotta go. I'll call you tomorrow, same time, okay?"

"Okay."

"I love you, Ri. I love you and I miss you." More than he could possibly express to a twelve-year-old. More than a grown, educated man could express with mere words.

"I know, I know, all the way to the moon," Riley said. "I love you, too. I'll talk to you tomorrow."

Asher said good night and waited until the line went dead.

All the way to the moon.

He tossed the phone onto the bed and opened the mini-bar. He fished out a beer and some peanuts. He chased the peanuts with the beer, then picked up his phone again and dialed Tara.

Tara, his assistant for more than ten years, answered on the second ring. "Hey!" she said brightly. "How's Germany?"

"I wouldn't know, I haven't seen the outside of an office or a hotel room in days," Asher said. "Listen, I hate to bother you at home."

"Not to worry. Chris is out. What can I do for you?"

"The night nanny quit," Asher said. "Tara, you have got to find me a nanny. I don't know how long I am going to be here—a week, two weeks—but my kids need some stability. I need someone who is there for them and can handle them, but someone I can trust not to take off or get in a huff over anything they say and walk out. You know what I mean?"

"I do."

"I know this is a huge thing to put on you, but I am at the end of my rope here, and I have no one else to turn to."

"I'm already on it," she said confidently. "We haven't had much luck with that service in Austin, so I found one in Cedar Springs. I figure there are some pretty nice resorts out that way, so surely there is a need for nannies, right? At least a part-time nanny until we find a permanent one."

"You found a service?" Asher asked disbelievingly.

"I've already got a call in to them," Tara said confidently. "Listen, Asher, I will find someone. I promise you I will, and if you need me to go out and hang out for a couple of days, I will. I don't think Chris will even notice I am gone. But the most important thing is to get BMW on track."

That was Tara—she was indispensable to him and obviously as worried about the future of the firm as he was. Guilt and regret began to pound at his temples. It was a bizarre thing to ask anyone, to find a nanny for his kids. He tried so hard to be there for them, especially when it mattered, but he also had a business and a livelihood to maintain for their sake and he felt like he'd been split right down the middle. He could not be everything he needed to be, but he'd be damned if he could figure out where to draw any lines.

At least he could trust Tara. He knew that if he couldn't find someone—which he couldn't, not from Germany—she would. "Please call me as soon as you have something," he said.

"Of course."

"Thanks, Tara. I'll talk to you soon." He hung up and looked at the clock. It was now a quarter after two. He couldn't sleep, not with this on his mind. He had to be at the BMW offices at eight in the morning. Asher pulled his shirt from his trousers, picked up a pen and a file, and started reading.

Focus, he told himself. Just focus, get the message down and get the hell out of here. Get home before all the wheels fall off the wagon of his life.

3

The road from Houston to Austin was a long stretch of horse farms and cattle ranches. Jane wondered about each and every ranch house she passed—did they have kids? Were they happily married? Had they ever given a child away? Adopted a child? Were their children happy?

Jane could not remember a time when she didn't know she was adopted. In fact, one of her earliest memories was standing on a stool in the kitchen, her head barely above the counter, watching her mother mix cake batter, hoping she would get to lick the bowl clean. "God brought you to us, Janey," her mother said to her, and playfully tweaked her nose. "He made a special delivery to us and gave us an angel."

She'd been more interested in the cake batter.

Her parents had never treated her adoption as anything other than normal. Once, when Jane had been a little older, she'd asked her mother why they'd adopted, and her mother had looked surprised by the question. "Because we really wanted a baby," she said, as if it had been perfectly natural to adopt another person's child when one wanted a baby. Jane was too young then to wonder why they hadn't given birth to her like they had the two sons after her, but Mona had told Jane years later that Terri and Jim hadn't believed they could have children naturally before Eric was born—he'd been a big surprise.

Nevertheless, Jane couldn't remember spending as much as a day of her childhood thinking about being the adopted one. That's not to say she didn't wonder about her biological parents from time to time. She had a healthy imagination and would envision what her life might have been like if her real parents had kept her. In grade school, she'd made a game of pretending she'd really been someone else, like Christie Heatherton, the cutest girl in school. She'd imagined walking around in Christie's skin, seeing everyone through Christie's eyes.

And there were times Jane wondered why her real parents gave her away. Was something wrong with her? Had she cried too much as a baby? Her mom said she was special, but Jane wondered what if she just *said* that, and the real reason her birth mother gave her away was because she wasn't special at all?

And sometimes, Jane would invent acceptable reasons her birth parents couldn't keep her. She pretended they lived on an island by themselves and there were no schools. Or they were very important—her father was the president's right-hand man, her mother on tour with the ballet. They were *rich*.

She'd once made the mistake of telling Michelle, whose last name now escaped her. She'd been a summer friend before her family had moved away. Jane had told Michelle about her real, *rich* parents, and Michelle had looked at her curiously. "But . . . if they're rich, why didn't they keep you?"

Suffice it to say that Jane hadn't thought through the logistics of giving herself extraordinary parents.

As a teen, Jane's focus had turned to her looks. What was she, part Italian? Hispanic? Mom said she was beautiful, but Jane felt ugly and ungainly. Her eyes were too big. Her nose was crooked. That's why they gave her away, she told herself—she was ugly. People would say to her tall, blonde brothers, "You look just like your father!" And then they would look at Jane with that awkward, blank look of not knowing what to say.

"*You* look like an angel," her mother would tell her. "You're so pretty, Janey, don't you know that?" The only thing Jane knew at that age was that she looked different from her family.

Still, overall, Jane had been happy and content with her family and herself. At what point that had changed, she wasn't entirely certain, but somewhere between college and teaching second grade, she'd begun to feel more detached from her family and the self she'd thought she'd known. Maybe it was because she'd taught in a part of Houston where there had been lots of kids without mothers or fathers or both, living with grandparents, or in foster care. Maybe it was because she'd read an author who wrote that our past is our present and our future, that we are all pieces of our past and our loves. Jane had so many invisible holes in her, so many pieces missing, that she'd begun to feel like her present was incomplete.

She was about twenty-eight and in her second semester of graduate school when questions had begun to simmer. Things she'd always accepted about herself and her life had suddenly seemed suspect to her, such as how everyone in her family liked to cook. Jane didn't like to cook, but she liked to eat. And when she overate, the weight went straight to her hips. She had the metabolism of a slug and had to run four or five times a week to keep from ballooning into a whale, yet everyone in her adopted family seemed to eat without the worry of putting on weight. Matt and Eric both had a talent for music, but Jane could scarcely carry a tune. Most of her family wore contacts or glasses, but Jane's sight was very good. She was good at science and math and considered herself to be a fairly good teacher. Now, Jane had wanted to know what other natural talents she might have had that she hadn't even been aware of.

She'd spent hours rummaging around her distant memories and thoughts, digging for clues as to who or what she was, convinced something was there if she was only smart enough to recognize it. On a whim, she'd signed up for the national adoption registry. She'd heard about the registries—both adoptees and birth parents could sign up, and if they were both looking, and indicated they were okay with being found, the registry would match and put them into contact with each other.

As she sped down Highway 71 on her way to Austin, Jane's hindsight was pretty clear. "You are *so* naïve," she muttered to herself and cranked up her stereo. She'd signed up for the registry, nervous and anxious, expecting something back within hours. Then days. When a few weeks had gone by, Jane had realized that no one had been looking for her all these years.

It had been a surprisingly stunning blow to her ego. Looking back on it now, Jane could see that was when her life began to slow to a crawl, really long before Jonathan asked her to marry him. She just hadn't understood that it was happening.

When the registry hadn't produced a response, Jane had asked her mother about her adoption again. They'd been at lunch at a new restaurant near Jane's apartment— her mother loved to check out the competition whenever she could—and Jane hadn't been able to get the registry off her mind.

"The soup is too salty," her mother had said as they'd eaten the first course.

"Mom, may I ask you something?"

"Shoot, sweetie. What are you having? I think I'll try the quiche. You can always tell the quality of a restaurant by their quiche, because it's nearly impossible to screw up, but it's hard to make it really, really good."

Jane had yet to look at her menu. "I've been kind of unsettled lately."

"You have?" Terri had asked, looking up from her menu. "Can I help?"

"Maybe," Jane had said. "Can you tell me . . . can you tell me more about who I am?"

Her mother had gone very quiet for a moment. She'd laid her menu down, tucked a strand of blonde hair behind her ear, and adjusted her rectangular glasses. "Mind telling me why you are asking about that now?"

"I just need to know," Jane had admitted honestly. "I want—I *need* to know, Mom. I don't have a complete picture."

"Are you going to go look for her?" her mother had asked bluntly.

The question had startled Jane. She couldn't believe her mother would think that, and furthermore, she hadn't really considered it. Not very seriously, at any rate. "Go and look for someone who gave me away? No, Mom! No, I'm just curious."

Her mother hadn't seemed convinced. "Let's order, then we'll talk." They'd ordered, and Terri had stared at Jane over her quiche, as if she'd been trying to read something into her daughter's expression as Jane had explained how unsettled she'd been of late.

When she'd finished, her mother had sighed, put down her fork, then looked Jane squarely in the eye. "Here is the

God's honest truth, Janey. I don't know anything about your parents. Nothing. They didn't want us to know, and it was all handled by a private attorney."

"Maybe the attorney knows something."

"He probably did, but he is dead. He had a heart attack and dropped dead at the office when you were about five."

Jane's heart had plummeted. "*Dead?* That's it, the only key to who I am is dead?"

"Who you *are* is Jane Aaron," her mother had said flatly. "You are just as much a product of your upbringing and environment as you are your genes. Whoever they were, they were nothing more than an incubator."

"Mom, I know that," Jane had said impatiently. "I am your daughter and I don't want to be anyone else's daughter. And I really don't want to *find* them. I just want to know a few things."

"Like what?" her mother had asked casually, picking up her fork again.

"Like . . . where did my ancestors come from? What is my nationality? Is there any history of heart disease or that sort of thing that I should be aware of?"

"Well I don't know how those questions can be answered unless you find your birth parents, do you? But I have to warn you that even if you do find them, they may not have the answers you want to hear."

"I *know*," Jane had said, feeling her frustration beginning to build. It had been so hard to explain what she'd been feeling, how empty the lack of knowledge about herself had left her. "But it's worth asking, isn't it? And they are the only ones who can answer the most basic question."

"What's that?"

"Why they gave me away," Jane had said flatly.

"Oh, Janey." Her mother had smiled sympathetically. "I

am certain whoever it was gave you up because they loved you so much and they couldn't provide for you."

"That's a stock answer, Mom. Why didn't they get a job?"

"It's a stock answer because it's true more often than not."

"Surely there is something," Jane had insisted. "Adoption papers. *Something.*"

"Of course we have adoption papers," her mother had said calmly. "But you will be disappointed. All the identifying information is blacked out and the court records are sealed. That means the only way you can find them is if you both sign up for an adoption registry."

"I know," Jane had said. "I already have. And I didn't get a match."

Her mother had clearly been stunned by her admission. It had been several moments before she'd spoken. "Lord," she'd said quietly. "Once you open that can of worms, you won't stop until you get to the bottom. It's human nature."

Jane had seen her mother's discomfort, the edge of fear in her gaze. "Mom, I love my life. I love my family," she'd said earnestly. "I don't want to mess that up with some new reality. I just want to understand what talents I have, and if I should worry about certain diseases—"

"You have plenty of talent!" her mother had said angrily. "Do you think knowing who pushed you out into this world will tell you who you are? Ask *me,* Jane. *I* know who you are. I know you have the warmest smile of anyone I've known, and you are wonderful with children. You trained all of our dogs growing up, and you are very perceptive about other people and you have a vivid imagination. You're beautiful and smart and funny. I *know* who you are. You don't need to find your birth mother for that."

Now Jane winced at the memory of that lunch, how

she'd given her mother a patronizing smile. "I know you *think* that, Mom. But right now you're being my mother. You don't really know."

"Don't you tell me what I know," Terri had snapped, her eyes tearing up as she'd dropped her fork with a clank against her plate. "I held you in my arms when you were two days old and I have never let you go. I fed you, I clothed you, I bandaged your boo-boos and I gave you Santa. I attended every school function, I stayed up with you the night Randy Davis broke up with you. I paid for your college, I helped you shop for your apartment, and now you're going to sit there and tell me I don't know who you are?"

"I'm sorry—"

"I didn't give birth to you, Jane," she'd continued angrily. "But I didn't love you one ounce less!"

"Okay," Jane had said, sitting back, holding up a hand. "I didn't mean it that way, honestly. I know you love me, I know you care. And I love you."

Her mother had stared at her a long moment, her jaw clenched. "I have to get back," she'd said abruptly and put her napkin on the table.

"What? Mom, don't go," Jane had cried, reaching for her mother's hand.

But her mother had squeezed her hand and smiled. "I need to get back to work, Janey. I am sorry for flying off the handle like that. I guess I didn't take my happy pills this morning. I'll see you later, okay?" She'd kissed the top of Jane's head and left Jane sitting there.

Jane hadn't said anything else about it for her mother's sake, and after that lunch, Jane really had tried to push it out of her mind.

But the questions had refused to go away.

Worse, things had started to slip through the cracks.

Jane had lagged in graduate school—she'd been trying to finish her master's in psychology with the hope of entering a PhD program. Nicole had finally asked, "Why are you wasting this opportunity? You'd be a *great* child psychologist, Janey, and all you lack is your thesis."

"I don't know, really," Jane had said. "I just wonder if I really want to be a child psychologist. I think the interest is coming from some buried need to understand myself," she'd said with a wry laugh. "I mean, where did I get the topic of children and loss for my thesis? I can't write something like that without working through my own loss, can I? And you know what, Nic? I'm not even sure I really suffered a loss. I am so confused about everything."

"Are you crazy?" Nicole had cried. "You don't have to answer all that now. But if you don't finish, you will always regret it. This is so unlike you, Janey."

"Is it?"

"Yes! Okay, what about sheer practicalities? You've put all this work into a master's the last two years, going to night school and working weekends. At least finish the damn thing! At the very least you'll get a raise from the school district for having a master's degree. That's worth it, isn't it?"

"Yes," Jane had agreed. Nicole had been right, of course, Jane had known she'd been right. She just hadn't been able to find the heart to finish her thesis.

And then there was Jonathan, her sweet musician with the soulful heart. She cared very much for Jonathan, and he was crazy about her. He told her frequently that he loved her and backed it up by writing songs for her and about her. He was cute, too, with shoulder-length, thick brown hair and tattooed arms. Jonathan Bauer was a free spirit, grounded in his reality, and Jane really admired him. Then Jonathan had gone and ruined it all by asking her to marry him.

Jane had known it was coming. She and Nicole had bet that it would be on Jane and Jonathan's two-year anniversary, and they'd been right. Jonathan had taken Jane out for a special dinner. It had been a lovely, beautiful evening, with rooftop dining at a swank little bistro, with prime rib and an excellent bottle of wine.

"Jane," Jonathan had said as they'd waited for dessert. He'd held out his hand to her, palm up.

That was the moment she'd known would come, and Jane's heart had begun to pound. But not in a good way. In a frantic, I-can't-breathe way. At first she'd assumed it had been a bad attack of butterflies. She'd smiled as Jonathan had risen from his chair and moved around to her side of the table. She'd tried to swallow as he'd gone down on one knee. He was nervous, she'd realized. "I can't imagine life without you. You know I love you, Janey—I love you so much. Will you do me the honor . . ." He'd paused, fished the box from his pocket, and fumbled a little trying to open it. "Will you do me the honor of being my wife?" he'd asked, and shown her the small diamond ring.

Jane had gasped. She'd gazed at the ring, tears in her eyes. She'd been thrilled! Overjoyed! But she hadn't been able to find her tongue.

An awkward moment had passed and Jonathan had laughed uneasily. "Hello?" he'd asked jokingly.

"*Wow,*" Jane had said. "It's really beautiful."

Jonathan's face had fallen. "God . . . are you turning me down?"

"No, no!" she'd said, but Jonathan had already come to his feet, looking sheepishly around them, and Jane had felt like she'd been outside of herself, like she'd just floated out of her body. "I'm not turning you down," she'd said softly as he'd resumed his seat, but she had been, they'd both known she had been. The ring had sat on the table between them. "I'm just not sure I'm ready."

Poor Jonathan—he'd looked so appalled, so hurt, and even now, as Jane pulled into McDonald's, her vision blurred with tears of regret.

She'd tried to explain. "I just have some questions that I need to answer—"

"Like what, for God's sake?" Jonathan had asked self-consciously.

"Like who I am, where I come from. Why I was given up for adoption."

"Are you *kidding*?" Jonathan had hissed angrily, then smiled at the waitress.

She wouldn't have blamed him if he'd walked out on her right then and there, but Jonathan really did love her. He'd stayed. They'd talked. He'd agreed, very reluctantly, that she should take some time. And they had continued to see each other, although things had never really been the same since that night.

Jane didn't feel worthy of a lifelong commitment. What if Jonathan left her? What if he cast her out to the world without knowing where she would land, like her birth parents had done?

"That's ridiculous," Jonathan had scoffed one night over burgers when she'd tried once again to explain her reluctance. "Your parents probably gave you up because they were teens and they couldn't care for you. They didn't cast you out to the cruel, cruel world."

That idea was easy for him to dismiss, but he hadn't been given up at birth. "I still can't help but wonder," Jane had said. "I mean, I work with lots of kids who were born to teen parents, and the kids and the parents have gone through some really bad times—but their mothers didn't give them up."

"I think a lot of people would argue that they should have," Jonathan had snorted. "Janey, your parents loved you. Come on, we're talking 1980. The world was a different place then. Unwed teen mothers couldn't keep their babies. I am sure they loved you so much they did what was best for you."

"Yeah, maybe," Jane had agreed for the sake of argument. But there had been something in the back of her mind telling her the world hadn't been that different in 1980, and that Jonathan had a Pollyanna view of it. Her parents could have kept her if they'd wanted her. "What if there is some hideous medical thing I should know about?"

"Don't worry about stuff like that," Jonathan had said, and he'd covered her hand with his. "Listen, if you're totally crazy, or have a tendency for bunions, or whatever, we'll deal with it." He'd laughed at his own joke. "You are going to marry me, right?"

Jane had smiled. "I'm pretty sure."

Jonathan had sighed. "I'm beating my head against a wall here. Again. Let's not talk about it tonight, okay? Are you going to eat those fries?" he'd asked, reaching for one.

She and Jonathan had gone on that way, in a sort of limbo, and Jane had continued to look. With the attorney gone and the records sealed, and the registry coming up empty, there had been only one other thing Jane could do: attack it from the other end. She could go to Cedar Springs, to the hospital where she was born, and begin there.

She'd decided to run her idea past Nicole first, and she'd shown up at Nicole's house one Saturday morning with cinnamon rolls Matt had made for her. Nicole's husband Colt had been out running errands.

"Ohmigod, that smells delicious!" Nicole had said as she'd padded into her bright yellow kitchen with the bag. Nicole had been dressed in Colt's University of Texas sweats, her dark hair clipped up. Her eight-month-old baby, Sage, had been in a high chair with a bib around her neck. She'd smeared strained carrots all over the tray of her high chair and on her face.

Nicole had made Jane some chai tea she kept around just for Jane. "How can you drink that stuff?" she'd asked, her nose wrinkling, and helped herself to a diet soda.

"Hey, I have some news," Jane had said lightly. "I think I am going to go to Cedar Springs."

"What do you mean, go to Cedar Springs?" Nicole had asked as she'd settled on a chair next to Sage. "Open up, angel."

"I am going to find my birth mom."

Nicole had gasped so loudly that she'd startled Sage, who'd instantly begun to cry. "I'm sorry, Sagey. Mommy is sorry, but she's so excited for Auntie Jane!" she'd cooed, wiping Sage's face and feeding her another spoonful. "I can't believe you're going to do it!" she'd said excitedly. "I'm really proud of you, Janey. That's a huge step and a hard one. What did Jonathan say?"

"Jonathan," Jane had said, and winced. "He was okay with it until I told him I was going to move there."

"*Move* there?" Nicole had cried, looking up. Sage had grabbed for the spoon, smearing more strained carrots on her tray. "Why do you have to *move* there?"

"Because I don't think it is something I can do in a couple of days. What if I find her, Nicole? I want to spend at least a *few* days talking to her."

"But what about your job?"

"I talked to Marilee," Jane had said, referring to their principal. "I'm taking an unpaid leave of absence for the rest of this term."

Nicole had gasped again. Sage had begun to wail for the food Nicole had been neglecting to feed her while she'd gaped at Jane.

Jane had calmly taken the spoon from Nicole and dipped it into the jar. "Here you go, sweetie," she'd said, giving Sage another spoonful. Delighted, Sage had slapped her palms onto her tray top.

"Wow," Nicole had said, incredulous, staring at Jane with wide hazel eyes.

"I don't know how long this is going to take. And you'll be happy to know that I plan to finish my thesis while I'm there so they don't kick me out of grad school. I should be back in Houston in the fall. . . ." Jane had shrugged. She really didn't know what she'd do after that. She couldn't think past this summer, past this quest.

"Do you have enough money to live?"

Jane had laughed. "You're a teacher. What do you think?"

"I think no. So are you going to get a job?"

"Yep," Jane had said. She'd smiled at Nicole.

But Nicole had shaken her head. "Now you have me worried. I mean, you have a great job here, and you have friends and family and Jonathan, who adores you. And you're *moving*?" She'd said it as if Jane had suggested moving to Siberia. "I can't believe it." Nicole had taken the spoon from Jane to finish feeding Sage. She'd shaken her head again, as if she'd been trying to make sense of it.

But Jane had methodically continued on. She'd arranged to sublet her apartment. She'd put things in storage. She and Jonathan had agreed that as soon as she found a place, he'd bring some of the larger things she couldn't carry in her Honda. The time to go had come.

Yesterday afternoon, Jane's mom and dad had skipped the family meal and come to see Jane. Standing in her half-empty apartment, Dad had stood with his hands in his pockets, looking around. "You have a flashlight and jumper cables in your car?" he'd asked, his gaze on some boxes.

"Yes," Jane had said.

"What about oil? Have you checked the oil lately? I better check the oil," he'd said and gone outside.

Jane's mother had closed up one box and run her hand over it. "Looks like you've thought of everything!" she'd said. "I can come over and finish up whatever you don't finish tonight," she'd offered.

"Thanks, but you don't have to do that. Jonathan is going to pick up whatever I leave and bring it to Cedar Springs."

Her mother had nodded; her father had stepped back into Jane's apartment. "Honda's good to go. Now you be careful driving out there, Janey. There are speed traps around Brenham, you know."

"I'll be careful," she'd promised.

He'd shifted his gaze to the floor. "Well. Guess we better get, Terri," he'd said, and glanced up at Jane. He'd smiled a little. "Come here, pumpkin," he'd said, opening his arms to Jane. She'd walked into his embrace, held him close, the scent of his aftershave bringing back memories of many Christmas mornings. Her father had kissed the top of her head. "You go do what you need to do, Janey. But you get on home as soon as you can."

"I will. I promise." She'd reluctantly stepped back. "Hopefully it will all go quick."

"Jim, go warm up the car," her mother had said, forgetting that it was humid and eighty-five degrees outside.

Jane's father had winked at Jane and sauntered out. As soon as he'd gone, Terri had grabbed Jane in a big hug, squeezing her tightly to her. After a moment she'd let go and reached into her purse, withdrawing an envelope. "Here," she'd said. "Here's a little money to help you get set up."

"Oh, Mom," Jane had said, her voice breaking a little. "You didn't have to do that."

"I know I didn't have to. I wanted to," her mother had insisted, and pushed it into Jane's hand. Her mother had cupped her face with her palm and smiled. "Janey, my love, I hope you find whatever it is you are looking for. That's my prayer, that you find it and then come home where you belong. I want my girl to be happy."

Jane had smiled gratefully. "Thanks, Mom."

"But you guard your heart," she'd added, tapping Jane's chest. "It is the wellspring of life, you know. You guard it with all that you've got."

So it had all come down to this, Jane thought as she pulled away from McDonald's with an enormous Coke and an order of fries. It was odd, really—there was such randomness to life, to her being given up, here but for the grace of God and all of that. For whatever reason, of all the babies born that day, Jane's mother had given her away. For all Jane knew, she was out there somewhere wondering if her baby was okay.

Or maybe she was out there not wondering at all. Whatever the truth was, Jane was determined not to leave Cedar Springs until she had it.

4

❧

*T*he house was huge, like something you'd see show-cased on House and Garden TV. It sat up on a hill, on its own natural pedestal, separated from the other houses just down the road in the swank Arbolago Hills subdivision. The entrance to the house was marked by tall iron gates with cursive Ps emblazoned in the ironwork. The house, which was so big that it had a name—Summer's End—was styled like a Tuscan villa with a red tile roof, a fountain in the middle of the circular drive, azaleas and roses flanking the entrance, and bougainvillea in flower boxes beneath the windows.

One would never guess tragedy shadowed the people who lived here.

Jane knew only because the woman from the placement agency who had sent her here for the interview had told her what had happened to Asher Price, the owner. He'd lost his wife in a tragic car accident a little less than two years ago. In the blink of an eye, his beautiful wife, the mother of his two children, a woman in the prime of her life, was gone. *Tragic,* the woman had said. *So tragic.*

Jane guessed there was nothing that could ever ease the pain of losing someone so quickly, so suddenly. Those poor children, losing their mother just before Christmas. *No one saw the kids during the holidays. No one knows how they coped,* the lady had said. Now Asher Price, a partner in a national advertising firm out of Austin, was looking for a nanny for his children.

Jane felt very bad for Mr. Price and his children, she did, but *nanny* was not the sort of job she was really looking for. It was not the sort of job she would *ever* look for. She was a schoolteacher on summer break—that did not qualify her to be responsible for someone else's kids. "Don't you have something else, something like a waitress, or maybe a hostess?" she'd asked the lady, even though Jane had already hit most of the restaurants in and around town. No one was hiring.

"I don't have anything like that," the lady had said. "With so many layoffs, people are taking those jobs now. Tourism is really down around here."

But a nanny?

"Not a nanny per se," the woman had cheerfully tried to sell it. "More like a babysitter."

"I need flexible hours," Jane had said.

"I am certain they'll accommodate you," the lady had said, and thrust the information about the interview into Jane's hand with a smile.

"I'm not really qualified."

"Don't sell yourself short."

"May I think about it?" Jane had asked.

Babysitter, nanny. The only difference was in how long one had to babysit, and she really wondered if she could babysit all day, every day. She was thrilled and exhausted by the time the last bell rang at school, glad the kids were out of her hair for a few hours. And overnight? Jane feared she might turn out to be the sort of nanny to do something remarkably stupid on nanny-cam and then watch it go viral.

She'd called Nicole from the parking lot of the placement agency. "What do you think about nanny?"

There had been a long moment of silence. "Are you kidding?" Nicole had asked.

"That's what I thought."

"Jane, you're a *teacher*. Not a nanny."

"I know, I know."

"That's not your thing."

But what was her thing? "I don't know," Jane had said, and squeezed her eyes shut a moment. "I'm not having any luck finding a job. The economy out here sucks. I think I am going to go check it out."

"God, Janey, don't do anything completely stupid," Nicole had cautioned her. "I mean that in the nicest possible way."

Jane had laughed. "Give Sage a kiss for me," she'd said, and gone back inside to tell the lady she'd go for the interview.

Jane didn't want to do it, yet here she was, sitting just outside the massive gates of Summer's End. "*Nanny*," she muttered under her breath and punched in the code the placement agency had given her, waited for the gates to swing open, then drove her Honda through and followed the drive up to the door, parking next to the fountain.

She got out and looked up. *That* was a house. She and her mother used to watch a real estate show that featured houses just like this. What was it, ten or twelve thousand square feet? More? She knew without seeing it that it was filled with marble and granite and hand-carved moldings. She did not belong in a house like that.

"This is so wrong," she muttered and pushed her hair behind her ears.

Mr. Price was undoubtedly expecting someone who had real experience in childcare, someone who was a nanny by profession. But he had the misfortune of being stuck in Cedar Springs, where, apparently, nannies did not congregate.

Jane did a quick check of herself in the side-view mirror of her car. Her long, dark brown and perpetually curly hair was loosely knotted at her nape. She wore a black pencil skirt and sweater set and some plain black pumps. The only thing this Mary Poppins was missing was a spoonful of sugar.

"Okay. Job. You *need* one," she reminded herself. She had no idea how long she'd be here, and her savings weren't so great that she could live on them indefinitely. So she slung her briefcase with extra resumés over her shoulder and walked determinedly to the front door. She rang the bell and waited, watching through the beveled glass as a figure moved toward her.

Jane was expecting Mr. Price to open the door, not a pretty young woman. She had short blonde hair and very high heels, and was wearing a very chic suit that Jane was fairly certain she'd not bought at Kohl's, where Jane had purchased her sweater set. The woman looked to be about Jane's age, around thirty.

"Miss Aaron?" The woman's voice had a slight East Coast twinge to it.

"Yes, Jane Aaron," Jane said and extended her hand.

"I am Tara, Mr. Price's assistant." She shook Jane's hand with a feather-light touch. "Please come in."

Jane's guess was right—the wide foyer was mostly marble under a soaring ceiling with elaborate crown molding. The décor was very minimalist and very white but for the pair of shadow paintings of a boy and girl on one wall.

"Would you like some iced tea?" Tara asked, gesturing toward a sunken living area.

And risk spilling it in this palace? "No, thank you," Jane said, following her.

The interior was spectacular. So spectacular that Jane was sorely tempted to text Nicole right there and tell her about it. She could smell a hint of jasmine, and she noticed candles on the carved mantel. The room looked like it had been styled for a photo in a glossy magazine. Every item was carefully placed: a sculpture of a Greek goddess, a large floral arrangement, a pair of tooled leather chairs at one end of the room, plush couches in the middle, and then another seating area arranged on an Oriental rug. The massive fireplace was on Jane's right, and the exterior wall of the living area was made up of east-facing windows that overlooked an edgeless pool and outdoor living area, and Lake Del Lago beyond. It was a very picturesque, a very expensive, view.

"Please have a seat," Tara said and indicated a pair of overstuffed white chairs near the windows.

Jane sat, but she had to shift to the edge to keep from disappearing altogether in the deep cushions. Tara did not seem to have that problem; she sat across from Jane, her long legs elegantly crossed. Above Tara's head and the fireplace mantel was a vibrant painting of flowers in a vase, their petals falling on a polished table.

Tara noticed Jane admiring it. "Mrs. Price painted that," she said. "She was very talented."

Jane had to agree—that painting looked like it ought to have been hanging in a museum. "Will Mr. Price be joining us?" Jane asked as she removed an extra copy of her resumé from her briefcase.

"He'll be joining us via telephone. He's in Munich at the moment." She smiled. "I hope you don't mind if I conduct the interview. I know his children and his preferences very well."

It seemed bizarre to Jane that Asher Price wouldn't be here to personally interview the nanny candidates. She couldn't imagine Nicole letting anyone near Sage without a full background check and a thorough grilling by her.

"It was an emergency," Tara added.

"Oh. Nothing serious, I hope," Jane replied.

"No. Just business."

Too busy, Jane guessed. Too busy to check out the people he might stick with his kids all day long. "I have a resumé—"

"That's not necessary. The placement agency sent one," Tara said, picking up a file on the table between them and opening it. "So you're a teacher?" she asked, peering at the contents of the file.

"Yes." Jane resisted the urge to push a bothersome strand of dark hair behind her ear. "I've taught second grade for a few years now and I've been attending graduate school around that. But I've reached the point where I need to devote myself full-time to finishing my degree." *Or get kicked out of the program.* "I am finishing my thesis."

"Do you like teaching second grade?" Tara asked, gliding right over the graduate school issue.

"Love it," Jane answered honestly. "Second graders are the perfect age for teaching. They aren't babies anymore but are still innocent. And they are so eager to learn."

Tara nodded. "We're a long way from Houston," she remarked and suddenly looked up, her gaze flicking over Jane.

"Yes, we are. I felt like I needed to be someplace where I won't have a lot of distractions so I can finish my thesis."

"What sort of distractions?"

Jane blinked. "Boyfriend," she blurted. "Family. That sort of thing." She held her breath, waiting.

"I understand that all too well," Tara murmured. "What is your thesis about?"

That was not something Jane really wanted to talk

about. Yet. "Ah . . . just how kids cope with loss." That was a very vague interpretation of what she was actually doing. "I'm still doing research. Lots of book work," she added, as if that explained her need to be in Cedar Springs.

"So the boyfriend . . . is he okay with you being here? Or is he going to be popping in every weekend?"

"Do what you need to do," Jonathan had said to her when they'd parted. *"When you get back, we'll see where we stand."*

"I don't think he will," Jane said and tried to smile. "You know how it is."

"I do," Tara agreed. "I suppose the placement agency described the job to you?"

"They said Mr. Price needed a nanny."

"For lack of a better term," Tara said. "Mr. Price is a partner in GSD&P—Green, Sutcliff, Dyer and Price, the advertising firm. Have you heard of them?"

Jane shook her head.

"They are national and handle several international accounts. They landed BMW a month ago, which is huge. But there are some issues. All of that to say Mr. Price's job is very demanding. He tries to be here as much as he can, but he is looking for someone who can keep an eye on his kids while he is working and when he is away."

Nanny is precisely the right term for it, Jane thought wryly.

"If you don't mind, I am going to call him now. He has a few questions he'd like to ask you."

"Sure," Jane said.

"Follow me?" Tara asked.

Jane followed her down a long hall and thick carpet. The hall was lined with paintings. Jane recognized Lake Del Lago in one. Tara led her into an office with hardwood floors and a wall of built-in bookshelves that were filled with books. There was a beautiful mahogany desk and an executive chair in the office; Tara walked around and sat in the chair, gestured to one of the upholstered chairs across from her, and picked up the phone.

Jane sat. "Hey," Tara said into the phone a moment later, as if she were talking to a friend. "Oh, sorry." She glanced at her wristwatch. "Yes, we can make it quick." She looked up at Jane. "Yes, everything looks good. Ah . . ." She glanced away from Jane. "The teacher. Second grade."

Jane shifted self-consciously, pushing her hair behind her ears again.

"Okay," Tara said and punched a button. "You're on speaker."

"Hello, Miss Aaron," a low male voice said. "I am sorry I can't be there today, but you're in good hands with Tara."

Even his children? Jane wondered. "Hello—"

"I only have a few minutes to ask a few questions."

"Okay," Jane said, leaning forward.

"Have you ever been arrested?"

"What? No, *no*," Jane said quickly, hoping they hadn't somehow learned about an unfortunate joyride when she was seventeen.

"Do you drink or smoke?"

"No."

"Have you ever been delinquent on a bill?"

Jane's eyes widened. "I . . . maybe one or two through the years, but no, I am not delinquent."

"Do you speak Spanish or French? Any languages?"

"No."

He paused, as if mulling it over. "I'll be frank, Miss Aaron. Your credentials indicate you have the sort of background I am looking for. My kids need a strong presence and a firm hand. Are you that person?"

Was she that person? Jane looked helplessly to Tara, who didn't even blink; she was jotting something down on paper. "I'm sure I can do the job, Mr. Price," Jane said.

"Great," he said. "Thank you. Tara, please pick up."

Tara picked up the phone. "Would you mind waiting outside?" she asked Jane.

Jane nodded and walked out, her thoughts spinning. This job sounded like too much responsibility, and she wanted exactly the opposite. She wanted only a quiet place to live, a place where she could hang out while she did what she had to do in Cedar Springs. *A strong presence? A firm hand?* Was that her?

The door swung open suddenly, startling Jane. "Well!" Tara said as she walked out with a big smile. "Thanks for talking with Mr. Price. Sorry we had to squeeze it in like that, but he's so busy."

And curt, Jane thought. So far, she was not a fan.

"He'd like me to show you the house."

Jane definitely wanted to see the house, if for no other reason than to tell her mother about it. "I'd love to," she said and followed Tara down the hall again, past the enormous living area. In another hall, Tara paused in front of a huge picture. There was the family on horseback. Another photo of them sitting on a big rock somewhere. Mrs. Price with the two kids—one of them a baby, one a little girl. Mr. Price stood to her right. He was tall and trim, his build athletic, but without being overpowering. He had dark golden hair and a handsome smile. Mrs. Price was beautiful, with sleek black hair that Jane instantly envied.

"This is Riley and Levi," Tara said, indicating the boy and girl. "They're older now. Levi is five and Riley is twelve. She'll be thirteen next month." Tara glanced at Jane and said low, "She could use some feminine guidance, you know? It must be awful to be without a mother."

"I can't imagine," Jane agreed.

Tara moved on, taking Jane through another sitting area with huge windows and floral chintz furnishings. "Here is the kitchen," she said.

The kitchen had a Viking stove and granite countertops, of course, and opened onto a very large den. This room looked the most lived in. There was a toy truck on the floor. Someone had written Piano lesson Tuesday on a chalkboard that was attached to a wall between the kitchen and den. There were shoes behind the couch and a pile of books scattered near the hearth.

"Let's move upstairs," Tara said, indicating a staircase. Upstairs, the family media room had theater-style seating. There was also a large playroom with chalkboard walls and built-in toy benches and a row of windows overlooking the pool. There were several bedrooms—Jane thought she counted eight in all—and every bedroom facing east had a balcony overlooking the lake.

The house was perfect, everything pristine. But it seemed a little off to Jane. The house where she'd grown up was always cluttered with her and her brothers' things. And Nicole's house—as meticulous as Nicole was about a clean environment, there was always evidence that Sage was about in the shoes and toys and books that were scattered everywhere. There was none of that lived-in look here. This house looked more like a showcase than a home, and Jane wondered if perhaps the kids were actually living elsewhere at present.

One other thing stood out to Jane: Mrs. Price was everywhere. There she was on a boat laughing at the camera. There she was with Mr. Price at a black-tie function. Again with a group of women dressed as expensively as she was. Mrs. Price was a beautiful woman with a brilliant, dazzling white smile and that beautiful mane of black hair. It was heartbreaking to think that the perfect family in the pictures had been torn apart by an automobile accident. How devastating it must have been for her children. And for Mr. Price.

"Last but not least, the nanny quarters," Tara said, leading Jane downstairs once again, using the back staircase. A middle-aged woman wearing an apron had appeared in the kitchen. She was a little butterball with graying hair and clear blue eyes and one of the kindest smiles Jane had ever seen.

"Hello, Carla," Tara said.

"Well hello there, Tara!" the woman said cheerfully as she wiped her hands on her apron and smiled broadly. "I didn't expect to see you back so soon. You may as well take one of the guest rooms as often as you come to Cedar Springs!"

Tara smiled. "This is Jane Aaron. Jane, Carla Petrie. She keeps this house in tip-top shape."

"I do what I can," Carla said, beaming. "Mrs. P liked a very clean house."

"It's beautiful," Jane said.

"Well, aren't you sweet," Carla said warmly.

Tara led Jane out of the kitchen and onto a breezeway, adjacent to the pool, that led to another door. Tara opened it and stepped aside. "*Voila*. The nanny quarters."

Jane stepped across the threshold and suppressed her gasp of delight. The quarters were at least as large as the small apartment Jane had looked at yesterday and definitely nicer.

There was a small kitchen with a granite countertop and stainless appliances. It was separated from the living area by a limestone bar with bar stools covered in cowhide. Over the fireplace hung a flat-screen TV. The furnishings were leather, and through a pair of French doors,

Jane could see what looked like a queen-sized bed and four posters.

"This room obviously hasn't been opened in a while," Tara said, and opened another pair of French doors, revealing the pool just beyond. "Have a look around," she urged Jane.

"This is where the nanny is going to live?" Jane asked, her voice full of awe.

"Yes. It's a guesthouse. Private, but close to the kids. You should check out the bathroom," Tara suggested, gesturing for Jane to go into the sleeping area.

Jane wanted to swoon when she saw it. It was all tile and marble, with a glass shower and a deep-jetted tub. She walked back to the doors opened to overlook the pool and the stunning view of Lake Del Lago beyond.

"So what do you think?" Tara asked.

"I think it's beautiful," Jane said. "All of it." She looked at Tara. "It's an amazing house, Tara, but I have to be honest. I'm not really a nanny. I've never been responsible for someone else's kids, and I don't plan on being in Cedar Springs very long. Maybe a couple of months at most. I'd think Mr. Price would want someone with more experience and a little more permanent."

Tara didn't seem remotely fazed by Jane's words. "Mr. Price has had a very difficult time finding someone with enough maturity and skills to be with his kids. Right now, he is interviewing people who can meet his needs at least for the summer until a more permanent solution can be found."

"Ah," Jane said.

Tara shifted closer. "Can you tell me if you are at least interested in the position?"

Jane looked at the pool and the guesthouse. She needed a job, and she wasn't stupid. This setting was hard to pass up. "I am interested," she said carefully. "But I need some flexibility to work on my thesis. I don't want to work weekends, and I'd also like to have Tuesday and Thursday afternoons after three. And I'd like to meet the kids before I say more."

Tara looked at her watch. "They'll be home from school in a half hour, if you care to wait." She gestured to the door. "Let's go back to the house and talk a little bit more about the job."

"Okay," Jane said. "Just out of curiosity, how many candidates is he interviewing?"

Tara opened the door leading onto the breezeway. "As of today, just one."

5

*J*ane took the job because she needed it and because she felt bad for the kids who had lost their mother and were left with such a rude, curt, absent father. She had not wanted to begin the job before Mr. Price had come back from Germany, but Carla left promptly at five every afternoon, and Tara had explained there would be a generous bonus if Jane could see her way to starting by the first of the following week.

Jane thought she could handle it after meeting the kids a couple of times. Levi was adorable. He was five years old with black hair and big blue eyes. His sister Riley was less adorable. She was a pretty girl with her mother's blue eyes, and her father's golden hair, but she was at an awkward age. The last time Jane had seen her, Riley had been wearing pencil-thin jeans that had made her legs look even skinnier than they were, and a black T-shirt with a mystic symbol on the chest.

She was quiet, eyed Jane warily, and Jane noticed that she tended to stand off by herself, moving back when someone moved toward her, like a pool toy bobbing just beyond one's reach. Riley had said more than once in Jane's presence—actually, it seemed like a dozen times—that they didn't need a nanny. Jane couldn't blame her for that. What kid wanted a nanny instead of a parent?

Nevertheless, Jane thought she could handle it.

Jonathan showed up that Sunday with her things and helped her move into the guesthouse on Monday. "Wow," he said. "This place is *sick*."

"Yes, it's unreal," Jane agreed, looking around.

Jonathan leaned back against the door of the guesthouse, his arms folded. "So you're sure you want to do this whole Mary Poppins thing, Janey?"

"No," she said, smiling sheepishly. "But it's the best thing going in Cedar Springs, and I need a job if I am going to be here. I'd eat through my savings in a month without it."

He pressed his lips together. "Okay," he said. He looked at Jane again, his eyes searching hers. He always looked at her like that now, a bit hopeful, a bit angry. "I guess this is it, then, huh? Where we take the totally cliché break?"

"It's just a summer."

"Just a summer," he repeated. "You and I have both been around long enough to know that summers sometimes turn into winters, and winters turn into years."

"Jonathan—"

"No, don't," he said, throwing up a hand. "Please don't try and explain again. It never sounds any better." He pushed away from the door. "I need to get on the road. I have to work tomorrow." He shoved his hands in his pockets. "I'm going to miss seeing you."

"Me, too," she said softly and moved to him, slipping her arms around his waist, laying her head on his shoulder.

Jonathan stroked her hair. "Remember the time we went rollerblading?"

Jane snorted. "Yes."

"I bet you fell twenty times. But you kept getting back

up and tried and tried again, and you never once complained."

"I was complaining in my head. I couldn't walk for a
week."

Jonathan chuckled. "I fell in love with you that day."

Jane sighed sadly and looked up at him. "It's just a
summer, Jonathan."

He looked dubious and kissed her softly. "Call me," he
said and slipped out the door.

Jane watched him go. She had a half hour before she
began her job, right at five when Carla left for the day.
She lay down on the eight-hundred-thread-count Egyp-
tian cotton bedspread and stared up at the beamed ceiling, remembering how Jonathan would sit on a chair in
her apartment with his guitar, creating a new song. He
would grin and grab her hand as she walked by, pulling
her back, kissing her knuckles, then her wrist.

That was the thing—she'd never grabbed his hand and
kissed it. She'd never feared that he was someone who
would escape her, that she had to hold on to.

Tears blurred her vision, and Jane sat up, wiping her
eyes. She moved to stand up and noticed a drawing on
the wall beside her. It was a mother and child in abstract.
Jane already knew Susanna Price's distinctive signature as
the artist. The drawing made her feel weird, particularly
given her reason for being in Cedar Springs. She stood
up, removed the drawing from the wall, and put it on a
shelf in the closet before she went to change.

In the kitchen, Carla had her handbag and a green grocery bag on the counter, ready to go. "Are you all moved
in?" she asked cheerfully as she thrust her hand into her
handbag and dug around for her keys.

"Yep. Jonathan is on his way back to Houston."

"He seems really nice," Carla said. "And he's cute, too." Jane nodded, blushing a little. "Okay, the kids are up watching a movie and there is dinner in the warming oven," she said, pointing to one of three ovens. "I thought on your first night you ought to have something fun, so I made you a pizza. Reheat it at three-fifty for about fifteen minutes and you should be good. Did Tara tell you how to use the monitoring system?" she asked, referring to the elaborate intercom and monitoring system built into the house.

"She did."

"Make sure you have that on at all times," Carla warned her. "Levi has been known to sleepwalk." She smiled fondly. "He thinks there are ghosts in the attic."

Jane smiled. "Have you worked here long, Carla?"

"Seven years!" she announced proudly and slung her black bag over her shoulder. "Okay, Jane! You call me at home if you need me. I'm probably easier to get hold of than anyone else if something comes up. Good luck!" she said cheerily and waved as she went out.

Jane sincerely hoped she wouldn't need to get hold of anyone.

She went in search of her charges, up to the second floor and the media room. The volume of whatever the kids were watching was so loud that Jane could hear it through the soundproofing. She knocked once, realized that was futile given the volume, and opened the door a crack. The sounds of a high-speed car chase blasted her. She saw Riley's honey blonde head just over the top of one of the theater chairs and walked into the room. "Hey, Riley!" she shouted over the din.

Riley hardly glanced at her.

"Could we turn that down?"

Riley refused to acknowledge her, so Jane picked up

the remote from the table beside Riley and turned the volume down to a reasonable level.

"I was watching that," Riley said.

"You're still watching it, but this way, you won't go deaf before you graduate from high school. Where's Levi?"

"I don't know," Riley said with a shrug and slumped deeper down into the leather theater seating. "It's your job to know. Not mine."

Okay, starting the new job with some good old-fashioned preteen attitude. "It is my job," Jane agreed pleasantly, "but I don't know where he is and I am asking for your help."

"I said, I don't know," she repeated, her blue eyes cold. "I'm not the nanny."

"No. No, you're not. That would be me. Tell you what—we'll talk about how we are going to navigate our way through the next few weeks once I find your brother."

Riley sighed and turned her attention back to the TV. "He's been shoveling dirt into the pool. I can't believe you didn't see him when you came out of the guesthouse."

Jane forgot what she was going to say. "Dirt?"

Riley suddenly laughed. "This is so great! He's been out there shoveling dirt and you didn't even know it!"

Fabulous. "I'll be back," Jane warned Riley, but she hadn't even made it to the door before Riley had pumped up the volume again.

Levi was indeed shoveling dirt into the pool. There was a very dark and very large circle on the grotto end of the pool where he was about to dump another bucket of dirt. From *atop* the grotto. "*Levi!*" Jane exclaimed, horrified. Startled, Levi turned and looked at her at the same moment he dumped the bucket of dirt into the pool.

"Levi, *no*," Jane said, hurrying forward and holding her

hands out for the bucket. "Come down from there! What are you doing?"

"I'm going to make mud pies," he said. He tossed the plastic bucket to her. Jane caught it easily, then caught his hand, pulling him down from the elaborate waterfall that flowed into the pool. Once she was assured the child would not plunge to a watery death, she looked at the pool, the bucket, and Levi's lovely round face.

He had dirt under his nose and another streak on one cheek. He was watching her with an expression of wishful expectancy, as if he believed she had the secret for hurrying his project along.

"Levi . . . you can't make mud in the pool," Jane said, and his face fell. "It would take you a *year* to put enough dirt in the pool to get mud. If you want to make mud pies, we can do that in the garden. Just not in the pool. Okay?"

"Do you have a garden?" he asked, confused.

"No, your garden. Don't you have a garden here?"

He shook his head.

Eureka. Jane smiled. "Oh wow, I thought all boys had a garden. Would you like one? You can plant things and dig a lot of holes."

"I want one," Levi said, his eyes rounding.

"Okay! We'll get to work on that tomorrow."

"What about the dirt?" Levi asked, leaning over to peer into the deep end of the pool.

"That is an excellent question," Jane said. "We'll think of something. In the meantime, let's get you cleaned up."

"I'm hungry, too," Levi said and broke into an odd, apelike dance. "Carla always gives me gummies."

"Really?" Jane said, gesturing toward the house.

Levi threw his head back, squeezed his eyes shut, and smiled broadly. "*Really,*" he said, mimicking her. He then began to imitate an ape leaping across the decking toward the house. "Then I want some grapes!" he shouted and disappeared into the kitchen door.

With Levi's help, Jane found the stash of gummies and followed him, doing his ape walk, up to the media room. The volume once again blasted them when Jane opened the door. She didn't bother to ask Riley this time; she just picked up the remote and turned down the volume.

"Can we watch *Phineas and Ferb*?" Levi asked his sister.

"No." Riley looked at Levi. Both kids lunged for the remote at the same moment, but Riley was there first, which prompted Levi to hit his sister.

"Hey!" Jane cried. She grabbed the remote from Riley and turned off the TV. That earned shouts from both kids.

"Okay, listen," Jane said, sensing a mutiny within the first thirty minutes of being on the job. "We need to establish some ground rules—"

"No, we don't," Riley said. "You can't really make us do anything. You're just a babysitter. You don't get to tell us what to do."

Levi, God bless him, was too young to realize he could question authority, and stared at his sister with wide-eyed horror. So did Jane as she frantically thought what to do next. "Okay, Riley, you have made it very clear you don't like me being here. I know this is a big change for you, and one you didn't ask for."

"I can't listen to this," Riley said and flopped back into her chair with dramatic flair.

"This is the way it has to be for a time," Jane stubbornly continued. "At least until your father comes home. You can take it up with him, but until then, we need to figure out how to make this work."

"Knock yourself out. I don't care what you do. All I know is that I don't want you here, I don't need you here, and I don't care what you say."

Teaching second grade had in no way prepared Jane for the cool hostility of a preteen. "I think you need to go to your room until you are ready to be civil." That was all she had, the thing her mother had used on her during the teen years.

Riley blinked. And then she laughed. "That is off the chain!" She unfolded her legs and stood up; she was almost as tall as Jane. "I'm not five, Jane."

"I'm five!" Levi said.

"And besides, I have a TV in my room *and* a computer. I can do whatever I want. For all you know, I am hooking up with sex predators online."

"Go," Jane said, pointing to the door. With her arms folded across her chest, Riley glared. For a moment, Jane feared Riley would refuse her. If that happened, she didn't know what she would do. But Riley walked out. Her exit was followed a moment later by the sound of a door slamming shut.

"Can I watch *Phineas and Ferb*?" Levi asked, as if nothing had happened.

Jane looked at him. She picked up the remote and handed it to him. "Have at it," she said, and as Levi settled in to watch the cartoon, Jane walked outside the media room and stood in the hall, wondering what in the hell she'd gotten herself into.

6

The late afternoon sun was slanting through the windows of BMW headquarters in Munich when Asher stepped out of a meeting to call Riley. He'd had several urgent text messages from her, the last one coming from Levi's phone. A couple of days, maybe three, had passed since the new nanny had begun work, and Asher figured Riley's urgent messages had something to do with her. Levi seemed to like the nanny. He'd said they were building a garden.

Riley hadn't said much at all, other than she didn't like the nanny. But then again, she hadn't liked any of the others.

"Mr. Price, would you like coffee?" an assistant asked as he waited for the number to connect.

"No, thank you—"

"Hello?"

Asher did not recognize the woman's voice. "Sorry, I have the wrong number—"

"Mr. Price? Oh, hi, it's Jane Aaron," the woman said. "You know, the new nanny?"

The new nanny's voice had a sexy, husky quality to it. Asher had missed that in their initial conversation. "Yes, hello, I know who you are. Why are you answering Riley's phone?"

"Oh . . . unfortunately, I had to take the phone away from her."

"Why? What happened?"

"She has some serious issues with me, Mr. Price. She doesn't want a nanny and is making it very difficult for me. But I think we are working things out."

Asher's stomach dropped. He knew better than anyone else how difficult Riley could be sometimes, but he suddenly thought of all those text messages he'd half ignored while working, and had a horrible vision of things going terribly wrong in his house. He imagined his children subjected to some Nazi Brunhilda without him there to defend them. "Where is Riley?" he demanded.

"She and Levi are swimming. Well, Levi is swimming. Riley is sitting in a chaise with her iPod so she can't hear me."

"I am a little distressed to hear you took her phone, Miss Aaron. I would have appreciated it if we could have discussed it first."

There was a moment of silence. And then Jane Aaron said, "Are you kidding?"

"What? No, I'm not kidding."

"No offense, Mr. Price, but you haven't called me, or otherwise communicated at all except through your assistant, and then you expect me to allow Riley to push me out the door, which is exactly what she'd like to do in case you haven't talked to her, because she really doesn't want me here—"

"I am fully aware," he interrupted. "I've received no less than one hundred text messages from her."

"Aha!" she cried triumphantly. "Then you *know* how hard this has been! Taking her phone seemed to be the only thing that would work, the only way I could get Riley to stop speaking so disrespectfully and calling her grandmother to complain just to see if she can get rid of me. I told her *you* could decide if and when she gets her phone back. If that's not okay, then maybe I'm not the right person for this job."

He should have been furious at the way she was speaking to him, but he was more incredulous. "Are you threatening me? Are you going to bolt and run after only a few days on the job? Where's your mettle?"

Jane Aaron gasped. "My *mettle*? Mr. Price, are you going to work with me here, or are you going to call up from around the world and issue orders without so much as a hello or welcome aboard?"

Asher blinked. And then he almost laughed. He couldn't remember the last time someone in his employ had spoken to him like this. "Point taken, Miss Aaron. I will be home Thursday by six o'clock, if there aren't any travel delays. After I spend some time with my children, you and I can talk about my expectations and Riley's phone."

"Great!" she said pertly. "And maybe we can talk about some of my expectations, too, if that's all right."

Who *was* this chick? "Fine. Now—how are the kids?"

"They're good," she said, her voice cheerful again. "They are adjusting as well as could be expected. Levi and I have begun a garden. I checked with your groundskeeper and he said that was fine."

The assistant leaned out the door and pointed to her watch. The meeting was starting up again and Asher still needed to call his office in Austin. "Okay, that's great," he said impatiently, looking at his watch. "Please tell the kids I'll call them at the usual time tonight. I'll be back on Thursday."

"Okay, see you then," she said, and hung up.

Asher hardly noticed; he was already phoning the Austin office.

* * *

Mr. Price had been away from home for over two weeks now, and his children could hardly wait for six o'clock Thursday to come around. School had ended yesterday and they were very excited that he was coming home—Levi talked about nothing but his daddy all morning, and even Riley was upbeat.

Carla had made a lasagna and salad for the grand occasion, with instructions for Jane on how to heat it. "It's one of Mr. Price's favorite meals," she said proudly.

Jane found it hard to believe that a demon actually ate food. She was still smarting over her conversation with the pompous ass.

About three that afternoon the phone rang, and Riley grabbed it before Jane could reach it. "Hi, Tara," she said. She was twirling around with the phone like a ballerina, her fingers trailing over the kitchen island. And then Riley stopped. Her face fell. "Why?" she asked, and as she listened, her shoulders visibly sagged. "Okay, fine," she said, her voice cool. "Bye."

"Who was that?" Levi asked from a row of trucks he'd lined up in the den.

Riley looked at her little brother. "Dad had to change his flight. He won't be home until tomorrow."

"What?" Jane said. "When?"

But Riley had already walked out of the kitchen. Jane looked incredulously at Carla.

Carla sighed. "The lasagna will keep 'til tomorrow," she said. She sounded as disappointed as the kids. "I think I have some chicken soup in the freezer I can dig out for tonight." She disappeared into the utility room to check the freezer.

Jane looked at Levi. He was staring glumly at his trucks. "Hey, you want to go check our plants?" she asked him.

"No," he said. "I'm gonna go watch TV."

As it turned out, there was no need for Carla to dig out the soup. Levi wouldn't eat anything but peanut butter and jelly, and Riley refused to come out of her room. *"I'm not hungry!"* she shouted through the door when Jane tried to coax her. So Jane ate soup alone, sitting in a huge kitchen where she didn't really belong, watching over kids who didn't really want her.

Later that night, she fell asleep on her laptop. Literally, on top of it—she'd sat with it on her bed, staring at an open page of her thesis, unable to find the words she needed. She didn't remember drifting to sleep, but she was awakened in the very early morning by the sound of doors opening and shutting coming through the monitor. *Levi.*

Jane found Levi in his room. Still half asleep, he'd changed into shorts and was pulling the sheets off his bed. "Levi, what are you doing?" she asked through a yawn as the boy stumbled by, dragging his sheets.

"Nothing."

He was clearly doing something. Jane followed him downstairs, to the utility room, where he pushed the sheets into the washing machine as if he'd done it many times before. When he put them in, he turned around and looked at Jane, his expression forlorn.

"What's the matter, Levi?"

He shifted his gaze away from her, to the washing machine.

Jane knelt down beside him. "Did you have an accident?" He still would not look at her but kept his gaze on the washing machine, pressing a finger against the glass front. "Did you forget to go to the potty?"

He shrugged, then looked at her from the corner of his eye. "Don't tell Carla, okay?"

Jane looked at the washing machine. Carla would know when she saw the sheets.

"Please don't tell her," Levi begged. "She doesn't like it when I do that and she'll tell Dad."

Jane's heart went out to him. She gathered him in her arms and hugged him tightly to her. "I promise I won't," she said, and kissed his cheek. She stood up, ran her hand over his head. "You want some breakfast?"

"Can I have Lucky Charms?" he asked, brightening.

While Levi ate Lucky Charms, Jane sipped coffee and perused the Neiman Marcus catalogue addressed to Susanna Price. When Riley appeared, Jane almost choked on her coffee. Riley had dyed her hair pink. As if that hadn't been enough, she'd painted her fingernails black.

Riley opened the refrigerator and fetched an orange.

"What did you do to your hair?" Levi asked.

Riley peeled her orange as if Levi hadn't spoken.

Carla walked in from the pantry, took one look at Riley, and said, "Oh, dear Lord."

"Riley?" Jane said.

"What."

"That's really cool. I like it." Riley shot Jane a suspicious look, but Jane smiled nonetheless. "But you probably should have checked with me first."

"With *you*?" Riley snorted. "It's my hair. I can do what I want. I don't need permission."

"I know someone who won't like it," Carla said. Riley shrugged indifferently and walked out of the kitchen with her orange.

Carla looked at Jane. "Mr. P is not going to like that at all," she said ominously.

At noon, Tara called and reported that Mr. Price was on his way and would be home by six. When Carla told them, Levi began to ask every half hour, "What time is it?"

"Three thirty," Jane said when he'd asked for the umpteenth time. "I'll tell you what—why don't we go get a smoothie while we wait?"

"I don't want a smoothie, I want my phone," Riley said as she chipped anxiously at her black nail polish.

"So you've said five million times," Jane said cheerfully. "But take heart, Riley—the end is nigh."

"I want a smoothie!" Levi exclaimed. "I want a *green* one!" he declared as he climbed up on the counter. Carla removed him with a loud sigh of exasperation.

"You don't even know what a smoothie is, Levi," Riley said.

"I do too!" He climbed up on the counter again. "It's *green*."

"Off the counter, please," Jane said. "A smoothie is like a milk shake, only better for you. And they make great ones at Daisy's Saddle-brew Coffee Shop. I was thinking it would be nice to get out of the house for a while."

"Yes, go, go," Carla said. "You kids are driving me crazy this week!"

"I don't want to go," Riley said. She was dressed in black pencil jeans and a black hoodie, in spite of the warm, humid weather.

"We're going," Jane said firmly but pleasantly. "Think of it as a field trip!"

Riley sighed dramatically, but she pushed away from the counter and walked toward the door. It wasn't much, but after the week Jane had had, she took it as a sign of progress.

They drove to the center of town in the Range Rover Mr. Price had made available to Jane to cart his kids around. At the Saddle-brew, Jane spotted Samantha Delaney's short dark hair behind the counter. Jane had met Sam her first day in Cedar Springs, and they'd become

friendly when Jane had stopped in for a coffee while she'd
been out looking for a job.

"Hey," Sam said, smiling at the kids. "So I guess you
took the job, huh?"

"I did," Jane said and forced a smile, as if it had been a
fabulous opportunity. She ordered smoothies for the three
of them—a special green one for Levi—and chatted with
Sam a moment before steering the kids to stuffed chairs
near the front windows.

"Hey, maybe we'll see Dad!" Levi said and hung over
the back of the chair, watching the cars pass by. "Riley,
there's your friend!" he said suddenly, turning so quickly
to Riley that he almost spilled his green smoothie before
Jane caught it and righted it.

"Who?" Riley asked, peering at the window. Her pretty
face suddenly paled. "Oh, *great*," she muttered, and
pushed deeper into the cushions.

"Tracy!" Levi shouted when the door opened, and he
waved his arm like he was flagging down a rescue plane.

"Levi, shut *up*!" Riley hissed, but Tracy had heard him
and, together with a large woman, walked to where Jane
and the kids sat. "Hi, Levi! Hi, *Riiiley*," she said, nudging
Riley's boot with her sandal.

"Hi," Riley said shyly.

Tracy was a cute girl with long brown hair and bangs.
She was wearing a halter top and a pair of turquoise short
shorts. She smiled easily at Jane. *Popular girl,* Jane thought.

"Hello," Jane said, coming to her feet. "I'm Jane Aaron."

"I'm Tracy, and this is my mom, Linda Gail."

"Linda Gail Graeber," her mother said and smiled
warmly at Jane. "Are you Riley's aunt?"

"Ah, no. I'm a nanny."

"*Nanny*!" Linda Gail said, as if that excited her. "Riley,
you didn't tell us you had a nanny."

"That's because I don't. She's only temporary until my dad gets back from Germany, and he's coming home today." Riley said all that without looking up.

Mrs. Graeber gave Jane a sympathetic smile.

"Why are you wearing that?" Tracy asked Riley. "It's hot."

Riley pulled the hood over her head and shrugged. Tracy had a sense of style that Riley did not yet possess, and it seemed to Jane that Riley shrank a bit in Tracy's presence.

"What did you do to your hair?" Tracy asked, leaning over, peering at the bit of pink that peeked out from Riley's hood.

"She made it pink," Levi said.

Jane glanced at Levi—and gasped with alarm. She made a lunge for him, grabbing his arm. He'd climbed onto the back of the chair and was balancing himself on two feet. She quickly yanked him down. "What are you doing? You don't want to fall and hurt yourself."

Levi responded by bouncing onto his seat in the chair.

"You're a handful, aren't you, Levi?" Linda Gail said cheerfully as she affectionately brushed her daughter's hair off her shoulders. "I've got two more at home and I'm still getting used to them," she said to Jane. "Are you from Cedar Springs?"

"No, Houston."

"*Houston*," Linda Gail said, nodding. "You came all the way out here to be a nanny?"

"*Mom*," Tracy moaned. "Don't start."

Linda Gail laughed. "All right, all right, I won't be nosy."

Tracy nudged Riley with her foot again. "Want to come over later this week? We can go swimming."

"Can't," Riley said. "My dad is coming home."

"At least call me," Tracy said. When Riley didn't respond,

Tracy shrugged it off. "Okay, see you," she said, and bounced up to the counter. Jane didn't think that Tracy would be lacking for any phone calls this summer. She probably had more friends than Levi had trucks.

"It was nice meeting you, Jane," Linda Gail said pleasantly. "Welcome to Cedar Springs."

Jane thanked her and watched her walk away before sitting in her chair again. She put her hand to Levi's legs to stop his kicking, and looked at Riley. "Tracy seemed really nice."

Riley looked down.

"I bet your dad wouldn't mind if you wanted to go over to her house one afternoon to swim," Jane suggested.

"I don't want to swim."

"Why not?" Jane asked curiously.

Riley sighed, as if Jane were taxing her. "Can we please go now?"

It would be nice, Jane thought, if she had a clue how to talk to this kid. She made a mental note to never, ever, teach middle school. *Talk to her like an adult,* Nicole had advised her. Jane would have to report back that speaking to this twelve-year-old like an adult wasn't exactly working gangbusters, either. She looked at her watch. It was early yet, but she said, "Yeah, let's go. Your dad could be home in an hour or so."

Levi bolted off the chair and raced for the door, almost knocking into a man who was entering at the same time. Riley walked out, too, leaving her caramel smoothie practically untouched.

Jane gathered up the cups and followed the kids out to her car.

And now, she thought as she started up the Range Rover, Mr. Warm and Fuzzy was coming home. As Jane drove the kids home, she wondered idly how long she'd last at Summer's End. She'd hate leaving that guesthouse, but she had a feeling she and Mr. Price were not going to hit it off. Especially when he saw Riley's hair.

At six that evening, Mr. Price called to say he would be late.

7

*A*sher called to tell his children his flight from New York was delayed and he expected to be home by ten. Unfortunately, he didn't account for summer storms in Texas, and it wasn't until half past midnight that his car service pulled up to the gates of his house.

He gave the gate code to the driver; the gates swung open, and the Lincoln Town Car eased through. Only a couple of lights were on in the house, and Asher felt a stab of disappointment. He was anxious to see his kids, to see their eyes, to hold them tight.

After he gathered his bags, Asher let himself in the front door and quietly put them down in the entry. A light was on in the kitchen, and another one over the stairwell. Beyond that, the house was dark and quiet.

Disappointment and fatigue weighed on him. So did hunger.

In the kitchen, Asher was surprised to find evidence of his kids. Carla and Maria, the girl who came in to do the heavy cleaning once a week, kept the house like a museum. But in the breakfast area, he spotted a calendar with stickers of plants affixed to different days of the week. There were two watering cans on the floor just inside the patio door, one big and one small, and next to that, two pairs of plastic gardening shoes. Packets of seedlings were piled on one end of the kitchen island.

He flipped on the overhead light. On the breakfast table were catalogues, which, he discovered on closer inspection, were of teen clothing. One catalogue was open and a little shirt or top or something was circled in red. Riley's iPod and laptop, covered in decals and the artfully painted letters R.A.P., were also on the table. His kid had an incredible artistic talent for a child . . . but she hadn't painted at all since Susanna had died.

Asher started toward the fridge, but his gaze fell on a picture that was lying on a small, built-in desk. Curious, he picked it up. It was a picture of Susanna poolside. She was dressed in a flowing gauzy swimsuit cover, the outline of her bikini visible beneath. He couldn't place the time or the occasion, but whatever it was, Susanna was wildly beautiful. A long tail of silken hair hung over her shoulder. She was laughing gaily, her mouth open, her blue eyes—Riley's eyes—bright and shining. She was holding a glass of white wine in one hand. A necklace dangled from the fingers of her other hand.

Asher's gut knotted. He picked it up and opened a drawer in the small desk, lifted up several papers and a phone book, and shoved the picture beneath them, then closed the door again.

He didn't want to be reminded. He'd spent the last year trying to forget.

He opened the fridge and studied the contents.

"Dad?"

That was his daughter's disembodied voice; he quickly shut the fridge, saw her slinking around the corner. She was wearing a ball cap backward, her hair tucked up underneath it. "Oh, man, you are a sight for sore eyes," he said and opened his arms.

Riley walked into them, slipping her arms around his waist as Asher folded himself around her, hugging her tight, lifting her off the ground. "God, I missed you," he said, and kissed her cheek.

"You're suffocating me," she protested, and Asher reluctantly put her down. Riley moved back, as if embarrassed by the display of affection. Things were strained between Riley and Asher, to say the least. He knew Riley blamed him for Susanna's death. She hadn't come right out and said it, but Asher sensed it, and God knew he blamed himself. He hadn't protected Susanna, he hadn't protected his children. It was a constant guilt, something that lived with him every moment of every day.

Now that Riley was almost a teen, it seemed as if the distance between them only deepened with each passing month.

"You were gone a really long time, Dad."

"I know," he said and cupped her chin, lifting her face so that he could look at it. "Longer than I ever wanted to be gone, that's for sure. I'm sorry I'm so late, kiddo."

She shrugged a little and turned her head from his hand, rubbing her nose with the tips of her fingers. Asher noticed the remnants of her black polish. He ran his hand over the crown of her ball cap; Riley ducked and moved away.

"What's under the hat?"

"Hair."

God, but she looked like Susanna. She had her mother's wide, blue eyes and classic high cheekbones. Sometimes it seemed as if Susanna hadn't really left them. "Levi's in bed?" Asher asked.

She nodded. "He's wetting the bed again. It's gross."

"He can't help it, Ri."

"I know," she said, yawning.

Carla had told Asher Levi's bed-wetting had picked up again. The kid was only five, and while the pediatrician had told Asher it wasn't so uncommon at this age, it was a concern for Asher. Levi was too young to understand why his mommy and daddy were gone. He was struggling like they all were, trying to find his way. The pediatrician had opined that Levi would grow out of it, and had recommended the usual remedies: no drinking before bedtime, get him up at night, etc. But Asher had noticed Levi's bed-wetting was worse when Asher was away, and in the last couple of months, he'd started having accidents during the day. There wasn't a pediatrician around who could convince Asher that was common at the age of five, that it wasn't some sort of psychological response to the things missing in Levi's young life.

The bed-wetting left Asher feeling completely helpless. He was failing his son. Levi needed stability, he needed everything to be all right so he could concentrate on things little boys should concentrate on, like getting to the potty on time and playing with his Transformers. Riley needed it just as much. Asher had figured out that as a father, he was good at providing all the material things, like a big house and toys and clothes, but he could not provide the most basic need for consistency in their lives. His was a constant struggle—his kids needed him, but so did the ad agency he'd helped found and grow into a respected national firm.

It had been a rough year for the agency. They'd lost accounts because of the economy and had been forced to lay off staff. Ron Sutcliff's illness had sent a ripple of fear through their investors and they'd weathered a very critical year right on the heels of Susanna's death. And through it all, Asher had been drowning in guilt and the need to be in two places at once.

"I'm making a sandwich," Asher said. "You want me to make you one, too?"

Riley nodded.

He fetched some ingredients from the fridge and spread them across the island. "I've missed talking to you," he said as he began to make the sandwiches.

"Yeah, well, the warden has my phone."

"And we are going to have a talk about that. But first, tell me what you've been doing."

"Nothing," Riley said. "What is there to do here? I've been hanging out. It's boring."

That only amplified Asher's guilt. "I know, Ri," he said, feeling wearier of a sudden. "I know it's been a real drag for you and Levi that I've had to travel so much lately. But you know that Mr. Sutcliff is sick and that I am trying to cover a lot of ground right now. Things will eventually settle down, but until they do, I need you to be patient with me."

"Whatever." She stretched her arm across the bar and laid her head on it.

"Do you like sprouts?" he asked. "Looks like Carla got a good deal on them."

"Oh yeah, she and the warden have decided we aren't eating enough healthy stuff. Like Levi and I are going to die if we eat one more candy."

Calling Jane Aaron "the warden" would indicate things had not improved between Riley and Miss Aaron. "About Miss Aaron . . . I understand you haven't been cooperating with her."

"I've been cooperating," Riley said insouciantly. "But she's kind of stupid, Dad. She's all like, 'Oooh, let's go get a smoothie,' or, 'Do you want to go to the gym and do some indoor rock climbing?' Like I am going to go climb a rock."

Rock climbing sounded fun to Asher. "I don't think those are necessarily crimes—"

"I don't need a nanny," Riley interrupted him. "I'm almost thirteen. I mean, Carla is here every day, and I don't see why Grandma Helen can't check in on us to make sure Carla hasn't killed us and stuffed our bodies in coolers and thrown them in the lake, or whatever it is you're afraid of. Why do we need a nanny?"

Did they have to have this conversation tonight? Again? "I know you don't want a nanny, Riley," he said calmly. "You don't want a stranger stepping into your life where Mom and I used to be, and God knows I get that. We've been on a roller coaster since Mom died. But we've been through this, and sweetheart, you are too young to live without supervision. And I've got a company that needs my attention. Obviously, something has to give, so we're going to have a nanny for a while."

"But why do *you* always have to travel?" she pleaded with him. "Why can't someone else do it?"

It was impossible to explain to a twelve-year-old how a business was run. "Because sometimes only a partner can make the deal."

She didn't say anything but laid her head down on the bar again. Only this time, her cap fell off. She quickly grabbed it and put it on again, but not before he'd seen the bright pink hair.

"Take that hat off," he ordered her.

"Fine," she said and took it off, staring at him defiantly.

Asher gaped at her. Her hair, beautiful golden hair, perhaps the only thing she had that looked like him, was covered in pink. "What did you do?" he demanded.

"Nothing."

"Riley—your hair is *pink.*"

"So? It's my hair." She leaned back, folding her arms.

"I don't care if it is your hair, it is not going to be pink," he said. "You're going to change that tomorrow."

"What do you care? It's not like you're ever here to see it."

"I am here now. And my twelve-year-old daughter is not going to have pink hair, okay? Don't argue about it—you're changing it tomorrow."

"That's so unfair," she muttered.

Asher methodically finished the sandwiches while Riley sulked. Once, Tara had suggested boarding school for Riley. Asher's first reaction had been hell no, he was not shipping his kid off because he was too busy . . . but then again, there were times he wondered if the idea didn't have some merit. At boarding school, Riley wouldn't have to face the fact that her mother was dead and her father was absent every day.

Asher stole a glance at his daughter and that horrible pink hair. He remembered the day she was born—she was so beautiful, so perfect, with a fuzzy patch of grayish hair on the top of her head. They'd called her their little miracle baby, and he'd been completely ga-ga for her. Could he really send his miracle baby away to school and not see her for weeks at a time?

But would Riley be happier? Would he?

Behind Riley, there was another picture of Susanna on a shelf. It felt a little strange, like Susanna was watching him, knowing what he was thinking and hating him for it. Let her hate him—she wasn't here to help him, she'd made sure of that.

"Here," Asher said, putting Riley's sandwich on a plate and pushing it toward her.

"I don't want it," Riley said and pushed the plate back.

"If you want to pout, pout in your room," he said and pushed the sandwich back.

"What about my phone?" she asked, ignoring the sandwich.

She got her hair color and her stubbornness from him, Asher figured. "Tell me what happened," he said, giving in, and sat back with his sandwich as he listened to his daughter. Even though it was full of complaint, her voice was the best thing he'd heard in a while.

8

A sound, something, awakened Jane the next morning, bringing her out of a fitful sleep. She glanced at the clock—it was 6:45 in the morning.

She hadn't slept well, waking every hour or so and glancing at the clock, wondering if the Pompous Prince had made it home.

She heard the noise again, a dull thud on the outside wall. Jane got up and pulled on a pair of shorts. She walked to the French doors that opened onto the pool and looked out. The sun was very low in the sky; there wasn't even a slight breeze. When she heard the thud again, she opened the door and walked outside and around the corner, where she spotted Levi standing in the small garden they'd planted, still in his pajamas, his shovel in hand.

"Levi! What are you doing up so early?"

He squinted at her clothing. "Did you wear that to sleep in?"

Jane glanced down at her denim shorts and camisole. "Some of it. Hey, it's awfully early in the morning for little boys to be up and around. What are you doing out here?"

"Digging a new hole for the new plants," he said, as if that were a normal thing for a five-year-old to do at dawn.

Jane guessed he might have had another accident, but he was still wearing his pajamas and they didn't look wet.

She walked into the garden, stepping gingerly over what they'd planted. They'd put the garden in a bare patch of yard with the blessing of Jorge, the groundskeeper. The area got full morning sun, but the shade of one old live oak saved the patch from a brutal late afternoon sun. Jorge had graciously tilled a few rows for them, and Jane and Levi had gone to the local hardware store to pick out tomato plants and seeds for watermelon, squash, and cucumbers. Levi had also begged for zinnias after seeing the seed packages at the checkout stand.

That very afternoon, Jane and Levi had planted while Riley had sat in a lawn chair with her skinny legs sprawled before her, earbuds in her ears, a book in her hand. Jane didn't think Riley ever turned a page; she'd used the book to keep from having to talk to Jane.

With the garden planted, Levi couldn't wait to come and check on things every day—but never this early. Then again, yesterday they'd noticed that the soil was breaking and little green shoots were starting to poke their heads through the cracks.

Jane squatted down next to Levi and examined the hole he'd dug. "That's a great hole," she observed and peeked up at him. "Why are you up so early, Levi?"

He shrugged. "We have a ghost in the attic. It woke me up."

"A ghost?"

He nodded solemnly.

"Did it scare you?"

"No. It's my mommy," he said matter-of-factly.

"Oh, Levi, I—"

"My daddy came home!" he suddenly and happily announced. "He went down there," he said, and pointed with his shovel at a path that led from the pool down the hill, toward the lake.

Jane stood up and looked down the path. "Down there?"

"I saw him. He was running. I like to run, too! Want to see how fast I can run?" He suddenly dropped his shovel and darted around her, running into the grass beyond their garden patch, running around in circles, his arms held wide.

"You are the fastest runner in the world!" Jane exclaimed, and caught him with one hand when he tried to run past her, causing Levi to collapse in a fit of giggles.

Jane set Levi up with *SpongeBob SquarePants* and a dry bowl of cereal in the media room, and returned to her quarters to dress, digging through her unpacked boxes for something she could wear to meet Mr. Price in person.

She hadn't had time—okay, she hadn't *taken* the time—to unpack much of anything. Frankly, she still wasn't convinced she was going to keep this job, or if she really belonged here. But then again, who knew where she belonged? She hadn't even gone to Cedar Springs Memorial Hospital to begin her search. Jane told herself she hadn't had time, but in truth, she was a big, squawking chicken. She was afraid. Once she got that ball rolling, who knew where it would go?

"First things first," she said aloud and pulled on a pair of Levi's and a Coldplay T-shirt. She decided that looked too casual, like she wasn't a real nanny. Which she wasn't, but that was beside the point of this morning's meeting. She tried a denim skirt and a blouse next, but that looked like she was trying too hard. "Why are you doing this?" she demanded of her reflection. She would probably be fired anyway, because just one word from him, one remark about anything she'd done in his absence, and it was *Hasta la vista, baby.* She'd be damned if she was going

to put up with some absent father's unrealistic expectations and superior attitude on top of that.

She put on the Levi's and T-shirt again, brushed her
hair, and pulled it back in a ponytail. It was, admit-
tedly, with something of a chip on her shoulder that she
marched across the breezeway, ready to wait for Mr. Price
to return from his run and ready for a confrontation.

She was not, however, ready for the sight of Mr. Price.

He happened to be standing in the kitchen, already back
from his run. Jane had seen pictures of him, of course—she
couldn't escape all the pictures of the happy family in this
blessed house. Hanging in the formal dining room was a
huge family portrait of all four of them in jeans and white
shirts, and there was even a dog. (Levi had explained to
Jane that the dog had gone to live on a farm so he could
chase cows. "We didn't have any cows," he'd added solemnly.)

But the man in those pictures did not catch her attention like the man standing before her did. She'd been so
transfixed by Mrs. Price—silky black hair, sparkling blue
eyes, and pearly white teeth—that she'd hardly noticed
Mr. Price in them.

Well, she noticed him now. The man standing before her
was quite handsome with his grayish-green eyes, the shadow
of a beard, and his thick, dark gold hair that reminded her of
baked sugar, wet and pushed back. The T-shirt he wore had
the arms cut out and the faded words Vandelay Industries, a
reference from the old Jerry Seinfeld show, which would suggest that he'd had a sense of humor at some point in his life.
His arms and shoulders were muscular, and his gray terry
gym shorts revealed a pair of muscular legs.

Altogether, he was astonishingly sexy in a sweaty kind
of way, and of all the things Jane had thought of him, *sexy*
had never been one of them—Caligula, yes; sexy, no.

"Good morning," he said, then downed a glass of OJ and put the empty glass on the counter. He looked at Jane again, then down at himself. "Is there something on me?"

God, had she just been *staring* at him? Yes, she was staring! "Sorry," she said quickly. "Good morning." Alert once more, she walked across the kitchen and extended her hand.

He took her hand in his very large one and grasped it firmly, giving it a good shake. Jane's hand felt warm; she quickly withdrew it and stuck both hands in her back pockets.

Mr. Price smiled a little lopsidedly as his gaze casually flicked over her. He nodded to a big coffee mug on the counter. "I just made a pot. Do you drink coffee?"

She glanced at the mug and noticed the pancake mix and bowl as well. "None for me, thanks." A cup of coffee sounded great, but Jane didn't want to come across as though everything had been hunky-dory in his little kingdom and they were just having a friendly cup of Joe. Mr. Price obviously didn't care one way or another; he helped himself to a cup, then leaned back against the counter, sipping from it.

Jane had never been good with silence and felt an insane need to fill this one. "So . . . when did you get in?" she asked, walking around to stand on the other side of the island from him.

"A little past midnight. Riley was still up, but Levi was asleep when I looked in on him."

They waited up for you, pal. "We decided that it might be very late and it would be better to see you first thing this morning."

He smiled a little. "No one was more bummed than me that I didn't get here earlier. I've been really anxious to see my kids."

The man actually looked chagrined, which surprised Jane. She had him down in the cold and heartless column.

Mr. Price suddenly glanced at his watch. "What time do they get up now that school is out?"

"Levi is already up this morning. He's upstairs, watching *SpongeBob*. But it's been pretty fluid. I wasn't sure what schedule to keep them on . . . since we haven't had a lot of time to talk." That would definitely let him know where she stood with this job, and Jane braced herself, ready for anything he might throw at her.

But Mr. Price did not respond right away. His eyes lingered on her. And then he surprised her by smiling. "We haven't, have we? I thought about what you said on the phone, Jane—okay if I call you Jane?"

"Yes . . . sure." He could call her whatever he wanted— she was not backing down.

"Anyway, you were right—I should have called you earlier and discussed expectations."

Jane blinked.

"The only excuse I have is that it's been an insane spring. I am the president and partner of our firm. We just landed a major account, so we've all been working to make sure it gets off the ground in the right way, which, unfortunately, it has not, and it has required my personal attention. I regret I couldn't be here, but the end of the school year necessitated I do something quickly. I understood you to be highly qualified and was confident you could handle this unusual situation."

"I was," Jane agreed. "I mean, I am."

"Then we're in agreement—we both thought you could handle it."

That didn't sound exactly as he'd meant it.

"Nevertheless, I'm sorry for not having talked with you sooner."

His speech was smooth, very neutral, very cultured. Jane could imagine him wearing a letter sweater on some Ivy League campus. She, on the other hand, had worn jeans and T-shirts on a Texas campus and somehow was feeling a little silly for having bothered him. "No need to apologize," she heard herself say, and inwardly winced at how easily she'd said it.

His gaze flicked over her again. "Are you settling in okay?"

"Sure," she said a little hesitantly. "Your house is so beautiful. And the nanny quarters are fabulous. I couldn't ask for better."

"Good." He sipped his coffee, pondering the cup a moment. "I had a chance to talk to Riley last night."

Oh yeah, here it was. This was where he'd say he wasn't comfortable with the way she did things, that he needed someone with more practical, hands-on experience with kids, and not someone who had just read about it in a textbook. Let him say it. Jane was ready for him— she had been since that phone call.

"I know Riley can be tough," he admitted. "She told me about the day you took the phone away, and I have to say, I probably would have done the same thing."

Wow. That was not what Jane had been expecting, not at all. In fact, it threw her so far off balance that she self-consciously pushed her hair behind her ears. "Okay," she said. "Thanks for that."

"And I apologize for our phone conversation. The most I can say for myself is that there is a current of fear that runs through a parent when they hear something about their kid when they are halfway around the world. I suppose I reacted from that fear."

"Sure," she said softly. "I should have realized that."

"However, having said that," he continued, as if she

hadn't spoken, "I would like for you to talk with me before you discipline my children or allow them to do something foolish like dye their hair pink."

"Yes, that pink—"

"I was shocked to find that bright pink hair on my twelve-year-old daughter, Jane. What were you thinking?"

She gaped at him. "*Me?* You have it wrong, Mr. Price. I didn't encourage her. In fact, I was as surprised as you. She just . . . she just did it."

"And you didn't think to correct it?" he asked flatly.

Jane's hands found her waist. "That sort of *correction* requires a salon," she said evenly.

"I would have reimbursed you for it. Didn't you think the pink was a little extreme? How long has she been walking around like that?"

"I don't think it's a good idea for any girl, no, but I also thought that it is just hair, and hair can be fixed. As for how long? She colored it Thursday night, Mr. Price, when you didn't come home as she was expecting."

He blanched. Then frowned into his coffee cup. "Well," he said. "I would like it to be fixed. And for future reference, I would like to know about things like that, and about Levi's . . ." He swallowed hard and put the cup down, his expression clearly pained. "What I am trying to impart is that I am striving to maintain what is normal and customary for my children to the fullest extent that I can."

Normal and customary. Like there was anything normal or customary about the kids' lives right now. "Okay," Jane said cautiously. "I understand that. But when you are away, it's clearly not always practical—"

"I don't think I am asking for anything that you wouldn't expect from any other parent."

"Right. But most parents are not in Germany."

"You can always text me. I will respond immediately."

He was crazy. "So . . . if you are in Germany, and I have a problem with one of the kids, I should text you and get a response before I do something like take Riley's phone?"

Mr. Price obviously could see where this was going. He pushed away from the counter, braced his hands against the island between them. He leaned toward her, his eyes locking on hers. "I don't mean that you should text me before you put Levi in time-out, Jane. But you should do so before you do something drastic. Taking Riley's phone was drastic—that is her primary connection to her only surviving parent. Now, I recognize that there is a certain learning curve in getting to know our family, but the three of us have been through a very rough couple of years. I trust that you will use your best judgment, but until we are all settled in, I would prefer you speak to me before you do anything. Okay?"

Her thoughts were suddenly jumbled around the notion that he was deigning to trust her, like he was cutting her a break, and the fact that his eyes were so *piercing*.

Mr. Price straightened up and looked at his watch again.

"If I could just clarify," she said quickly, before he could walk out or change the subject. "In the event you do not respond quickly, I have the latitude to do what I think I need to do to correct behavior, right? I mean, it's not really practical to try and nip a situation in the bud when I have to wait for . . ." She was going to say something to the effect of having to wait for orders to come from on high, but she thought better of it. ". . . for you if there is a delay. I would lose any credibility I had with them if that happened."

He glanced up from his watch. He probably wasn't used to people questioning him. She'd had a principal like that once, and he—

"I agree."

He *agreed*? She didn't believe him. "Really?"

He allowed her the barest hint of a smile. "Really."

"Okay," she said, nodding. "And if that happens, I need you to back me up," she added warily. "Like with Riley's phone. I don't think you can just give it back and leave her the impression that all she has to do is bide her time until you show up again."

One of his dark brows rose above the other. "You don't, huh?" He chuckled. "I will definitely clarify my expectations with the kids."

Jane was having a very difficult time reading him. "Fair enough," she said, and nodded. "There is just one other thing, Mr. Price."

"Asher. God, please, call me Asher. 'Mr. Price' sounds so . . . official."

"Okay . . . Asher. I took the job with the understanding the hours were flexible and I'd have time to work on my thesis. Tuesday and Thursday afternoons after three—and weekends."

"Right, Tara explained the terms to me. You can start now."

"Start what?"

"Your days off. You can start today." He looked at his watch again. "If there is nothing else, I'd like to make breakfast for my kids."

Jane debated telling him about the dirt in the pool, which had required Jorge's intervention and his entire morning. "No. Nothing else."

"Then I'll see you back here Monday morning."

Ooo-kay. Orders given; troops dismissed. He was going to trust her with his kids but treat her like a servant. She wasn't some girl just out of school. She was a teacher, a professional. Did he honestly think he could treat her like that?

He looked at her impatiently, as if she should have been gone already.

"Have a good weekend," Jane said curtly and walked to the door, pausing momentarily to steal another look at him. But as she turned, she saw that Riley had slipped into the kitchen and wondered just how much of that conversation she'd heard.

9

Jane's unplanned freedom presented the dilemma of what to do first. Obviously, her thesis was the most pressing thing that required her attention. And there was certainly the hospital, where she would begin her search.

But Jane followed her pattern of late and chose avoidance; she opted to run.

She put on a pair of knee-length running pants, running shoes that had seen better days, and a T-shirt with the neck cut out, which she knotted at her waist.

The trail Levi had indicated his father had taken began in a corner of the backyard and went down toward the lake, disappearing into a thicket of cedars and oaks. It was a shaded path, an important consideration in Texas in early summer.

Jane jogged down the hill and into the trees. At the bottom of the hill, the trail forked and a smaller path turned into deeper woods. Jane followed that one, and a few moments later, she ran into a clearing with a small spring.

Nice. Judging by the picnic table and a tire swing, it was a private swimming hole. There was a little house, complete with a porch and windows. It was an extravagant little playhouse, but that didn't surprise Jane; everything at Summer's End was extravagant.

Someone had been here recently. Brush was stacked in a pile, and a leaf blower and extension cord had been left behind on the porch of the playhouse. Jane walked around the spring, dipping down to put her hand in the water. The temperature was startlingly cool, and the small leaves constantly shed by the live oaks were floating on the surface. But the trail ended here, so Jane reversed course and ran back to the other path.

She ran through oaks and cottonwoods, past blooming cactus and limestone, running parallel to the lake about a mile until the trail met a wider, public trail. She ran until she began to feel her legs, then turned around and started back.

The day was heating up; she was running out of steam. When she reached the last stretch of trail to the house, she slowed to a walk, eyeing it. All uphill. "No way," she muttered, and with her hands on the small of her back, she strolled down the smaller path to the private swimming hole to catch her breath.

It was a rustically pretty setting. Jane could imagine herself here on her day off. With a couple of beers. She could sit under the big oak tree, stick her feet in the water, and relax. Even better—she could work on her thesis at the picnic table. Maybe this was the sort of setting she needed to get those creative juices flowing.

She decided to check out the little house. Jane tried the door, but it was locked, so she peered inside through one of the windows. The glass was filmy and it was hard to make anything out inside, save one remarkable thing— the walls were wildly and colorfully painted.

Jane cupped her hands around her eyes to have a better look. The walls were, indeed, covered with bright paints, and mostly pink. On one wall, it looked as if someone had splashed the bright pink paint over a mural.

Directly across from where she stood, the name *Riley* had been written in childish scrawl.

"Aha." This *had* been Riley's playhouse, her own private art studio. "Not a bad idea," she said aloud with some admiration. Riley had painted her laptop, and Levi said she had more paintings, which, predictably, Riley had refused to show Jane. But Jane had an idea—maybe this was one way to reach the girl. Maybe she could bring Riley down here and encourage her to express her obvious frustration in a creative way. Maybe it would help her loosen up a bit.

"Great idea, Janey," she congratulated herself as she started back. If she could have patted herself on the back as she'd run up the hill, she would have.

Jane's cell phone was beeping when she reached the guesthouse; she had a missed call from Jonathan. She got a glass of water and ran cold water on her face before calling him back. "Hey," she said when he answered the phone. "Sorry I missed you. I was out for a run."

"Out running, huh? Do you have time for that? I thought you might be working on your thesis or something," Jonathan said lightly.

"Right," Jane said, and looked at the untouched files and laptop on the table. "Got it right here. So how are you?" she asked, turning her back on her thesis.

"I've got some news—we finally got booked into the Foghorn," he said, referring to his band, Orange Savage.

"Jonathan, that's fantastic! When?"

"In a few weeks. Do you think you can come?"

Jonathan's band had been trying to get booked into that venue for what seemed like forever. "Are you kidding? I wouldn't miss it," she said sincerely.

"Really?" He sounded a little surprised. "Great. So . . . how are you, Janey?"

She looked around at the boxes. "I'm definitely getting settled," she lied.

"And the kids? Is that situation any better?"

"Ah, well . . . ," Jane said. She sat down and began to unlace her shoes with one hand. "Their dad finally came home."

"Yeah? What's he like?"

"He wasn't as bad as I feared, but he's no Uncle Barry." She laughed. Uncle Barry was the type who had never met a stranger. The moment you showed up at his house, you were wrapped in a tight bear hug and comfort food was shoved at you while Uncle Barry talked up a storm.

"Cool. Maybe now you can relax and start looking."

"Yep. I'm going to do that." She tossed one shoe into a box.

"Like . . . when?" Jonathan asked.

She tossed the other shoe into the box and rubbed the back of her neck. "This week. I told him I need time off and he said okay, so—"

"So . . . this week," Jonathan said. "This week you're definitely going to take some steps to find your birth mother. Right?"

"Right," she agreed automatically. *Right, right, right.* No more excuses.

"I hope you do," Jonathan said and laughed a little. "I'm starting to wonder, you know? You've been out there a little over two weeks, and every time I talk to you, I don't sense any urgency on your part in finding your birth mother."

She was supposed to have a sense of urgency? Jane didn't agree with that, but she couldn't disagree that she'd been dragging her feet. In all honesty, she was afraid. She didn't really know what she was doing anymore, or what she might find. It just seemed nice, for a bit of time, to exist in this space between not knowing and knowing the truth about herself.

"Aren't you going to say anything?" Jonathan asked.

"I'm working on it?" Jane offered hopefully.

Jonathan was silent for a moment. "Okay. Okay," he said, but Jane had the sense he wanted to say more. "Well, look, let me get off the phone. I've got to get to rehearsal. I'll call you later, okay?"

Was she imagining an issue where there was none, or did he seem a little angry? "Sure," she said uncertainly, and Jonathan hung up before she said anything else.

She stared at her cell phone, debating whether or not she should call him back and try and smooth things over. Unfortunately, she had nothing promising to say to him. She couldn't answer her own questions, much less his.

Jane headed for the shower instead. She dressed in a cotton dress and gladiator sandals, determined to get out of Summer's End, get some air, and clear her head. She dashed on a bit of blush and mascara and gathered her purse and cell phone. She was walking out to her car when a BMW pulled up in the drive.

Tara got out of the car—or rather, Tara's legs got of her car. Long, slender, tanned legs. "Hi, Jane!" she called out as if they were friends. She ducked her head into the car again, then emerged with a shoulder bag and some files, which she tucked under her arm. "Hey, cute dress."

Next to Tara's short shorts and halter top, Jane felt slightly frumpy. "Thanks," she said.

"So you have the day off, huh? Where are you off to?"

"Just running a few errands. What about you?"

"Oh, the usual. Asher and I have some work to go over." Tara smiled, as if working on a Saturday made her happy. Maybe it did. Maybe what they had to go over was each other, and Jane had a sudden image of Tara's long, tanned legs wrapped around Asher's bare back.

"He's been gone so long and things have backed up," Tara added. She opened the back door of her car and pulled out a beach bag, which she slung over her free shoulder. "And it doesn't hurt that we can work next to such a great pool," she added with a wink.

"No kidding," Jane said. He hadn't been home for twenty-four hours and he was already pouring himself into his work. Poor Riley and Levi.

"Okay! Have a great day off!" Tara pointed her keys at her car and punched a button. The car beeped as she walked on to the house.

Definitely, Jane thought, there was definitely more than work going on between Asher and his lovely assistant. Well, they made a perfect couple. She could just picture the two of them decked out and presiding over some fabulous society party, while she sat up in the media room with Riley and Levi in her favorite Pearl Jam T-shirt and cutoffs eating frozen pizza.

Jane called Nicole on her way into town. "I met my boss," she announced when Nicole answered.

"Still an asshole?"

"I think so," Jane said, pondering that. She'd vented to Nicole about him earlier in the week, but she wasn't exactly sure now. "Whatever he is, I can say this—he's gorgeous."

"Oh *really*."

"It's actually kind of breathtaking," Jane confessed. "He's hot. Remember Tom Cockrell?" she asked, referring to a bartender they both knew. "He's that kind of hot."

"Wow," Nicole said. "I used to dream about Tom Cockrell. Speaking of hot, have you talked to Jonathan since he left?"

Jane sighed. "This morning. He always sounds so bummed."

"Well God, do you blame him?" Nicole asked with a snort.

That response bugged Jane because a part of her *did* blame him. "That's not what I mean," she said petulantly. "I just wish he'd be more understanding, that's all."

"How much more understanding can he be?" Nicole asked.

"So, because I was honest and didn't jump into a marriage I wasn't sure I wanted, Jonathan is the victim here?" Jane asked irritably.

"I didn't say he was a victim," Nicole shot back. "But you have to admit, Jane, you didn't give him any indication you were going to say no. You gave him every indication you'd say yes."

"Because I thought I was going to say yes!" Jane cried. "You know that, Nic! I honestly didn't know I was going to balk until he asked me. Would it have been better for me to have said yes? God, I feel like I have to conform to everyone else's opinion of my life. Everyone seems to think I should be content and happy with the way things are, but I'm not, and I seem to keep apologizing for that. What am I supposed to do? Something at the very core of me is gasping for breath and I can't ignore that."

"Don't drive off the road," Nicole said. "I am not saying you should ignore it, but . . ."

"But *what*?" Jane pressed. "Marry Jonathan so he won't be mad?"

"No, but maybe you can try and appreciate how everyone is trying to support you and how hard that is sometimes. It's really hard to watch you give up a great guy, and squander the master's degree that you have worked toward for *three years*."

"I am not squandering it."

"Yes, you are! If you don't give them something in the next couple of months, you are out of the program! I don't see why you can't look for your birth mother but keep up with your life at the same time. Why is that so hard?"

Nicole had a fair question, one that Jane had asked herself. "I don't know either," she admitted. "Do you honestly believe I want to be stranded like this? I am doing my best to get off this island I have put myself on." Jane pulled into the parking lot of the Saddle-brew. "Listen, I'm at this place . . ."

"Yeah, okay. Call me later?" Nicole asked.

"Definitely. Kiss Sage for me," Jane said and hung up. She really couldn't blame Jonathan or Nicole or anyone else for being frustrated with her. Jane was fully aware that she must look completely crazy to the people who loved her, now that she'd managed to isolate herself from them all. She didn't want to be isolated, yet she had this weird, pervading sense of loneliness that was pushing her away from everything and everyone she knew, into the unknown. It made no sense, least of all to her.

"Look it up in your textbook," she scoffed to herself. She supposed she could do just that, but that seemed a little too black-and-white, and frankly, Jane didn't really want to know why. Right now, she just wanted to continue on this slow path to learning the truth about herself. She'd face reality later.

"Hey Jane—where are your kids?" Sam asked when Jane finally walked inside.

"Home with dad," she said with a relieved smile. "Got any strawberry smoothies today?"

"Coming right up," Sam said.

"And a cinnamon roll, please," Jane added.

"Miss Aaron?"

Startled to hear her name, Jane turned to see Linda Gail Graeber's curly hair and smiling face. "I thought that was you! Are you alone? You are, aren't you? You have to come sit with me. I want to introduce you to some friends," Linda Gail said.

"Oh, I—"

"Come on, now," Linda Gail said quickly before Jane could decline her offer. "You're new in town and this is the best way to meet people from Cedar Springs," she said as she linked her beefy arm through Jane's and pulled her away from the counter. "My friends and I are going to the Cedar County Arts and Crafts Fair. Oh, hey, if you're not doing anything—"

"Oh! Thanks, but I can't—"

"That's okay, it runs all week, so maybe later this week you can get by there. *Gir-rls!*" she warbled, stopping beside a table. "I want to introduce you to Jane Aaron. She's *Asher Price's nanny!*"

The three women at the table stopped talking at once and looked at Jane, wide-eyed.

"Hi," Jane said uncertainly.

"Sit down, sit down!" said one of the women, who jumped up to pull a chair out. She had dreadlocks and was wearing a tie-dyed knit dress.

"This is Reena," Linda Gail said, indicating the tie-dyed woman. "And Anne," she said, gesturing to the woman with the graying bob, who looked the complete opposite of Reena and the oldest of the four. "And Cathy."

Cathy had brown hair pulled into a short ponytail. The crumbs of her muffin had caught on the appliqué of a potted plant that graced the middle of her shirt. "I am so glad Asher got a nanny!" she said as she moved her purse aside for Jane. "Those kids deserve having someone home with them every day."

Jane wondered how they knew Asher was gone frequently.

"Where are you from, Jane?" Reena asked as Linda Gail squeezed herself into a chair.

"Houston."

"Oh, yeah? Did they bring you all the way from Houston to be the nanny? I'm not surprised. The Price family has always gone top shelf in anything they do. Asher's daddy is an oilman, you know. They have a *lot* of money. Speaking of *not* a lot of money, Taylor is buying a car—all by herself! It's one of those hybrids—she's into the environment now that she moved to Austin."

The other women laughed.

"Smoothie and a roll!" Sam called from the counter.

Linda Gail patted Jane's arm. "I'll get it."

"Taylor is my daughter," Reena explained to Jane. "She got a job with a real estate firm in Austin. You know that Austin is a hippie town, right?"

Jane smiled. "I've heard that."

"So Asher advertised in Houston this time?" Cathy asked.

"Ah, no . . . at least, I don't think so. I found the job here in Cedar Springs," Jane said.

"You found it *here*? I didn't know there were jobs like that in Cedar Springs or I would have told Taylor," Reena said.

"Where are you living?" Anne asked.

"Summer's End."

"Oh, that's so beautiful," Cathy said wistfully as Linda Gail returned to the table with Jane's order. "Say what you will about Susanna Price, but if nothing else, she could at least decorate a house."

"*Cathy,*" Linda Gail said low.

"What?"

Linda Gail frowned; Cathy blinked, then looked at Anne. Jane smiled. "Did I miss something?"

"Inside joke," Linda Gail said. "Now listen, girls, if we want to get good parking at the arts and craft show, we've really got to get moving." She said to Jane, "Let's do try and get Riley and Tracy together this summer. I know Tracy would love it, and I really think Riley needs to get out. She was locked in that big old house all of last summer. She needs to be a kid again, you know? All right, girls, are we off? Jane, you have a good day!"

The other women said their good-byes, and when the four of them had finally collected all their handbags and keys and whatnot, they walked out of the coffee shop, already arguing about where exactly they would park.

That was weird, Jane thought as she watched them walk out the door. *"Say what you will about Susanna Price."* What was it that people said about Susanna Price?

Jane finished her cinnamon roll and thought she'd head to Walmart to pick up a few personal items. She drove around the picturesque town square with its newly planted flowerpots and banners hanging over the street announcing the upcoming June Bluebonnet Festival. She drove past the old part of town with the tidy Craftsman homes and rambling Victorians and manicured lawns, out to the edge of town, where Walmart was located.

But at the light, instead of turning right toward Walmart, Jane suddenly turned left and followed the road that skirted the southern edge of town until she reached the Cedar Springs Memorial Hospital.

She pulled into the parking lot of the hospital and looked at it. It had two wings, an emergency entrance, and a main entrance. It was a small hospital. So why, then, did Jane feel so intimidated? Why did she look at the door and wonder how she would ever make herself walk through it?

She *would* do it. Not today, because it was Saturday, and she doubted that the administration staff was working. But she'd do it, and soon, no matter what anyone else thought. She might be afraid of what she'd find—or not find—but she'd come all this way and she had no hope of moving on with her life, or going home to her family, or finishing her degree, or banishing that persistent, distant ache until she walked through those doors and started asking questions.

10

*T*hat's it, Asher," Tara said, jotting down a note. "Looks like we've covered everything."

They were in the den off the kitchen, Tara wearing a bikini top and shorts, Asher in swim trunks and a T-shirt. Tara had worked for Asher for so long that he considered her family, and like family, she'd spent some time in the pool with Levi while Asher had paid some bills and made some personal calls.

Still miffed about Asher's less than enthusiastic response to her hair, Riley had stayed in her room.

When Asher had finished with the things he'd needed to take care of, he'd served up lunch, diving into the batch of Waldorf chicken salad Carla had left. Afterward, while Levi had napped and Riley had sullenly watched TV, Tara and Asher had caught up on the work he'd missed while in Germany.

"Is there anything else?" Tara asked as she closed her notebook.

Asher glanced out the window. It was late afternoon, the heat of the day. He wouldn't mind a mojito. He idly wondered if he had what he needed to make one. Rum. Sugar and mint. "I can't think of anything," he said. "I won't keep you any longer, Tara. You probably need to get back to Austin."

Tara winced a little. "Yes," she said with a sigh. "If I don't, there will be hell to pay. Chris and I . . . we're going through a rough patch."

Surprised, Asher looked at her. "I'm sorry to hear that. You're still living together, right?"

"Oh yeah, yeah," Tara said, studying the inlaid scroll on the table. "We haven't split up or anything drastic." She looked up. "But honestly, I don't know how long we can go on like this. Have you ever heard someone say they were lonely in a relationship? Well, that's me. I never felt as lonely as I do with Chris these days, you know?"

Oh, yes, he knew. He was the poster child for loneliness in a marriage. He knew what it was like to sit next to someone and feel invisible. Or to lie in bed beside her and feel utterly alone. "I'm sorry."

"Yes, well . . ." She sighed and smiled sadly as she gathered her things. "I better go. Thanks so much for letting me hang out in the pool, Asher. That was heaven."

"You know you're always welcome."

"I know." She walked to the door and paused. "You'll be in on Monday?"

Like he could be anywhere else. "Early," he confirmed, and followed her out onto the drive. He watched her leave, and when the gate had swung closed behind her, he wondered what he was going to do with his evening. He used to have some buddies in Austin he'd hang out with on occasion, but after Susanna died and he had the kids and then had to travel so much . . . well, he didn't get out much. It had been so long that he didn't even know where he'd get out to if he had the chance. Sometimes it felt like he lived in a bubble—work, kids, and back to work again. That was his existence.

Asher walked back into the house just as Levi walked through the kitchen, headed for the back door.

"Wait . . . where are you going, buddy?" Asher asked.

Levi paused, his hand on the doorknob. "To show Jane something."

"Not today, okay? Today is her day off." Levi looked at the door, debating. "She needs time to do her own thing," Asher explained. "What were you going to show her?"

Levi's hand slipped away from the doorknob, and he held out a DVD case. "This movie. Want to watch it with me, Daddy?"

Asher saw the unmistakable blue-and-white cover of *The Hedgehog's Holiday,* a movie he had watched with Levi a thousand times if he'd watched it once. He forced a smile for his son's sake. "Sure thing. After supper, okay?"

"What are we having?" Levi asked, walking back into the kitchen.

That was an excellent question. Asher looked at the doors of the walk-in pantry and imagined all the wholesome food items contained within. "Pizza," he said. Easy to make, and he could throw on some broccoli to make himself feel like a responsible parent.

"*Yeah!*" Levi shouted as Riley walked in behind him. "We're having pizza, Riley!"

"Don't have a coronary, " Riley said with a roll of her eyes. "It's just pizza and we eat it, like, five times a week."

Riley had dyed her pink hair yellow, a brassy and unnatural shade of her natural gold. When Asher had mentioned the pink to his mother on the phone earlier— and his displeasure—she'd clucked her tongue at him. "She gets that from her mother. But it's summer, Ash. Who is going to see her?"

He was.

Asher realized that Jane was right; Riley's hair needed the intervention of a professional. He decided not to say anything about it tonight, however, and risk the fragile peace. "I make pizza maybe once a week," he responded jovially.

"At least twice a week, Dad. Mom made something different every night."

"She was a very good cook," Asher said patiently. Susanna had been a creative cook, and she'd engaged the kids in her ambitious creations. "But I'm not. I have to stick with my strengths." He winked at Riley.

"Is Tara gone? Her perfume was giving me an epic headache," Riley said.

"She's gone."

"Good. I thought she was going to spend the night."

"Would it have been so bad if she had?" he asked. "It's not like you would have had to bunk with her. We have four guest rooms upstairs, remember?"

"*Yes*, it would have been so bad. You see her all the time."

"Well, I'm going to see only you guys tomorrow," Asher assured her. "I was thinking we could go to Austin and have lunch at Guero's, then swim at Barton Springs. How does that sound?"

Riley regarded him warily. "Really? Just us?"

"Yes, really, just us. Want to go?"

"Yes!" Levi shouted.

"He was talking to me," Riley said, and looked at Asher. "Yes."

One small step for Dad . . . "Good. Come help me get this pizza going so we can watch the hedgehog movie."

"I'll help!" Levi offered, and he began to dig in one of the cabinets for a pizza pan.

"The hedgehog movie *again*?" Riley complained.

"Yes, again," Asher said and handed her plates. "After that, we can watch *Twilight* and drool over that guy."

"*Da-ad*," Riley said with a grimace and turned her

back on him, walking into the dining room with the plates. Gone were the days when Asher's little girl told him everything in one long stream of consciousness. *I fed my turtle spinach and he ate it but Carla said it was for supper and I had to find some grass or something, and oh, Mom was crying again this morning, but she's okay, she's in her bed now.*

"Here, Daddy," Levi said, handing up a jar of pizza sauce.

"Good job, buddy," Asher told him, and turned his attention to supper.

After pizza, they watched the hedgehog movie that had Riley rolling her eyes with teenage disdain but held Levi enthralled. They made some popcorn and watched a second movie about a family mistakenly stuck on a strange planet with endearing, one-eyed creatures. When it was over, Asher picked up Levi, who had fallen asleep, and carried him to bed.

As he tucked Levi in, Levi woke up and watched Asher through heavy lids. The sound of a heavy thud in the hallway reached them, and Levi's eyes widened. "What's that?"

"Riley dropped something," Asher said. He leaned down to pick some toys off the floor.

"Sometimes I hear Mommy upstairs."

Surprised, Asher paused and looked at his son. "You do?"

He nodded. "She walks around up there."

As there was no upstairs, and no Susanna walking around, Asher thought he should call an exterminator.

"Do you hear her, too?" Levi asked.

Only in his thoughts. *"Why do you make everything so hard? Can't you just enjoy life?"* she'd asked him once. No, he hadn't been able to just enjoy life, not with her ups and downs wreaking havoc on them. "No, I don't hear her," he said.

Levi considered that a moment, then asked, "Do you miss her, Daddy?"

"I wish she were here," he said, and he did, for Levi's and Riley's sakes. But he didn't miss her, not in that way. He kissed Levi's forehead. "Go to sleep now. We've got a big day tomorrow."

The hall was dark when Asher emerged from Levi's room. Riley had apparently turned in for the night, as there was no sound coming from the media room.

Asher went downstairs to clean the kitchen. As he walked into the mess, he remembered that he'd never had that mojito. He opened the fridge and took out a beer, drinking it as he started to clean. He opened a second beer to finish up, and when he finished, he turned off all the lights except one over the stove, then helped himself to a third beer.

He leaned back against the counter, sipping, listening to the silence. Asher didn't care for silence, because he had a tendency to fill silence with thoughts that collected like birds on a wire, reminding him of a life he might have had once but had lost forever, of the lonely, empty road stretching far beyond him.

He abruptly walked outside to escape the silence and paused to look up at the night sky and the full moon. He drank his beer.

That moon reminded him of Susanna. Once, when they'd first been married, Susanna had had a bad day and told Asher she was going to take a long bath. But he'd found her outside on the patio of the little house in central Austin, their first home, reposing in a lounge chair, completely naked. She'd laughed when he'd looked around, anxious about neighbors. And then they had made love, right there on the lounger. Susanna had been completely uninhibited, crying out when she'd come, and laughing when he'd frantically tried to shush her. *"Don't worry so much, Ash. Our neighbors have sex, too,"* she'd said.

Asher strolled out a little farther, looking up, remembering the stars from that long-ago night, twinkling over the heads of two lovers. And they had been lovers then. Intimate, passionate lovers—

"Hi."

The voice startled Asher, and for a brief, stunning moment, his mind let him believe that Levi was right, that it was Susanna. He peered into the darkness. A movement in the pool caught his eye, a woman in one of the thick foam chairs that Susanna had favored. But the hair was wrong. It was too . . . messy.

"I'm sorry, I thought you saw me. Did I scare you?"

He realized it was Jane Aaron. Asher could see her now in the moonlight, her head resting against the back, her legs dangling in the water. She hadn't even turned on the pool lights; she was just floating in the moonlight. "Jane? What are you doing?" He started forward, hesitated, and then moved again, to the pool's edge.

"Nothing. Just floating. It's such a beautiful night, isn't it? Do you mind?"

"Of course not. You're floating in the dark?"

"Absolutely. Better to see the stars that way." Her hands drifted in the water, languidly moving to keep her facing him. "You can't see stars like this in Houston because of all the lights. But out here . . ." She sighed and looked up. "They seem so close. It feels like you can almost touch them," she said and lifted her arm, as if she thought she might.

Asher looked up, too. All those stars made him feel small and insignificant.

"But then again, it's so vast, it makes me feel . . ."

Alone. Small. All the clichés, all the things he felt about those stars.

"Hungry." She laughed softly.

Surprised, Asher shot her a look. Jane didn't notice; she lowered her arm, dipped her hand into the pool. "Hungry?" he asked, curious now.

"In a roundabout way," she said lightly. "The starry sky reminds me of Italy. I went there last summer, and I was in this little Tuscan village, on a piazza, and there was this sea of people, all these happy Italians sparkling around me. But they all spoke Italian. I don't speak a word of Italian, and it occurred to me that theoretically, I could say anything and no one would know. It was a strange feeling. And looking up there, at all those stars that can't hear me or see me . . . I thought about Italy. And then I thought about pasta." She laughed again.

He pictured Jane in Italy, bobbing in a sea of sparkling Italians. Alone. He'd just been thinking that himself, and it gave him an odd prickle on the back of his neck. "You didn't go with a boyfriend? A friend?"

"No, just me." She laughed. "I was trying to find myself," she said, playfully adding gravitas to her voice and making imaginary quote marks in the air.

Asher's curiosity was suddenly raging. He recalled a strange day he'd spent in Hong Kong.

"Great. Now you think I'm weird."

"Just the opposite," he said. "I was remembering that the same thing happened to me. I was in Hong Kong, and I decided to walk from my hotel to the office where my meeting would be held, but I got lost. I ended up in a park, sitting on a bench in the middle of a bunch of old Chinese guys. No one spoke English—believe me, I tried. I remember thinking that I could get lost and never find my way back. I could spend the rest of my days hanging out with old guys on park benches."

No one had even looked at him that day. He'd felt like

a useless bag of bones. He was no one to anyone, except two kids who would outgrow him one day.

Jane giggled.

He couldn't imagine that she'd experienced something similar, that feeling of being invisible in a world of people. "So did you?" Asher asked.

"Did I what?"

"Find yourself."

Jane laughed. "Not exactly. Truthfully, I think I've just begun to look."

She suddenly slipped out of her chair, hooked one arm over the side, and pulled it along as she swam to the edge. Asher watched as she got out of the pool. She was wearing a one-piece swimsuit, the sort someone would wear to swim laps. Jane had a lush figure—not pencil thin like Tara, but curves in all the right places. Asher was surprised that he found her so . . . *attractive*.

Jane picked up a towel and began to dry off. "I guess you did, though."

"Pardon?"

"You found yourself."

"Ah . . . not really," Asher said. "But I found my way to the office."

She smiled. "Well, thank goodness you did. What would Riley and Levi do if you hadn't?"

Asher didn't answer. They stared at each other for a moment. A long moment. "I'll just . . ." Jane nodded toward the guesthouse and wrapped the towel around her.

"You don't have to get out. Or go in," Asher said. Maybe it was the beer, but he suddenly wanted her to stay and float in the moonlight. "I'll leave you alone with your stars."

"No, I should turn in. I have so much to do tomorrow. Good night." She turned and walked to the guesthouse. A long tail of dark, wet hair looked like it had been poured down her back. At the door to the guesthouse, Jane paused and glanced back at him before slipping inside.

Asher turned his back to the guesthouse and looked up at the moon. "Note to self," he muttered. "Lay off the beer." He shouldn't be looking at the nanny that way; it was way out of bounds. He didn't want to be the guy who ogled the young, pretty nanny, because those guys were asses, and Asher was not an ass.

He just wished Jane didn't look so damn good in a bathing suit.

11

*A*sher roused his kids the next morning with a very loud and off-key rendition of Alice Cooper's "School's Out" and helped them get their things together for a trip into Austin. They had brunch at Guero's, a taco bar on South Congress Avenue where Austinites went to see and be seen. Levi liked the pictures on the wall and the variety of salsas that accompanied the constant flow of chips.

Riley, apparently unhappy with her hair and her bathing suit, which she proclaimed baby-ish, wore a goofy hat and ate only a few bites of her enchiladas.

After lunch, they headed for Zilker Park and Barton Springs, one of the largest natural swimming holes in the state. It was an Austin institution, a city-maintained, spring-fed pool that maintained a constant temperature of sixty-eight degrees year-round. It was heaven in the hot summers, and warm enough in the winter for serious swimmers.

The best part about Barton Springs was the setting. Large pecan and cottonwood trees hung over the grassy slopes, providing plenty of shade. The pool itself was enormous, one thousand feet long. Nevertheless, in the summer, it could get very crowded, and this warm Memorial Day weekend was no exception.

Levi had a dangerous like of jumping off things, and he had reached the side of the pool and jumped in in expert cannonball fashion before Asher could stop him. Riley was more reticent. She fussed with her bathing suit and her hat and finally made her way into the pool, easing in one inch at a time, complaining that the water was too cold, complaining when Levi playfully splashed her.

The water felt great to Asher. Barton Springs brought back a lot of memories of his childhood. He and his buddies would hang out on the grassy slope above the pool, and when they tired of that—meaning there weren't any girls taking their bait—they'd head for other parts of the park, such as Town Lake, where they would rent canoes, or over to the disc golf area, where they would heave Frisbees well past their mark.

He'd forgotten how weightless those lazy summer days of his youth had been, with nothing more than a bright future looming on his horizon. As Asher floated on his back, he had a moment of wistfulness, of wishing he could go back and do it all over.

The moment was washed away when Levi splashed him and said, "Let's race, Daddy!" and he realized no matter how difficult or unfair his life might have been, he wouldn't trade a single moment with his children.

After a couple of hours in the water, the three of them moved down to the area below the dam. Riley wanted shade so she wouldn't get burned, although that seemed impossible, seeing as how the sun hat she insisted on wearing dwarfed her. But Asher obliged her and tossed out a blanket beneath a cottonwood and fed them his version of a snack—grapes, crackers, and Cheez Whiz.

Dogs were allowed to swim below the dam, and Levi eventually wandered a few feet away to watch them. Riley and Asher remained on the blanket, Asher watching Levi.

"Oh, God, that's Dax," Riley said suddenly, and twisted around so that she was facing Asher, her back to the pool.

"Who?" Asher asked, peering over her shoulder.

"Dax Hawkins. He goes to my school." She stole another look over her shoulder. "He's the one in the blue."

Asher saw a skinny kid with a mop of dirty blonde hair in the company of two younger boys. "Want me to call him over?"

"*What?*" Riley gasped. "No! I don't like him!"

"Why not?" Asher asked curiously.

Riley shrugged and drew her knees up to her chest. "He's always talking to Anna Greenberg."

"Anna who?"

"*Greenberg,*" Riley said and pulled her hat lower over her eyes. "She's, like, the cutest girl in school. Is he still there?"

"He's still there. Anna can't be cuter than you, baby girl. You're beautiful."

Riley snorted. "You have to say that. You're my dad. Where is he now? Is he coming over here?"

Asher leaned up to look around her. "No, he went off in the other direction. And I don't have to say that because I am your dad, I am saying it because it's true. You're really beautiful . . . especially when your hair isn't pink. I bet all the kids at school think so, even if they don't say it."

Riley dipped her head. "Highly doubtful. No one likes me."

Asher tried to see her face, but her hat prevented it. "I don't believe that for a minute."

"Dad," she said impatiently. "You don't understand."

He did understand—he just didn't know how to deal with it. It was moments like this when Asher missed Susanna most of all. She'd been Riley's rock; the two of them had discussed everything. Asher knew that Riley missed her mother so hard and deep that it colored everything in her life. To make matters worse, he was so dumb about things like boys and hairdos and the cruelties of the middle school years.

"Anyway, I don't care, because I don't want to be friends with anyone who likes the Jonas Brothers. Anna *loves* them."

Riley said it as if Anna liked to eat ants, and Asher couldn't help but smile. "What's wrong with the Jonas Brothers?"

"They're just the biggest losers in the world," Riley said, picking at the blanket. "Tracy Graeber asked me if I wanted to go to their concert, but I wouldn't waste money on that."

That was the first Asher had heard of that. "When?"

Riley shrugged. "When you were in Chicago that time."

Chicago. American Airlines account. He'd been so crazed in trying to get that pitch together. They'd lost the account to another firm. Had Riley said something then, something that hadn't registered? He tried to see his daughter's face again. "Did you want to go?"

"No, Dad, are you listening? I *hate* the Jonas Brothers. They're so lame."

"They seem to be doing pretty well to me," Asher said innocently.

Riley looked up with an expression that suggested he was a moron. "They can't even sing. It's totally dubbed."

He honestly didn't know if they could sing or not or if they were dubbed. The only thing he knew about the Jonas Brothers was that one of his partners had paid a hefty premium to get his daughter and her friends prime seats at the concert. It had never occurred to him that Riley might want to go. She'd never mentioned them, and he had certainly never thought to ask.

Those were the sorts of things that Susanna had always known.

Riley needed a woman in her life. Asher knew it.

The older she got, the more it was apparent to him. He wished he or Susanna had had a sister. "Maybe you want to call Grandma Helen when we get home," he suggested, thinking Susanna's mother might know better than he about hair and other things that might be bothering Riley.

Riley cast a suspicious look at him. "Why?"

"Why? Because she likes to hear from you."

Riley's eyes narrowed. "You always do that."

"Do what?"

"You always push me off on Grandma Cheryl or Grandma Helen. It's like you can't even talk to me, like I'm a loser or something. You think I'm like her."

"Like who?"

"Mom! But I'm *not* like her, I am my own person, and you don't have to always freak out if I don't like something."

Asher had to tread carefully here. "I am not freaking out, baby girl. I know you are *you,* but I thought maybe Grandma Helen knows about hair and the Jonas Brothers more than I do."

"Trust me, Grandma Helen doesn't know anything about hair *or* the Jonas Brothers," Riley snapped and looked away, toward the dog swim. "Maybe *you* would know if you were ever here."

That comment, delivered by his twelve-year-old daughter, was a harsh reminder to Asher of the disagreements he and Susanna used to have. His long work hours had been a point of contention between them. *"You hide from me, from us, in that job!"* she'd spat at him once. *"I work that job so you can live like this,"* he'd responded just as hotly, gesturing to the expensive house and designer furnishings that had been breaking his back.

"Riley, I can't read your mind. If you want to go to a concert, or get a haircut, all you have to do is ask," he said irritably. "Listen, I know you miss Mom, and I wish she were here, too—"

"Really? You don't act like it. Sometimes I think you're glad she's dead—"

"*Hey*," he said sharply. "Don't speak to me like that."

Riley turned her head so that he couldn't see her face.

"Now listen here, Riley Ann—"

"Levi is bothering that lady," she flatly interrupted.

Asher looked up; Levi was talking to a young woman who had a chocolate Lab on a leash. Levi had his hand on that leash and was tugging on it. "Great," Asher muttered and leaped to his feet. He paused to look sternly at Riley. "We're not through," he said. "Levi! Take your hand off that leash!" he called to his son.

Startled, Levi looked up, saw Asher striding toward him, and guiltily dropped his hand.

"I am sorry," Asher said to the young woman as he put his hand on Levi's shoulder and pulled him back. The dog eagerly sniffed Asher's legs, tail wagging. "My son loves dogs."

"I can tell," she said, smiling. She was pretty. "It's okay. Molly doesn't mind."

"Hey, Molly," Asher said, leaning over to pet the dog. He straightened up again. "Come on, Levi." The young woman smiled at him, and Asher felt a tiny flicker of desire. He smiled back, let his eyes take a quick inventory of her body. "Have a good day," he said.

"You, too."

Asher turned Levi around and started him in the direction of Riley and the blanket. "Buddy, you can't walk up to people and try to take their dog. That's not good."

"I wasn't!" Levi insisted. "I just wanted to take Molly to the water."

"That's not your call. That was her dog."

"Can we have a dog, Daddy?"

A dog was the last thing Asher needed; just the thought of trying to take care of one on top of everything else overwhelmed him. "Not now. Maybe someday." He left it at that, as Riley was standing with her arms folded.

"I want to go home," she announced imperiously.

"I don't!" Levi cried as he flopped onto the blanket. "I want to swim some more! Okay, Daddy?"

"No, Levi, it's time to go," Asher said.

"I don't *want* to go!" Levi cried and rolled over onto his stomach.

"Come on, I'll take you over to Sandy's for a frozen custard," Asher said as he began to gather their things, but Levi began to sob. "Grab the bag, Riley," Asher said, and hauled Levi up to his shoulder, carrying him to the car. When he had his kids in the car—Levi on his booster, still crying—Asher jogged back to get the blanket.

As he was folding it, he saw the young woman with the chocolate Lab again, standing on the water's edge. He suddenly had an image of him, holding himself over her, sliding into her. What would it be like? What would mindless, killer sex, no strings attached, be like? Asher hadn't had sex in so long he guessed it would be pretty explosive. But as he looked at the woman, who was now talking to some young stud, he figured she would not want to have sex with a guy like him. She might have ten years ago, but Asher wasn't that guy anymore. Hell, he didn't even know what kind of guy he was now.

He picked up his stuff and walked back to the car, where Riley was sulking and Levi was whimpering.

Riley sulked all the way home, then disappeared into her room. Levi was refreshed after his car nap and wanted to play trucks. He'd built an elaborate track in the playroom and demanded that Asher watch a variety of cars speed down the track and crash into the wall, which, Asher noted wryly, had obviously been used as a crash pad for some time.

He obliged his son for a half hour or more. He even sent a few cars down and helped Levi make some track adjustments for better velocity. But more pressing things were playing at the corner of his mind and creeping into the forefront. "Okay, buddy," he said. "I need to go check on supper."

"No, Daddy, don't go! I want you to stay here!"

Asher winced. "Come on, Levi. I've got to make some phone calls, and then I have to make dinner."

"You don't have to call anyone tonight! They're not home!" Levi's face, dirtied from a day of food and sun, was earnest. "And you don't have to make dinner because Carla makes it all the time and leaves it!"

"What if you bring some of your trucks down to the office, and you can play with them while I do a few things?" Asher suggested.

Levi's response was to slump onto a window seat, dejected. "I don't want to play down there. I want to play up here. I made this track so I could show you."

"Levi, I . . ." Whatever Asher meant to say was suddenly lost when he noticed the dark stain spreading down the leg of Levi's board shorts. "Shit, Levi," he said, squatting down next to his son. "Why didn't you run to the potty?"

"I'm sorry," Levi said, tears welling.

What was wrong with his son? "It's okay," Asher said evenly. "But you have to try and make it to the potty."

"I'm sorry," Levi said again, hanging his head.

Why did this keep happening? What was Asher doing wrong? Perhaps a better question might be, what was he doing *right*? How could a five-year-old be so troubled?

"Come on, buddy," he said, taking his son by the hand. "Let's go change."

12

*O*n Monday morning, Jane was the first one in the kitchen, drawn in by the smell of breakfast. "Something smells delicious!" she said as she walked in through the back door.

Carla grinned. "Huevos rancheros. I thought you especially might like them."

"Me?"

"Oh, I'm just teasing. I just said that because you're Hispanic, right?" Carla said cheerfully.

Who knew? "I love huevos," Jane said and opened the fridge, pulling out the orange juice. When she closed the door, she looked right into the steely gray-green eyes of her employer.

He gave Jane a curt nod. "Morning." He was wearing suit trousers, a crisp white shirt, and a tie. He looked much different than he had Saturday night in the moonlight, in shorts and a polo. This morning he looked stiff. Aloof.

"Good morning," Jane said.

"Carla, if you would, make something I can take with me. I want to be in Austin before the traffic hits."

"No problem," Carla said.

He turned toward the door.

"Ah . . . Asher?" Jane said.

He paused impatiently.

"Just a reminder that I'll be off tomorrow afternoon at three."

"I remember. I'll be home."

"Thanks," Jane said, but Asher had already walked on. She glanced uneasily at Carla.

"You may as well get used to it, hon," Carla said. "Mr. P is so busy he doesn't have time to breathe, much less chat. Do me a favor, will you?" she asked as she shoveled eggs onto a piece of toast, making an egg sandwich. "Run this out to him, will you?"

"Sure," Jane said.

"That's his coffee," Carla said, nodding toward a coffee tumbler. She wrapped the sandwich and handed it to Jane.

Jane was standing in the foyer when Asher came striding out of his office, shoving into his suit coat. He looked at her warily, as if he expected a confrontation. "Your breakfast," she said, holding out the sandwich and coffee.

"Ah." He looked at her again as he put his cell phone into his pocket. "Thanks." He took the items from her, his fingers brushing against hers. "Have a good day," he added and walked out the front door.

Aloof and sexy, she thought to herself, and watched him get in his car.

"Daddy!" Levi called from upstairs and ran down, sliding into the sidelight just as Asher's sleek Mercedes headed up to the gate.

"I didn't get to say good-bye," Levi said.

"That's okay," Jane said and squeezed his shoulder. "You can say hello when he gets home tonight. Come on—Carla's making breakfast."

"Hello, Levi!" Carla called out cheerfully when Jane and Levi entered the kitchen.

"Hi, Carla. Can I have Lucky Charms?"

"You may not," Carla said. "We're having eggs."

"Guess what, Levi?" Jane asked before Levi could complain. "I found an explorer camp!" She'd found the brochures in town for the daily summer camps held at one of the local parks. This one focused on exploring the flora and fauna of the Hill Country, and it included swimming, fun projects, hikes, and lunch. "See? Here are some pictures of the explorers," she said, showing him the brochures.

Levi stared at the brochures. He didn't seem as excited by the pictures of kids planting trees as Jane had hoped. "What do they do?" he asked.

"They . . . they dig dirt and throw rocks into water. And they get to look at lots of cool bugs."

Levi eyed her suspiciously. "What type of bugs?"

"The biggest, hairiest ones."

"*Eeewe.*" This from Riley, who had somehow managed to rouse herself before noon. She was wearing a My Chemical Romance T-shirt and Texas Longhorn pj bottoms. "Where is the camp?"

"At City Park. It sounds like fun, don't you think, Levi?" Jane asked.

"Levi is already growing tomatoes," Riley said as she opened the fridge. "How much more fun can he have?"

"I can have fun if I want to!" Levi protested. "When can I go? I want to go, Jane."

"We're going to talk to the camp director right after breakfast."

"Yeah!" Levi shouted, leaping up.

Riley watched him, then leveled a superior look on Jane. "He'll get kicked out."

"Why would you say such a thing?"

"Because I know Levi."

"Excuse me, but what happened to the cows?" Carla asked.

Her question surprised Jane; she and Riley both looked at Carla, who was standing at the breakfast table. "Where are the cows?" she asked again, twirling around in a circle to look around the room.

"Cows?"

"The *drawing* of the cows. It was right *here*," Carla said, pointing to a blank spot on the wall.

"Oh, that," Jane said. "Sorry, I forgot to put it back up. Levi and I moved it so we could put up his glue project to dry—"

"You can't move that!" Carla said sharply. "Mrs. P made that drawing and it always hangs *right here*."

"I'll get it, Carla!" Levi said and darted into the utility room, returning almost instantly with the framed drawing. "Here it is."

Carla clamped a hand over her heart and sighed with relief. "Thank God. Mr. P would never forgive me if I lost it." She gestured for it. As Carla hung the drawing again, she actually looked a little shaken.

"I'm sorry, Carla," Jane said again.

"Please don't move anything. Everything in this house is where it is for a reason," Carla said curtly, and she looked at Riley, who gave her a halfhearted shrug. "Come and get your plates," Carla said.

She banged around the kitchen while Jane and the kids ate breakfast. Jane thought Carla was being a little ridiculous. Mrs. Price had been dead a year and a half now, and moreover, there were more drawings and paintings than anyone in this house could count. But Jane had learned her lesson: Susanna Price wasn't going anywhere. It was little wonder Levi thought he heard her in the attic.

After breakfast Jane took Levi upstairs to get him dressed. They were picking up his room when Riley appeared in the doorway. "What am I supposed to do while Levi is playing with bugs?" she asked.

"You can go to camp with me," Levi offered.

"Here, Levi," Jane said, handing him clean clothes. "Go in the bathroom and brush your teeth and wash your face, then get dressed, okay?"

"Okay," Levi said. Taking the clothes, he frog-hopped into the bathroom. "I have a few ideas for us," Jane said to Riley. She had great ideas. Ideas that were guaranteed to wow her young charge into utter devotion.

"Please don't say I have to go to camp."

"No camp," Jane said cheerfully. "Much better than that. I thought we could make an appointment to get your hair cut and maybe some highlights. Highlights are cool, right?"

"I guess," Riley said, glancing at herself in the mirror above Levi's dresser.

"Then, while Levi is at explorer camp, you and I can do something I think you will find really fun. I thought we could go down to the hidden springs and open up the little playhouse and do some painting." She grinned, waiting for Riley to proclaim it a great idea.

Only Riley didn't do that. She seemed more astounded than surprised. She gaped at Jane, her blue eyes wide. Then the girl paled, anger washing over her features. "You went *down* there?"

"I found it when I was out for a run," Jane said, her smile fading.

"You didn't go *in*, did you?"

"No, I didn't go in," Jane said. "But I—"

"I can't believe you went down there," Riley said coldly. "That was mine and my mom's private place. I don't want you in there."

So much for Jane's brilliant, I'm-such-a-cool-nanny

ideas. "I didn't go in, so calm down," she said evenly. "I happened across it, that's all."

But Riley's eyes flashed with anger. "This isn't your property, Jane. You can't just walk around wherever you want. You're supposed to be with us or in the guesthouse."

Jane had to draw a breath to keep from saying something she'd regret or get her fired. "Okay, I get it is obviously someplace that is very special to you. I just thought that maybe, now that a little time has passed since your mom died, we could go down there together and you could take up painting again."

Riley turned back to the mirror. "Don't try and act like you know anything about me, because you don't. It's not special to me. That was my mom's studio and it's where she painted and I just don't want you to ruin it."

By the strength of her protestation to the contrary, Jane gathered that it was a very big deal indeed. She watched Riley fidget with her hair a moment. "I know you must really miss your mom," she said quietly.

Riley snorted. "Now you're like the school counselor. What do you think?"

"I think that you do miss her, Riley. And I am only trying to help."

Riley sighed and turned around to Jane. "I don't need your help. And besides, you would never understand because you *have* a mother. My mother was . . . she was . . ." Riley shook her head and looked away from the mirror. "You wouldn't understand." She tried to pass Jane, but Jane put her hand on Riley's arm.

"You don't know me very well, either, Riley. The thing is, I understand maybe better than you know."

"Oh yeah, like your mom was killed in a car wreck," Riley scoffed.

"No, my mother is alive and well," Jane said. "But

I have another mother who gave me away when I was a baby, and I know what it's like to miss her."

"What?" Riley looked up, clearly confused. "What do you mean? Either you have a mother or you don't."

"I mean that I was adopted. So I know what it's like, because I miss a mother I never even knew. I know it's not the same," she said quickly before Riley could argue. "But I do understand a little of what it's like not to have your mother around."

Riley frowned. "Why'd she give you away?"

"I don't know," Jane said. "I hope to find out."

"Where does she live?"

"I don't know that, either, but I think maybe somewhere around Austin."

"At least she's alive."

"But that doesn't change the fact that in some ways, both of us are missing our mothers."

Riley looked at her appraisingly, as if she was seeing Jane through some new lens. She looked at Jane's hand, which was still resting on her arm. Jane silently removed it, prompting Riley to look up again. "Where am I going to get a haircut?" she asked.

It was only a tiny step of progress, but it was a step just the same, and Jane smiled faintly. "Let's check some places out after we sign Levi up at camp."

13

Asher had agreed to giving Jane Tuesday and Thursday afternoons, meaning that through the summer, he would work at home those afternoons unless he made alternative plans. It wasn't ideal, but Tara had said it was a deal killer, and Asher had desperately needed Jane.

He desperately needed her to come home Tuesday night. An impromptu, but important, meeting with prospective clients from AT&T had cropped up, and Asher was expected at Steiner Ranch Steakhouse near Lake Travis at seven. The client had agreed to see Asher for drinks.

At ten until six, Asher was wearing a sixteen-hundred-dollar Italian suit, making peanut butter and jelly sandwiches for the kids. It seemed easier than baking the meat loaf Carla had made for them, which would have required firing up the monstrous Viking stove Susanna had insisted upon installing (Asher's preferred method for food preparation was the microwave). He didn't have time to prepare anything else. He needed Jane to come walking through that door right about now. In fact, he kept walking to the window and peering out at the drive, hoping to see the red Honda.

"Does Jane have a cell phone number?" he asked Riley.

"Are you serious?" Riley picked up a neon pink Post-it from the kitchen desk and held it out to him. "She left this in case we went to the bathroom and couldn't find our way out."

Asher smiled. Riley had painted her toes and finger-nails bright pink, perhaps in silent protest to the loss of her pink hair. He'd been informed, the moment he'd walked through the door yesterday, that she had a hair appointment Thursday and she was getting *highlights*. He was not fool enough to come between Riley and her highlights.

He checked his watch again. He could be at the Steiner Ranch Steakhouse in twenty minutes; he still had time.

"Guess what, Riley? We painted alligators today!" Levi said. He was on his knees on a stool at the kitchen island, where he was playing with a pair of Transformers. He had them locked in a deadly grip.

"I know, doofus, I was with Dad when he picked you up."

"Then we made a volcano and blew it up," Levi continued. "It blew all the way to the sky!"

"Dad, where's my laptop?" Riley asked, lazily looking around.

"I don't know, Ri. Where did you put it?" Asher asked as he dialed Jane's number.

"Alligators can *eat* you!" Levi informed them both, opening his mouth as wide as he could, then snapping it shut.

"*Hello, you've reached Jane Aaron,*" Jane's softly husky voice said from somewhere in cyberspace. "*Please leave a message and I will return your call as soon as I can.*"

"Jane, this is Asher Price calling. I've had something come up and I need you back at the house. It's almost six—please call and let me know when we can expect you."

"*Stop,* Levi!" Riley shouted.

Asher looked up; Levi was on the floor now, trying to bite Riley's leg like an alligator. "Levi, no one likes an alligator clamped to their ankle. Leave your sister alone."

Asher closed his cell phone and tossed it aside to continue with the sandwiches.

Levi climbed back on the stool and picked up one Transformer. "Daddy? Was Mommy crazy?"

Asher paused with the knife in the peanut butter jar and stared at his son.

"*Dad*," Riley said, clearly horrified.

"Where did you hear that, buddy?" Asher asked calmly.

Levi shrugged. "Jackson said it."

"Jackson? Who's Jackson?"

"He's in my camp. He has a bear whistle."

"No, Mommy was not crazy," Asher said firmly. "Jackson was teasing you."

That seemed to satisfy Levi, who turned back to his Transformers. Riley, however, stared at Asher as if she desired more of a denial, more defense of Susanna. When Asher didn't offer it, she walked into the den.

Had Susanna been crazy? That depended on whether or not one would call bipolar disorder—a medical condition affecting the chemical balance in her brain—the result of a bad set of genes or just . . . crazy? Asher didn't know and didn't care anymore. If Susanna had or hadn't been crazy had no bearing on their life now. She'd been bipolar and the drinking hadn't helped, and she'd been selfish and cruel to him, but in her own way, when she'd been sober and on an even keel, she'd been a great mom. Asher was determined to keep as much of Susanna's troubled history from his children for as long as he could. He knew he couldn't hide it forever, but he wanted his children to have the memory of the mother they loved, of the mother who'd taken them for picnics and done art projects with them and read to them every night. He wanted his kids to have that Susanna. Not the other one. Not the one he'd had.

The sound of a car in the drive was a relief. "There she is," he said. He wiped his hands on a dish towel and strode to the door, the kids on his heels.

Jane didn't seem to notice them as she walked up the drive; she was on her phone and juggling a few canvas grocery bags. She was wearing sunglasses on the top of her head, jeans that rode low on her hips, and a tight-fitting tie-dyed T-shirt with a peace symbol painted on the chest. It matched the small peace symbol on the bumper of her car. A part of a tattoo peeked out from the top of her jeans, and that caught Asher's attention, intriguing him. Her hair, which he'd only seen wet or tied in a funky knot at her nape, was down, wild and wavy, hanging below her shoulders.

Here he was once again thinking that his nanny was sexy, and he tried not to look at the tease of a tattoo.

"It wasn't like that," she said into the phone. "It was more like I'm not entitled to know. Like I have no right to ask who—"

She happened to look up and see Asher and his children standing almost shoulder to shoulder, looking at her.

"Ah . . . hey, can I call you back? I just got back to work and the family is . . . is right here." She smiled. "Something like that. No, I'll call you later tonight. Bye." She snapped the phone shut and shoved it into the pocket of her jeans. "Hi," she said warily to the three of them.

"We've been waiting for you forever!" Levi said loudly. Asher put his hand on his son's shoulder.

"You are waiting for me?" Jane looked at Asher. "But . . . I had the afternoon off. I reminded you."

"Right, I know you did. But I've had something come up at the last minute and need you to cover for me, please." He glanced at his watch again. Tara would be here any moment. "I need to leave in about fifteen minutes. I was making the kids a PB&J," he said, gesturing to the kitchen. "If you could finish that up, that would be great. Thanks." He started inside.

"Wait . . . are you leaving?" Jane asked, sounding a little incredulous.

"I have to go to a meeting. It can't be helped."

"But I had the day off."

"You had the *afternoon* off," Riley corrected.

"Riley, butt out," Asher said, and to Jane, "Look, I'm sorry about the last-minute change, but I can't miss this opportunity. And you're here now, so . . . no problem, right?" He thought there better not be—he was paying her a small fortune and providing her room and board.

"It's just that I thought I had the rest of the day off," Jane said, heaving her bags into one hand so that she could push her loose hair behind her ear with the other. "We agreed, after three on Tuesdays and Thursdays."

"Jane, we painted alligators today!" Levi said loudly.

"Wow, you did?" she asked, but her gaze—amber brown and challenging—was locked on Asher.

Those eyes, the hair, and the bit of tattoo he could see were distracting to the man in Asher. "Jane. I am going to meet with two representatives from AT&T. We could potentially land a huge account here." The sound of Tara's car on the drive reached him. "I obviously can't miss this, so I am asking you to please stay with the kids tonight."

Jane frowned. "All right."

"Thank you. I often have these sorts of events. We'll just have to be flexible." He started toward the house again.

"I guess you mean that *I* should be flexible."

Asher hesitated, uncertain if he'd heard her right. He glanced back. Oh, he'd heard her right—Jane bore the international expression of feminine ire. "Is there a problem?" he asked.

"Jane, do you want to see my alligator?" Levi asked, oblivious to the tension. Riley, however, took a seat on a stone bench, as if she was enjoying it.

"Hello, everyone!" Tara called, sashaying into their midst wearing a gold minidress. "What are you doing out here?"

"Getting ready to leave," Asher said. "Do I need anything?"

"Just your brilliantly creative mind."

"Then we should be going."

"Excuse me?" Jane said, drawing his attention back to her. "I am not available Thursday night—just in case you have an emergency, that is."

Tara's smile faded.

Again, Jane pushed her hair back, but in a way that made Asher think she was anxious. "I mean, tonight, you have an emergency meeting, which is fine, but you gave me the time off and now you are basically taking it back. I'm doing some research and there are some people I need to see, and I've made plans Thursday, and I want to make sure we are on the same page here."

"Is Jane in trouble?" Levi asked of no one in particular.

"Close," Riley said gleefully.

"Hey, Riley, Levi, will you show me the pool?" Tara asked, gliding past Asher, holding out her hand to Levi.

"You've seen the pool, like, a million times," Riley said.

"Riley, go with Tara," Asher said low.

"Dad—"

"*Go,*" he said sternly. With a sigh, Riley stood and followed Tara and Levi, who was racing to the wrought-iron gate that led to the pool area.

Asher motioned to the house. "Come in, Jane," he said tightly and stepped back, allowing her to pass by him.

"*Thanks,*" she said and swept by him, her bags inadvertently banging against his leg as she passed. She stepped into the narrow mudroom, where she dropped her bags and faced him.

Asher shut the door behind them and leaned back against it. "All right, Jane. Whatever the problem we're having here, let's get it out in the open."

She hesitated, studying him a moment. "Okay, here it is. I am usually a team player and I wouldn't mind, under normal circumstances, filling in. But you're taking back the time you gave me to work on my thesis and I want to make sure we are clear about that."

"Oh, I think you've made it very clear," he said sardonically.

"Good."

"Now allow me to be clear," he said, pushing away from the door, stepping closer to her. "Sometimes things come up. Sometimes I need you to do a little more than what we agreed, and I think I'm paying you enough to expect a little flexibility."

"Good point," Jane said pertly. "But I will point out that I'm working enough overtime that I should expect you won't take advantage of me."

Jane Aaron had some spunk to her and some amazing amber brown eyes. And that damn tattoo was going to kill Asher with curiosity. He narrowed his gaze on her. "Do you think that perhaps you are making a big deal out of a little thing?"

"Do you mean a little thing to you? I think if I allow you an inch, what's to keep you from taking a mile?"

No one ever challenged Asher so boldly. When someone disagreed with him, it was usually with deference. Jane Aaron was interesting, and Asher moved closer to her in the mudroom, stepping around her bags. "I think you could give me the benefit of the doubt, Jane. I don't like time away from my kids, and I wouldn't ask you to do this if it weren't absolutely necessary."

She lifted her chin a little. "I'm just protecting my boundaries."

"Don't worry about your boundaries. I will protect them for you."

They were locked in a standoff, one that was scented by her perfume, which, he realized, he was close enough to smell. Then Jane suddenly smiled, as if she'd won the debate. "Then I guess we're on the same page. Have a good evening, Asher," she added, and dipped down to pick up her bags.

"I'll be back in a couple of hours," he said, regarding her suspiciously.

"Okay. See you then." She passed him so quickly that Asher didn't have time to move. Her arm brushed against him as she made her way with her bags into the kitchen, leaving the scent of her perfume to linger after her.

14

Asher did not return in a couple of hours as he'd said, and Jane ended up putting Levi to bed. When she walked by Riley's room, she saw Riley at her desk, writing furiously in a bound notebook. When Riley saw Jane, however, she got up and came to the door.

"Want to watch TV?" Jane asked.

"No, thanks," Riley said and closed the door.

Nothing like a little rejection to end the evening.

Jane retreated to the guesthouse and called Jonathan. "Hi," she said, smiling when he answered. "It's me. Sorry about earlier, but they were all standing in the driveway when I got home."

"No problem," Jonathan said. "I got that the king was on his throne. So tell me what happened at the hospital today."

"Oh, man," Jane said and sat on one of the leather armchairs. "Talk about an exercise in futility. The woman was nice enough once we got past who I was and why I was asking, but it's such a chicken and egg thing."

"How so?"

"She said they don't keep records by year, and that if I wanted to know who was born on April twenty-fifth, nineteen eighty, I would have to bring her specific names. I told her I couldn't do that, obviously, because I don't know what my name was, and she said there was nothing she could do."

"That really sucks," Jonathan said. "So what are you going to do now?"

"I don't know," Jane said. "I've already Googled everything I can think of and came up empty. It's like I don't exist." She thought about the night she'd been floating in the pool, talking with Asher about how invisible one could be in the world.

"What about the local paper?"

"It's really small and comes out once a week. It's mostly about kids and local sports. I mean, there's not even a website, can you believe it?"

"Still, you could go to their office. I bet they have microfiche. It's at least worth a shot."

"It's the only shot I have unless I can think of another angle or, by some divine miracle, come up with a name." She sighed and pressed her palm to her forehead. "Let's talk about something else. What's going on with you?"

"Not much," he said lightly. "Just getting ready for the Foghorn gig. It's on the nineteenth."

"Perfect. I'm putting it down now," she said, jotting it on her thesis folder. She yawned. "Listen, I should go. I've got to get up early and get Levi to camp."

"Yeah, okay. . . . Janey?"

"Yes?"

"I miss you," Jonathan said softly.

Jane hesitated. She cared deeply for Jonathan, but she didn't know what to say to that, because in that moment, she didn't miss him like she should. Honestly, she had yet to miss him like she should.

"Wow," Jonathan said. "Your silence is devastating."

"I didn't mean it that way."

"I love you, and you can't even say it anymore," Jonathan said, his tone hard. "When did that happen?"

"God, Jonathan, please just . . . *stop*," Jane pleaded.

"Stop loving you?" he asked sharply.

"Stop *pushing* me. Please stop pushing me! I know you aren't happy with the way things are, but I can't . . . I can't make it better right now."

She heard the slow release of his breath. "That's pretty definitive, isn't it?"

"I don't know. But at least it's honest."

"Okay. Great. Got it."

She closed her eyes. "Please don't do that," she said wearily.

"So let me get this straight—I can't talk to you, I can't be with you, I can't say I love you, and I can't be mad. Am I forgetting anything?"

"You're making it worse, Jonathan."

"What do you want from me, Jane? To pretend it's all okay for your sake? You broke my heart!" he exclaimed, his voice rough with pain.

Jane caught her breath. That she couldn't be what he needed her to be was also heartbreaking. "I know," she murmured.

"Okay, Jane," he said, sounding resigned now. "Look, you're coming to the Foghorn gig. Just . . . just do what you have to do, and think about it, and we'll talk then. All right? Let's just call a truce for a few weeks."

She wanted to argue. She wanted to assure him that was unnecessary, but in truth, it was freeing. "Okay."

Jonathan was silent for one long minute, almost as if he expected her to clarify or take it back. When she didn't, he said simply, "I'll see you then," and clicked off.

It was a little frightening, Jane thought, that she didn't

feel as sad as she did relieved. She didn't feel right at all, didn't feel like she belonged there with him now.

The thought startled her.

"You don't believe that," she said aloud. She was just angry and tired of arguing. Maybe it was that she didn't know where she fit in this world just now. The longer she was here, the more she wondered if Houston was really right for her. But it wasn't as if she believed Cedar Springs was really the right fit, either.

She was floating along, looking for something to anchor her, and she wondered, sitting in that posh guesthouse, with the phone still in her hand, how long she could float before she sank.

"I need a drink," she muttered and glanced at the clock. Ten past ten. She remembered Asher had been drinking a beer the other night, and where there was beer, there might be vodka and cranberry juice. Carla had told her to help herself to anything in the kitchen. Jane wasn't certain she'd meant the alcohol, but then again, she hadn't specifically ruled it out, so . . . Jane tossed the phone aside.

In the kitchen, she flipped on the light over the stove so she could see what she was doing and opened the fridge. Damn. No vodka. No wine. But there was beer, and that would do.

Jane took a seat at the kitchen island. She'd taken only a sip when Asher suddenly walked into the kitchen, still wearing a tie, but the suit coat gone. Jane froze, the beer bottle halfway to her mouth. "Ah . . . hi," she said self-consciously. "I didn't know you were home."

"About ten minutes." He looked at her beer.

Jane did, too. "Oh. Carla said I should help myself—"

"Of course," he said, cutting her off. "I think I'll join you." He walked to the fridge and retrieved a beer. He twisted off the top, took a swig, and said, "I'm sorry I'm late."

He said it tightly, as if he had to force himself to say it. "It's okay," Jane said, waving her hand loosely.

"No, it's not okay." He turned around to face her, leaning back against the counter. "I told you I'd be gone only a couple of hours, but I ran into a problem. I should explain something here. My firm has been struggling the last year. Our managing partner is fighting cancer, so now I have his job, plus my old one. We've lost some major accounts in the last year with the downturn in the economy, and we really need a big account like AT&T. This opportunity popped up, and I felt like I needed to stick around." He took a sip of beer. "Just so you know I am not jerking you around."

Wow. Jane had no idea. He looked tired, too. Jane smiled a little. "It's really no problem, Asher. You were right—I was here, so it was no big deal." She lowered her gaze to her beer. What else would she have done? Work on her thesis? What a joke.

"What's your excuse?" Asher asked.

That brought her head up. "My excuse?"

He nodded to her beer.

"Oh yeah," she said sheepishly and gave him a shrug before taking a small sip. "Boyfriend."

"Oh." He nodded. "That's never easy."

"That's an understatement," she said with a snort. "He wants to get married," she blurted. She had no idea why she'd told him, and she honestly expected him to say something like *That's nice* and walk out.

But Asher didn't do that. He studied her a moment. "Are you going to marry him?"

"That is the problem," Jane said, squirming a little in her chair. "I don't know what I am going to do. I don't know if I am ready for that. The thought of planning a wedding right now is so . . . alien."

"It's a big decision," he casually agreed.

It was a huge decision, growing bigger and bigger each day. "It's not him," she said, feeling the need to vindicate Jonathan somehow. "It's just that I want to be really, really, one hundred percent sure, and I'm not even that sure of myself."

Asher shrugged a little and drank from his beer. "I don't think you can ever be one hundred percent sure. You never know what marriage is going to be like until you are in it and breathing the same air."

Jane laughed a little. "We've breathed the same air."

"But marriage is different. I can't really describe how it's different—it just is. Trust me."

He said it as if he was warning her. She wondered what he knew. "Do you mean you weren't certain when you decided to get married?"

He gave her a wry smile. "No. I was one hundred percent certain."

He was confusing her.

"For what it's worth, here's some unsolicited advice. Don't let anyone push you into anything."

Had he been pushed? Had *he* pushed?

"But you probably know that. And I'm the last guy to hand out marriage advice, so . . ." He straightened up, took another swig of his beer. "I need to prepare for tomorrow. I have a feeling you will make the right decision, Jane. You don't strike me as the type to do things lightly." He leaned across the island and clinked his beer bottle against hers. "Cheers," he said and walked across the kitchen, yawning. But before he went out, he looked back at Jane. "You're okay, right?"

"Definitely," she said and smiled. "Before you go, I

should tell you that I made an appointment for Riley at Envy Salon on the square to help with her hair. But the only time they have is Thursday afternoon, and I—"

"I know—you have plans," Asher said, and with a wink, he walked out, leaving Jane with a half-drunk beer and a deepening interest in that man.

At a quarter to three Thursday afternoon, Jane was convinced Asher wasn't coming home after all, but at the last moment, Carla found her and told her he had returned. At a quarter after three, Jane was standing at the door of the *Cedar Springs Standard*. The paper was so small that it didn't even keep regular office hours. They were closed Monday afternoons and Thursday mornings, and all weekend.

The nameplate on the office entrance listed only two people—the managing editor, Ed Brewster, and Macy Lockhart.

"May I help you?" A young woman with short, honey blonde hair and blue eyes smiled warmly at Jane.

"Are you Macy?" Jane asked.

"Ah, no. I'm Emma, Macy's sister. Macy is on maternity leave. What can I do for you?"

"I need some information that is about thirty years old, and I was hoping Mr. Brewster is in."

"Who, Ed?"

"The managing editor," Jane clarified.

Emma chewed the corner of her lip a moment and glanced at a closed door at the far end of the office. "Are you sure you want to talk to Ed?"

Surprised by the question, Jane glanced at the closed door, too.

Emma leaned forward. "Listen, the only reason I ask is because Ed is kind of old, and he usually takes a nap in the afternoons. I don't like to disturb him unless there's something happening. Like news." She laughed.

"Okay," Jane said uncertainly.

"Don't worry. Whatever it is, I am sure I can help you!" Emma said cheerfully. "I mean, yes, I am only filling in for Macy, who just had a baby. Why she had to get a part-time job six weeks before she had a baby is beyond me. It's not like they needed the money, they've really been doing pretty good with Finn's book deal and the donations and all that, but never mind, here I am, filling in. It's okay, because trust me; part-time is about all anyone needs for this job. What is it you're looking for?"

"I was hoping to find the names of the babies born in the Cedar Springs hospital on April twenty-fifth, nineteen eighty."

"Nineteen eighty?" Emma's brow wrinkled. "That might be a problem. There was a fire in the warehouse that burned a lot of the *Cedar Springs Standard* records, but I'm not sure what years." At Jane's horrified look, Emma said, "Faulty wiring. You didn't hear about that?"

"No . . . I'm kind of new to town."

"Oh, it was quite a big to-do around here," Emma said as she walked to a filing cabinet. "The good news is, the library had some of the issues dating to the fifties. Not *all* of the issues dating back to the fifties, because that would be too easy, right? Macy said it was hit or miss. But still, they had some. And then Ed wrote an editorial about the whole thing and who would have guessed it, but old man Turnbow, who owns the hubcap place out on seventy-one? Turns out he is a history buff and a bit of a hoarder and he had a bunch of the old printed versions of the paper going back to the thirties. The *thirties,* can you imagine? So now Ed is in the process of having everything scanned in and put on microfiche so we can re-create a record and every score of every Cedar Springs high school football game since the fall of the Alamo."

Emma opened the filing cabinet and pulled out a manila folder. "Give me just a second," she said, and sat down at a desk with the open folder.

As Emma read the contents of the file, Jane looked around. The room looked a lot smaller than it was because of all the filing cabinets. They lined every wall. On Emma's desk was a picture of a woman who resembled Emma with a handsome man, holding a baby girl. The picture reminded Jane of all the pictures around Summer's End, pictures and portraits proclaiming to the world that the Price family was a happy, beautiful family.

"This doesn't tell me anything," Emma said, drawing Jane's attention. "I'm going to have to do some research. Translation—call Macy." She laughed. "Unfortunately, the baby had an appointment today, so she's in Austin." Emma closed the file. "I need to ask her what years we have records for, and then I need to find out if the library has it, and if so, if it's on microfiche yet."

"Oh," Jane said, disappointed. "How long will that take?"

"I hope not more than a couple of days," Emma said. "But between you and me . . ." She glanced at the closed door, leaned forward again, and whispered, "Ed has a serious lack of organizational skills, so it might be a bit of a hunt," she whispered.

Jane was crestfallen.

"Is there a number where I can reach you?" Emma asked cheerfully, and picked up a pencil to jot down Jane's cell number.

15

While Jane was sitting in the offices of the *Cedar Springs Standard*, Asher was picking up Levi from explorer camp. He was actually surprised and relieved that Jane had found this outlet for Levi. The kid needed some structure and meaningful activity and, moreover, he seemed to enjoy it very much.

As Asher pulled into the parking lot, Levi raced down the path to the Range Rover, a flag in his hand. But when Asher stepped out to meet him, Levi's face fell. He stopped in his tracks. "Where's Jane?"

His son's disappointment pricked Asher a little. "She had something else to do today. Hey, that's a cool flag."

Levi's face lit up. "I made it all by myself!"

"Mr. Price?"

Asher glanced up to see a woman marching toward him. She introduced herself as Charlotte, the camp administrator. Her hair was cut shorter than Asher's, and she was wearing shorts and a shirt that reminded Asher of his Cub Scout days.

"May I speak with you? We are having a couple of issues with Levi."

Levi instantly ducked around behind Asher. "Like what?" Asher asked.

"He is not minding the camp counselors. We have a

three-strikes policy here, and Levi was up to two today. He was throwing food at lunchtime, and this afternoon, he kicked two sand mountains the kids had built."

Asher looked down at Levi, who was studying the tips of his hiking boots.

"Earlier this week, we made volcanoes. Levi deliberately disobeyed and poured more vinegar into the baking soda than he was instructed." Charlotte frowned slightly. "The result was a massive volcanic explosion in the small room we have for such activities. It created a huge mess that two of our counselors had to stay late to clean up."

"I didn't know it would explode that much, Daddy," Levi mumbled.

"We ask that the kids respect our authority, Mr. Price. For the safety of the other kids and the shared experience, it is very important that all the children obey the camp counselors."

"I am sure Levi respects authority, Charlotte," Asher said shortly and looked at his son. "Levi, you know you have to mind Miss Charlotte and her"—*flying monkeys* was the phrase that came to mind—"counselors," he said.

"Yes, sir," Levi mumbled.

"Why did you kick the sand mountains?"

"Because Jackson said I was weird because I don't have a mommy."

Asher's heart twisted a little. "Okay. We'll talk about this on the way home. Go hop in the car so I can talk to Miss Charlotte a minute."

Head down, Levi walked to the car and crawled into the backseat. When he was out of earshot, Asher asked Charlotte, "Were you aware that some kid was taunting my son?"

"I have talked to the other child," Charlotte said confidently.

"Are you threatening to kick him out as well?"

"Mr. Price, that is hardly what I said."

"You certainly implied it. But Levi was obviously pro-voked."

Charlotte sighed. "Believe me, Mr. Price, children can be mean."

"He is *five*, Charlotte. He needs protection from bullies. He needs *your* protection and your defense."

Charlotte's face darkened. "I can assure you that Jackson Harvey will be dealt with. We do not tolerate bullying at our day camp. Nevertheless, Levi has to obey the rules."

"He will obey the rules," Asher snapped. "You need some order in your camp."

Charlotte bristled. "Thank you for speaking to Levi," she said tightly and walked briskly away in her little explorer outfit.

Fuming, Asher walked to the car and got in.

"I didn't know it would explode that much, Daddy," Levi said fearfully when Asher closed the driver's door.

"I know, but you have to listen to the camp counsel-ors," Asher said, then lectured Levi on the importance of minding camp counselors and being a team player on the way to the hair salon, where he was to collect Riley from Helen, Susanna's mother.

They pulled up outside Envy Salon on Main Street just as Helen and Riley emerged. Helen had her arm around Riley's shoulders, and Riley was smiling at her grand-mother. God, it made Asher's heart swell to see Riley's smile. It reminded him of Susanna, and he was sure Helen thought the same.

Riley's hair looked closer to her natural blonde, and moreover, she'd cut it. Her hair was swinging just above her shoulders; long bangs swept down the side of her face. As she drew closer to the car, he noticed one slender faint stripe of pink in her bangs. If that's all there was, he could live with it. She was wearing a tight black T-shirt with some silver insignia, tight black jeans, and some goofy-looking high-top tennis shoes. Asher noticed something else—Riley had curves. And *breasts*. Good God, how had he missed that?

Riley and Helen walked around to the passenger side of the car. Helen was a striking woman with blondish silver hair and a tan. She looked a lot like Asher's mother, really—one of the thin, wealthy, fit senior citizens milling about this part of Texas. Asher's mother's hair was darker and highlighted, but she was pencil thin, wore a lot of jewelry like Helen, and spent her summers in New Hampshire or Europe, out of the Texas heat.

Riley opened the door and climbed in. Helen leaned over, propped her arms on the open window, and smiled warmly. "Hello, Ash. The pink wasn't my idea. I just thought I should state that for the record."

"Somehow, I knew that," Asher said.

Helen poked her perfectly coiffed head through Riley's window and looked into the backseat. "Hello, Levi!"

"Hi, Grandma."

"When are you coming to see me? We haven't made cookies in a long, long time, have we?"

"I don't know," Levi answered honestly.

"I would very much like for you and Riley to come spend the night. Will you do that?"

"Yes," Levi said.

Helen missed the kids. She'd all but accused Asher a couple of weeks ago of keeping them from her, and she'd grudgingly accepted his excuse that he just wasn't home much.

"Any weekend you'd like to have them, Helen," Asher offered now.

"I can never get hold of you, Ash. But I'll try again.

Now tell me quickly how the new nanny is working out before I melt in this heat."

"I like her!" Levi announced.

"I think we're settling into a routine," Asher added.

"I am so relieved. I know that's been a real concern."

"Can we go now?" Riley asked impatiently.

"Can you tell your grandmother thank you?" Helen said, playfully punching Riley in the arm.

"Thanks, Grandma."

"You're most welcome, my love." Helen reached over the seat and tweaked Levi's toes. "Good-bye, Levi. Don't forget those cookies, now."

"Bye!" Levi shouted, and kicked the back of Riley's seat.

"Don't kick my seat, Levi," Riley said. She opened the care visor to examine her hair as Asher backed the Range Rover away from the sidewalk and pointed the car in the direction of Summer's End.

They hadn't even left the town square when Levi said, "Your hair looks weird," and kicked the back of Riley's seat again.

"Shut up," Riley said and closed the visor.

"It's *weird*."

Asher gave his son a look in the rearview mirror. "No one asked you for your opinion, Levi."

"Yeah, Levi, no one wants your opinion. No one really even wanted *you*."

"*Riley!*" Asher snapped.

"What?" she asked, looking at him wide-eyed. "It's true. You and Mom used to fight about it all the time."

"Dammit, Riley, you have no idea what you are talking about! That is *not* true," he said angrily and looked at Levi in the rearview mirror. "That's not true, buddy."

"Don't *say* that, Riley!" Levi shouted and angrily kicked the back of her seat again.

"Stop kicking my seat!" Riley cried.

"Riley Ann," Asher said low. "There are a lot of things you think you understand that you don't. Watch what you say, do you understand me?"

"I'm sorry! I know you want Levi *now,* Dad," she said and sank lower into her seat. "I didn't mean to make everyone mad."

Asher glanced in the rearview mirror. Now Levi was staring pensively out the window. Not wanted at camp, not wanted by his parents. What more could a kid take? And Riley! She'd been only a little older than Levi was now when Susanna had discovered she was pregnant again. It had been a huge blow to them. Susanna had had a habit of getting off her meds, claiming they'd impeded her creativity. Asher, Helen, and her doctors would convince her to get back on them. But somehow, in spite of their best precautions, Susanna had gotten pregnant again. They'd argued about her pregnancy and her inability to really care for a baby, and about her drinking while she was carrying Levi. When Levi was born prematurely, Asher had feared the worst. So had Susanna. She'd feared her son would die, and even though Levi had been fine, Susanna's anxiety had begun to spiral out of control.

Riley had been the miracle baby, but Levi had undone the miracle, and Riley remembered it all.

Asher suddenly turned right.

"Where are we going?" Riley demanded.

"You'll see when we get there," he said curtly.

The Saddle-brew had to be the most successful business in all of Cedar Springs. Every time Asher stopped by, regardless of the time of day, the place was packed. Today was no exception.

Samantha Delaney was working the counter. She had a pencil stuck behind her ear and was holding another one in her hand. Asher ordered a latte for himself, juice for Levi, and nothing for Riley, who couldn't make up her mind.

"Asher Price!"

Asher turned around at the sound of his name; Linda Gail Graeber was standing behind him. "Well look here, it's old home week!" she said happily.

Asher had a soft spot for Linda Gail. She'd organized what he now thought of as the funeral food brigade when Susanna had died, enticing the women around town to pull out their standby casseroles from the deep-freezes in their garages and dole them out to Asher and the kids in a steady stream for about three weeks after the funeral. It had been an invaluable gift to him as a newly widowed, grieving father. "How are you, Linda Gail?"

"Oh, I'm right as rain, right as rain. We hardly see you around town anymore."

"I've been tied up with work."

"Can't work too hard, else you'll drown in your own sweat," she said with a wink. "Riley, look at your hair! That's just too cute! Asher, I swear, I've been trying my hardest to get Tracy and Riley together this summer," she said, stroking Riley's hair. "Maybe they could go swimming or something fun like that."

"Consider it done," Asher said instantly, ignoring Riley's look of horror.

"I wanna go!" Levi said.

"You, too, buddy. Linda Gail, bring your kids out to Summer's End." He opened his wallet and pulled out a business card. "Let me give you the number of our nanny, Jane Aaron. You can call her and set it up."

"That would be great!" Linda Gail said. "Jane and I have already spoken about it—I'll give her a call."

Asher looked up from his wallet. "Jane? Our Jane? You know her?"

"Oh, I met her! She's great, Asher. My friends and I liked her instantly. You did good."

Asher borrowed a pen from the counter, jotted down Jane's cell phone number on the back of his business card, and handed it to Linda Gail. "I'll let her know you're going to call," he said.

"Thanks! I know Tracy will be thrilled."

Riley, however, was not thrilled. The moment they left the Saddle-brew, she said, "You're killing me, Dad. Why are you making me do this?"

"It's not torture."

"It's not to *you*, but it is to me."

"Why is it so hard to have some friends over, Riley? Think about it—what's the worst that could happen?"

She looked down. Her hair fell forward, covering her face. "I don't want to hang out with Tracy or anyone else."

"This is an opportunity for you to stop hiding from the world, baby girl. Tracy is a great kid. So are you. And you could use some friends, Riley."

"*God*," she said and folded her arms across her body. She tossed her head, just like Susanna would do when she was angry with him.

This will be a telling couple of years, Ash, his mother had said a few months ago. *If Riley is going to follow in Susanna's footsteps, you'll probably begin to see it during puberty*. That remark had made Asher angry at the time, but sometimes he couldn't help but wonder.

But at the moment, he hardly cared. They were going to have a swim party, even if it killed Riley Ann to do so.

16

One of the benefits of Jane's job, she quickly discovered, was the running trail down to and around the lake. Carla didn't mind if Jane ran early before the kids got up. Of course on weekends, Jane could run as far and as long as she liked.

That Sunday morning, she had her iPod and was running a quick pace to the beat of Pearl Jam. As the trail was a little rocky, she had her head down, her thoughts a million miles from the trail, shuffling between her untouched thesis, the news from Emma Harper about the state of the paper's records, and, naturally, Jonathan.

On the public path next to the lake, Jane happened to look up and see another runner approaching her. His stride, fast and strong, looked easy for him. She envied that kind of runner, the sort that didn't seem the least bit winded by three miles.

As he drew closer, Jane realized it was Asher. She quickly put her head down and ran past, hoping and praying he didn't notice her—

She jumped when his hand touched her arm. She reluctantly stopped, pulled the earbuds from her ears, hoped she wasn't too sweaty, and said, "Hi."

An unshaven Asher, dressed in shorts, another butchered

T-shirt, and a cap, looked confused. His gaze flicked over her, and then he grinned.

He *grinned*.

His face was transformed with that smile. His good looks were suddenly approachable. His green eyes shone and one cheek, Jane couldn't help notice, was dimpled. "You're a runner, huh?" he asked, seemingly pleased by it. "I didn't know that." His gaze slid down to her bare legs.

Jane looked down, too. "In the loosest interpretation of the word, maybe," she said and glanced up again.

"You seemed like you were running to me. What are you listening to?"

"Pearl Jam."

"Good choice," Asher said, nodding approvingly. "I lost my iPod in Germany."

"Bummer."

"I'll say," Asher said. His eyes were shining with amusement, and Jane was surprised by how that seemed to trickle down her spine. She could only imagine what it must be like to be romantically involved with him, to have the smile bestowed on her on a daily basis. Lucky wench, Tara or whoever it was, because *that* was a sexy, charming smile.

"So what kind of distances are you running?"

"Distances? Oh no," Jane said, waving a hand at him. "No distances. I mean, I've run a couple of five ks to see if I could, but mostly I run to . . ." Her mind went blank. She tried to think of the right word, any word. She ran for release, to think, to *not* think, to mourn.

His smile deepened at her inability to speak. "Me, too," he said, as if he understood the complex reasons she ran. Was that even possible?

Asher looked down the path from where he'd come.

"Want to run together? It's another mile to the trail's end and I could use the extra mileage."

Jane instantly had the image of him practically sailing along and hearing her make some awful wheezing noises as she tried to breathe, not unlike a wounded cow. "Oh, no," Jane said. "I'd hold you up."

"I doubt that." His smile was slow and easy. "Come on. I'm going to run down there. You're going to run down there. So let's run." Jane hesitated; Asher put his hand on the small of her back and gave her a nudge forward. "You can't pretend I'm not here, can you?"

"Ah . . ." No, she could not ignore him. Not possibly. So Jane started at her normal pace, and Asher easily fell in beside her.

Neither of them said much as they ran down to the lake. While Jane concentrated on breathing, Asher pointed out a couple of things to her—the crumbling remains of an old one-roomed schoolhouse from the pre-lake days when a settlement was built on the banks of the river. The first bait shop on the lake that was now a private boathouse.

Mostly, they just ran. Jane was keenly aware of him beside her, of his strength and the easy way he ran with what seemed to her as a serious lack of exertion.

When they reached the end of the trail, Asher pointed her to another trail she'd never seen before. It went up in the hills. "It's an alternate route back," he said. "Want to see it?"

The trail looked more vertical than horizontal to Jane, and she didn't want to make a fool of herself trying to navigate it. But her tongue ignored her brain and she said, "Sure."

It was a rough go. Jane's butt and thighs were beginning to scream at her, and Asher still looked as if he'd hardly broken a sweat. About halfway back, when Jane's chest was about to burst, they reached a peak in the trail, and Asher pointed to the lake. "See that building on the north shore?"

Jane took her eyes off the path to look, and when she did, she misstepped. She went down so quickly that she didn't even make a sound before hitting the ground.

"Hey, are you okay?" Asher asked, reaching down to help her up from the ugly sprawl.

"I'm good!" she cried, but she was mortified to her toes. She was on all fours; in her haste to pop up, she hopped, and the moment she did, she grabbed her leg. *"Ouch. Ouch ouch ouch,"* she hissed. Asher caught her with one arm around her waist before she toppled again. He was warm and damp, and in a panic, Jane tried again to put weight on the offending foot.

"Whoa, wait," Asher said. "Sit here and let me have a look."

"I'm okay, really," she insisted. "I just need to walk it off."

"Spoken like a true jock," he said jokingly. "Let me have a look first," he insisted, and helped her to a seat on a big chunk of limestone.

"I don't know what happened," she said as he knelt before her.

"You landed on a rock." He lifted her leg in one hand and felt gingerly around her ankle with the other. "Happened to me once. You really need trail running shoes around here. Does this hurt?" he asked, bending her foot back a little.

It hurt like hell, but Jane was pleasantly distracted by his touch. "A little," she said.

He knew exactly how much pressure to apply as he moved her foot around. He moved his hand up her ankle again, probing it. "I don't think anything is broken." He lifted his gaze to her and for one slender moment, Jane believed she felt a spark between them.

Then again, it seemed that she—silly girl that she was—

had imagined it, because Asher looked down and put her foot on the ground. "Let me help you up," he said and stood, reaching his hand out to her. Jane slipped her hand into his; he closed his fingers tightly around hers, put his other hand around her waist, and helped her stand. "What do you think?" he asked as Jane tested her ankle.

She thought her heart was going to jump right out of her chest. He held her so easily, so securely, and his body was hard against her. The sensation was intoxicating and maddening; what was she doing? "It's okay," she said. "I think I can walk." She needed to step away from him, breathe some air, find her bearings again.

But Asher had other ideas. "Try a few steps," he suggested and tightened his already firm hold of her. On the second step, her knee buckled.

"Okay, that's it," he said and pointed to a tree. "Sit." Jane looked at the tree. "Right there," he commanded. "With your back against the tree."

"I don't—"

"*Sit*," he said sternly.

Jane sat. Asher sat, too, propping her foot up on his thigh to elevate it.

They sat that way for a moment until Jane pulled her hat low over her eyes and said, "This is awkward. I feel like a moron."

"Nah," he scoffed. "Could have happened to anyone."

"It didn't happen to you. Now the kids will wonder where you are."

He smiled and looked up to the treetops. "Riley is watching Levi. They'll be fine."

"Wow," Jane said. "You have better luck getting her to watch Levi than I do."

Asher chuckled and looked at Jane again. "My little girl can be stubborn, there is no doubt."

A breeze lifted up from the lake, cooling them. Jane looked at Asher's hand on her ankle. She liked the feel of it. Very . . . masculine. "She's a puzzle," she said, working to keep her mind clear of such thoughts. "I can't find anything to really interest her. I discovered the little playhouse just below the house, and I thought she might want to go there and paint or do some artwork. But she refused to step foot in it."

Asher's smile faded. He looked at Jane. "That studio holds some painful memories for her."

Jane blinked. "I'm sorry. I didn't realize . . . she said it was her mother's."

"Did she say anything else?" Asher asked curiously.

"Just that she wouldn't go in. And that I shouldn't either." She smiled.

Asher smiled, too. "She had a complicated relationship with her mother." Jane had the sense he was choosing his words carefully. "Living with Susanna wasn't always easy."

Her curiosity piqued, Jane waited for him to say more. She wanted to ask him why it hadn't been easy, but she didn't want to pry.

"She was an artist with an artist's temperament. You could say she was a little mercurial."

Mercurial. Jane thought of Alice in Wonderland for some reason.

"Riley didn't always understand her mother's moods. She was so young, and . . . and I think now she struggles to reconcile the memories of a mother she loved and misses with a mother who could be different at times."

So vague, yet so intriguing. "I had no idea," Jane said.

"I know Riley can be difficult," he said apologetically. "She's a little different herself."

"She's cool," Jane said. "A really cool girl. Levi is cool, too."

Asher smiled skeptically. "Thanks. I think they're both pretty cool. I'm glad you think so. By the way, I invited the Graebers for a swim party. Linda Gail is going to call you to arrange it. Make sure the kids are available, and especially Riley." His smile was charmingly devilish. "That girl is going to go, even if I have to drag her dead body myself," he confided.

"Wow, Asher, I hope it doesn't come to that," Jane said in all seriousness. "But if it does, I'll help you."

He laughed, patted her ankle. "Speaking of the little devils . . . want to try your ankle again?"

"Yes."

He helped her up and took firm hold of her again. She gripped his arm as she tested her ankle, his earthy scent tickling her nose.

"I can walk," she said, taking a few steps. "I just rolled it. I'll be fine." Jane risked a look into those eyes. "Thanks."

"You should lay off a few days," he advised and let her go. Jane took several steps forward. "We're only a mile or so from the house, right?" she asked, looking down the trail and away from him. It seemed saner that way. "You should go on. Don't worry about me."

He laughed. "Now what kind of guy would I be if I left you for the armadillos?"

Another jovial remark from a guy Jane had pegged as the least amusing man in Texas. "Thanks! I really didn't want to be eaten by armadillos." She began her gingerly walk.

"I had forgotten how nice it is to run with someone," Asher said absently as he strolled alongside her hobble.

"Oh? Did you used to run with your wife?"

"No." He looked at the lake. "Running wasn't her sport. I meant that I used to run with a couple of buddies. We've lost touch in the last few years."

"What was her sport?" Jane asked. When Asher didn't answer her, she looked at him.

His smile was gone, his expression impassive. "To be honest, I don't really remember."

That response seemed a little odd to Jane. How could he not remember?

"Who do you run with?" Asher asked. "Your boyfriend?"

Jane laughed. "Hardly. Running isn't his sport, either. I took it up a couple of years ago." She peeked up at him. "I needed to get out."

"Ah," Asher said. "So . . . were you running from, or running to?"

She thought about that a moment. "I was more like a hamster, running to and fro." She laughed at herself.

"I know what you mean."

"Really? You don't seem like you'd have the kind of life-muddling questions I seem to have."

"Whether or not to get married?"

"We'll start there," Jane joked, and Asher laughed.

"How is the injured ankle, by the way? You seem to be moving much better."

"I predict a full recovery by the morning with a little ice, elevation, and chocolate. As for the klutz in me, I'm not sure that can be corrected. This isn't exactly the first time I've done this," she confided sheepishly. "I ran right off a curb once."

He laughed. "How can you run off a curb?"

"Allow me to enlighten you," Jane said, and she told him about her flying off a curb she hadn't seen. And leaping to avoid what she thought was a snake—which had turned out to be a stick—and landing half on, half off the trail, spraining her foot.

By the time she had finished, they'd reached the gate to

the house. "Maybe, for the sake of the running public, it's a good thing you go solo," Asher suggested.

"Exactly," Jane agreed.

Asher opened the gate and stood back so that Jane could limp through. "This is where I leave you to put some ice and chocolate on your ankle. You're okay?"

"I'm good," she assured him.

He smiled as his gaze wandered over her a moment. "See you later, Jane. Take care of that ankle." He walked on to the house.

What ankle? Jane wondered and limped to the guest-house.

17

🞸

*J*ane's ankle had recovered Monday morning, but she decided she would not risk running. Instead, she went into the house hoping for breakfast from Carla. She got that, and two hundred dollars.

Jane stared at the ten twenties after Carla explained the money was to buy Riley a swimsuit. "He left two hundred dollars to buy a swimsuit?" she asked incredulously. "How much does he think one costs?"

"Oh, he has no idea," Carla said as she resumed chopping cucumbers. "You can't blame the poor man—Mrs. P had some expensive tastes." Carla stopped chopping and glanced slyly at the door before leaning across the kitchen island. "Between you and me, Mrs. P could *shop.*"

"Really?" Jane said, sliding onto a bar stool.

Carla's cheeks puffed out and her eyes rounded. "Never seen anything like it. Once, she came home from Austin with six Coach purses. Six! Now, I'm no purse expert. I've had the same bag for twelve years now and it still suits me fine. But I know the name Coach, and I know they aren't cheap. And she had *six* of them in the same color! She also had six bracelets, six pairs of Stuart Wisenheimer—"

"—Weitzman?"

"Weitzman, Wisenheimer, I don't know. Some fancy shoemaker. She said six was her lucky number."

That sounded bizarre. "Were they gifts?" Jane asked, trying to make sense of it.

Carla shrugged and picked up her knife again. "Don't know. What I do know is that she had a problem with the credit cards. And that time, it was more than Mr. P was willing to pay. They had an awful fight about it."

Jane could not imagine the couple in the portrait in the living room engaged in an awful fight. They seemed far too sophisticated for awful fighting. "So what happened?" she asked as she swiped a cucumber from beneath Carla's knife.

"That's just it," Carla said. "When I left that day, I was so worried about little Levi. Riley was at school, but Levi had just started crawling, and while they were fighting, he just howled. But when I came back the next day, it was like I dreamed the whole thing." She dumped some cucumbers into a bowl. "Never did see those Coach bags or the shoes again. Maybe she took them back, I don't know, but Mr. P and Mrs. P were all lovey-dovey again."

Jane looked at the money she held. That definitely sounded mercurial. "Just out of curiosity, how old is Mr. P?"

"He was forty in March," Carla said and winced. "I forgot it, can you believe it? Been with the Prices for seven years and flat forgot it. I felt so bad, but in my defense, he treated it like another day. Didn't do anything special for it. He never did, really, I think because Mrs. P was a little sensitive about the fact she was four or five years older than him. You'd never know it to look at her." She paused and sighed wistfully. "She worked hard at being beautiful and she was *so* beautiful. Such a pity that she died so young."

"Tragic," Jane agreed, and glanced up at the picture of Susanna on the shelf behind Carla. Beautiful. Sleek and shiny, highly polished. Not a mark, not a blemish.

"There's a real cute little shop down on Simpson Road," Carla said. "It's called Molly's Closet. They have swimsuits for girls." She turned around to the fridge and went back to work.

When Jane went in search of the kids, she found Riley in her room, applying makeup and, particularly, a lot of deep blue eye shadow. Jane watched the twelve-year-old curiously for a moment. "Did your dad say that was okay?"

"Why not?" Riley asked insouciantly. "It's my face."

"I can think of a million reasons why not," Jane said and leaned down to pick some clothes off the floor. She spotted a swimsuit and picked it up, holding it out. "Good Lord," she said, wrinkling her nose as she examined the two-piece with the tiny little cuddly bear appliqué on the breast. "How old is this?"

"I don't know. I don't really use it," Riley said. "I don't like to swim."

"I wouldn't either if I had to wear that," Jane said, and Riley actually laughed.

"We are going to improve on that, my friend."

Riley stopped applying blush. "What do you mean?"

"Your dad left money to get you a new swimsuit. Carla told me about a place we can go after we drop Levi at camp. Are you up for a little shopping?"

"Yes," Riley said and immediately put down the blush.

Jane and Riley spent the morning looking for the shop—it wasn't on Simpson Road as Carla had directed but on *Sandhurst* Road—and then discovered that Molly's Closet had swimsuits for little girls. Not for teens, which Riley would be in a matter of days.

"Let's get out of here," Jane said softly and put down a truly horrible pink suit.

"*Thank* you," Riley breathed and headed for the door.

In the car, Jane said, "Remind me never to ask Carla where to shop for swimsuits."

"That was epic bad," Riley agreed.

"Where is the closest mall?"

"You mean like Barton Creek?" Riley asked uncertainly.

"Yep. Like that. Where's Barton Creek? In Austin?"

Riley nodded.

Jane glanced at the clock and sighed. "It's too late to go today—we won't have time to shop before we have to come back to get Levi." She looked at Riley. "Tell you what. We'll go early tomorrow and make a day of it."

Riley's face suddenly brightened. "*Really?*"

"Yes, really!" Jane said and started her car.

"Cool!" Riley said happily.

The radio station was blaring an ad, and Riley grimaced. "They're always shouting like we're deaf or something." She punched a button and Janis Joplin came up, crooning "Piece of My Heart."

Riley paused a moment, listening. "Who's that?" she asked as Jane pulled out onto the road.

"Who's *that?* That is Janis Joplin, the mother of rock and roll."

"I never heard of her," Riley said.

"Are you kidding?" Jane cried. "She's classic. She was from Port Arthur. You know where that is, don't you? Down near Corpus?"

They listened a few moments. "She has an epic voice," Riley said. "Is she on the radio?"

"Not anymore. She died a long time ago, before even I was born."

"What happened to her?"

Jane looked at Riley. "Heroin overdose. Janis had a rough life."

"Why?"

"Well, I think because she was really gifted, but when she was growing up, kids in school gave her a hard time. She wasn't part of the in-crowd, and they made fun of her."

"Oh," Riley said. "Like me."

"I don't think like you, Riley. But you know, it's true that sometimes really talented people have a hard time fitting in because they're not like all the rest. They're special. You're special. You're really smart and you have a lot of talent. So was Janis. She went on to be a rock legend, paving the way for other female artists, like Madonna. But here is the difference—Janis had a lot of emotion in her and didn't know how to release it in a positive way. A lot of people like her release it through music or art, and she did, too. But she dulled a lot of it with heroin. She destroyed herself with it. But I think it's really cool to be different and talented and not one of the herd."

"That's really sad," Riley said. "I like her voice."

"You should see *The Rose* with Bette Midler. It's the story of her life."

They listened to the end of the song. When it was over, Jane turned down the volume. "So who do you like?"

"I don't know," Riley said. "I like Amy Winehouse. I like her voice. And I like Lady Gaga, too. I like her outfits."

Jane laughed. "She's very creative with them, isn't she? She's got a new song out, did you know?"

"No," Riley said.

"Maybe we can download it later."

"That would be awesome," Riley agreed.

The rest of the morning with Riley was surprisingly easy. Even when Linda Gail called to suggest Friday as the date for the pool party, Riley was very cheerful in her announcement that she would not attend.

Jane, on the other hand, felt herself increasingly on edge. She was hoping to hear from Emma, and every time her phone rang, her heart skipped a beat. Only Emma did not call. Jane was the recipient of one wrong number, a call from Vickie asking where Jane bought the cute pair of boots she wore a few months ago, and the last from Tara.

"Hi, Jane, hope your day is going well," Tara asked as if they were chatty friends.

"So far so good. What's up?"

"Asher is going to be held up tonight, and he wondered, could you please feed the kids?"

Jane's jaw dropped. He'd made it two whole workdays before breaking his promise to her that he'd not take advantage.

"Now, before you say anything, he is fully aware that you will not be happy with this, and he promises to make it up to you," Tara added quickly.

"Really? How so?" Jane asked.

"Umm . . . I'd say that's between the two of you. But honestly, Jane, he was blindsided this morning by a very big problem."

Jane sighed heavenward, but she thought of how tired he'd looked the other night. "Okay," she said reluctantly.

"Oh, great! Thanks so much, Jane!"

"But he owes me!" Jane reminded her.

"Sure, sure," Tara said, but she was already hanging up.

Jane was inclined to be miffed, given her testy mood, but her other option for that evening's entertainment was working on her thesis.

Her thesis only mocked her now. She couldn't remember what she'd already written, couldn't remember why she'd landed on children and loss as a topic. It was obviously too broad, too . . . uninspired. Watching the kids was a lot easier than trying to think her way out of that debacle.

At least Carla tried to make it easy for Jane by leaving a dish of fish and vegetables for them, but when Riley and Levi saw the dish, they both protested.

"But that's dinner," Jane said. "We don't have anything else."

"No, I don't want it!" Levi insisted.

"Can't you make something?" Riley asked.

"Me? Oh, you guys, I am *horrible* in the kitchen. You have no idea how horrible."

"But you can make spaghetti," Levi said hopefully.

"Everyone can make spaghetti," Riley echoed.

Jane gazed at their expectant faces and sighed. "On one condition," she said, pointing at them. "You're both helping me."

"Yeah!" Levi said and rushed into the pantry.

As they prepared the meal—Levi stirring the bottled sauce, and Riley making a salad—it occurred to Jane that this was the scene Susanna had seen most nights of her life. She would have stood where Jane was standing, watching her children, talking to them about their day. She would have seen her husband, too, when Asher had come in from work. This had been hers. A perfect picture. Susanna Price must have been a very happy woman.

Jane and Levi were playing Chutes and Ladders, and Riley, who had deigned to grace them with her presence that evening, was painting her nails blue when Asher arrived home at a quarter to nine.

Levi heard his car and bounded for the door just as Asher walked through. He put down his briefcase and kissed the top of Levi's head. "How was camp today, kiddo?"

"Good," Levi said, and followed him into the den.

"Hey, baby girl," Asher said, running his hand over

the top of Riley's head. He paused, looking down at her fingers.

"It will come off, Dad. Don't freak," Riley said, lifting her head when he leaned down to kiss her cheek.

"I won't freak," he promised her and collapsed into a chair. He smiled ruefully at Jane. "Thanks," he said, loosening his tie. "I owe you. Again."

He looked exhausted, and Jane took pity on him. "Do you want something to eat?" she asked.

His expression was one of sheer gratitude. "Do you mind? I'm beat and I'm starving."

"Carla made fish. But they ate spaghetti."

He grinned. "Fish is perfect. Thanks."

As Jane warmed a plate, the kids chattered away—Levi about camp, Riley about how lame Molly's Closet had been. Levi began to tell how Jackson had been stung by a bee at camp today, and mimicked his cry. Jane laughed and looked up; her gaze met Asher's. She realized he was watching her, and a flush spread quickly through her body. He held her gaze a moment before turning his attention back to his son.

A little flutter tickled Jane's belly. "Soup's on," she said, her eyes on the plate.

"Great," Asher said.

He walked into the kitchen and Jane offered him the plate. When Asher took it, his fingers brushed hers, and Jane felt that touch spark all the way to her toes.

"Smells great," Asher said. "Thanks for helping out, Jane. I know you need your space."

"No problem. Really." She pushed her hair back, wiped the countertop. "Another tough day, huh?"

"Definitely," he sighed, taking a seat at the island. "Sometimes I wonder why I thought this would be a good business to get into."

"I know the feeling," Jane said.

"Don't you like teaching?" he asked, forking a bite of fish.

Jane hesitated. She didn't know anymore. She couldn't remember all the fine details of why she'd become a teacher. Everything had felt so fluid and up in the air for so long that she didn't know what she liked or disliked.

Asher looked up, expecting an answer.

"I don't know," she said. "Maybe. I mean, I love the kids. And I love to see them learn, but for me . . . I don't know. I feel like I've been looking for the right fit . . ." Her voice trailed off. It was too difficult to explain.

"What about the degree you're working toward? Is that what you want to do?"

"Child psychology?" She laughed sheepishly. "I'm not even sure about that anymore. I'm not making the progress I ought to be making—" She fluttered her fingers at her head. "Can't seem to find my mojo. Does that ever happen to you? Do you ever lack creative juice?"

He considered that as he took a bite. "Not really," he said with a shake of his head. "For me, work has become my sanctuary."

Sanctuary. What an interesting choice of words. And what an interesting sanctuary his work was, seeing as how it seemed to be eating him alive. What sort of refuge was that? And a refuge from what, exactly?

"Jane, I can't make this turn!" Levi cried, fussing with one of his Transformers. Jane helped him transform the robot back into a motorcycle. When she was done, Asher was standing.

"Thanks for this, Jane. I feel like a new man," he said. "If you want to go, I'll take it from here."

Jane blinked. She looked around. "I'll clean up. You've had a long day."

"So have you," he said. "And you've already gone above and beyond. We'll be fine here. The kids will help me."

"Not me," Riley said instantly.

"Especially you, smartypants." He smiled at Jane. "See you tomorrow, right?"

"Okay," Jane said uncertainly. She didn't want to go. She wanted to remain in this perfect picture.

"Bye, Jane!" Levi said. Riley waved her blue fingers at Jane.

Asher opened the door for her. She stepped past him, her body moving dangerously close to his. She looked back at him. "Good night," he said softly, his gaze on hers, and Jane felt that little flutter again.

"Good night." She walked on. But halfway to the guest-house, she glanced back, saw Asher in the kitchen with Riley and Levi. Levi was leaning across the island, and Riley was holding out her hands, examining her fingers, while Asher put his dishes in the dishwasher. He was talking to them, no doubt asking after their day. It was a little fairy tale in there, and Jane hadn't realized that she'd even wanted in on a fairy tale.

She turned away and walked on. "Don't kid yourself, Janey," she muttered. No matter how much she imagined to the contrary, she was the nanny here. Nothing more.

18

Riley, in fine spirits, was up before everyone the next morning, ready for a trip to Barton Creek Mall in Austin. She hurried Levi through his waffles and up to his room, then chastised Jane for not moving faster.

"You know that Barton Creek will be there all day, right?" Jane asked laughingly after they dropped Levi off. She'd downloaded some Lady Gaga and Amy Winehouse for them to listen to on the way into Austin.

"Right, but we don't *have* all day. And I don't want to miss any time, because I never get to go there, not since Mom died," Riley said. "Dad's never around to take me."

"So you like to shop, huh?"

Riley shrugged. "I guess. It was fun to shop with Mom. She liked to buy stuff for me."

Jane wondered if she'd bought six of everything for Riley.

"Once she took me out of school and we went to the mall and bought a bunch of clothes, and then we went to Six Flags in San Antonio," Riley said.

"She took you out of school for that, huh?" Jane asked. She had parents like that, parents who thought nothing of taking their kids on little excursions instead of leaving them in school.

"It was *awesome*." Riley giggled. "Dad was so mad."

"How come?"

"Because he didn't know where we were. Mom forgot to tell him. And we didn't come back until the next day. But Dad . . . you know, he doesn't like stuff like that. He's not fun like Mom was. Mom was cool."

She *forgot* to tell him? Jane looked at Riley, who was twisting her hair around her finger. "I wish I had a sister," Riley said suddenly and looked at Jane.

"Me, too."

Riley stopped twisting her hair. "Do you have a brother?"

"I have two," Jane said. "Matt and Eric. They're younger than me and they both work at the restaurant."

"What restaurant?"

"The Garden," Jane said. "It's the restaurant my family owns and operates in Houston. President Bush eats there sometimes."

Riley's jaw dropped. "Your family owns a *restaurant*?"

"What?" Jane asked. "Is that weird?"

"I mean . . . no offense, but your spaghetti wasn't that good."

Jane couldn't help laughing. "Hey, I warned you—I am a terrible cook. But I'm adopted, remember? I don't have the cooking gene."

"So what's that like, being adopted?" Riley asked.

Jane shrugged. "It never bothered me. I have a great family and we're all very close. But sometimes . . . ." She looked at Riley again. "Sometimes, it feels a little like you're outside looking in through the window."

"That's totally weird," Riley said.

She asked Jane more questions about her life in Houston. Jane told her about Nicole, and about teaching second grade, which seemed to interest Riley. She laughed when Jane told her some stories about her kids, like Trystan Walsh, who had an obsession with Hannah

Montana, and Lily Criswell, who was double-jointed and would sit at her desk with her legs folded back.

Riley's good mood was infectious. But once they reached Barton Creek Mall, her good humor dissolved with her impossible standards. By lunchtime, Jane and Riley had been to half a dozen stores with no luck in their search for a new bathing suit. They were all too yucky for Miss Riley Price.

At one of their last prospects for suits, Jane found a cute bikini in blue plaid, which seemed to be all the rage this year. She showed it to Riley.

"No," Riley said.

Jane sighed. "Okay, look, Riley. The Graebers are coming over whether you want them to or not. Are you going to sit on the edge of the pool dressed in black jeans and a hoodie?"

"Maybe."

"Come on, give me a break. Look, I'll make you a deal. You find a swimsuit and promise me you'll wear it, and I'll take you to get a henna tattoo."

That brought Riley's head up. "Really?"

"Really."

"Dad would kill me."

Jane winked. "He's never here, remember?"

Riley suddenly grinned. "What's your tattoo?" she asked.

"A Celtic cross."

"Mom had a half moon with stars around it on her shoulder. She and Dad always say they love us to the moon and back, and she said that's why she got the moon and the stars, to remind her how much she loved me." Riley looked at the swimsuit. "That's what I want, too, the half moon and the stars. Okay?"

Jane held out the swimsuit. "You know the deal, so you tell me if it's okay."

"Deal," Riley said. She snatched the plaid swimsuit Jane was holding and disappeared into the fitting rooms.

An hour later, Jane carried a bathing suit that looked fantastic on Riley and another one she'd picked up for herself.

In the car, Riley leaned over to admire the tiny henna moon and star pattern on her ankle. "I can do that, you know," she said. "I can draw pretty good."

"I know. Levi told me. Do you draw now?"

Riley's expression changed almost imperceptibly, but Jane noticed it. "Not really," she said and bent over her lap, her hair sliding down to hide her face. "I wasn't as good as Mom. She was a *real* artist."

"I bet she started out by drawing."

"No, it wasn't like that. Mom was *really* good."

If you liked the sort of overdone paintings Jane had seen. "Do you have a sketchbook?" Jane asked. "I know a cool website where you can get a bunch of different ones."

Riley shifted her gaze out the window. "I don't want to talk about that now."

She didn't want to talk about sketchbooks? Why did that make her uncomfortable? Jane wanted to ask more, but her cell phone buzzed.

"Miss Aaron?" a woman said when Jane answered. "This is Charlotte, from the explorer day camp?"

"Is Levi okay?" Jane asked instantly, imagining Levi lying on the ground, his leg broken. Or worse.

"He's fine. But I must ask that you come get him. He threw a rock at a child."

"He *what*?"

"He can't stay the rest of the day. In fact, I need to talk to his father about his continued participation in our camp."

"Wait—did something happen to him? Did someone say something to him?"

"He and Jackson Harvey had words again, but I can assure you we are dealing with Jackson just as firmly. Is Levi's father somewhere I can reach him?"

"He's working. I'll have him call you," Jane said, vying for time. To do what, exactly, she had no idea.

"He needs to call me today, Miss Aaron."

"He will. I'll be there soon."

Jane clicked off and looked at Riley. "Levi," she said simply. "He's been acting out in camp again."

"Told you," Riley said. "He's always gets like this when Dad is gone a lot."

"Like what?"

"Wild," Riley said. "You haven't seen it yet. It starts small, then gets really bad."

Jane sped up.

Levi was unrepentant. He told Charlotte he didn't have to do anything she said, and Jane could scarcely make him apologize. In the car, he climbed into his booster, then kicked the back of Riley's seat. "Hey!" Riley snapped. "I'm on your side, doofus!"

"Levi, what is the matter with you?" Jane demanded as they drove away from the camp. "I thought you liked camp."

"I *hate* camp!" he shouted. "It's stupid!"

"*Stupid* is not a word we use," Jane said automatically, the habit ingrained from teaching. "What happened today?" she demanded of Levi. "Did someone say something to you? What happened that made you throw a rock at a kid? You could have hurt him!"

Levi kicked the back of Jane's seat. "I just don't *like* camp."

"Levi, this is very serious. I am going to have to call your dad just so you can go back tomorrow."

"No! Don't call him. I don't want to go back."

But Levi loved camp. Jane looked in the rearview mirror at him. "Come on, buddy, tell me what happened."

The poor kid looked down. When he looked up again,

he had tears in his eyes. "Jackson said my mommy is dead because she was crazy."

Jane gasped with fury. Her hands closed painfully around the steering wheel. "That is not true, Levi, not true at all. Your mother had a car accident, that's all. I don't want you to worry. I am going to call your dad, and he is going to take care of this," she said.

Levi didn't say anything to that; he just stared out the window, looking terribly forlorn. He needed his father. *Both* these kids needed their father.

Back at Summer's End, Jane tried to call Asher, but she was told he was in meetings and could not be reached. So she texted him and told him she had removed Levi from explorer camp, that Charlotte desired a call, and if someone didn't do something about Jackson Harvey, she would. She got one word back from Asher: *Done.*

Early that evening, Jane dispatched Levi to get a trowel from the garage for some work in the garden. She was watering the tomato plants when Asher appeared at the garden's edge. He was still in his suit, holding his briefcase. "I called Charlotte," he said simply. "I called Jackson's mom, too."

Jane dropped the hose. "And?"

"She claims that Levi is doing a good job of name-calling himself and that he's the one doing the bullying. It's a he-said, he-said thing."

"Levi is not a bully," Jane said adamantly.

Asher frowned a little. "No, he's not a bully. But Levi can act out with the best of them. I'll talk to him."

"Are you going to keep him in camp?"

"Are you kidding?" Asher asked, and for a moment, Jane's heart sank. "Of course I am. He'd be crushed," Asher finished, and Jane sighed with relief.

"*Daddy!*" Levi flew around the corner of the guesthouse with his trowel in hand.

Asher whirled around, squatted down, and caught Levi in his open arms. He picked his son up, hugged him closely. "Hey, buddy. I love you, man. I love you all the way to the moon, you know that? What happened today?" he asked, dipping down to get his briefcase before walking away from the garden.

Jane stood staring at the spot of ground where Asher had just stood. A moment later, she picked up the hose and the trowel Levi had dropped and continued working.

That night, after a frozen Kashi dinner and a lot of time staring at her thesis, Jane was unable to sleep for thinking of her many ponderous issues.

When at last she did sleep, it was fitful. She tossed and turned her way into an erotic dream. There was a man on top of her, his hands stroking her skin, his mouth hot and wet, moving down her body. "Who are you?" Jane whispered. He looked up and smiled. *Asher.*

Jane bolted upright, wide awake, her heart pounding, her body inflamed. *Jesus, Mary and Joseph.* What in the hell was going on with her?

19

Whatever Asher said to Levi must have worked, for the rest of the week passed without incident at camp and at home. Jane didn't see Asher at all; her only contact with him was a couple of text messages inquiring about preparations for the pool party.

"Linda Gail Graeber must be beside herself," Carla said midweek. "She'll be bragging about this to all her friends."

By Thursday, Jane still had not heard from Emma, and when she dropped Levi off at camp, she decided to swing by the offices.

"Hey, Jane!" Emma chirped when Jane walked in. "I was just about to call you."

"You were?" Jane asked, her heart suddenly racing. "Did you find out anything?"

"I sure did. I'm sorry it took so long, but Macy had to find time to come down and look through some files, and that took forever—but the good news is, we have it all on microfiche, and let me tell you, there is no rhyme or reason to the way things have been filed around here. I'm going to talk to Ed about it. It's ridiculous and a huge mess. Now here is the bad news . . ."

Jane's heart skipped.

"We had to order the microfiche from storage, and it's

not indexed, so you'll have to go through about thirty years' worth on an ancient old reader."

Okay, okay, that was not so bad; she could deal with that. "When?" she asked.

"We'll have it on Monday. When would you like to come in?"

"Tuesday afternoon," Jane said instantly.

"Great!" Emma said brightly. "I'll see you Tuesday."

Friday dawned a cloudless, beautiful-blue-sky day. Levi was up before nine, dressed in his board shorts. Riley woke up two hours later and began complaining the moment she did. She had a headache, she didn't want to go, she would get sunburned.

"You're coming to the party, and that's that," Jane said. "If you say another word, I am going to call your father."

Riley snorted. "What's he going to do, come racing home to spank me?" she said as she disappeared into her room. But an hour later, she came out again, wearing the new suit.

At the appointed time, Jane met Linda Gail and company on the driveway. The big gold minivan cranked to a stop, and a boy, who looked to be about ten, jumped out first. He was holding two big water blasters. "This is *so awesome,*" he cried, looking up at the house.

Linda Gail and Tracy followed. Linda Gail was wearing a black cover-up and flip-flops. "I see you've met my son, DJ. That's short for Davis Junior. DJ, if I so much as see that gun pointed at anything beyond the perimeter of the pool, you will be taken home. Do you understand?" Linda Gail commanded, but she failed to wait for DJ's reply before turning a bright smile to Jane. "Thanks so much for arranging everything, Jane," Linda Gail said. "These kids have been looking forward to this all week. I hope you don't mind, but I brought some pimiento cheese and Cheetos." She handed a big Tupperware container to Jane and hoisted a shopping bag onto her arm. "The house is beautiful," she continued as she grabbed giant beach bags, towels, and sunscreen, which she pushed into the hands of her children.

"Please come in," Jane offered. "Riley and Levi are already in the pool. I'll take you out."

As they walked through the house, Linda Gail said again, "The place is really spectacular."

"Isn't it?" Jane agreed. "I still can't believe I'm working here."

"Susanna Price did all the decorating herself. She had a very good eye," Linda Gail said with great authority as they stepped outside.

The patio area was something else to behold. It was covered in satillo tile and padded red teak furnishings. There were two mosaics embedded in the tile, pretty patterns that broke up the monotony of the red. Huge clay pots contained crepe myrtles with impatiens planted at their base.

Jorge had helped Jane set it up for the party, arranging two of the teak lounges under an enormous umbrella. Underneath a vine-covered pergola was a teak table with chairs arranged around it and a large cooler with snacks and drinks for the kids. Jane planned to grill hot dogs later.

Linda Gail and Jane settled under the umbrella. DJ and Levi were already in the pool, making pretzels out of neon-colored pool noodles. Riley and Tracy were standing a little apart on the edge of the pool, Tracy chattering away, Riley with her big sun hat and arms folded tightly across her body. There was a breeze coming up off the lake, rustling the tops of the cottonwoods, and the view of

Lake Del Lago was stunning. It was really a perfect day for a pool party.

Jane fetched iced tea for her and Linda Gail, and settled in to watch the kids.

"This is nice. *Really* nice," Linda Gail said. "I could definitely get used to living like this," she added with a laugh. "I like Riley's hair pulled back like that. You can see her face. She's going to be a beauty, just like her mother." She settled back in her seat. "You know Summer's End was the first mansion they built up here."

"I didn't know that," Jane said. Riley and Tracy were now climbing on the grotto, up to seats carved into the stone. Jane considered that a promising sign.

"Oh yes," Linda Gail said. "I heard Asher paid a small fortune at the time just to get out of Austin."

The way Linda Gail said that—*paid a small fortune to get out of Austin*—sounded strange to Jane.

"So tell me about yourself," Linda Gail said before Jane could ask what she meant. "Do you have family in Houston?"

"I do," Jane said with a smile. "A big one." She told Linda Gail about her family and the restaurant.

"That sounds like a fun group," Linda Gail said. "Really, Jane, you're so pretty and vibrant to be stuck in this town."

Jane laughed. "I don't know about that. This seems like a great place to be." She looked at the kids, the boys engaged in a noodle war now, and the girls talking. Riley had dropped her arms and was facing Tracy, who, by the look of things, was still doing all the talking. "It's your turn, Linda Gail. Where do you work?"

"I work for Wyatt Clark," Linda Gail said. "I bet you've heard of him."

Jane shook her head.

"You haven't heard of Wyatt Clark? How long have you been in Cedar Springs, now?" Linda Gail declared and sat up. "He just might be the most tragic man in all of America. That man has cried tears as big as your fist."

"Really? Why?"

"I'll tell you why. Listen to *this* story," Linda Gail said, and proceeded to tell Jane about the love triangle her boss had been caught up in. "I run his office," she said, finishing her rather long-winded tale of the poor man's convoluted love life. "He may have put the deal together for the Hill Country Resort and Spa, but I am the one making sure that thing stays on track. It opens next summer."

"I've seen it," Jane said. "That's a huge resort."

Linda Gail smiled proudly. Then frowned. "You never heard of Wyatt, huh? That honestly surprises me, because let me tell you something, there are no secrets in Cedar Springs."

Jane blinked with surprise.

"Oh, don't worry," Linda Gail said cheerfully. "If you think no one knows about the Price family, you're wrong. Everyone knows. They just won't say."

Stunned, Jane slowly put her tea down. "What about the Price family?"

"Didn't they tell you at Marty's?"

"Marty's?"

"The placement agency," Linda Gail said impatiently. "Marty Wilson owns it. They didn't tell you?"

"Tell me what?"

Linda Gail waved a pudgy hand at her. "I'm probably making a bigger deal of it than it is," she said. "It's nothing, really. Susanna Price had a couple of issues, that's all."

Now she had Jane's undivided attention. "What sort of issues?"

"I'll put it this way. The Prices are a good family, don't

get me wrong. And Lord knows Asher has worked hard to be a good husband and a good father. But it wasn't any great secret that the Prices weren't the most normal family in Cedar Springs."

"What are you saying?" Jane asked. "I don't know what you mean."

"Asher's mother plays bridge with my aunt, and, you know, I've heard things."

"Like?" Jane pressed.

"Not anything to be alarmed about," Linda Gail added hastily. "It's just that Susanna Price did things that people in Cedar Springs don't do. For instance, just before she died, she went down to Hilltop Photography Studio on the square. She told them that she was going to turn forty-five in the next couple of years and she wanted a portrait of herself before she got too old and didn't look so beautiful."

"That doesn't sound so strange," Jane said. Self-indulgent, maybe. Hardly crazy.

"Well, no . . . but what Susanna wanted was a *nude* portrait of herself. And they did it! Several different poses, all black and white. People in Cedar Springs don't do stuff like that, and I thought . . . I thought maybe you'd heard. Or seen it," Linda Gail added hopefully.

Jane shook her head. "Is that all?"

"Is that all?" Linda Gail laughed. "Some people think that's art, and I suppose Susanna was one of them. But some people think you do something like that, you're knitting with only one needle."

Jane didn't think a nude portrait made Susanna crazy, but she could see that some might believe the slightest deviation from the norm was suspect. "Mr. Price never said anything—"

"Oh no. He wouldn't. In spite of their problems, he

was entirely devoted to her. Honestly, if you want to know what I think, I think the only *real* issue was Riley."

"*Riley?*"

Linda Gail nodded and leaned over the arm of her chair. "I suppose you know she was suspended from school for fighting last year."

"No," Jane said, her thoughts racing now.

Linda Gail chuckled. "They didn't tell you much of anything, did they, sugar? Well, my Tracy has always liked Riley, even though Riley has made it hard. Apparently it's not hard to pick a fight with her. Tracy says that Riley and her dad don't get along. But you know how that is with these preteens, they—*hey!*" Linda Gail suddenly shouted.

Jane was startled, too, by the blast from DJ's water blaster. She looked up; Levi was bent over with laughter, and DJ was grinning like a little devil, filling up the blaster again.

"That little stinker!" Linda Gail said, and heaved herself out of the chair to give DJ a lecture.

Jane got up, too, to have a word with Levi. She maneuvered him away from Linda Gail, who was giving DJ a good dressing-down. But Levi was so intent on the tongue-lashing DJ was receiving that Jane was having trouble steering him. She heard Riley say, "Dad, what are you doing here?" and thought she'd misheard.

Jane turned around and was surprised to see Asher standing on the patio, his gaze on her.

On all of her.

20

*J*ane Aaron was hot; there was no pretending otherwise.

Asher had not fully appreciated how hot she was the night he'd seen her floating alone in the dark. He'd been aware of her lush shape, but standing here now, in the light of day . . . *hell*. She was hot.

He shoved his hands in his pockets, abashedly glad he'd had Tara rearrange his schedule so that he could come home and join the party. He'd expected to find them all playing in the pool, maybe even lounging on towels around the edge. He had not expected that Jane would have ditched the functional bathing suit for a neon green bikini and one of those short little skirts. Or that she would look so amazing.

She seemed startled that he was there. He smiled; his gaze flicked down to the tip of that tattoo on her abdomen that taunted him, then up again. "How are things?" he asked, concentrating on keeping his eyes on hers.

"Great!" Jane said. Her hair was tied in that loopy knot at her nape, but she smoothed back the curls that had escaped it. "Is everything okay?"

Apparently he needed an emergency to be home. "Perfect." He meant her, of course, and the force of that secret admission rocked him back on his heels.

"You're home so early," she added, as if he'd misjudged the time and mistakenly left the office too soon.

"It is shocking, I know," he said with a wry smile. "But it seemed like a good day for a pool party."

"Asher! What a great surprise!" Linda Gail called to him. Asher looked over Jane's shoulder to see Linda Gail in her big straw hat waving her fingers at him. "We weren't expecting you!"

"Slow day," he called back, and to Jane he said, "I'm going to change and join you, if that's okay."

"Sure, of course." She pushed those pesky strands of hair back again, but they floated back over her brow.

"*Daddy*!" Levi shouted. "Daddy, watch me!"

Asher forced his gaze away to Levi and watched him jump off into the deep end, then swim to the edge and climb out.

"Cool!"

"That's DJ!" Levi shouted, pointing at Linda Gail's boy. "He brought his water blasters!" Levi jumped back into the pool.

Asher noticed Riley sitting up on the grotto in one of the built-in seats. He had to admit, she looked great in her new swimsuit, although he wasn't crazy about the henna tattoo. She was sitting with Tracy, their heads bent together, talking, Tracy's hands moving as she talked. "Hello, Riley!" he called to her.

Riley lifted her hand and waved, then quickly turned back to Tracy.

"We are going to put some snacks out," Jane said, drawing his attention back to her. She was looking at him curiously and, he thought, a little suspiciously, as if she didn't believe he really had come home to join the pool party.

"Great. I'll be back." He was smiling as he retreated to change. This was going to be a good day.

Asher took a detour by the garage on his return, remembering that he'd stored an old blaster there. He used a garden hose to fill it, then entered the party blasting, getting Riley and Tracy up on the grotto. Just as he knew they would, the two girls shrieked and scrambled down from the grotto, but young DJ, a veteran at having older siblings, shouted at Levi to get his gun. The boys were ready for Asher when he cannonballed into the water. When he came up for air, Levi and DJ dog-piled him in the shallow end, trying to drag him under.

He thrashed around with the boys, feeling the stress of the week float away from him. As Jane and Linda Gail grilled hot dogs, Asher gathered the boys and plotted an attack on the girls. It didn't go precisely as planned, because Riley figured it out and ran and DJ, in his eagerness to blast her, missed and hit Jane.

Jane whirled around. "Who did that?"

Asher and the boys froze.

"DJ did it!" Tracy shouted, pointing at her brother.

"Is that so?" Jane asked, handing the barbeque fork to Linda Gail. "Do you mind, Linda Gail?" she asked sweetly. "DJ and I are going to have a little talk."

"Good. He needs one," Linda Gail said.

Jane lunged for the blaster Levi had left on the edge of the pool and deftly filled it as DJ frantically swam to the other side of the pool with his. She fired at DJ, hitting him squarely.

"Game on!" Asher called to the boys.

"That would imply you *have* game," Jane said and blasted him, which earned a burst of laughter from Riley. Asher responded by grabbing his daughter and dragging her into the pool, laughing at her sputtering protests and her attempt to shove his head underwater.

The afternoon was a blast, one of the best Asher had

had in a long time. He'd always been a competitive guy, and he discovered Jane was competitive, too. As the girls battled the boys, she was not afraid to take him on while directing Tracy and Riley in coordinated attacks on DJ and Levi. Linda Gail sat in her chaise and called out suggestions to both sides.

The game of pool war gave way to Marco Polo. Jane delighted in taunting Asher when he was Marco, drawing very near and whispering, then swimming just out of his reach. Nevertheless, Asher refused to be bested by her. When he at last sensed her behind him, he swirled around, launching himself at the same moment he shouted, *"Marco!"* He heard her little cry just as he landed her, pinning her up against the side of the pool with both arms.

He opened his eyes. She was trapped within the circle of his arms, her breasts breaking the surface of the water just inches from him. Her amber eyes were sparkling beneath the V of her devilish frown, her hair dark and wet on her shoulders. His gaze fell to her mouth.

"Polo," Jane said, and splashed him in the face before dipping beneath his arm and swimming away, much to the delight of the kids.

Much to Asher's private delight.

By the time they had played a couple of rounds of Marco Polo, they had all worked up a ravenous appetite. Jane lined the kids up like a pro, handing out plates, tossing hot dogs onto them, sitting them down at the table. Linda Gail handed Asher a plate full of food and sat with him at one end of the table, while Jane sat at the other end with Levi and DJ.

"You should find someone, Asher," Linda Gail opined as she munched on some Cheetos. "The kids need someone, and so do you."

Who was he going to find? It wasn't as if women were lining up at his door. "We're doing okay," he assured her.

"Sure you are. But a man can't live on kids alone," she said with a wink. "I've got a friend—"

"Oh, no," he said, throwing up a hand. "Thanks, Linda Gail, but I'm good."

"Okay, fine, I won't set you up with one of the loveliest women I ever did know, and she's pretty, too. But you call me, Asher. You call me when you're ready to stop being lonely up here at Summer's End."

Linda Gail had no idea how lonely it was at Summer's End, but Asher merely smiled and ate his hot dog.

Linda Gail and her kids left an hour or so later—reluctantly—and Asher followed them out to the drive. Linda Gail lingered another ten minutes chatting about Cedar Springs before finally getting in the minivan and starting it up to the gate.

By the time Asher returned to the pool to help clean up, his kids had disappeared inside. Jane was still there, picking up empty juice boxes and soda cans.

Asher picked up the cooler. "Great party," he said to her. "Thanks for pulling it together."

"Honestly, I didn't do much. Carla and Jorge did most of the work."

"Ah. Nevertheless . . . thanks."

She smiled. "You are welcome." She shifted the bag of trash she held.

Asher supposed it was heavy. Still, he just stood there, holding the cooler.

Jane smiled and shaded her eyes with her hand, looking toward the breezeway and a large trash can. "I'll finish up."

"Have dinner with us," Asher said.

Jane turned her head and looked at him with surprise.

She couldn't have been as surprised as he was—he suddenly felt like a bumbling sixteen-year-old. "I mean . . . Carla's not here, and I am going to make something, and after all the work you did today—why not have dinner with us? One less meal you have to make for yourself." He tried to say it easily, like it was no big deal, like they were friends. But they weren't friends, and Jane's expression confirmed it. "Unless you have to work on your thesis," he added quickly.

Jane shifted.

"Whatever you want," he said and took a step toward the house, alarmed by his complete lack of finesse.

"You're cooking, right?" she asked. "Because I really am not much of a cook."

Asher paused. "Yes. I'm cooking."

Jane suddenly smiled. "Thanks. I'd like that. I'm about to overdose on frozen dinners as it is. What time?"

He hadn't thought that far ahead. He hadn't thought at all. "Ah . . . whenever you're ready."

"Cool. Thank you." She padded across the decking in her bare feet to the trash.

Asher tore his eyes away from Jane's derriere, walked into the kitchen, and deposited the cooler. He looked blankly at Riley, who was doing something on her phone, and told her he was going to shower before he started dinner. He continued upstairs, his mind's eye full of Jane in that sexy swimsuit, blushing when she realized he was looking at her in a not disinterested manner.

And then he'd blurted that invitation to dinner like some lovesick kid. Asher cringed; he was really starting to question himself. He was *thinking* about Jane, and thinking a lot. He knew men who were dogs, who would take advantage of their nannies if the opportunity presented itself. But he'd never been one of those guys. Asher was not a playboy, and in spite of his troubled marriage, he'd been painfully faithful.

He couldn't help but remember the first time he'd met Susanna. Lord, but he'd thought she was the most beautiful woman he'd ever seen—she'd had beauty queen good looks, with long, sleek black hair and sparkling blue eyes. When she'd agreed to go out with him, Asher had thought he was the luckiest guy on the planet.

They'd begun to date, and everything had seemed perfect to Asher. Susanna had been so vibrant, an exciting lover, and she'd seemed to adore him. They'd played like young couples play—dinner out with friends, weekend trips to South Padre. He'd thought it was cool that Susanna was an artist and had studied at some art school in New York. Before they'd married, she'd spent hours in a little studio in the back of her parents' house, working on her art. She'd never really had a job, but Asher hadn't been surprised—she'd come from money. She'd been a little spoiled, but that had been part of her charm.

Every once in a while, Susanna would get a little down. She'd said she'd suffered from anorexia when she'd been a teenager. That had boggled Asher's mind—Susanna was gorgeous and educated, and he hadn't understood how she could possibly have had self-esteem issues. God, what a joke. *Here, Susanna, eat something,* they'd all said when she'd get down, as if food was the answer. Her mother, Helen, had seemed especially hell-bent on preserving some image of Susanna as a happy, confident person. Asher had chalked that up to her being overly protective, but for him, Susanna's occasional blues had been a minor blight on an otherwise beautiful relationship. She'd been everything to him.

They'd married a year later in a big wedding at the Four Seasons in Austin. They'd set up house in Clarksville. Susanna had painted while Asher had worked. She would complain from time to time that the ideas weren't coming, but for the most part, she'd seemed happy.

About six months after they'd married, Asher had come home from work one day and discovered Susanna had been shopping. She'd found a shoe sale, she'd said, and she'd bought two dozen pairs. Asher had been shocked by that. He'd known women liked their shoes, but two dozen pairs seemed extreme to him. He'd asked her to take some back. That request made Susanna livid. Asher had never seen her like that—she'd screamed at him, accused him of wanting to keep all the money for himself, of keeping her prisoner in that house. She'd locked herself in the bathroom with a bottle of vodka and sobbed.

Even now, Asher shook his head as he ran the water for his shower. He'd been a young man then, about as equipped to handle that scene as he'd been to fly a space shuttle. So he'd called Helen, who'd appeared promptly the next morning and whisked Susanna to a doctor. "I'll handle it," she'd said firmly, and honestly, Asher had thought Susanna was acting like a spoiled child. But later that afternoon, when Helen and Susanna returned from the doctor, Helen said, "The doctor can't be sure without some tests and therapy, but he thinks it might be depression."

Asher had nodded. "She's been depressed before."

"No, Ash. I mean clinical depression," Helen had said. "The doctor recommends therapy and more evaluation."

"Of course," Asher had said instantly. "Whatever she needs."

Anything for Susanna. His life, his happiness, his future, all for Susanna. And with therapy, Susanna had recovered and improved greatly, and Asher had thought everything was okay. But it wasn't okay; it was the lull before the proverbial storm. Asher had often wondered if signs of impending doom had been there all along and he'd been so blinded by lust and young love that he'd ignored them.

He hadn't known then—he couldn't have known then—he wouldn't know until much later that Susanna had bipolar disorder.

Yet in spite of it all, he'd never wanted anyone but Susanna. Not even when their lovemaking had gone from the frenzied passion of true desire to the frenzied desperation of holding the tatters of their marriage together. Even when he'd had to work so hard to hold on for his kids' sake, to find that place they could exist, he'd only wanted Susanna.

And when the wanting had stopped, he'd still been loyal, still faithful, because he had married her.

He'd never been the type of guy who couldn't get the nanny off his mind. He supposed that now it was due in part to his need for sex—he hadn't been with anyone but Susanna since he'd married her. Sex only added to his ongoing sense of frustration.

Asher stripped down and showered quickly. He toweled off, wrapped the towel low on his hips, and lathered his face for a shave. He wiped the steam off the mirror, then picked up his razor. He hesitated, studying himself in the mirror a moment. What would a woman like Jane think about him? Was he attractive to her? He was older than she, and while he was fortunate to have a full head of hair, there were a couple of gray strands in it now, and a hint of gray in his whiskers.

He glanced down at his abdomen. It wasn't exactly washboard anymore, but he wasn't fat, thanks to the running he did. Asher's gaze drifted up, to his shoulders. They were fairly broad—he'd played football in high school—and he had a scar just above his right pec, where he'd run into a barbed-wire fence as a kid.

What would she think of him?

Jane could probably have any guy she wanted, he thought as he began to shave. But then again, she was different from the other women he knew. She was pretty in an exotic way, but she wasn't highly buffed with hair and skin treatments. Susanna had been a high-maintenance kind of woman. Jane seemed . . . real. What you see is what you get. She had a great smile, the best smile he'd ever seen. Not only that, she looked at him like *he* was real and not all-powerful, like so many young women at the firm with stars in their eyes.

Asher liked the way Jane was with the kids, he liked that tease of a tattoo, and he liked her wild hair and honey amber eyes. . . .

"Get a grip," he muttered to himself and took an angry swipe, nicking his neck. "Great."

He was stupid to even think this way. It was inappropriate as hell, and besides, looking at himself now, he believed himself too vanilla and too old for someone like Jane Aaron.

He sighed, washed his face, pulled the towel from his waist, and walked into the adjoining dressing room to dress.

When he returned to the kitchen wearing a Willie Nelson concert T-shirt and a pair of old khaki shorts with a couple of holes and frayed at the hems—his cooking pants, Riley liked to call them—he found both kids and Jane already there. Levi was, as usual, the first to see him, and in the way of a five-year-old, he dispensed with any greeting. "Daddy, can I have the water gun you brought? It was so cool!"

"It's yours," Asher said as Jane turned around from the refrigerator. She was wearing a sundress, a slinky cotton thing that hit her about midthigh. Her skin was glowing from a day in the sun; she looked like a poster child for natural beauty.

"Hi," he said.

"Hi," Jane said and smiled brightly. "You got a little sun today."

Asher self-consciously put a hand to his forehead. "Hello, Riley. Did you have a good time today?"

Riley shrugged as she put a stack of plastic cups in the cupboard. "Like it's possible to have fun at a swim party over the age of five."

"Riley!" Jane said laughingly. "You and Tracy have been texting each other since she left. You said you had a great time."

"I did not say *great*," Riley said. "That would be so lame. I said *okay*." But she was smiling.

There was something different about the kitchen, Asher thought. It seemed brighter somehow. Lights? No, the usual lights were on. Maybe it was the fact that his kids were actually helping Jane. Riley and Levi, who heretofore could hardly have been convinced to pick up their dirty socks, were helping Jane clean up from their party. Riley was putting away the paper goods, and Levi was wiping out the inside of the cooler.

"So . . . what's for supper?" Jane asked. She was standing, her hands on her hips, with an irreverent smile, as if she didn't believe he could cook.

For one fleeting moment, Asher imagined that cotton dress sliding down her body and pooling silently at her feet. "Steak," he said.

"*Yes!*" Riley cried with a fist pump.

"And roasted potatoes," Asher added.

"Wow. I'm impressed. Can I make a salad?" Jane asked.

"That depends," Asher said. "Will we die?"

Her smile deepened. "I really can't say for certain."

"Let's risk it," he said with a wink. "Thanks."

He gathered up all he'd need to fire up the grill and enlisted Levi as his helper. Riley stayed in the kitchen with Jane, chattering away like she used to do with Susanna. Jane had finished making the salad when Asher and Levi came in again. She'd also put the steaks on a tray, ready to be seasoned and grilled.

"You can't cook, but you do good prep," Asher remarked.

Jane grinned. "It's insurance. I figure this way, I get out of cleanup. What else can I do to help?"

"You could help with the potatoes," he said as he began to season the steaks. "I have a special herb packet I put on them. If you don't mind, I can tell you what herbs to mix together for that."

He waited for Jane to get a bowl and rattled off some of the herbs he used, laughing out loud when she actually tried to measure.

"What?" she demanded, spilling sage on the counter.

"Just a pinch, Jane," he said as Riley giggled.

"I hate that 'just a pinch,'" Jane complained. "What exactly is a pinch?"

"A *pinch*."

"Yes, but is that an eighth of a teaspoon? A quarter?"

"I think it's like a spoonful," Riley offered.

"I know how to pinch!" Levi said.

"Not that kind of pinch, buddy," Asher explained. "We're talking about herbs."

"What's herbs?" Levi asked.

Jane explained it to him. "It's like dried grass," she said, to which Levi said, "We have to eat grass?" Riley laughed.

Asher felt happy. Truly happy. This was what he'd always pictured, what he'd always wanted. A family who laughed together. Who knew how to be happy together.

When the meal was ready, Asher opened a bottle of wine and the four of them sat down in the dining room. Riley and Levi filled the room with their bright chatter about the day and the swim party. It was good to see them happy; they'd had more than their fair share of heartache, and Riley especially. The girl could build a staircase to heaven with all the heartaches she'd suffered.

Tonight, his kids were at their best. He was proud of them. Riley spoke with great animation and detail about what Tracy said a girl named Lindy had said, and what Riley had said to that, and so on. It was the effortless, thoughtless chatter of a pubescent girl, a surprising and welcome change from the gloom Riley had cast over a table of three in the last year.

"Oh, Jane, I downloaded that new song by Lady Gaga," Riley announced. "She's mad cool."

"Who?" Asher asked.

Riley and Jane exchanged a look. "She's a singer," Jane said.

Asher had never heard of her. He never saw TV anymore.

"Haven't you heard her on the radio, Dad?" Riley asked.

"I don't think so," he said, and Riley and Jane laughed again, sharing some private joke. Jane was pretty when she laughed, he thought. Her eyes sparkled. And he . . . he felt even more vanilla. *Lady Gaga.* He made a mental note to look her up.

Riley's speech was peppered with little shout-outs from Levi, who claimed he'd seen a turtle, and when that did not elicit a reaction from the table, he upped it to a snake. As Asher helped himself to another helping of salad, Levi was talking about the school of sharks that he and DJ had seen in the lake.

"There are no sharks in the lake," Asher said.

"Remember, we talked about that, Levi," Jane added. "Sharks live in the ocean. Way, way out in the ocean."

"How do you know?" Levi asked. "Have you seen them?"

"I have. My dad used to take us deep-sea fishing when I was a kid and I saw them once."

"Where was that?" Asher asked curiously.

"Dad, seriously, how can you hire a nanny and not know these things?" Riley asked. "She's from *Houston*. She's a *teacher*."

"I knew that, smartypants," he said, but Riley was right. He really knew very little about Jane, other than that she was pretty, she couldn't cook, she was a runner, she thought Italians sparkled, and he had a growing and indefensible desire to sleep with her. He wasn't just thinking it, he was imagining it in full-scale Technicolor. *Sex in a bed, on the floor, in the shower.*

"Her family owns a restaurant."

Asher almost sputtered his wine. "Now that, I haven't heard," he said, looking at Jane. "A restaurant? And you don't know what a pinch is?"

She laughed, the sound of it velvet. "I know—pathetic, right?"

"What sort of restaurant?"

"Continental," she said, fingering the stem of her wineglass. "Or, as we like to say, whatever Mom and Uncle Barry feel like today." She told him about The Garden, and the family history with it, about the accolades it had received through the years. She said the Bushes were regulars there, and that her family gathered for an early supper each night in one of the private rooms. She made them all laugh with her descriptions of them. "Aunt Mona wears these big black button earrings. Uncle Barry says it makes her look like a tagged cow."

On the roof, in the car, on a boat. "Do you have any siblings?" Asher asked.

"Two brothers," Riley said. "She feels my pain."

Jane laughed and tousled Levi's hair.

"So how come you don't cook?" Asher asked, leaning back in his chair. "Didn't anyone teach you?"

"Oh, they tried, believe me, they *tried*," she said laughingly, her smile illuminating. "It's a huge joke now. But I don't have the cooking gene. I don't know why that is; I can't taste things like they can." She shrugged.

"Maybe because you're adopted," Riley suggested.

"Adopted," Asher repeated and looked at Jane. Another surprise.

"Yep. Adopted." She smiled.

Asher wanted to know more, but the sound of a cell phone interrupted them. "Oh, that's mine," Jane said. "Will you excuse me?" She hopped up from the table and hurried to her bag, fished inside it for her cell phone, then walked into the kitchen, her back to them as she answered.

"I bet it's her granola boyfriend," Riley said.

The boyfriend. Asher had conveniently forgotten about him. He looked at his plate and worked very hard to be disinterested. A boyfriend definitely put a damper on his game of imagining sex with Jane—he'd just imagined it in the pool. The boyfriend probably knew how Lady Gaga was. He was probably a very un-vanilla kind of guy.

Suddenly wanting up from the table, Asher pushed his plate away. "Anyone up for a game of Chutes and Ladders?"

21

*A*re you going to stay, Jane?" Riley demanded when Jane stepped back to the table after asking Nicole if they could catch up later.

"Stay?"

"To play Chutes and Ladders! Dad and Levi are going to be a team if you will be my partner. Will you stay?"

Jane hesitated. Today, in the pool when they'd been playing Marco Polo, Asher's bare, muscular chest and surfer shorts riding just below a trim waist had had her believing she'd need to drive off a cliff to keep from launching herself at him. She didn't think hanging out with him was the best idea. Actually, it was a very bad idea, but she was like a kid in a candy store lately—she couldn't help herself. Jane had thoroughly enjoyed this day. The kids were in great spirits and she'd actually seen an endearing side of Asher, a softness and attention to his kids that surprised her.

"Please?" Riley begged.

"Don't press her, honey," Asher said and stood up, picking up his plate as he did. "She probably has plans."

"You don't, do you?" Riley asked.

"Actually . . . no," Jane said, mentally kicking herself for being weak.

"That means you'll play, right?"

Jane looked at the three of them looking at her. "Okay," she said, to which Riley and Levi both shouted *yay*. "But on one condition, Ri. We have to win."

"We'll *crush* them," Riley said, pumping her fist.

"Are you sure?" Asher asked Jane. "I don't want to keep you."

"I think you're afraid of a Riley-Jane team."

"Ha!" Riley cried.

Asher chuckled. "Maybe a little. All right, you two," he said to the kids. "Let's get the kitchen cleaned before you take down the game."

"I'll get it!" Riley shouted and was quickly out the door, Levi on her heels.

"Hey! Carry stuff to the kitchen!" Asher called after them, but they were already racing upstairs. He glanced sheepishly at Jane. "My kids are spoiled," he sighed.

Jane laughed, picked up their plates, and carried them into the kitchen after Asher.

He opened the dishwasher and groaned. "It's full. I'll have to wash."

"I'll help."

"No," he said sternly. "You are off duty and we've imposed enough as it is."

"Let me dry," Jane urged him. She opened a drawer and withdrew a dish towel. "I can't stand here and watch you like some guest. That would be weird. And besides, I have the towel," she said, holding it out for him to see.

Asher looked at the towel. "Never argue with a woman and her dish towel," he conceded. "Thank you. And thanks for today," he added as he filled the sink with warm, sudsy water. "I think the Price family needed that."

"A pool party?"

Asher smiled, his green eyes soft. "Time to be a family

without any demands on us. It was fun." He leaned around her and picked up a plate from the island.

Jane felt that little flutter in her belly again. She wished he wouldn't move so close to her. She hoped he'd do it again.

"It's cool you can stay," he said. "I thought you might have some work to do tonight," he said.

Work that kept piling up and up and up. Jane hadn't written a word on her thesis. Her excuse was that she felt stymied waiting for Emma to get back to her. "I do," she admitted, taking the plate he'd washed. "But I felt honor bound to stay and make sure you don't cheat."

Asher made a sound of surprise. "Excuse me?"

"Come on, Asher," she said slyly. "You cheated at Marco Polo. You opened your eyes."

"I did not," he protested with a guilty grin.

"Then how do you explain that miraculous grab of DJ at the end?"

"Hey! That was a highly skilled tactical maneuver, I'll have you know. Did you think you were playing with a novice?"

"Do you mean I was playing with a *professional* Marco Poloist?"

He dropped his head back with a laugh. "Sweetheart, I wrote the manual on Marco Polo," he said roguishly, and a tiny thrill skated down Jane's spine.

Asher handed her another plate. "Here's how you do it. First, you miss a lot. It makes the enemy complacent. Then, when you have them thinking you couldn't find them in the bathtub, you make your move." He reached around her again, his body brushing across hers, sending another, stronger shiver sizzling through her. He paused, still reaching, and looked directly into her eyes. "And then you pin them down. No mercy."

He was standing so close that she could see the flecks of brown and gray in his eyes. It rattled her, sparked a shock of desire through her. She wanted to say something witty, something charming, but words failed her, and before she could summon her thoughts, Asher faded away from her.

He tossed a serving spoon into the sink. "*That* is how you play Marco Polo."

Jane released the breath she was holding. "Or . . . you peek."

Asher suddenly smiled at her, the flash of it startlingly white and warm. "Busted," he cheerfully agreed. "But I did it for you."

"For *me*?"

"Yes, wasn't it obvious? There was no way DJ was going to let that game end without some serious intervention."

Jane laughed. "Then I owe you a debt of thanks."

"That's more like it," he said with a wink. He washed the spoon and handed it to her, then slipped behind her again to grab a bowl, leaning in so close—or maybe it was she who leaned in so close—that she caught the scent of his cologne. It was subtle, but enticingly masculine.

Come on, Jane, she thought to herself. As if her life wasn't muddy enough right now. But she couldn't resist his charming smile or the sparkle of warmth in his eye. Lord, how things had changed! She had warmed to Asher Price, was even fantasizing about him. It was so interesting to see how different he was when he wasn't working. He was relaxed and charming and sexy. *Jesus,* the man was sexy.

"So have you worked things out with your boyfriend?" Asher asked.

"Huh?" Jane mentally shook her head, trying to clear it.

"Boyfriend," he said with a sultry smile. "The guy who wants to marry you."

"Oh. Him." Yes, Jonathan—this was good, this would keep her feet firmly planted on the ground, and she forced herself to summon an image of Jonathan. "Not yet."

"Have you decided?"

Decided? She'd hardly thought of Jonathan the last couple of days, a fact that stirred up a healthy dose of guilt at the moment. "No," she said softly.

He looked at her a moment, then turned back to the dishes. "Sorry. I didn't mean to pry."

"You're not prying." She didn't know how to tell him all the things that went round in her head when she thought of Jonathan and marriage. "I'm not any closer to a decision than I was a few days ago. The thing is . . ." She didn't even know where to begin.

When Jane didn't continue, Asher turned to her. "The thing is?"

Jane smiled self-consciously. "The thing is, I am in the process of looking for my birth mother, and I need to do that before I make any decisions about the rest of my life. It's just this . . . this thing I need to do," she said with a tiny shrug.

"Oh. I didn't know."

"Yes, well . . . the truth is, that is the reason I chose Cedar Springs to finish my thesis. I was born here. This is where I've started looking."

"Really?" he said. "That must be pretty intense for you."

"It is," she said, nodding. "I feel like a pioneer. I have no idea what I am going to find, you know? It could be good, it could be bad. I'm throwing myself out there, let the chips fall where they may."

"That's admirable," Asher said as he handed her a glass. "I think that would take a lot of guts."

No one had ever said that to her. No one at home had

given her credit for taking the steps or acknowledged that it *did* take a lot of guts. More courage than Jane sometimes believed she had in her.

"So . . . if you don't mind me asking, how is the search going?"

"Not so well." She told him about her trip to the hospital, and then to the *Cedar Springs Standard*. She told him that on Tuesday she would get to review the microfiche for the first time. "Sometimes I feel like I am standing on this bridge between Houston and whatever is out there," she said, gesturing vaguely to out there.

"I'd bet it gets lonely on that bridge," Asher said.

A different kind of shiver ran through Jane when he said that. He said it as if he knew, as if she'd confessed how alone she felt at times. How could he possibly know that? She looked up from drying a fork.

Asher smiled a little and handed her a plate. "I'm just guessing." He plunged his hands into the sink. "But the good news is, you have a boyfriend waiting at the foot of the bridge, right?"

"Right," Jane said absently. "I'm going to see him next weekend."

"Ah, well . . . great," he said. "I look forward to meeting him. We'll have drinks."

"No," Jane said quickly. The thought of the two men meeting disturbed her greatly for some reason. "I mean I'm going home." She put the plate down. "He's a musician, and he's got an important gig. He wants me there to hear it."

"A musician. Cool," Asher said, nodding. "Classical? Jazz?"

"Rock. His band is called Orange Savage." Jane turned away from Asher's curious green eyes. Yes, this was better. If she just didn't look at him—

"I'm an alternative rock guy myself," he said casually.

Jane picked up the bowl he'd just washed. Asher leaned across the sink to fetch a glass, bracing himself with one arm against the edge. An image popped into Jane's head of Asher bracing himself like that over her on the kitchen island, his golden hair hanging over his brow as he moved inside her. . . .

Good God, stop it, she silently chastised herself. She looked at the bowl. She'd all but polished the glaze from it. "Where does this go?"

"Up there." He nodded to a pair of tall cabinets.

Jane opened the cabinet. There was a spot on the top shelf, naturally. She went up on her tiptoes and reached up to put the bowl away. Her sundress skimmed up the backs of her thighs and pulled tight across her back and bottom. Asher was suddenly behind her. "Let me help." His voice was low; he put his hand to her back, reached up beside her, took the bowl from her, and slipped it into its spot on the top shelf. The thrill of his touch flooded Jane, warming her skin, prickling at her nape.

She sank down to her feet beside him and glanced up. It didn't help at all that she thought she was seeing the edge of want in his eyes, too.

His gaze dipped to her mouth, then slid lower, to her chest. "Just one or two more," he said quietly. His hand slid lightly across her hip as he dropped it and moved back to the sink.

He washed one more plate and the last of the silver while Jane wiped down the countertops. "I think that does it," he said a moment later. He drained the sink, wiped his hands, and shoved them into his pockets, then smiled at Jane. "Okay, Miss Aaron," he said. "Let's see if you're as tough at Chutes and Ladders as you are at Marco Polo."

"Tougher," she said. "Didn't I tell you? I'm the southwest regional champion of Chutes and Ladders."

"Wow," he said, pretending to be impressed as he gestured for her to precede him. "A tournament girl. I'll have to show you my trophy case."

"You, too?" she asked, feigning surprise.

"Monopoly," he said with a wink. They both laughed.

Three hours later, after several rounds of Chutes and Ladders and Chinese checkers, Jane tapped her wristwatch and looked at Asher meaningfully. "All right," he said reluctantly. He'd had a wonderful time with Jane and the kids, and while he was still imagining Jane naked, the need to see her naked had subsided somewhat. Asher could thank Chutes and Ladders for returning him to the world of reason.

He said good night to Jane, put Levi to bed, told Riley not to stay up too late, and retreated to the huge cavern of a master suite, where he'd spent some of his darkest hours. He never entered this room without remembering.

The suite had an adjoining study and a sleeping porch between the bedroom and the outside balcony. Susanna had decorated the suite so many times that Asher had lost track. At the time she'd died, the room had been painted in blues and greens and the bed and window coverings had had an aqua feel to them, which Asher supposed was apropos of his life with Susanna—in the last two years of her life, he'd felt as if he'd been constantly struggling to reach the surface of a marriage in which he'd been drowning.

He still hadn't completely come to terms with her death. There was part of him that believed that if she'd kept taking her medicine, she would still be here and his kids would still have a mother. There was another part of him that wondered whether she hadn't been destined for that fiery death all along, and there was nothing he could have done to change the course of her fate.

He looked around him now; he'd painted the walls and removed most of her art, replacing it with a flat-panel TV and Riley's and Levi's baby portraits. He'd left only one of Susanna's paintings that was really quite good; it was the vista outside their bedroom windows, a view of the lake and the cedars. In it, one could see the rooftop of the studio he'd built for Susanna and Riley through the trees. The other paintings she'd made for this room were nonsensical color messes. She'd argued that they were contemporary art. Asher called them nightmares. He'd stored them all in the attic in case Riley or Levi wanted them someday.

He'd thrown one portrait in the trash after her death. Susanna had had it done just after her forty-third birthday, a few short months before she died. In it, she was completely nude, lying on a fur rug, her expression full of sexual desire. Asher had never really been able to shake the thought that maybe the portrait had been intended for someone.

He was certain it had not been intended for him.

This place was his now, his retreat, the one place he could escape Susanna in this damn house. His clothes were draped over a chair. His basketball sat on the floor next to the wardrobe. The bed coverings were muted and suitable for a man.

Asher stepped out onto the balcony and looked up at the night sky.

A movement caught his eye and he looked down. He could see Jane below in the light of one of the solar lamps, watering Levi's tomatoes. It was strange, watching her. With Susanna, it had been about what they could do for her. With Jane, it was . . . well, it was something he needed to get over, that was certain.

He thought of the vulnerability he'd seen in her tonight

when she'd talked about searching for her birth mother. It had sparked something deep in him, a need to protect, to help, to do for her. And then he'd actually touched her, had put his hand on the small curve of her back, had felt the heat of her body through her thin cotton dress, and it had felt good.

Ridiculous. He was forty years old, well past the point of adolescent cravings and meaningless flirtations. There were boundaries to respect here. He was her employer. She was his nanny. There was a man who wanted to marry her, and Asher thought too much of her to have some summer fling.

But God, he wanted her.

For that reason, he was glad his parents were flying in later this week for Riley's birthday. It wouldn't hurt to have something to remove the distraction of Jane from his thoughts.

22

*A*pparently, Jane liked flirting with disaster. In spite of the long, hot bath she'd taken last night in which she'd engaged in some strong self-counseling, her head was not any clearer this morning. She kept thinking about Asher's hand on the small of her back, the way his smile crinkled the corner of his eyes. And then she ran a couple of extra miles Saturday morning. She told herself it was making up for lost time after she'd sprained her ankle. But the real reason was that she hoped Asher would appear on the trail.

He did not appear on the trail Saturday. Or Sunday.

Jane didn't see any of the Prices, actually, and by Sunday evening, she'd convinced herself that she'd really made a huge thing out of nothing. He was growing more comfortable with her, that was all, and with comfort came a sense of familiarity. She was not living out her own private version of *Pretty Woman*. Asher was not going to sweep her off her feet into some meaningful relationship. Even if he tried, she still had all the same issues that prevented her from committing to Jonathan. Why would she jump from the frying pan into the fire?

God, what about Jonathan, good, loyal Jonathan? He was the man Jane had believed herself in love with the last two years, and suddenly she had trouble even thinking about him. It was the height of self-destruction, and she owed Jonathan so much more than this.

Jane didn't know herself anymore. It was her face staring back at her in the mirror, but the person inside was beginning to feel like an alien to her.

Her doubts about her judgment did not keep her heart from skipping a beat Sunday night when she heard a knock on her door. She jumped up from the table, where she was mindlessly surfing the Internet, and opened the French doors. Asher was standing there with Levi before him, his hands on his son's shoulders.

"Hey!" Jane said brightly. "What are you guys doing? You want to come in?"

"I do," Levi said and started forward, but Asher held him back.

"Thanks," Asher said, "but we just came out to tell you that my parents are coming in Thursday for Riley's birthday. We're going to head out to their ranch for a long weekend, so if you want to knock off a couple of days, that would be fine."

"Oh." Jane pushed her hair behind her ears. "Okay . . . I guess I'll head for Houston early then, if that's okay."

Asher's gaze shifted to Levi, who was twisting back and forth. "Of course. It sounds like you have a lot to work out there." He lifted his gaze to hers.

"Right." Jane couldn't quite meet his gaze. She had no hope that she'd work anything out, but she was determined to try.

"Okay, then, Levi and I are going to water his garden now, so . . . I guess we'll see you later."

"Come on, Daddy! I'll show you the cucumbers!" Levi broke free and raced around the corner of the house. Asher hesitated; he looked at Jane, his gaze intent. "Good night."

"Good night," Jane said and watched him walk on.

That was it? Not even an invitation to come check out the plants with them? Jane slowly shut the door and walked to the living area, collapsing onto the couch. "You are *such* a moron," she said aloud and fell, facedown, onto the couch with a groan of exasperation.

Monday was off to a roaring start when Riley caught Levi playing with her laptop and the two argued loudly.

"Calm down," Jane commanded them, retrieving the laptop from Levi. "It's not the end of the world, Riley."

"It *is* a big deal. I have personal stuff in there," Riley said sharply. "Anyway, he has his own computer—why does he have to mess with mine?"

"Where's my computer, Jane?" Levi asked curiously.

Jane sighed. "I don't know. Let's go look for it."

But Levi's computer was not recovered before Levi left for camp. Riley's good mood was not recovered for the rest of the day.

Monday afternoon, while Levi was parked in the playroom with his Play-doh Backyardigans Playset, and Riley was shut in her room, Jane was picking up Levi's cars—they seemed to multiply overnight—and was surprised when Tara walked into the house. "Hello, hello!" Tara said cheerfully, as if they were pals. "How are you, Jane? How was your weekend?"

"Ah . . . fine," Jane said, looking at her curiously. "I didn't know Asher was here."

"He's not," Tara said. "I just ran out to pick up a few things. Asher has to pop up to Dallas tonight."

"Tara, is that you?" Carla called from the kitchen. "I've got it all right here." Carla appeared, rolling an overnight bag behind her.

Jane looked at the bag, then at Tara. "*Tonight?*"

"It was a very last-minute thing," Tara said. "But not to worry, Jane! Mrs. Freeman, his mother-in-law, is coming to get the kids this afternoon. They'll spend the night with her, but she's got a golf game in the morning, so she will drop them off, then swing around again in the afternoon."

"No, wait," Jane said a little frantically. Tomorrow was her appointment at the *Cedar Springs Standard*. "When will Asher be back?"

"Tomorrow night. But he is not going to impose on you. He was very clear about that. 'Do not impose on Jane,'" she said, playfully mimicking him. "Mrs. Freeman will be here. Trust me, it's all worked out. Can you have the kids ready to go at five?"

"Yes, but tomorrow . . . tomorrow I have an appointment I absolutely cannot miss."

"You won't," Tara said cheerfully. She took the bag from Carla. "Okay, I must run. Have a great day, you two!"

"Good-bye," Carla said and shut the door behind Tara. She turned around to Jane. "Helen Freeman will be late to her own funeral," she said matter-of-factly and walked back to the kitchen.

Jane would not miss her appointment, even if she had to drag Levi and Riley with her.

That evening, Helen Freeman arrived at seven o'clock, exactly two hours late. "You must be Jane. What a sweet thing you are! Sorry I'm late, but the traffic from Austin is horrendous. I'd love to stay and get to know you better, Jane, but Bill is probably ravenous. Come on, kids! You know how Grandpa Bill can get when he's hungry! I'll have them back here at eight. I'm playing golf with Derinda, and she fades in the heat."

Helen did return the next morning as promised. But not at eight. At nine. "I'll be back at three," she promised Jane.

Jane spent a frantic forty-five minutes getting Levi ready for camp.

She'd been home an hour and was trying to coax Riley into a trip to the Saddle-brew when Charlotte called her. "We've had a fight," she said bluntly.

"Oh, my God. With Jackson?"

"Yes. Both boys are being sent home. I am going to recommend that Levi be moved to one of the afternoon camps. Will you call Mr. Price, or would you like me to do so?"

"I'll call him," Jane said. On her way back to camp to pick Levi up, she called Asher's cell, which was answered by Tara. "Oh. Hi," Jane said uncertainly.

"Surprise!" Tara chirped. "Asher's cell has been forwarded to me."

If Jane didn't know better, she'd wonder if Tara had kidnapped Asher. "Is he around? I need to speak to him about Levi."

"Oooh, 'fraid not. May I give him a message?"

"Is it possible that I might speak with him?" Jane asked.

"It's possible, but it's going to be hard. He's in back-to-back meetings all day, and then he's catching a flight back to Austin at four."

"I really need to speak to him, please," Jane said. It irked her that she couldn't get through to him without going through Tara. This man was such an enigma! He'd been warm and charming and fun Friday, so much so that she'd believed that, at the very least, they could be friends. More than friends. Not that she wanted to be more than friends, but what did it matter? He had completely closed her off.

"I'll let him know," Tara said.

By the time Asher returned the call, Jane was on edge. She was waiting for Helen to arrive, was feeling nervous and even a little flighty, preoccupied with what she might find at the paper.

Asher sounded rushed. "What's up?"

"Levi was fighting in camp today," Jane said bluntly. She could hear a tapping noise in the background. Computer keys, she thought.

"Jackson again?"

"Yes. Charlotte said she didn't know how it started, but both boys were to blame. She wants to move Levi to the afternoon camp."

The tapping sound stopped.

"Levi doesn't want to do that. Apparently he's made a friend in the morning camp he doesn't want to lose."

The tapping noise started again. "Why Levi?" he asked irritably. "Why not move Jackson?"

Jane winced. "According to Charlotte, because of child care issues. Apparently, his mother works mornings."

"Bullshit," Asher said abruptly. "I've got to run, but I'll call Charlotte. Thanks, Jane. See you."

"What did he say?" Levi asked when Jane clicked off her phone.

To her it was more what he *didn't* say. She looked at Levi's worried face and cupped his chin. "He said he was coming home later. Do you want to tell me why you fought with Jackson?"

Levi frowned. "No. But he said Mommy was crazy and so am I."

"Oh, Levi, I—"

"Is *SpongeBob* on yet?" Levi asked quickly and moved his head away from her hand.

Jane's heart ached for the little guy. In spite of Levi's part in the dustup, which she could not excuse, it was obvious to her that he was unsettled, and for all her training and education, she felt powerless to help him.

Levi was tucked in front of *SpongeBob* and Riley on her laptop when Helen arrived, still dressed in her golf clothes. "Look what I've got!" she said happily and held out two stuffed McDonald's bags. It was only ten after three. Jane supposed that was Helen's idea of an afternoon snack.

Jane had no time to worry about their nutrition at the moment—she had only a small window to work with, and she hurried out to her car. As she turned the ignition and put the car in drive, she felt a whole new level of disquiet in her bones. This was it, the moment she'd been wanting for so long. "Don't be nervous," she said to herself. It was just information. It wasn't as if her birth mother was going to meet her at the offices of the *Cedar Springs Standard*.

The jarring ring of her phone startled her; she grabbed it, thinking, for some deranged reason, that it was Asher.

"Hi, sweetie," her mother trilled.

Not Asher. "Hi, Mom. How are you?"

"I have an easy day shift, so I'm good. Your father, however, twisted his ankle playing basketball with the boys yesterday."

"Is he okay?"

Her mother laughed. "His pride is wounded—they trounced him. But his ankle is fine. Never mind that—I wanted to call because today is the big day, huh?"

"Yes."

"How exciting, sweetie!"

"I'm nervous, Mom. What if I get a name, the real, actual name of someone who gave birth to me?"

"That would be great! Isn't that what you want?"

It was so hard to explain the emotions Jane was feeling—the desperate need to know mixed with the fear of knowing. "I do . . . but at the same time, I'm afraid of finding out why I was abandoned."

"Oh, Janey, I wish you'd stop saying that. Abandoned,

given up, whatever. Can't you just accept that it was part of God's larger plan for you? It happened for a reason. A *good* reason."

Jane didn't say anything. She didn't know that, and she didn't know that it was a particularly good reason.

"It is what it is," her mother said. "Just remember that you don't have to do anything with the information you get. You can stop this at any time, or you can go forward. Just don't expect there to be a silver lining, or anything at all, really, and you'll be okay. And know that your father and I will always be here for you."

"That is about the only thing I know for sure anymore, Mom," Jane said. "I'll call you when I find something out, okay?"

"I'll be waiting by the phone," her mother assured her.

At the *Cedar Springs Standard* offices, Jane didn't allow herself to think; she pushed through the glass doors into cool, moist air, the smell of old paper, and the sound of a baby fussing.

"Jane, is that you?" Emma called from somewhere behind the filing cabinets.

"Yes . . . Emma?"

Emma appeared with a baby in her arms and a happy smile. "Come on back."

Jane followed Emma around putty-colored filing cabinets, her sandals silent on the blue carpet.

Behind the cabinets was a woman sitting in a chair at Emma's desk, a portable car seat at her feet. She had a very pretty smile and gold blonde hair and green eyes. She resembled Emma.

"Jane, this is my sister, Macy Lockhart," Emma said, handing the baby to her. "And this adorable little munchkin is my niece, Grace. Or, as I like to call her, the-reason-I-am-stuck-here."

"Oh, Emma," Macy said cheerfully as she put the baby in her car seat.

"Your baby is beautiful," Jane said to Macy, and bent over the infant to have a look. Grace was only a month or two old, and her mother beamed down at her with an expression full of love. A bit of jealousy pricked Jane—it was not the first time she'd felt jealous of a baby. When Jane saw mothers with babies, she couldn't help wondering what her birth mother had seen. Had she loved her at first sight? Had she counted her fingers and toes? Kissed her?

"Okay! Here's the microfiche we found that includes 1980!" Emma said proudly.

"*We?* You mean me," Macy said as she dangled a pair of tiny bears above the baby.

"Okay, *you*. It would take the entire rocket science lab from UT to make sense of this mess. I mean, really, can't y'all hand this over to someone and get it straightened out?" Emma complained to Macy. She handed the film to Jane. "The readers are just there. Do you want me to show you how to use it?"

"No, thanks. I used them at school," Jane said.

"Okay. We'll leave you alone. The files are not indexed, except by year, and there are three decades on each roll, so you'll just have to dig."

"Thank you," Jane said.

A pair of readers sat side-by-side in a dark, cool corner of the office. Jane could hear the sisters chattering and laughing softly, the baby cooing as Jane began to scroll through the years of Cedar Springs history.

Emma was right, Jane quickly discovered—not much had happened in Cedar Springs in the last several years. It seemed there had been a big rain and flood about a year ago that had fed stories for a month. *Disaster on the Lake,* followed by *Cleanup Begins,* and then later in the month, *Mold a Problem on Ave A.* The high school sports teams got the most coverage, with highlights of every game followed by profiles of the key players.

Jane scrolled through the last two years, but when she reached 2008, she was startled to see the headline *Local Women Die.* She gasped softly at the picture that accompanied the small article—had it not been for a tire lying in the road, Jane would not have realized she was looking at two cars. The only thing left was a heap of twisted, burned metal. Behind the wreckage, cows grazed in a field as if nothing had happened.

> *December 5, 2008: The Cedar County Sheriff's Office is investigating a fatal collision that occurred about midnight Tuesday on Highway 16 near the intersection with Highway 71. Sheriff's deputy James Penn said that a Mercedes driven by Susanna Price, 43, of Cedar Springs, was traveling north at a very high rate of speed when her vehicle crossed the lane divider and collided head-on with a Chevy Tahoe driven by Sandra Fallon, 64, of Fredericksburg. Both drivers were pronounced dead at the scene. Investigators suspect alcohol was a factor and are awaiting the results of DNA tests. The sheriff's office is asking any witness to the accident to call the county hotline. This is the county's fourth fatal accident of 2008.*

Jane read the article again. Drunk driving? That was not something Jane would have guessed in a million years, and certainly no one had mentioned it to her. It was startling to think that Susanna's life had ended that way, or to imagine that the beautiful, sophisticated woman might have had a drinking problem.

But then again, maybe that explained things. Maybe Susanna had been different from people around town, and had drunk too much from time to time, and people had put a label on her. Linda Gail had said she was strange. Little Jackson told Levi she was crazy, which he'd obviously heard from somewhere. *Crazy* was such a harsh word, so full of indictment. It reminded Jane of Crystal Ross, an administrative aide in the school where Jane worked. Everyone said Crystal was crazy. They made remarks about her "being off her meds." Jane wasn't sure how Crystal had gotten that reputation, but the result was that everyone cut a wide berth around her, fearing she'd go off.

But Crystal never went off. She was a little odd, sure, but she was a perfectly nice and sane person. Jane knew, because she couldn't stand how Crystal was ostracized and had begun to have lunch with her. Crystal wasn't crazy; she wasn't even close to crazy. She just marched to the beat of a different drummer, and frankly, it was not an unlikable drummer.

Surely the same could be said of Susanna. Jane could not imagine that the charming, sexy man of Friday night could have been married to a crazy woman for fifteen years.

Jane continued to scroll, her pace a little slower, looking for any other clues about Susanna. She found only one: a charity event at which Susanna had been listed as a cochair. There was a picture of her, front and center, her smile luminous, her gown sumptuous. She had her arm around a portly gentleman, and he around her. Susanna was leaning into him, her hand on his chest, and she was smiling broadly. Her long tail of silky black hair hung artfully over her shoulder, jewels dangled from earlobes, and her décolletage plunged almost to her navel. She was so glamorous, so beautiful, and so enviable.

But what caught Jane's eye was Asher. He was standing slightly behind and apart from Susanna. Holding a highball glass, one hand in his pocket, he looked very handsome in his tuxedo. He was gazing at Susanna, but his expression was sullen. Was he jealous? Tired? Angry? His was not the look of a happy man, but there was something else . . .

He looked alone.

That was not the smiling face of the man sitting beside Susanna in the portraits around Summer's End. That was the look of a man who was living on the outside.

His expression left Jane feeling sad and a little uncomfortable.

She continued on, scrolling through years of high school sports and county bonds projects, finally reaching December 1980. To her horror, her hand had a slight tremor in it. *November, October, September, August.* She felt strange, as if the walls were shifting closer to her. *July, June, May.* In the office behind her, the baby started to fuss, and tears suddenly clouded her vision.

Monday, April 28, Weekly Edition. On the right-hand side, in a small table of contents, she found *Death and Birth Notices, Page 4.*

Jane stared at the page. Page four was where she would see the name. She'd have that one thing—a name—that would be the key to her past. It suddenly all seemed so simple, and Jane couldn't understand why it had taken her almost thirty years to find that single, tiny bit of information about herself.

Did she want to know?

She gasped softly, shocked that she'd just had that thought. *Not want to know?* She'd left everyone and everything behind to know. But suddenly, the moment left her feeling like she was about to throw the only life she truly had under the wheels of a gigantic bus.

She scrolled to page two. And to page three. She took a deep breath, plunged past her fear, and moved to page four. There it was: *Births*. Jane held her breath. *Births* . . . there was a little box with an announcement:

> *Cedar Springs continues to grow! Five babies were delivered at Cedar Springs Memorial Hospital the week of April 21: a boy on April 22, and a bumper crop on April 25: three healthy girls!*

Jane blinked. She shifted closer, peering intently at the screen, thinking surely she'd missed the names. She scrolled down. And up. She scoured all of April, frantically moving between the weekly editions. In the first two weeks of April, five children were born, their names all listed. In the last two weeks of April, there was nothing but that box and a headcount. *There were no names.* All she had was a birth announcement that wasn't, a small box smashed in between an ad for a hardware store and the results of the high school basketball game.

"I don't understand," Jane said aloud. "How can this be?"

"Jane? Are you talking to me?" Emma called to her.

"How can this be?" Jane asked again.

Emma and Macy appeared at her back, leaning over her shoulder, peering at the screen.

"I don't understand why there are no names!" Jane exclaimed.

"Oh, for Chrissakes," Macy said with some disgust. "This is such a rinky-dink little paper that Ed called the hospital and asked for baby names just so he'd have something to fill an empty column. And the hospital staffer was probably on vacation or too busy to do Ed's job for him, so he printed what they gave him. It's so typical!"

The week of April 21 . . . Jane's stomach was advancing on her throat. Only moments ago, she'd been afraid to find the one thing she'd been looking for. Now she was furious that she'd been robbed of it, that she didn't know, *couldn't* know. Disappointment and frustration were choking her and could not be forced down.

"I'm sorry, Jane," Emma said. "Is there something else we can look up?"

Jane shook her head. Macy and Emma were watching Jane like they expected her to fall apart. But Jane was too stunned to fall apart. "Thank you. That's all I need today. Thank you." She tried to force a smile as she stood, but her thoughts were bouncing around like popcorn in her head. "Thank you," she said again, and walked out of the office, her stomach churning, the taste of bitter disappointment in her throat.

23

*J*ane was still sitting on the couch in the guesthouse when someone knocked at her door. She'd been sitting in the same spot since she'd returned from the *Cedar Springs Standard* office, staring blindly at the wall. She hadn't eaten, she hadn't done anything but brood.

The knock came again; Jane glanced at the clock. It was nine.

She tossed aside the pillow she was clutching and opened the door. "Hi, Riley," Jane said dispassionately when she saw Riley standing there. "Come in."

Riley walked in. "Dad said to tell you he's home," she said as she looked around.

"Great," Jane said, uncaring.

"What's that?" Riley asked, pointing at Jane's boxes.

"My things."

Riley wandered over to peer into an open box Jane had been using to hold her clothes. "Why haven't you unpacked them?"

Ah, the million-dollar question. "Well . . . I don't really know," Jane said.

That earned a suspicious look from Riley. "Are you lazy?"

Jane smiled thinly. "I guess." She resumed her seat on the couch. "What did you do today?"

"Nothing. Watched TV." Riley flopped dramatically into one of Jane's chairs and fidgeted with a little charm that hung from her cell phone. "I talked to Tracy. She says Michael Howser likes me." She gave Jane a wary sidelong glance, as if she expected Jane to argue.

"Oh, yeah? Who is Michael Howser?"

Riley dropped her gaze. "Just this guy at school. I don't think he really likes me. I think Tracy is just saying that."

"Why would she just say that? She doesn't strike me as the type to make things up."

"She's not," Riley said. "At least I don't think she is." She bowed her head, letting her hair fall to cover her face. "But I don't know why Mike Howser would like *me*."

"I do," Jane said. "I think you're great. You're funny, you're cute, you're smart, and you're talented."

Riley snorted. "Not really."

"Yes, really. I wouldn't make things up, either."

Riley didn't say anything. She bent over her lap and touched her fingers to the floor. "I kind of feel like Janis Joplin sometimes, you know?"

"I know. Me, too. But you're not really like Janis. She had problems. You don't have those kinds of problems."

"You don't know," Riley said. "I've done things."

"Like what? Fighting?"

Riley's head came up, her eyes narrowed. "How do you know?"

"Just heard it. What happened?"

Riley suddenly stood up and walked to the kitchen bar. She touched Jane's laptop, keeping her head down, hiding behind her hair. "Sometimes people say things I don't like," she said with a shrug.

Jane thought of what she'd read about Susanna today. "Do you mean about your mom?"

"*No*," Riley said impatiently. "I'm not Levi. I mean they

say things about me. Stupid things. And please don't try to be a counselor and ask me what, because it's so stupid I forgot already."

Jane knew that was a lie, but she was in no mood to be a counselor. "Okay," she said.

Surprised, Riley looked at Jane. But when Jane offered nothing else, Riley walked to the door. She paused there, her hand on the knob. "It's really weird that you haven't unpacked your boxes. You've been here, like, forever now." She walked out, closing the door quietly behind her.

"Some days it feels like forever, I'll give you that," Jane muttered and sank lower onto the couch.

She couldn't sleep. She wasn't tired; she was keyed up and anxious. She kept seeing that headline: "Cedar Springs Continues to Grow!" Lying on her bed, watching the ceiling fan drift in a lazy circle, she heard Levi crying over the monitor. Jane looked at her clock; it was half past midnight. He would have been in bed for three hours or more now. She got up, pulled on some shorts under her camisole, and hurried to the house.

But when she reached Levi's room, she found Asher at Levi's dresser, rummaging through it. He was bare-chested, wearing a pair of lounge pants that rode low. He looked up and started at the sight of her. Jane pointed at the monitor to explain her appearance. "I heard him. Is everything okay?"

"An accident," Asher said softly and glanced over his shoulder at the bathroom door. "He's in the tub. He's embarrassed."

"Poor little guy," Jane said quietly. "Can I help?"

"Thanks, but I've got it. Go back to bed."

"Daddy?"

Asher and Jane both looked toward the bathroom. "Coming, buddy," Asher said, and with a halfhearted smile for Jane, he walked into the bathroom carrying clean pajamas.

Jane wasn't leaving. She stripped Levi's bed, found clean sheets in a hallway linen closet and made the bed up again. She took the soiled sheets down to the utility room and began to fill the washtub.

"Hey, I can do that."

She hadn't heard Asher come in. He'd put on a shirt and was carrying Levi's wet pajamas. He took the jug of detergent from her. "Please, I'll do it."

He seemed determined, so Jane moved back and folded her arms across her chest as she watched him. She thought she ought to go, but her curiosity about his coolness to her was swallowing her practical side. "Poor kid," she said.

"Yeah, poor kid." Asher dropped the pajamas into the washer. "He's worried about Carla finding out."

"I won't tell her."

Asher glanced at Jane, his expression cool, shuttered. She smiled, feeling suddenly out of place. "He must really miss his mother," she said. "He thinks he hears her in the attic."

"What he hears is mice," Asher said shortly.

"Yes, but I . . . I meant—"

"I'm sorry," Asher said and shoved his hand through his hair. "Sorry. I'm just worried about my son."

"Me, too," Jane said. "He's such a great kid." She bent down to pick up the sheets and handed them to Asher. "I was just thinking how awful to hear those things said about his mother and then to imagine he hears her in the attic. It must be frightening for a little boy." Particularly as five-year-olds tended to have rather vivid imaginations anyway. "You must miss her, too," she added quietly.

If Asher missed her or not, he didn't respond. He

looked down into the washtub. Apparently satisfied it was doing what it should, he closed the lid.

His silence was unnerving. "I know this is hard for you all."

"Do you know that, Jane?" he asked and turned his head to look at her. His eyes were blazing. "It's been a while. I don't think we're missing her quite as much as you'd like to have us miss her."

"What?" she asked, confused. "I think you misunderstood me. I just meant that she died so suddenly and so young. It's obviously weighing on Levi, and you yourself said that Riley needs her—"

"Their *mother*," he said coldly, "went on a drinking binge and killed herself in a fiery car crash. She wasn't much help to them then, and I can't honestly believe she'd be much help to them now."

Jane's jaw dropped. His voice was so bitter, so hard. "What are you saying? Maybe she drank, but at least they *had* a mother. Children need their mother—"

Asher suddenly moved, grabbing her head in both hands, lifting her face to his. Jane made a small cry of alarm, but he ignored her. "They don't need her, they *never* needed her. They loved her, but they never needed her the way . . . the way they need *you*, even after a few short weeks. My children learned not to need their mother because she always put herself first. Don't romanticize it."

Jane's heart was pounding from surprise at both his words and the fact that he was holding her. "I don't believe you," she said breathlessly, trying to back away from him, not knowing quite what to do in this situation. She wanted to touch his face. She wanted to flee.

"Believe it. It happens." His gaze fell to her mouth.

Her pulse began to race. "Was she crazy?" Jane whispered.

"Not as crazy as I am, apparently," he said low, and his mouth descended to hers.

Jane grabbed his wrist. After days of imagining it, of wanting it, Asher's mouth was on hers, warm and soft, moving on her lips, his tongue against hers.

Jane's reaction was purely visceral; she opened her mouth to him. One of his hands dropped from her hair and slipped around her waist, pulled her hard into his body, pressing her against him. Desire was suddenly burning Jane up, turning her insides to ashes. His kiss was devastatingly sensual and full of need. The sensation was potent and spilled over Jane, filling up the space around them, filling her lungs and mouth and eyes with Asher.

But then, just as unexpectedly as he'd kissed her, Asher broke away. He pressed his forehead to hers, his breathing ragged. Jane slowly realized that she was still gripping his wrist, holding on to keep from slipping beneath the surface of all that want.

Asher stepped back. She let go of him. "I'm sorry," he said. "Jane, I . . ."

"Don't apologize." They stood looking at each other for a long moment, his eyes searching hers. But a river of questions and confusion began to flow through Jane. Her knees felt weak. "I should go," she said.

He nodded.

She hurried out, did not look back. She hurried through the kitchen, to the breezeway. She could still feel his arms around her. She could still taste him. Her body was smoldering. She had the very uneasy sense that she'd finally done it; she'd finally crossed some invisible line from which it was impossible to go back and be the person she'd once been. She was no longer standing in the middle of the bridge.

In the guesthouse, behind closed doors, she leaned against the wall and bent over. *"Stupid, stupid, stupid,"* she whispered. She'd walked right into the scene of a TV movie script, the nanny and the dashing man of the house—how clichéd! She couldn't believe what had just happened, that he'd kissed her, that she'd responded so easily, so *eagerly,* and now . . . *now* what was she supposed to do with all this longing?

Longing hardly described what she was feeling. When Jonathan kissed her, it was with the desire for sex. But when Asher kissed her, it felt as if there was more, so much pent-up desire, so much need in his kiss. It was as intoxicating as it was wrong.

Stupid, stupid, stupid.

The next morning, Jane walked cautiously in the house, expecting to be confronted with the evidence of that illicit kiss. But nothing had changed. Carla was her usual cheerful self. When Jane peeked into the laundry room, the evidence of Levi's bed-wetting had disappeared, and that searing kiss along with it.

Mr. and Mrs. Price arrived late that morning and took the kids for lunch. "Mr. P said this morning that you should take a few days," Carla said to Jane as the kids trooped out with their grandparents. "They are leaving first thing in the morning for the Price ranch down by San Antonio."

"Great. I'll leave tomorrow, too," Jane said. Part of her couldn't wait to get out of here. Part of her didn't want to go.

She felt restless and antsy, so she drove down to the square, to a cute little art supply shop, and bought Riley's birthday present: a sketchbook and colored pencils. She wrapped the gifts prettily and left them on Riley's bed.

The day continued to drag, so Jane decided to go for a late afternoon run. She waved to Jorge on her way

down the little path to the running trail. But as she jogged
down, she saw where the path split, one trail to the hidden springs and the playhouse, one down to the lake.
Jane veered onto the path to the hidden springs.

The little house was still locked up. A humid breeze
kept the tire swing twisting lazily. The leaf blower and the
pile of debris were gone, the only change since the last
time Jane had been here.

She walked up on the little porch and, shielding her
eyes, peered into the window. She could see the swaths
of color, the scattering of paper on the floor. She walked
around, checking the windows, looking for an opening,
but the little house was locked up tight. She returned to
the door and fiddled with the lock and doorknob. It was
definitely locked.

Jane stepped back; with hands on hips, she stared at
that doorknob. There was something about that little
house that drew her, something that she had to see without the filter of dirty windows. She didn't really know
what answers she was seeking, but something told her
there was a key to them in there. She pulled a bobby pin
from her hair, which she used to keep her bangs from her
face when she was running.

Don't do it, she told herself as she straightened out the
bobby pin and stuck it into the little hole in the center
of the doorknob. *Don't, Jane. Don't do it, don't do it.* But
she continued to jimmy the lock with the hairpin until
it caught and released the lock. The door popped and
swung open onto a dank room.

Jane peered inside, feeling a little guilty. But as her eyes
adjusted to the dim light, she began to sense something
was off about the room. *Not normal,* Linda Gail had said.
She was so creative, such a talent, Carla had said. *Crazy,* little Jackson Harvey had said.

Jane stepped hesitantly across the threshold. A thick layer of dust covered everything, and a sour, vinegary smell permeated the air. A set of shelves and cabinets were built onto one wall, two paint cans sat side by side, but there was nothing else. Across from the shelves on the opposite wall was a small table built into the wall. A stool was tucked up neatly underneath the bar, undisturbed.

Everything else was a wreck. Another stool lay broken under the bar. Construction paper and canvas littered the floor. Several easels were stacked like pick-up-sticks in a corner.

The mess of the room was pretty spectacular, but not quite as spectacular as the paint that had been flung about. The quantity astounded Jane. Paint cans were everywhere. Shoe prints, some of them on the end of a long slide, were all over the paint, almost as if someone had been dancing or fighting. In one spot, Jane swore there was the outline of an entire leg, as if someone had fallen. Gallons of colorful paint covered the walls, the ceiling, the windows.

And there, in a corner, was a child's painting. It was a picture of a house, a sky and a sun, and a little brown dog lying on the porch. Jane thought it might even have been this little house. It was good, but it was torn, and paint had splattered on it, and strangely, a shoe print was stamped across the middle of it.

This room didn't look artistic or creative. This room looked like madness. It took Jane's breath away, really, and she wished she hadn't opened the door and looked. She'd been wrong to snoop, so wrong. The last twenty-four hours of her life had been so off-kilter.

She turned toward the door, wanting out of there and away from the madness, but another painting caught her eye. It was lying on the floor near the door, another by the child artist. Jane bent down to pick it up, pushing the door closed a bit to dislodge it. The painting was of a person, a woman with long black hair. It was only half finished, and it had suffered the same fate as the other painting: a shoe.

Jane let it flutter to the floor and was about to leave the house when she heard the sound of someone running.

She froze. The footsteps were coming closer, and with them, the sound of someone sobbing. Great, wet gulps of air. Jane's heart suddenly leaped with fear and began to pound in her chest. She looked wildly about, but there was no place to hide. So she crouched down below the window and held her breath.

"Riley!"

That was Asher. Jane put her hand over her mouth and squeezed her eyes shut. He was coming after Riley, and she, Jane, was in deep, deep trouble.

24

Asher wanted to kill his mother. She could never let it go, could never stop talking. He'd known where Riley had gone when she'd run out of the house, and he found her on the picnic table outside the studio, her arms wrapped tightly around her legs. She had her head down on her knees and was sobbing.

Asher sat beside her. "Come here, baby girl," he said and wrapped her in an embrace, held her head against his chest as she cried.

For a moment. She suddenly jerked up and rubbed her hand beneath her nose. "You're probably on *her* side. Go ahead and say it, you're on her side!"

"No, Riley, I'm on your side. I'll always be on your side, no matter what."

"I hate her, Dad. I swear I hate her!"

"No, you don't," he said soothingly. At least he hoped she didn't. His mother didn't mean to hurt Riley, but she could be incredibly insensitive.

"She always says mean stuff about Mom, and then *me*. Why does she have to do that?"

He didn't know the answer to that. It was so clear to him that his mother's offhanded remarks were agitating his daughter, and he couldn't understand how his mother didn't see it. Even when he'd asked her to stop, she'd looked at Asher and said, "Do you think I'm wrong? Don't you think we should at least have her evaluated?" It was his mother's standard refrain: Bipolar disorder could be hereditary. Better to know sooner rather than later.

"She's not trying to hurt you, Ri," he said. "She's just . . . she just doesn't understand things." And she was opinionated. And could be something of a bully.

"I can't stand it, Dad," Riley said tearfully. "I know what Mom was like, but still, I miss her so much, and it's not like I don't already hear about it at school, and then from my own *grandmother*. She was my mother!"

"I know, honey, I know," he muttered, and felt a familiar, painful ripple through his heart. It was so unfair that Riley had to suffer his mother's cruel remarks on top of losing her mother. Asher would do anything to make her life happy and whole, to take all the pain and suffering from her young shoulders and return her to a state of happy childhood innocence. It was such a hopeless feeling to know that he couldn't protect his daughter from the truth. There was nothing he could do, nothing that could change all that had happened in her young life.

"It's like no one misses Mom but me," Riley said, rubbing her nose again.

"That's not true," he said. "Mom was so vibrant, so alive, and a lot of people miss her. She loved you so much, Ri, more than the air she breathed."

Riley smiled a little, thankfully; the tears had stopped, but her eyes and nose were swollen from crying. "What about Levi?"

"Oh yeah, she loved Levi just as much, but in a different way. Levi was a surprise, and he was early, remember? He had those health issues at birth that really scared her, and she was always a little protective of him. But *you*? Riley, she planned you. She couldn't wait to have you.

She even had your name picked out before she knew she was pregnant. Your mom wanted you as bad as she'd ever wanted anything, and she loved you even more for it."

Riley's smile deepened. She was so pretty when she smiled, but she smiled so rarely. He brushed the hair from her eyes. "Do you know what Mom would say to you now?"

"Not really." She looked down. "I can't remember some things anymore. Like what her voice sounded like, or what she'd say."

"Well, I know what she would say," Asher said. "Right now she would tell you that it doesn't matter what anyone else says or thinks, the only thing that matters is what is in your heart. Riley, you knew your mother in a way that no one else on this earth knew her, including me. You knew Mom like you know yourself, and she knew you the same way. No one can ever take that from you. No one can ever change the special bond you two had. Everything Grandma said today is just words. She knew Mom from a distance, but you knew her up close and for real."

"Yeah," Riley softly agreed, nodding. "I did." She looked up at the cottonwoods towering above them almost as if she were looking for Susanna.

"Don't worry about Grandma," Asher said. "She's not all bad. In her own way, she loves you very much. Besides, once we get to the ranch, you'll be out riding horses and she'll be in the air-conditioning."

Riley smiled. She rubbed her eyes and stood up. "Thanks, Dad."

His heart swelled. "No need," he said. "Grandma and Grandpa took Levi for ice cream. Why don't you go back and pack in peace?"

"Yeah, good idea," she agreed. Riley stepped away from the table, but when she realized Asher hadn't moved, she looked back. "Aren't you coming?"

"In just a minute. I'm going to check on things around here. Go on, and I'll be right behind you."

Riley obediently started up the path.

Asher watched her until she had turned the corner onto the broader path, then stood up and looked at the door of the studio. It was only slightly ajar, and he might not have noticed it at all if he hadn't stopped by here the other day to check on things when he'd been out for a run.

He guessed teens or someone up from the lake had found it and used it to do whatever kids did these days.

Asher walked up on the porch, gave the door a push, and watched it swing slowly open. He expected to see graffiti or beer cans.

He did not expect to find Jane, or for his heart to drop.

"What are you doing in here?" he demanded, his mind racing through any plausible explanation, then wondering if he cared. He'd not seen her since the night he had so impulsively and foolishly kissed her, the night when he'd felt himself crack open like parched earth and felt her seeping into his bones. He'd thought of little else but Jane since, struggling with the monstrous desire she stoked in him, knowing it was wrong, feeling disoriented, guilty, and perhaps even a little happy.

"Ah . . ." She looked around. Rubbed the back of her nape. She looked . . . delectable in running clothes that hugged her curves, her hair in a big knot. She looked moist, damp, and oh so guilty. But when she looked at him, her eyes were full of sorrow. "I am so sorry, Asher. I . . . I was curious. I know what you must be thinking," she said, holding up a hand. "You must be thinking that I have no right. That this studio was locked and I came in and I have no right."

Yes, he'd thought that. But at present he was thinking of how much he wanted to touch her.

"And you're right, I shouldn't have. I was leaving, and I . . . I didn't *want* to overhear," she said, looking contrite.

"Yet you did overhear. Quite a lot, too."

"I did, but I honestly don't know what I overheard. I know that Riley is . . . she was obviously in pain. She obviously came here for solace, but it must be so hard for her."

"I doubt she came here for solace," he said, looking around at the ugly walls. "She doesn't know, Jane."

"Excuse me?"

"She doesn't know everything about Susanna. She obviously knows her mother died in a horrible crash. She and Levi both know it. And they know there was nothing identifiable about their mother, that she was just bits and pieces, and we couldn't see her to say good-bye." He would never forget the DPS trooper at his door, the harrowing news of how Susanna had died. It had been so horrific, and guilt had grabbed him by the throat and forced him to his knees, right in front of that trooper. It felt as if someone had ripped his heart from his body. For all her faults, for all their troubles, he had loved Susanna once, and he couldn't imagine how painful her death must have been.

Nor could he have imagined that Riley would witness their final argument, here, in this very room.

"They know some, but they don't know all." It had been so long since he'd thought of that awful day. "I don't want them to know all. Riley adored her mother so much, and Susanna adored Riley. I have never told Riley that the night her mother died . . ." He swallowed. He couldn't say it. This room, this horrific scene of madness, brought back painful memories. He wondered what Jane saw in this room, if she could sense the insanity.

"Don't," Jane said. "You don't need to say more."

"Yes, I do. My daughter is a very talented artist. Her talent is raw yet, but it's an obvious talent. Susanna saw it, too. She nurtured it along, she taught Riley what she knew. But . . . but Susanna struggled with drinking," he admitted. "And vanity. That's a very dangerous combination. The day she died, she'd been drinking vodka. Down here, with Riley. And she'd had enough that when Riley showed her some painting, Susanna couldn't handle the idea that Riley might one day be a better artist than she. She flew into a rage of jealousy and destroyed Riley's paintings."

"You're kidding," Jane said, her gaze shifting to the pictures Riley had drawn that still littered the floor.

"I wish I were," he said. Asher had never been able to clean this room after what had happened. He wished it had burned with Susanna. "She said some terrible, hurtful things to Riley. So horrible that Jorge came to get me. She and I had a hellacious fight, right in front of Riley." If he'd had the chance to do anything over, it would have been that. He would have sent Riley to the house, he would have spared her that, but he hadn't thought, he'd been so angry. "Maybe I was dismissive of Susanna, maybe I could have handled it differently, but I told her I wouldn't speak to her until she sobered up." He looked at the walls. "I was pissed, Jane. I was so very angry with her for tearing down Riley's talent—for Chrissakes, she was only eleven. But there was no talking to Susanna when she drank like that. I took Riley and left Susanna here. Riley was devastated, as you can imagine."

"No," Jane said, her amber eyes wide. "I can't imagine."

Who could? What mother would begrudge an eleven-year-old her painting? Only a bipolar alcoholic. "I heard her come in a little later, heard her go up to our room. I never thought she'd leave, but that evening, when I went to check on her, I discovered she was gone. She'd taken my car, she was driving, and she was drunk. She killed herself and that poor woman."

"Oh, my God," Jane whispered. She looked sick; she folded her arms across her body.

"Fortunately, grief has a funny way of making us remember things. I don't think Riley remembers a lot of that day. Not yet, anyway, and if I have my way, not ever. I know people say things about Susanna, but I am doing my level best to protect my kids from the truth as long as I can." He looked at Jane. "Riley hasn't been in this studio since the day her mother died. It holds too many painful memories."

"Oh, dear God," Jane said, her voice and eyes full of sorrow. "And here I was, trying so hard to get her down here." She looked down. "Asher . . . I can't begin to tell you how sorry I am for . . . for everything. That must have been horrific."

It had been the blackest day of his life, and Lord knew that he'd known a few. Black was the color of the days and weeks that had followed. He'd struggled with guilt and grief and trying to work at the same time he'd been learning to be a single parent to Riley and Levi. There had been moments when he'd felt relieved of the burden that was Susanna, and moments he'd longed to see her face. "You just don't know how much you love someone until they are gone," he said quietly and felt a dull twist in his gut. "In spite of her problems, I had truly loved her."

He'd never said that to anyone, and oh God, there was a time he'd loved Susanna deeply. It was strange—he'd wanted to leave her so many times, but he'd never been able to bring himself to do it. He'd always believed it was for the sake of the kids, but on some level, he'd understood how much Susanna had needed him. Even when the romance was dead, the marriage in shambles, she had needed him desperately. Yet in the end, he hadn't been able to protect her from herself. He'd failed her.

"I'm so sorry," Jane said.

Asher suddenly felt very drained. He hadn't talked about Susanna to anyone in a very long time. His life had been spent on pins and needles for so long that he was still getting used to terra firma. He looked away from Jane, remembering.

"How are you?" Jane asked.

He didn't understand.

"Are you doing better?" she asked.

Better than what? The wound didn't feel open anymore, but the gash, the scar, was there. He studied Jane's face, her pretty, open, expressive face. Yes, maybe he was healing a little, or at least beginning to heal in the sunshine Jane had infused in their lives.

"It's none of my business," Jane said apologetically. "But I think you worry about the kids so much, and, you know, you have to think about yourself, too."

Unthinking, drawn to her softness, Asher took a step toward her.

Jane's eyes widened slightly. "I just wondered if you were okay because I know how that is, how you keep busy thinking of what you need to do for everyone else and you don't leave time to think about what you need for yourself."

At the moment, he was thinking of her. Gentle Jane. Such a contrast from his late wife! He moved toward her, his eyes on her lush mouth, the memory of their kiss suddenly racing in his blood.

Jane backed up, held out her hands as if she thought he meant to tackle her. "I mean, I do it, too," she said, speaking quickly. "I forget that I have to take care of myself, and it was only recently that I finally understood I need—"

He caught her by the shoulders. "What do you need, Jane?" he asked low. "Tell me. Tell me whatever it is you need."

Her lips parted. She looked as if she meant to speak, but instead, she melted, curving into him. She smelled like lotion and lavender, and her skin was warm. Asher shoved his hand into the knot of her hair, splayed his fingers against her jaw. "Whatever you need," he said again, and kissed her.

Her lips singed him; he could feel her in every pore, his body drinking her in, hungering for more. He had not remembered a kiss could be like this, so full of want and hope. He pressed his hand to her breast and covered it, felt the blood in his veins turn to fire. He was erupting, his desire so powerful that he feared he'd not be able to control it. *"Jane,"* he whispered and pressed his lips to the salty hollow of her throat.

Jane's hands were moving on him, inflaming him. They were in his hair, on his shoulders, on his chest. He pushed her back, up against the windowsill, fighting himself as he wildly sought her mouth with his. Jane arched into him, clung to him, countering with as much heat as he gave her.

His hands explored her shape, moving over her full hips, her slender waist, her lush breasts. But when he cupped one breast and began to knead it, Jane suddenly twisted in his arms. "No," she said, gasping for breath. "No, Asher."

It took all of the strength Asher could muster to lift his head from her mouth, to slacken his hold of her. He gritted his teeth, tried to catch his breath.

Jane touched his face, her fingers light on his skin. "You astound me," she said. "And as much as I would like . . . this," she said, "I can't. I didn't come here for this. I came to Cedar Springs to find my birth mother. I have put my life on hold for that single quest. I came to put all the pieces of me together, and I don't know how to fold this . . . this incredible attraction into that."

God no, don't say that, please don't say that. Asher groaned. He made himself step back and away from her. He slowly ran his hands over his hair and locked his fingers behind his head, trying to find reason and duty and the suffocating responsibility that had guided him these last few years. "I've taken advantage of you," he said roughly and dropped his hands.

"Not at all," Jane said. "That's not what I meant."

Asher looked at the door.

"I don't know what this means, this thing between us."

That was fair. "Neither do I," he reluctantly admitted.

"I need to think," she said uncertainly.

That was the least he could do. He looked at her. "Yes." It was all he could say. His body was still thrumming, his blood still sluicing hot in his veins. He didn't want to think right now, he wanted to make love.

"I'm off to Houston tomorrow, and you and the kids . . ."

"Right." He suddenly wanted out of this studio. He hated this place. He hated the evidence of Susanna all around him. How had he believed, if only for a moment, that he could escape her? He looked at the door again. *Just get out. Get out of here, get away from Susanna, get away from your lust.*

Jane must have read his thoughts. She started moving. "So, I'll just go now," she said carefully.

But as she walked past him, Asher impulsively reached out and tangled his fingers with hers. She paused and gazed up at him, and Asher saw a depth of emotion in her eyes that sent a small shiver through him.

Jane didn't say anything more. She put her head down

and walked on. She was running when she stepped outside, jogging onto the path. Away from him, Asher wondered, or away from her desire?

He waited until he felt in control of himself again, then closed the door and shoved against it twice to make sure it was locked before walking back to the house.

25

*J*ane was gone from Summer's End the next day as soon as she could get her things together. Not only had she completely overstepped her bounds but she'd reached yet another dead end in the search for her birth mother, and she'd made no progress on her thesis.

Jane felt awful about herself. She didn't *know* herself.

She arrived in Houston in time for the family's nightly meal. They were all very happy to see her. Eric and Matt, her freakishly handsome brothers, did their favorite thing and sandwiched her between them. "Neanderthals 'til the bitter end," Jane said laughingly.

"You're so skinny!" her mother cried, wrapping Jane in a tight embrace.

"Mom, I have been gone a month. I have not gained or lost a pound. And I was never skinny."

"I am so glad to see you!" her mother said, ignoring her.

"Let her go, Terri. She'll be gone six months if she thinks she has to endure that every time she comes home. C'mere, kid, your old man wants a hug, too," her father rumbled.

She said hello to Aunt Mona and Uncle Barry, and answered their questions about Cedar Springs, about the kids, about the house. When they sat down to eat— grilled pork medallions with red potato mashers, roasted corn, and tarragon aioli, the evening's special—Jane's cousin Vicki asked her bluntly, "Did you find your birth mother?"

"For heaven's sake, Vicki," Aunt Mona said irritably.

"What?" Vicki asked. "It's what we all want to know, isn't it?"

Everyone looked hopefully at Jane.

"Ah, no . . ." She forked some of the potatoes. "So far, I haven't had much luck."

"So have you found *anything*?" Eric asked. "Mom said the hospital wouldn't tell you anything."

"Nothing. The hospital has to have a name to even consider looking. So I went to the local paper to look at birth announcements, but that didn't work out, either. There was a little box that announced three girls had been born at the hospital that day, but there were no names. Nothing. I guess the hospital was short-staffed that week or something," she said with a shrug.

"You're kidding!" Uncle Barry said, looking confused. "I don't understand. I thought those little country papers always printed that kind of stuff."

"I guess this paper is more of a hobby for this old guy than an actual paper. They get the *Austin American Statesman* for real news."

"So what does that mean? Are you going to give up?" Vicki asked, and everyone paused in their dining to hear her answer.

Jane flushed. "I don't think so. I just have to figure out how to continue."

"In Cedar Springs?" Matt asked.

"Well . . . yes, in Cedar Springs. That seems logical. At least for a while."

She noticed the look Matt and Eric exchanged.

"So how is the thesis coming?" her dad asked.

Jane dropped her gaze to her plate. "Hmm. Well, that's . . . kind of in limbo," she said with a wince.

Everyone looked at their plates then. It was fairly apparent to Jane that they all thought she was a flake. Maybe she was. Maybe she was discovering how deep her flakiness went. Maybe all that go-getting, motivated ambition she'd had all her life had been a fluke.

Her mother suddenly stood up. "Anyone need refills?" she asked, wiggling her empty glass at them, and walked out of the room.

No one said much about Jane after that.

Later, when Jane was at her parents' house for the night, she called Jonathan. "Hey, guess what? I'm a day early," she said brightly.

"Oh. Great," he said. "I wish I'd known. I've got a gig tonight."

She had figured as much. "What are you doing tomorrow?"

"I have to work, Janey."

"Okay. Then I guess I'll see you at the Foghorn, right?"

"The set starts at ten. Thanks for coming, Janey. I've got to run . . . but I'll see you there, okay?"

He clicked off before she could ask anything else.

Nicole's husband agreed to watch Sage so Nicole could accompany Jane to the Foghorn. Nicole was excited about her night out without a toddler, and she ordered appletinis for them. They found a table near the stage and caught up while they waited for the set to start.

Jane told Nicole what had happened at the paper in Cedar Springs.

"Well, someone gave the old coot the information," Nicole said. "You should go and ask."

"I did. The hospital has to have a name."

"Not the name of your birth mother—of whoever was working that day."

At first Jane laughed. "That was thirty years ago. You think they still have the work schedule hanging in a back room?"

"No, but I bet they can figure out who was working then. The doctor on duty, that sort of thing. It can't be that hard. It's not like it was the dark ages. It's a fairly modern hospital, right?"

Nicole had a point.

"Hey, there's Jonathan!" Nicole said. Jonathan's band was taking the stage to check equipment. Nicole whistled; Jonathan looked up, and Jane waved at him. He lifted his chin in response.

"What is that, that chin thing," Nicole complained. "Is his hand too heavy? He looks hot, Janey," she said, nudging Jane.

He did look hot. And he looked completely different from Asher. Edgier, maybe. Rock and roll sexy. Any woman would be thrilled to have him as a boyfriend. Jane should have been thrilled. Jonathan was a great guy, perfect for her, and she couldn't understand why it was so hard for her to love him like he loved her. It wasn't as if she could do better than Jonathan. Asher wasn't perfect for her, Asher was a dream. Jonathan, on the other hand, had been there for her for three years. Jonathan was real. Maybe she could make this work. Maybe she just had to focus on it, and it would all come flooding back.

Once the music started, Jane was reminded what an excellent musician Jonathan was. She'd always thought his guitar playing was soulful, but tonight, it transported her. And Jonathan seemed happy to see her when she went up to the stage between sets. He asked her to meet him at his place after the gig. "You still have a key, right?" he asked her.

"Of course!" she said and gave him a quick kiss.

Jane was asleep on his couch when Jonathan came home. He woke her up by smoothing back her hair. "Hey," she said sleepily. "Dude, you were so good tonight."

"Thanks." He eased down onto the couch beside her, pushed a hand through his long hair, and sighed.

Jane touched his chest. "Hey, you," she said. "I'm really happy to see you." She *was* happy to see him. Much happier than she would have guessed she'd be a couple of weeks ago.

Jonathan caught her hand in his and kissed it. "I need to talk to you," he said. Jane stilled. She could hear it in his voice, could sense it coming, and as if to prove it, Jonathan leaned back and dropped her hand. "I am seeing someone else."

Stunned, Jane gaped at him. "Are you kidding?"

"No, baby," he said and pushed a wild piece of hair from her face.

"When?"

He shrugged a little. "Last couple of weeks. It just sort of happened."

Jane suddenly scooted away from him, climbing around him to get off the couch. "Wow," she said. "I don't know what to say."

"Really? I thought you'd be relieved."

"Relieved?"

"Come on, Jane," he said. "It's not like you've really been into us the last year or so."

"What do you mean? I have too been into us. Yes, I moved to Cedar Springs, but that doesn't mean I'm not into us," she insisted, but in her heart, she knew that wasn't true.

"So into us that every time I broached the subject of marriage, you had some excuse about why it wasn't going to happen."

"I said not right now—"

"Not right now, not ever," he said firmly. "Don't kid yourself, Janey. You have been avoiding the whole commitment question for a long time now. And when you went off to Cedar Springs, it was pretty much over. We both knew it."

"I never said it was over! I said I'd be a little while, maybe the summer. What's wrong with that?"

"You can't deny that you left it open-ended."

"Only because I couldn't tell you how long it was going to take."

"Exactly," he said. "A few months, a few years?"

He was right, he was so right. She'd been stringing him along, hoping he'd still be around when she'd gotten through whatever it was she was trying to get through. She hadn't allowed herself to think of what would happen then. It just seemed too big a question, too weighted, too important to consider until she at least knew who she was.

"You're right," she said sorrowfully and sank onto her knees next to the couch. "I've been horrible to you."

"Hey, I never said that."

"But it's true," she said. She laid her head on his lap. Jonathan stroked her hair. Funny, but Jane was already feeling the void. "Who is she?" she asked.

"No one you know. Her name is Elissa. She's a violinist with the Houston Symphony."

That actually sounded cool. "I'm sorry, Jonathan," Jane said tearfully. "I tried."

"I know you did. But it would have been worse if you'd married me because I wanted it. It's okay, Janey. I am cool with the truth." He took her hand in his and squeezed it. "I really hope you find what you are looking for, you know? I don't think there will be any peace for you until you do."

Maybe. Jane wasn't so certain of that anymore.

She left an hour later after the two of them had gathered up the few things she'd left behind in his apartment. "Can I call you to see how you are?" Jane asked a little tearfully as they stood beside her car.

"I'll be mad if you don't." He wrapped her in an embrace and kissed her cheek. Myriad images flashed in her head; their first meeting, the days they'd spent in Galveston. His band. Making love . . . A tear slipped from the corner of her eye, trailing down her cheek.

She got in her car, waved good-bye, and had the sense that now she really didn't know where she belonged.

It was late when Jane got home. She felt a weariness in her bones that felt more like days than hours without sleep. She collapsed onto her childhood bed and fell asleep thinking of Jonathan. She was startled awake by a hand clamping down on her foot.

Jane opened her eyes, squinting.

"Is it true? You and Jonathan are *over*?" Eric demanded.

"What?" she asked grumpily and pulled a pillow over her face.

Eric pulled it away from her face. "Janey, did you and Jonathan break up?"

"How do you *know* that?" she asked and sat up, rubbing her eyes.

"I heard it at the G Street club."

That was impossible. The G Street club was across town. "Man. News travels fast."

"Janey—"

"Yes, Eric, yes. Jonathan broke it off. It's over. Why?"

"Why?" Eric exclaimed. "Because I *like* him? Because you guys have been together for almost three years and we all thought it was going to be Jonathan forever and no one saw this coming? Or because you're my sister and I am worried about you? Come on, Janey, what happened? Is it the adoption thing?"

"The *adoption* thing?" she echoed, pushing her hair from her eyes. "No, it just ran its course. It's over. Couples break up sometimes."

"Do you want me to talk to him?"

"God, no," she said quickly. Her brothers had always been so protective of her, Eric particularly. When they'd been kids, he'd been very disturbed by greasy little Jason Kelvin telling Jane she was the black sheep of the family because of her looks, then making bleating sounds behind her back. Eric had tried to fight him. He'd been six to Jason's nine and the fight had not gone so well for Eric then, but when high school had rolled around, Eric had been a lot bigger than Jason. He'd caught Jason behind the Dumpsters one day and paid him back for all the cruel things he'd ever said to Jane over the years.

"I don't mean about you. Just to see how he is doing, if—"

"Eric—he's with someone else."

Eric stared at her a moment, then sat heavily on his bed. "God, I feel so used."

"It's okay, it really is," Jane assured him. "Jonathan and I . . . it just wasn't going to work. We wanted different things." But as she spoke the words, she couldn't help wondering if they were true. Last night, at the club, she'd thought she'd wanted him. She'd thought she'd always wanted what Jonathan had wanted, and he'd never wanted anything but the best for her. How could a few weeks in Asher's company suddenly make Jonathan an also-ran?

"Man, Janey . . . are you okay?"

"I'm fine." She fell back, covered her eyes with her arm.

"Are you sure? Three years is a long time."

"I'm sure." She was, wasn't she? She suddenly thought of Asher and the way he'd looked at her in the studio, like he'd wanted to crawl inside of her, like she'd been the most gorgeous thing and he hadn't been able to let go. Sex with Jonathan had been good, but he'd never *looked* at her like that. No one had ever looked at her like that, no one had ever made her feel quite that alive and desirable and—

"Hell-oooh, I am talking to you, and you're off in la-la land. What are you going to do?"

"Do?" She hadn't really thought about it. "I'm going back to my job," she said, realizing that she would in that moment.

"When are you going to come back here, where your family is?" Eric asked, squeezing her knee.

"When did you turn into such a family guy?"

"I guess when my sister took off," he said gruffly. "So? When?"

"I don't know. It's all going a lot slower than I thought." Or in a different direction. Everything was in the air and she was drifting along, trying to find her footing in something or someone.

"Janey, look. We're all worried about you. You're giving up so much. And for what?"

That was a good question, and one she wouldn't be able to answer until she finished her search. "I know what I'm doing."

"Really?" he asked skeptically, sensing her lie.

"Eric! I am moving as fast as I can." She was going at least as fast as her heart and emotions would allow her to go.

Which, when she thought about it, wasn't very fast at all, because fast suddenly equated to leaving Summer's End.

26

Riley was happy and radiant the day of her thirteenth birthday.

Asher had surprised her by inviting Tracy, thinking her friend would be a good buffer between Riley and his mother. He'd asked Linda Gail at the last possible minute if Tracy could come along, but Linda Gail had been accommodating.

They rode horses all morning, then Asher's mother took the girls shopping in San Antonio while Levi and Asher rode the Gator. That night, Asher's dad barbequed a brisket. Riley wore a new swimsuit and a thing that tied around her waist and hung to her knees. She and Tracy both had bracelets and lizard tattoos on their ankles, picked up that afternoon during their shopping spree. Asher wasn't crazy about the tattoos, but his mother had assured him they were harmless.

He watched Riley laughing and dancing with Tracy on the pool decking. His daughter was thirteen today, and her transformation was nothing short of remarkable. Just a few short weeks ago, she'd been dressing in hoodies and black T-shirts. Today, he could see in her the stunner she was going to be. She had budding breasts and curves in her hips. Asher had to look away. He really had no idea how he would survive the dating years.

They opened gifts poolside. From Asher, Riley got the iPhone she had desperately wanted. But it was Jane's gift that seemed to make an impression on her. She stroked the thick paper of the sketchbook, examined the colored pencils. She didn't say much, but her expression relayed her pleasure.

"Are you going to draw?" Asher asked her.

She shrugged and smiled a little. "Maybe."

On Saturday, Asher took the kids to Schlitterbahn, a giant water park in San Antonio. He left Riley and Tracy sunbathing on the mock beach while he and Levi tackled some of the slides. When they returned, Riley and Tracy were talking to three boys. *Already?* He was stunned by it and chased the boys away.

"You're funny, Mr. Price," Tracy said with a laugh.

No, he wasn't funny. He was scared.

Fatigued from a morning spent navigating enormous slides, Asher sent the kids off for food and lay on the beach, holding their spot. A beautiful woman with a tail of sleek blonde hair and long, tanned legs strolled by him. She was wearing a very revealing bikini with a transparent cover-up, and she smiled at him the way women smiled when they wanted to be approached.

Asher's body reacted—movies of hot sex with the woman instantly took up real estate in his brain, images that might have heated his blood, but damn it all if Jane Aaron didn't pop into his head and crowd out the images. Happy, smiling Jane and her wild hair was pummeling the sex goddess into smithereens.

It was the same image he'd had running in his brain since that first kiss in the utility room. He heard her laugh, saw her smile, could see her running, or hanging out with the kids.

But Asher wanted her off his mind. He did not want

to imagine what sex with her would be like, or how his days might be a little easier if he woke to that smile every morning. It was a dumb fantasy—he couldn't take up with the nanny. *Get a grip, pal. Think of the complications, think of the kids.*

But the more he thought of the complications, the more they began to erode.

Invariably, however, the pleasant memory of Jane was ruined by the memory of her standing in the studio, looking so shocked. Yeah, well, who could blame her? The signs and symptoms of a bipolar mind could be very shocking, especially for those who were not familiar with it. Jane had been smart to stop him from kissing her any longer. She probably recognized a wagon full of baggage when she saw it. Asher didn't think for a minute that he was worth that kind of baggage to Jane. No one was worth that—well, maybe she was—but not him, and he had no illusions. She could have anyone. She didn't need some forty-year-old guy with a history of heartache hanging around.

It was so unfair, all of it. Unfair to Susanna, unfair to those who had loved her, unfair to her children. Asher had been struggling with her disorder for years. He knew it had not been her fault, that it had been an imbalance in her brain chemistry, but he'd never quite accepted the maddening characteristics of her illness, or the raw fear that his children would inherit it.

And his mother, God bless her, would never be convinced that Riley, especially, didn't have a propensity for the illness. Asher had learned that even the mention of bipolar disorder could put the suggestion in some people's minds. Last year, when Riley had had such a hard time at school and attacked that boy for some perceived slight, the school counselor had said, "Have you considered that Riley might have a treatable condition?" She had not meant the measles.

But Riley had been to therapy after Susanna's death—they all had. Asher had told the school counselor in no uncertain terms that the psychiatrist in Austin had told him flatly that Riley was fine, that she was grieving the loss of her mother.

Nonetheless, Asher had put a lot of energy into hiding the truth about Susanna and keeping his kids safe from remarks and assumptions. Yet Susanna sat like a ghost perched on his shoulder, her presence everywhere, in his children, in their family's collective memories. When he'd told Jane about Susanna and the studio, he'd felt as if a burden had been lifted from him . . . but only for a few short hours. The full truth had crept back into his consciousness, had sunk into his bones again. It was the burden he feared he would never shed. And now it was a burden he had handed to Jane.

Saturday night, while Asher's mother made chicken fajitas, Levi and Tracy walked down to the stable with his father to feed the horses. Asher was on his way there, too, when he saw Riley sitting on the diving board of the pool, her feet dangling just above the water.

"Hey, baby girl," he said as he strolled out onto the decking. "What are you doing? Don't you want to feed the horses?"

"Dad," she said, looking up at him with clear blue eyes, "today Grandma told me I should never be afraid to talk to you if I'm blue."

"Are you blue?"

"No! I was just tired. But Tracy is so bubbly and she talks all the time, and Grandma thinks I should be like her, and if I'm not, I must be blue. It's epically annoying."

Asher smiled. "I can imagine that it is. My advice is to ignore Grandma. That's what I do."

Riley smiled. Then sobered. "But why does she say those things?"

Asher shrugged. "She cares about you."

"No," Riley said, twisting around on the diving board to face him. "What makes her think she needs to say it? What was wrong with Mom, Dad? I mean, I know she got drunk a lot, but what was really *wrong* with her?"

Asher hesitated. God, Riley was growing up fast. He'd always known these questions would come, if for no other reason than Riley would eventually confront her memories. For some reason, he thought of one of those dark days when he'd discovered Susanna had been off her meds and had been cheating on him. "You disgust me," he'd told her.

"Get over yourself, Ash," she'd said hotly, teetering on a pair of perilously high and expensive heels, a drink in her hand. "You think you're so above promiscuity? Don't you ever look at a woman and just think you'd like to fuck her and nothing else?"

"No, Susanna," he'd said hotly. "I don't think that or have a lover because I am married to you. I *love* you. And we have a child who deserves to have a mother she can respect."

Susanna had thrown her drink at him.

It had been all he could do to keep himself from leaving Susanna then, but there was Riley, just three or so at the time, and then Susanna had flamed out of her mania and straight into suicidal depression within a matter of days. He'd come home to find Riley crying and banging on the bathroom door for her mommy, promising to be good. He'd found Susanna inside, on the floor, her wrists bleeding.

The doctor at Shoal Creek Hospital—Fleming was his name—was thin as a reed, with an Adam's apple that bobbed up and down like a cork in the water when he talked. He'd told Asher that leaving Susanna was the worst thing he could do for her and her recovery. He'd said Susanna needed her family's support now more than ever. He'd said that now she was on her meds, she wouldn't act on what the doctor called "hypersexual impulses" with the proper combination of medicine.

"So let me get this straight," Asher had sneered. "If your wife was out banging one of your patients, you'd stick with her, no questions asked?"

"Mr. Price," the doctor had said with strained patience, "would you leave Mrs. Price if she had diabetes? Or would you recognize that something was obviously wrong and seek to help her? Without the proper medications, your wife really can't control her hyper-impulsivity. She has a chemical imbalance in her brain. She's sick. Very seriously ill."

Hyper-impulsivity. Asher had thought of the Energizer Bunny when he'd said it, and it had made him shudder. It had been difficult to wrap his mind around the idea that his wife was seriously ill, that her actions were because her brain didn't function properly, but the more he'd thought about it, the more things had begun to make sense. Susanna couldn't help the drama she created. She was sick. Really sick.

Asher looked at Riley now, wondering if she remembered that day, or the dozens of other days that had followed. He'd thought—hoped—she'd be older than thirteen before she questioned him, but maybe it was time he told her about Susanna. He went down on his haunches at the pool's edge. "Mom was bipolar, honey."

Riley frowned. "What does that mean?"

"It's when people can't regulate their moods and they go from extreme highs to extreme lows. It means that Mom tried really hard not to get depressed and drink, but her brain wouldn't cooperate."

Riley frowned suspiciously. "That doesn't make sense. Like her brain made her drink?"

"In a roundabout way, yes," he said. "The chemistry in her brain was off. People who are bipolar find some sort of relief from it when they drink. I can't explain it very well, but it was something she worked really hard to control with medicine."

Riley looked at the water. "Does that mean . . . does that mean she was really crazy?"

"No, baby girl. She wasn't crazy, just sick. She loved you guys so much, and for the most part, she was fine. But sometimes the medicine didn't work and she got sick and she drank too much and got really depressed."

"Riley!" Tracy suddenly bounced out of the sliding glass doors. "Your grandpa says we can go riding now. Are you coming?"

"Yes," she said and backed off the diving board. She paused uncertainly and looked at Asher. "Will I, Dad? Will I get sick like that?"

He looked into her blue eyes and smiled as confidently as he could. "No," he said. And he truly believed it.

"Are you riding Socks, Ri?" Tracy asked, bounding into their midst. "If you're riding Socks, I am going to ride Bailey."

"I'm riding Socks!" Riley said and looked at Asher. "Thanks," she said. It seemed to Asher that she wanted to say more, but she didn't. She hurried to join Tracy.

Asher stood up by the side of the pool, staring into the water. How could he explain his wife's illness to his children? What could possibly make them understand mania?

It had taken several years of living with it for him to understand it. His first taste of it had been when he'd converted a room in their first house to a studio. Susanna had been thrilled with it and had painted every day, filling the room with easels and canvasses. She'd taken some samples of her work to a local gallery. They'd said they'd wanted to exhibit her work in a fall show. Susanna had been ecstatic. She'd been brimming with ideas and had begun to keep odd hours, sometimes painting through the night. On more than one occasion, Asher would get ready to go to work and find Susanna still up, still painting. She'd made colorful, spirited pieces and talked constantly about her exhibit. "It's going to be a *huge* show," she'd told him, puttering around in her smock. "It could get national attention."

Asher had known nothing about art or the art world, but he'd been proud of his wife. How could he have known she'd been manic then? It wasn't as if he'd gotten a checklist when they married: Behaviors to Clue Spouses into Manic Behavior.

He learned never to say much about her work, however. She'd asked him once what he'd thought about a particular piece. She'd painted the canvas with orange and pink, big swaths of color. "Does it represent the colors of the sun?" he'd asked, trying to be appreciative of the abstraction. Susanna had gaped at him. And then she'd thrown a bottle of paint across the room, barely missing him.

"You're so cruel!" she'd accused him.

It had shaken Asher, but a friend of his had laughed about it when he'd told him later. "Dude, haven't you learned anything yet?"

Still, he hadn't realized anything was wrong, and hadn't until Susanna went shopping again. That time, she didn't just run up a credit card or two. She'd almost destroyed them financially.

Asher would never forget the sick feeling he'd experienced that day. He thought the pain and fear of that afternoon had been what cancer felt like, devouring him from the inside out. He'd come home from a long day to find a pink Jaguar convertible in their middle-class driveway in their middle-class house. Asher hadn't known it was even possible to purchase a pink Jaguar. When he'd gone inside, Susanna had met him at the door, her blue eyes bright, too bright, dangerously bright. "Darling!" she'd cried, and had showered his face with kisses.

"Whose car is that?"

Susanna had laughed, caressed his cheek. "I've had the *best* day," she'd said in her sultry voice. "I found the greatest deals." She'd twirled around and skipped into the living area, and that was when Asher noticed the bags and boxes. They'd been everywhere, covering the furniture and the floor. Susanna had ignored him as he'd walked into the room, gaping at everything. She'd been busy pulling out clothes and shoes and jewelry to show him. And even as she'd chattered away, he hadn't been able to fully grasp that she'd *bought* all of it. It had taken several moments of watching his giddy, excited wife. She'd seemed high to him.

"*High?*" she'd echoed when he'd asked, and laughed, long and loud. "I'm not *high,* Ash! I'm happy! I needed these things and they have made me so happy! Don't they make you happy? Look, look, I bought you this," she'd said, thrusting a watch at him. "You know how your watch is always skipping ahead? I bought this."

That was probably the moment Asher realized she'd bought the car. "We can't afford this!" he'd cried, panicking. "Susanna, what have you done?"

Her bright smile had faded, and a pall had come over her. She'd collapsed as if he'd hit her onto the couch in between the bags and things. "You're always like that," she'd said hopelessly. "You expect so much, and the one time I do something for myself, all you can do is criticize!" And then she had kicked the glass coffee table with enough force to crack it.

Asher had called Helen again. Unfortunately, neither of them had been able to calm Susanna. She'd wound up in the hospital the following day, having gone from raging to suicidal in the dizzying space of twenty-four hours. Helen and her husband, Bill, had accompanied Asher and Susanna, and Asher had sat numbly while Helen had explained to the doctors that Susanna had had anorexia at one point in her life, but that she'd been cured. Asher remembered Helen saying those exact words: "Susanna was cured."

The doctor asked several questions that had made no sense to Asher. But at the end of a stupefying session, the doctor had said, "Mr. Price, based on your wife's history and symptoms, I believe she suffers from bipolar disorder."

Those words had shocked him. Asher had looked at his mother-in-law, but Helen had been gaping at the doctor. It had been the first time anyone had used that term when talking about Susanna.

Susanna had remained in the hospital a week for observation. They'd gotten her on an even keel by beginning what would be a long tail of medications she would take for the rest of her life, cocktails of Ativan, Librium, Klonopin, Xanax, Stelazine, Thorazine, lithium, and more. Some of them had made her groggy. Some of them had made her anxious. In addition to seeing a psychiatrist weekly, Susanna also had to see a psychopharmacologist to keep track of all her medicine combinations. But they'd seemed to work—Susanna had evened out, and Asher had remained cautiously optimistic that they could manage as long as she stayed on her meds.

Their sex life had returned, and it had been good. Hot. But something had seemed a little different—Asher hadn't felt connected to his wife when they'd made love. It seemed to have been all about the sex. It had been a minor complaint.

The happy days had stretched into a year. One day, Asher found empty pill bottles in the bathroom. Alarmed, he'd called her in there. "What's going on here?" he'd asked, holding up the empty bottles.

Susanna had been beaming. "I don't need them."

"You do, sweetheart, you know you do—"

"I'm pregnant!" she'd cried and thrown her arms around his neck. She'd told him excitedly that she'd poured all the pills down the toilet, that she'd never take those things and risk harming her baby. "I don't need them, Ash," she'd assured him. "I'm over it."

She'd been right. In the days and weeks that had followed, she hadn't needed them. It had almost been as if the bipolar thing had never happened, and Asher had wondered if maybe she'd been misdiagnosed again. Susanna had been her old, beautiful self. They'd called Riley their miracle baby. Something about the pregnancy had reset the balance in her. Even Susanna's doctors had agreed her chemistry might have been altered with a change in her hormones.

Riley was a healthy, happy baby, and Susanna had been a great mom. She'd doted on her daughter, and everything was perfect until Riley was about three, and then, just like the first time, Susanna had surprised him completely.

Asher hadn't seen it coming.

At least, Asher didn't think he'd seen it coming, but ten years later, he had a bad habit of second-guessing himself. Had he really not known that his wife was sleeping with another man? Could he have been so blind? Hadn't he worried that Susanna's need for sex was at times insatiable?

It had been the most humiliating period of Asher's life. It was one thing to discover his wife had been unfaithful. It was another to have had one of his partners tell him what everyone else in the office knew.

Asher had been working long hours. He'd hired a housekeeper-slash-nanny because Susanna had begun to paint again and complained she had too much to do and never had a moment to herself. When Rosa had started, Susanna had joined an art appreciation class. "I have to get out of the house," she'd told Asher. "I need to clear my head after being cooped up with a toddler all day. You have no idea how stifling that can be."

Perhaps that should have been a warning.

The class had met twice a week at the Austin Museum of Art. Jeff Green, Asher's partner, had told him that Susanna had met the gentleman there. Susanna had failed to mention him to the man she was married to. And she'd failed to mention to Asher that her lover was a client of GSD&P.

The ensuing confrontation with Susanna had been painful and mortifying. He'd come home to find Susanna ready to leave for her so-called class. She'd been wearing makeup and earrings and high-heeled shoes, and no wedding ring. Asher wondered if he'd ever noticed how she'd dressed for class, if he'd been that blind to what his wife had been doing behind his back.

Worse, Susanna had had the audacity to look annoyed that he'd come home early. She knew. Asher could see in her expression that she knew why he'd come home, and worse, that she was determined to go in spite of it. "What are you doing here? I have to go, Ash. I have to get to class."

Asher had expected shame or denial, not a determination to go to her lover. He'd been as baffled by it as he'd been angry. "You're not going, Susanna. I know what's up."

Yet Susanna had tried to pass him, and Asher had caught her elbow, forced her into their bedroom. Susanna had gone wild, then. Crazy wild. He'd been shocked by it. And Riley, God—his poor baby girl. The little girl had screamed and cried and cowered in the corner as her mother had kicked and scratched at Asher because he would not let her go. Susanna had ridiculed Asher, she'd flailed at him, but when Asher had announced that he was leaving and taking Riley, Susanna had gone tumbling over the edge of reason.

She'd been hospitalized again. Dr. Fleming had used terms like electroshock and mixed-state, and medication and therapy. Asher's wife had been dangerously sick, and as angry and heartbroken and bewildered by it all as Asher had been, he'd had no choice but to take care of her and Riley.

It was Helen's idea that they move to Cedar Springs, away from the art class and closer to her mother. Asher had agreed, but naturally, the move had come with a price—Susanna had insisted on Summer's End. It was more than he'd been able to afford at the time, but it seemed to make her happy, and he'd given in. He'd always given in. As angry as he'd been with Susanna, she'd been so frail and so ashamed, and he'd never been able to deny her; she'd always had that kind of power over him.

In Cedar Springs, the struggle for balance had been a constant in their lives. Susanna had begun to cycle more frequently. She would do something outrageous, like the time she'd disappeared and turned up in Cabo San Lucas. She'd called him. "Let's move here, Ash! It's *gorgeous* here!"

Asher had to take off work to fetch his wife from Mexico.

Then she'd cycle into depression again, ignoring Riley, going for days without getting out of bed, or bathing, or eating anything other than junk food. Helen would have to come to tend her daughter and granddaughter. But somehow, Susanna would rally, and Asher's sex life would go from nonexistent to once or twice a day.

When she cycled, she'd be fine again, but only for a while. Asher had learned to recognize the signs: incessant chatter, grandiose ideas. He'd take her back to the doctors, they'd adjust her meds, and they'd wait. Once, when they were driving back from the doctor's office in Austin, Susanna had put her hand on his thigh. "I am so sorry, Ash," she'd whispered.

He'd looked at his beautiful wife, her eyes full of tears.

"I am so sorry. I know you never asked for this. But I don't know how to stop it."

He'd covered her hand with his. "It's okay, baby. I love you." That much was true. As frustrated and scared and tired as he'd been, he had always loved her on some level.

On the day she died, Asher had known she'd been cycling. She'd been talking about colors and ideas, that incessant chatter. She'd announced she was going to make a painting for the National Museum of Art. She could see it in her mind, this brilliant work, and she'd taken Riley down to the studio to get started on her vision, and it had all gone so horribly wrong.

Asher could not protect his children from all of that truth, especially Riley, and honestly, there were days like today, when he wondered if he should even try. He wanted them to remember the loving mother who maybe had a couple of problems beyond her control—not the maniac. But perhaps that was too revisionist, too unfair to his kids. Maybe the truth would help them. Maybe it would hurt them. He had no idea what to believe.

But one thing he was certain of, as he thought back over the last fifteen years—his kids had been traumatized enough. He couldn't freak them out by acting on his desire for Jane, no matter how much that tiny voice in the back of his head asked, *But what about you?*

Riley didn't say any more about Susanna that weekend. They stayed through brunch on Sunday, but Asher was growing increasingly restless. He'd left things so abruptly with Jane, and he had no idea what he was going back to, or where he'd go from here. Nevertheless, he couldn't stop thinking about her, couldn't stop wanting her. And it was the most agonizing of wants, because he didn't know how to have her—the complications were so damn glaring.

But he'd kissed her, and she'd been a presence in his house, a sun to his children, and he realized that this thing in him, the thing he was feeling for Jane Aaron went well beyond a physical attraction. Jane stirred him up, mixed his thoughts and desires and made him feel like a living, breathing man again. Like a man who wanted a woman.

That thought continued to drum in him, the beat different and tenacious. He wanted Jane. He didn't know if she wanted him, but he wanted her, and he was determined to find out a way.

Asher and the kids were on the road by two Sunday afternoon, and a sense of anticipation was building in his blood. He dropped Tracy off, said a few words to Linda Gail, but was anxious to be on his way. He continued on to Arbolago Hills. He was only mildly aware that Levi was talking about horses.

"Dad, what are you doing?" Riley asked.

"Hmm?" he asked, glancing at her. She pointed to his hand. He was tapping his fist against the wheel. "Nothing," he said and put his hand down. "I just want out of this car."

They pulled up to the gates at his house and he groaned; the gates were too slow to open. Why did he have them, anyway? They were an ostentatious pain in the ass. They finally slid open, and he punched the gas, causing Levi to cry out as he made a sharp right and headed down to the garage. He drove around the curve . . .

His heart sank. There was no red Honda in the drive.

Jane had not come back from Houston, and Asher honestly didn't know if she would.

27

As usual, Nicole was much more grounded about Jane's feelings than Jane. On the drive back to Cedar Springs, Jane phoned Nicole to tell her what had happened with Jonathan, and she confessed to feeling guilty that she didn't feel worse about the breakup. "I'm sad. I will miss Jonathan," she said. "But after three years together, I can't help thinking, that's it? I'm just sad? I should be devastated, but I'm not. I'm really okay. I swear, Nic, my family is brokenhearted, but I'm not. Maybe there is something wrong with my ability to connect."

Nicole laughed.

"I'm not kidding," Jane said. "I could descend from a long line of sociopaths, have you ever thought of that?"

"God, Jane," Nicole said. "Did you ever think that maybe the reason you aren't devastated is because it's been over with Jonathan for a long time now? I mean except for sex and occasionally having something to do on weekends, you haven't really *been* with Jonathan for several months. Think about it. You spent a lot of time looking for your birth mother, you couldn't commit . . . why do you think he found someone else?"

Jane couldn't argue with Nicole's logic. She loved Jonathan—or had loved him at some point—but that love had turned into something else. Deep affection, maybe, she didn't know. But it wasn't heart-stopping all-out love.

It was early evening when Jane turned onto the windy road that led up to Summer's End. She glanced at herself in the rearview mirror—her hair was pulled back into twin bobs, and she was wearing a pink skirt with tiny yellow and white flowers, sandals, and a white T-shirt. She didn't want to think about how she looked. She didn't want to admit to herself that she was eager to see Asher. Hell, he'd probably written her off as a flake, too. After all, she'd practically begged for a kiss, then had run away. That was part of her pattern lately—so uncertain, always in that fog of indecision. She could see that about herself, but she couldn't seem to stop it.

At Summer's End, she punched the code and waited for the gates to swing open, nervous about what she'd find. She continued on, down the drive to the garage, and parked just outside the gardener's shed. She got out of her car and opened the trunk. She was retrieving her bag when she heard Levi.

"Jane!"

Amazing, she thought, how much lighter she instantly felt at the sound of his voice. She whirled around. "Hey, buddy!" Levi ran for her and threw his arms around her legs. Jane leaned over him and hugged him.

Riley was right behind him.

"Wow, Ri," Jane said, smiling. "You *look* older."

"Really?" Riley asked, smiling. "Look, Tracy and I got tattoos." She turned her ankle for Jane to admire it.

"That is mad cool," Jane said. "How was the birthday?"

"It was great. Thanks for the sketchbook."

"You are very welcome. Have you used it?"

"Not yet," Riley said, her smile brightening a little.

"Hello, Jane."

Jane looked up; Asher was standing in the doorway, his hands in his pockets. One lock of golden hair fell over his eye. He looked cool and relaxed, and maybe a little reticent. "Hi, Asher," she said, unable to help her smile. "How are you?"

"Good. You?"

"Me, too."

He nodded. Glanced down. "I'm ordering pizza. Are you hungry?" He lifted his gaze to hers.

Jane's smile broadened. "Actually, I'm starving."

"Then I'll order two," Asher said and smiled a little lopsidedly.

There was a flurry of activity as Jane returned her bag to the guesthouse and then allowed Riley to drag her to her room and show Jane all the things she'd bought on the shopping spree with her grandmother. Not to be outdone, Levi insisted on showing her his new car.

"Yeah, he got a toy for *my* birthday," Riley complained as they descended the stairs. "What am I going to get for his birthday?"

"A piece of cake," Asher said, appearing in the foyer. "The pizza is here. Let's sit on the patio."

They sat around the teak table with their pizza and sodas for the kids, wine for Jane and Asher. Levi regaled them, in seemingly one long breath, about his trip as they ate.

"We went to Schlitterbahn and Daddy and I went down a big slide and Riley and Tracy were talking to boys and Daddy said they had to leave and then we went home and I *threw up* and it was *green* because I was eating a lot of green popsicles and Dad said I was going to turn into a popsicle but I didn't and Tracy has a new boyfriend and they are so dumb they just hold hands and Daddy said Riley can't have one."

Jane cocked a questioning brow at Asher with that one; he playfully rolled his eyes.

Levi continued talking about horses until the pizza was gone, intermittently corrected by Riley. More than once, Jane glanced at Asher, and they exchanged a quiet smile over the kids' chatter. But Asher didn't say much. It felt to Jane as if he was watching her.

By the time they finished the pizza and cleaned up, the sun had begun to slide into the lake, and the kids decided to go swimming. They splashed around the pool while Asher and Jane sat at the table, finishing the bottle of wine. There was an empty chair between them, and to Jane, it felt as wide as the lake. Asher was very quiet and seemed distant to her.

"Sounds like you guys have had a great few days," Jane said.

"It was a good birthday, I think." He looked at Jane. "You look great. Houston obviously agrees with you."

She blushed. Actually, being out of Houston agreed with her more. "Thanks."

Asher turned his attention to the pool again. "I guess the boyfriend was happy to see you."

"*Ahem.* Well . . . not exactly." She self-consciously shoved her hair behind her ear. "It would seem he has moved on."

That prompted Asher to look at her again. "Moved on?" he repeated, as if he hadn't understood her.

Jane splayed her fingers on the table before her. "In other words, we broke up," she said and smiled sheepishly. "He has a new girlfriend."

"Then he's an idiot," Asher announced decisively.

Jane couldn't help but laugh. "He's not an idiot. But I think he was tired of waiting."

Asher snorted, but when Jane shrugged, he said, "Seriously?"

"Seriously."

He shook his head. "He will definitely regret that."

"Thank you," she said, giving him an appreciative smile. "However, to be fair, I wasn't exactly giving him the right signals." She looked at her hands a moment, uncertain how to say what was really on her mind, had been on her mind since the first night Asher had kissed her. "Actually, I've been kind of confused."

When she looked up again, Asher was watching her. "Interesting," he said, his gaze moving over her face. "That would make two of us."

She wanted to ask him why he was confused, if it was the same thing that confused her and had kept her up a few nights, thinking. But all she could manage was, "Really?"

He nodded, his eyes locked on hers.

Jane's belly fluttered. Now she had to ask, she had to know. She felt a little short of breath, as if she'd walked out on a limb without even realizing it. She turned a little in her seat to face him. "I don't know about you, but somehow I have managed to get myself into a situation I probably shouldn't be in . . . but the truth is, I like it."

"That's a dilemma," he agreed, his expression inscrutable. "What are you going to do about it?"

The fluttering in her belly took a little dip. "I don't know . . . do you have any suggestions?"

He pursed his lips together and shook his head. "Unfortunately, no," he said quietly.

Jane's heart leaped painfully. She hadn't understood how badly she'd wanted him to say yes until he'd said no.

"Daddy! Can we watch the hedgehog movie?" Levi shouted.

"Ohmigod," Riley said at the same time Asher sighed and glanced at his watch. She hopped up to the side of the pool. "I'm going to my room."

"Okay, buddy." To Jane, he said, very casually, "Hedge-hog?"

"Ah . . . no thanks." She self-consciously rubbed the back of her neck. She was feeling uncomfortably strange all of a sudden. "I should get ready for work tomorrow." She smiled and stood up, gathering the wine bottle and the glasses. "I'll get this."

She started for the house. She could hear Riley complaining about the hedgehog movie. She could hear Levi splashing in the pool. She could feel Asher's eyes on her, and yet he did not call her back. Jane wasn't sure what to make of it, whether she should be grateful or hurt.

The following morning began as if nothing had ever been out of place at Summer's End. Asher was at work before Jane made it to the house. Carla was her usual cheery self. Jane took Levi to camp and took Riley to Target to buy fingernail polish. She didn't hear from Asher, and she didn't see him Monday night.

Her sense of unease grew. Had she alienated him? She desperately wanted to see him and talk to him. *Just tell me what is going on. Just explain the landscape to me so I know what it is.* In the absence of knowing, Jane took a long, soaking bath. She reminded herself that she'd brought this uneasiness on herself. She'd been up and down and sideways for several months, spinning wheels and kicking up dust, all the while going nowhere. It was time, she told herself, to get her life in order.

It was time to focus on those things that were actually within her control and stop the spinning wheels in her life. She wasn't going to beat herself up about her thesis any longer. She would finish it when she could focus on it. She wasn't going to lie awake every night worrying how Asher felt about her. Right now, and for the next few weeks or however long it took, she was going to focus on the one thing that kept her spinning, that kept so many things beyond her reach and her control: finding her birth mother.

"That is the number one goal, girlfriend," she said to herself. She was resolved. She would search until she could search no more. No excuses.

Toward that end, she was definitely looking forward to Tuesday. She was going to the hospital, and this time, she would not take no for an answer.

28

Tuesday afternoon, Jane marched into the administration section of Cedar Springs Memorial Hospital. The clerk—a box of a woman whose name tag said Brenda—smiled when she saw Jane walking toward her. "You're back. I knew you would be. You guys always come back."

By *you guys*, Jane assumed she meant people involved in adoptions searching for birth records.

"Did you find a name?"

"No." Jane put the copy of the microfiche down on the counter between them. "But I found this."

Brenda picked up the microfiche and read it. She frowned. "That's it? That's all they've got?" She rolled her eyes. "That is such a Mickey Mouse operation."

"That's all I have—but I have an idea," Jane said. "Maybe you could help me find the name of the physician who delivered me. There had to be a doctor on duty that day, right? One who could deliver babies? Maybe the doctor might remember something? You know, Brenda— is it okay if I call you Brenda?—the more I thought about it, I wondered why I didn't think of this before!" She said it brightly, like it was a fabulous idea, like Brenda should jump at the chance to help her.

Not that Jane really expected Brenda to jump to help her, and Brenda did not disappoint. She instantly shook her head. And rather emphatically at that. "I can't do that. I can't give you employee files."

"No, no, not files," Jane said quickly, as if that were preposterous. "Just a name. All I need is a name and I can take it from there."

Brenda frowned.

Jane leaned across the counter. "It's the only thing I've got, Brenda."

"Sorry," Brenda said, not unsympathetically. "We have rules we have to follow. HIPAA regulations have us hamstrung."

"Oh, for heaven's sake, HIPAA doesn't have anything to do with the name of the doctor who delivered a baby."

Startled by a woman's voice, Jane turned to see an attractive woman with strawberry blonde hair and a figure Jane would kill to have. She looked to be in her late forties, early fifties, and her smile was as striking as her cleavage. "I don't mean to interrupt," she said demurely to Jane, and then to Brenda, "now Brenda, hon, you know as well as I do that Dr. White has been delivering babies here since Sam Bass was shot up and laid out in Round Rock. What's the harm of helping the lady out?"

"The harm, Laru, is that we have rules to follow," Brenda said, folding her arms across her chest. "I can't just hand over personnel information to anyone who asks."

"I should introduce myself, shouldn't I?" the woman asked pleasantly of Jane. "I'm Laru Friedenberg. You're Jane Aaron, right?"

"I—yes, I—" Jane was momentarily dumbstruck by how Laru Friedenberg could possibly know who she was, and in that breath, Laru turned her attention to Brenda again and began to tap a manicured finger on a counter, causing the very large diamond she was wearing to glint in the abundance of fluorescent lights. "I know you have rules, but don't you think it's a fair assumption that Dr. White was the one delivering babies . . ." She paused and glanced at Jane. "About twenty-five years ago?"

"Thirty, actually," Jane said.

"Really? I wouldn't have guessed you a single moment over twenty-five." She looked to Brenda again. "About thirty years ago?"

"It was probably Dr. White if he was on duty," Brenda conceded.

"Well all right, then, we're getting somewhere!" Laru said cheerfully. "And if Benny wasn't on duty?"

Brenda shrugged. "I have no idea. But I am not allowed to give personnel information to people without some sort of official documentation. You know that, Laru."

"You mean like a warrant?" Laru sweetly suggested.

Brenda sighed. "You are such a trial."

"Just asking," Laru said with a wink. "Thank you, Brenda. You've given me and Jane enough to get started."

"Whatever," Brenda said with a sigh of resignation. "If you are through manipulating the situation, I have work to do."

"I am," Laru said. "Don't forget book club is meeting at my house this month."

"Are you kidding? I wouldn't forget that. I can't wait to see what rooster is hiding out with you these days."

Laru laughed and looked at Jane. "I'd guess you're wondering how I know you," she said.

"I am," Jane agreed.

Laru tapped that manicured finger to her temple. "I'm clairvoyant. And Macy and Emma are my nieces and they told me all about you. I figured it was you when I overheard your conversation. Not that I was eavesdropping, mind you, but you may have noticed that Brenda's voice carries."

Jane had noticed.

"Now hon, if you will give me fifteen minutes, I will take you around and introduce you to Dr. White. He's a close friend."

"Oh!" Jane said. "Okay—yes, thank you!"

"That is what I call a thousand-watt smile," Laru said with a wink. "Isn't she cute, Brenda? Just as cute as a spotted puppy." She walked away, her heels clicking on the tile floor.

Jane looked at Brenda, who was standing there with a file clutched to her chest. "Oh, she knows him, all right," Brenda said. "Laru almost married him about ten years ago, and it wasn't from a lack of trying on Dr. White's part." She snorted. "And if she needs a warrant, don't think she won't get that, too. She'll call up to Judge Reinhold's office and get one just because she can. They had a little fling, too."

True to her word, Laru came bouncing back about ten minutes later. "Come with me," she said to Jane. "That is, if you've got time."

"I do!"

"We're going to go have a coffee in the perfectly awful cafeteria, and then, in about a half hour, we're going to have an audience with Dr. Benny White."

"Are you kidding?" Jane asked, incredulous.

"Don't look so surprised! Benny and I go way back," she said, flicking her wrist in the direction of back. "I'm sure Brenda gave you an earful," she said, her gaze narrowing. "I'll tell you the truth, Jane—I'm fond of Benny, but I'm a lot fonder of my freedom and the fact that I don't *ever* have to put a roast or anything else in the oven like I had to with my previous marriages." She laughed at Jane's expression. "Did you think I'd sugarcoat it? I'm guessing you're adopted, am I right?"

"You're right. And I'm not having much luck. It's like my birth mother just disappeared off the face of the earth."

"It's a good idea for you to talk to Benny. For one, he's notoriously anal. I think he's bronzed every time card he ever punched. And two, if he doesn't know the answer, he'll find out for you. He's a good guy that way."

"That would be wonderful. I can't tell you just how wonderful," Jane said gratefully.

"So you're living up at Summer's End, huh? I helped Susanna Price decorate that place," Laru said, pausing to tell the lady behind the counter that they needed two coffees. "Randy King, my fourth and last husband, owned a fine furnishings store, and Susanna bought a lot of stuff from him. It's a little palace, isn't it?"

"It's incredible," Jane said.

"And how is Ash treating you?"

The question caught Jane off-guard. She could feel the rush of heat to her face, as if she'd been caught spying on someone through a bathroom window.

"Treating you pretty well, huh?" Laru said wryly. "Well, he is a handsome man, at least as good-looking as the last winning horse of the races. But a word to the wise, sweetie—Ash was completely devoted to Susanna."

Jane's gut twisted.

"I'm so glad you met my nieces!" Laru said, patting her hand. "Did you see little Gracie? She is just about the cutest thing. Let me tell you about Macy," Laru said, and proceeded to tell Jane how Macy had lost her husband in Afghanistan, and had eventually remarried, only to find her first husband was alive after all. And then, in the middle of an entire summer having two husbands, she'd turned up pregnant. Jane was so caught up in the story that she didn't realize the time had gone by until Laru looked at her

Rolex and said, "Oh goodness, there I go again bumping my gums. Benny is probably waiting for us."

Dr. White had thick, wiry brows that matched the gray mop of his hair, and he was sympathetic to Jane's plight. But he was very little help.

Laru was right in that he had records of work schedules that went back three decades. He confirmed he'd been a resident in the pediatric ward then, but that was the only thing he could tell her. "Miss Aaron, I'd like nothing better than to tell you something you could use, but the truth is, I've delivered hundreds of babies. I can't recall anything about your birth. I'm sorry."

"Maybe there was an adoption agency involved," Jane tried.

"There very well may have been. I just don't recall. I am really very sorry."

Jane was dejected. Once again, a door had closed on her. She stood to go. "Thank you so much for your time."

"Well, now, hold up. You know who might remember an adoption or anything like that would be Debbie Carpenter. She worked that maternity ward for years."

A fragile surge of hope filled her. "Debbie Carpenter?" Jane said, repeating the name, making sure she had it just right.

Dr. White nodded. "She's retired now. Lives out on a ranch somewhere. Where is that she lives again, Laru?"

"Now Benny, how would I know?" Laru said with a wave of her wrist.

"Out near Fredericksburg," Dr. White said. "On about sixty acres. Don't think they run anything bigger than goats and dogs. Debbie was a gardener. I wouldn't be surprised if she's not selling homegrown tomatoes at one of those organic places. Is she selling produce, Laru?"

"For God's sakes, I don't know her," Laru said with an impatient shake of her head.

"She was a fine gardener," Dr. White said again. "I used to look forward to all those summer vegetables. Wait here." He walked to his desk and computer and pulled up a screen. Laru looked at Jane and shook her head.

"I had her number at one point, but I'm not sure I still have it." He took a moment, scrolling through some screens. He bit his lip and shook his head, but jotted something down. "Take this," he said. "I don't think that's any good, but it's the only number I have for her."

Jane looked at the number she held in her hands. "Thank you."

"If that doesn't work, I bet you could stop in at the visitor's center and they could tell you where Debbie and John Carpenter live."

"Thank you," Jane said again. "Thank you so much."

"Wish I knew more," Dr. White said.

"Good luck, Jane!" Laru trilled as Jane went out, the number clutched in her hand.

As soon as she reached her car, Jane called the number Dr. White had given.

The phone rang several times. Jane was just about to hang up when a man answered with a gruff hello.

"Ah . . . Mr. Carpenter?" she said hopefully.

"Who?"

"I am looking for a John or Debbie Carpenter, and—"

"Wrong number," he said abruptly.

"Are you sure? I—"

"Yeah, I'm sure—wrong number. I've had this line for five years now, and there ain't no Debbie here." He hung up.

Okay, well—not the answer she'd been hoping for, but Jane was nonetheless buoyed. She had marched into that hospital on a mission, and she had come out with a name. A name! Thanks to Laru, whom Jane never would have met if she hadn't come in today. And now, for the first time since she started her search, Jane had something concrete to work with.

She felt good. She felt like she was finally taking steps in the right direction.

Debbie Carpenter was out there, and Jane was going to find her.

29

*W*hen Tara told Asher that a meeting with the AT&T representatives would be happening in Dallas at the end of the week, he told her to send Scott.

Tara instantly stopped what she was doing and turned fully around to look at him. *"Scott?"*

"Scott."

"Scott Blakely, the junior, still-wet-behind-the-ears Scott?"

Asher glanced impatiently at her. "He is an account manager. And he's going to be very important to the AT&T account."

"Okay . . . but *you* always go."

Asher shrugged and looked at his computer. "I need to spend time with the kids. Scott can handle it. If he gets in over his head, I'll make the next trip."

He didn't hear Tara move. When he looked up, she was staring at him. "Is everything okay?"

"What? Yes," he said, and gestured to his desk. "I've got work to do."

"Yep," she said briskly and went out of his office.

Asher sighed guiltily. Tara had been his stalwart assistant since long before Susanna died. He'd always been pretty open with her, but he could not tell her what was on his mind now. He wondered if he was falling in love. It had only happened to him once before, and he couldn't

recall what that had felt like. But this . . . this was con-
suming him. It was almost surreal; his children weren't
as impossible to deal with as they had been. He suddenly
enjoyed sitting at the dinner table with them, listening to
them talk about their day instead of a litany of their com-
plaints.

Jane's presence in their lives made him believe all
things were possible. Her presence made him think of
family and hearth and home, all of which was new for
him, because for years, his castle had also been his dun-
geon. It was brighter and warmer at Summer's End than
he could ever remember it being.

He wondered if it was possible he might have a happy
future. He'd dared not think it until now, but he'd come
to believe that he had to at least try for something different for himself before his hope dissipated and life
returned to the same heart-aching drudgery he and his
children had known since Susanna died.

With that in mind, Asher went home early Tuesday,
but Jane had already left for the afternoon. He had dinner
with his kids, did a little work afterward, but it was pointless—he couldn't focus. He was determined that today he
would step out of the shadows and no longer pretend his
desire didn't exist. If Jane didn't want that, then he'd go to
Plan B. Not that he had a Plan B, but he would deal with
it. Somehow.

When he had Levi in bed and Riley was in her pajamas
in front of her laptop in her room, he returned downstairs
to see if Jane had come in yet, disappointed to see that the
red car was not in the drive.

He was sitting on the patio in the dark, trying to think
of what he might possibly say, when he heard her car pull
into the drive. A moment later, Jane stepped in through
the gate. She was carrying a book and a cup he recog-

nized as coming from the Saddle-brew. Her head was down, and she looked lost in thought.

"Jane?"

He startled her; Jane gasped and her head jerked up. "Asher!" She pressed her book to her heart a moment. "You scared me." She looked around, peering into the dark. "Where are the kids?"

"In bed. I didn't mean to startle you. I was hoping we could talk," he said.

"Oh." Her hand fell. "Okay."

He wasn't very good at this. Frankly, he sucked at this. He gestured to the loungers. "Would you like to sit?"

Jane glanced at the guesthouse, then at the loungers. "I, ah . . . okay," she said hesitantly. She sat carefully on the end of one.

Asher sat across from her. He wasn't entirely sure how to proceed. "I've done some thinking."

"I think I know what you're going to say," she said low, her gaze on her hands.

That surprised him. Was he that damn obvious? "You do?"

"Yes. And I completely understand."

Asher arched a brow. "Understand what?"

"Us," Jane said, looking up. "Not *us*," she quickly clarified, "but . . . you know."

"No." His heart began to flag. All that wanting, all that hope, sinking before he could even express it. "No, I don't know."

"Come on, Asher," she said softly. "You made it pretty clear Sunday night, didn't you? I know this is not a good situation. I mean, obviously not, with the kids, and everything you guys have been through, and you being the boss and me being . . . well, me not being the boss. And I know that you . . . well I would guess that you have a lot of choices and opportunities that don't include teachers from east Houston, *especially* the type that probably seems a little flaky, which, trust me, I know I am, and if I had any doubt, my brother made it painfully clear. So don't feel like you need to . . . finish this off," she said, gesturing with her book between the two of them.

"No, Jane, you've misunderstood me—"

"I can be pretty astute at times. I know that's not obvious, but yeah, I can be," she said, folding her arms across her body now.

"Wow," he said. "You've got it all figured out."

"Yep." She smiled thinly. "No worries."

"You've got it all figured out, but you left out one important detail."

"Right," Jane said, but her brows knit. "I did?"

"You left out the part where I am crazy about you. I want you."

Jane gasped. Her shoulders suddenly softened. "You do?" she asked hopefully.

Completely. Insanely. "I do." He glanced at the house. "I apparently should have said so sooner, but I'll let you in on a secret," he said, and shifted his gaze to her again. "I'm not very good at this. Honestly? I have no idea what I'm doing."

She smiled. "Me either."

"I only know that I can't continue just walking through life, Jane. I can't be a monk for the sake of my kids, and until you came along, I didn't realize how dangerously close I was to being one. I would like . . . I would like to spend time with you." *I want to make love to you.* "I would like to get to know you." There. He'd said it. He might have lost his touch, but he'd gotten his point across.

But Jane didn't answer right away, and his heart

skipped a beat. "What are you thinking?" he asked her warily.

"That I wasn't expecting that. I thought, after the other night—"

"Right," he said. "Like I said, I'm not very good at this."

She smiled, and a small shiver skirted his spine. "Actually, you're pretty damn good. And I would really like that, Asher. I would really like to know you, too." She stood up, smiling down at him. "Would you like to come in? I've got some beer."

Oh yes, God yes. Asher nodded.

Jane walked to the door of the guesthouse, opened it, and looked back at Asher before stepping inside and leaving the door standing open.

He slowly stood up and looked around the patio. Okay. He followed her to the guesthouse, stepped across the threshold, looked around, and saw packing boxes along one wall. "Are you leaving?" he asked, alarmed.

Jane looked at the boxes and smiled. "No. I never unpacked. I wasn't sure if I was going to stay here." She laughed a little nervously and put her book and coffee down, then tied her hair at her nape before turning to look at him. She smiled.

"Are you . . . are you sad about your breakup?" Asher asked as he stepped deeper into the room.

Jane pressed her lips together and shook her head. "Remember what I told you about my search? I think I've been searching so long that I accidentally left some things on the trail. I think my relationship with Jonathan was over before I realized it. Before I even came here. It just took me a while to get it."

"I know the feeling."

"You do?" She didn't look as if she believed him.

Asher sighed. "I think I should explain some things."

"Oh. Okay," she said. "Would you like a beer?"

"No, thanks," he said, waving her off. "I just need to get this out in the open."

Jane blinked. She slid onto a bar stool. She gestured to the one beside her, but Asher shook his head. He needed to stand for this.

"I told you about Susanna's drinking, but there was a little more to it than that." He took a breath and steeled himself. "She was bipolar. Extremely so. She cycled between mania and depression."

Jane's eyes widened. "Oh, my God . . . I had no idea."

"Not many do," he said, and told her some of Susanna's history, leaving out the more gruesome details. As he talked, Jane stared at him, unblinking, her eyes full of horror and sorrow. "My point in telling you is that I think I tried to keep it together for so long that I lost some things along the way, too."

"I'm so sorry. How horrible that must have been for you."

"No," he said, shaking his head. "I don't want your pity or sorrow. It's over and done. I've moved on. The kids come first, obviously, but you said . . . you said, take care of yourself, and I realized that I've been alone in my heart for so long that I don't know how to ask anymore."

"Oh, Asher," she said, sliding off her stool.

"I want . . . I want life, Jane. I want to be part of your life, if you'll let me." *Let me step into the light.* "I need to be part of it, if only for a time," he added, and swallowed. "I'm not asking for more than that. Only that you let me be here. With you. For as little or as long as you'd like."

Jane gaped at him.

Asher had asked too much. He knew it, he'd asked too much, and now he had to leave before he humiliated himself further. He turned toward the door, but Jane caught his hand before he could take a step. He half turned, wary of her.

Her amber brown eyes twinkled up at him. "Be in my life," she said. "I don't know where this will go, I don't know what to expect, and I don't want to make any promises I can't keep . . . but I really want to be in your life. So yes, Asher, please . . . be in my life." She rose up on her toes and kissed him.

That kiss roused a fire-breathing dragon that roared to life in Asher. His heart began to beat a hard staccato. Her words, her kiss, all of it, was intoxicating; he was drunk with relief and joy and desire. He cupped her head in his hands and kissed her fully. He could feel the life spread to his limbs, stirring inside him. He ran his hand over her shoulder, down her arm, laced his fingers in hers. "I missed you," he said, the words sliding off his tongue before he knew they were there.

"I missed you, too."

Asher tangled his free hand in her hair, undoing the knot, lifting it to his face. "This was never my intention. I wanted you, but I told myself I wouldn't touch you."

"Touch me," Jane urged him, and pushed her face into his neck and kissed him as she wrapped her arms around his back. Her breath was warm, her lips soft and moist against his skin. A raw shiver shuddered through him, and Asher twisted her around, put her on her back on the bed and crawled over her. He cupped her lovely face and looked at her sparkling eyes, her luscious mouth and sexy smile, and her hair spilling all around her. His mind moved past the questions and the fears, raced headlong into the need to be with this bright, vibrant, beautiful woman. Jane could do that to him—somehow she made him need her, physically, emotionally.

There was an erotic chaos and eagerness to their love-making, Jane's lips singeing his skin every place they touched him. Her fingers trailed down his body, to his hips, to his cock. She tasted sweet to him, and the cool, airy scent of her cologne aroused all of his senses. She felt just as he'd imagined she would in his arms—soft, yet strong, and sweetly eager.

Somehow her shirt opened, and he moved down her body, to her breast, pushing her lacy bra aside. With his mouth he ravished her, with his hands, he caressed her. He traced his fingers over the tattoo that had tantalized him, outlining the cross, kissing it.

Jane's breath grew shorter, her lips warm and moist on his skin. She inflamed him, forced him to bear down, to hold on, to savor every sensual moment of it. There were two kinds of lovers, Asher thought wildly. Women who could satisfy a man's lust, and women who could destroy a man's reason. Jane was definitely destroying his reason. She was moving provocatively with him, her touch as tantalizing as it was demanding, her gasps and groans awakening even stronger desires.

His hand slipped under her skirt and between her thighs and Jane sighed with pleasure, as if she'd been waiting for his touch. He got out of his clothes and looked down at her. Her lids were heavy, her mouth slightly open as she drew deep, quick breaths. Her body, so perfect to him, so voluptuous, seemed to almost shimmer in the low light. Asher sank into her with a long sigh of relief from the years spent in his own private prison.

Being inside her was the salve to an old wound, a slip of heaven. As he moved in her, stroking her with his body and his hands, Jane moved with him, her breath coming in pants, her hands and mouth more insistent until she cried out in ecstasy. Asher's own tsunami of desire flooded over him then and washed him away with her, tumbling him in wave upon wave of sheer rapture.

He had no idea how long he held her or how long they lay there, wrapped in each other's arms. He no longer worried that he was falling in love with the nanny.

He had fallen.

30

*W*ith his leg draped over Jane's, Asher was propped on his elbow, tracing the outline of the Celtic cross tattooed on her hip bone. They had not moved from the bed, but lazily talked about little things.

"Why the cross?" Asher asked, leaning over to kiss it again.

Jane giggled. "That," she said, touching her finger to his, "was something I picked up in Ireland on my way to Italy. I was moved by some of the more mystic parts of the Emerald Isle. And there was excellent Irish whiskey involved."

He chuckled and pushed her hair from her face. "So do the Irish sparkle, like the Italians?"

She grinned, happy that he remembered. "I'd say the Irish are a little gloomier." She laughed at herself. "It's so beautiful there. Have you ever been?"

"Only Dublin. I had an account there a couple of years ago, but I never had time to get out and look around."

Jane had an image of them standing on the cliffs or walking through the forests there. Maybe someday, who knew? She looked at him now, his hair falling over his brow, his muscular shoulders and thighs. She could picture him in Europe, a lone traveler.

"Where else did you go that summer?"

"Ireland and Italy. Paris. Greece."

"Wow," he said, nodding. "That's quite a trip. And you were alone for all of it?"

"Yep. It's kind of funny—I felt edgy, but I thought it was wanderlust. I thought if I just got out and saw the world, then I'd feel right. I didn't want to go alone, but my best friend, Nicole, wouldn't come because she was pregnant, and there wasn't really anyone else I would ask who was free. Honestly, I was okay to go by myself. I thought I needed the time to explore me."

Asher didn't say anything. He ran his hand over her thigh.

"Does that sound weird?"

"Not at all. It sounds enlightened. Did you find you?"

"No," she said with a giggle. "I just brought home more questions. I think I realized that what was making me edgy was all the missing information about me. That's when I resolved to try and find out more."

"And how is that going?" he asked as he pressed his palm against the plane of her abdomen.

"Suddenly pretty good. I met a woman at the hospital, Laru Friedenberg—"

"Ah, Laru," he said, nodding. "I know Laru. Everyone knows Laru."

"Really? Well, she helped me find the name of the nurse who was working in the hospital when I was born."

Asher lifted his gaze from her body. "Where? Here?"

"She is somewhere near Fredericksburg. I have to find her. There's a good chance she might know something about my adoption. It's a long shot, but at least I actually have a shot for once." It felt good to say that. She had a shot, an actual shot.

"That's really good news," he said.

"You have no idea," she agreed, and at his curious look, she smiled as she touched her finger to his lips. "It's the first lead I've had. It seems like the closer I get, the harder it becomes, so I really need this to turn into something."

"Harder? I'd think it would get easier."

Of course he'd think that. Jane shook her head, ran her hand over the top of her head. "It's not like that for me. It's been really hard, and God, you'd think a psych major might have some insight into what's so hard about it, but I don't. I had a lovely childhood, you know? I have wonderful parents and two great brothers and aunts and uncles and grandparents and cousins. I always knew I was adopted, and I was so well loved, and honestly, I never really thought of it until . . . until one day I read something about how we are all our past, and our pasts are our present, and our present is our future. . . ." Jane smiled. "That sounds ridiculous, I know. I'm really not very good at explaining what I am feeling."

Asher laughed. "Join the club. But I think I know what you are saying."

"All I know is that my past is lacking in my present. There are things I want to know, that I *need* to know, and not knowing seems to color everything. Not knowing somehow has prevented me from moving ahead with my life in certain areas. But I've made up my mind. I am entirely focused on finding my birth mother. I am not going to worry about anything else until I have exhausted all the leads."

"I admire you for even trying." He leaned down and kissed her. "And I will help you in any way that I can."

"Ah," she said, and cupped his face and looked into his eyes. "That's so sweet."

Asher pulled her in close to his body and kissed her

deeply, then reluctantly lifted his head. "I have to go, babe," he said softly. "It's after two."

She nodded. He touched her chin, then stood up and pulled on his pants. Jane sat up and wrapped her arms around her knees, watching him. "So . . . where do we go from here?" she asked.

He pulled his T-shirt over his head, combed his hair with his fingers. "I don't want the kids to know, not yet."

"Yes, I think it would be a little weird for them."

He frowned. "I don't like sneaking around," he said. "This feels so right, Jane, you have no idea how right it feels. I need to do this for myself—but at the same time, I have to think of what's best for my children. I think we need to be sure of what we're doing before we even think of telling them." He paused. "Are you okay with keeping this to ourselves for a while?"

"More than okay," Jane said, somewhat relieved. "I don't think either of us wants to be the cliché here. I'm all for taking it slow and seeing where it goes first."

"Thank you." He smiled, leaned over, and kissed the top of her head. "Did anyone ever tell you that you're cute?"

"Yes. Casey Randall told me in the ninth grade."

He laughed and kissed her good-bye for the time being.

Did you take some happy pills or something?" Riley asked with a hint of disdain early the next afternoon. They'd just returned from the library, where Levi had picked up a book about dinosaurs. "You're so laughy."

"Laughy? Is that a word?" Jane asked cheerfully. She felt excited and fulfilled, and perhaps most notably, Jane felt as if she was where she truly belonged for the first time in months.

"You're just like, weird," Riley said.

If this was weird, Jane was weird, because she felt happy.

They walked through the kitchen into the den. Jane paused to look around at the familiar furniture. This was surreal. Just a few days ago, she'd been in this very room with no clue of what was to come, of how her thoughts and feelings and even her disposition would change. It was so sudden, so complete. Maybe . . . maybe she'd fallen in love with Asher. Was falling.

"Can I have a snack?" Levi asked.

"You can have some grapes," Jane said and walked back into the kitchen. *Do I love him?* she asked herself. She certainly hadn't thought about much else besides Asher for the last several days, and today, with the exception of Debbie Carpenter, Asher had been the only thing on her mind. She kept thinking of last night, of the way they'd come together. It just seemed so perfect, so meaningful to her. *Are you romanticizing it?* No, no . . . this was real. She could feel it in her bones.

Jane put some grapes on a plate and returned to the den. "Nothing else before dinner, Levi," she warned him, knowing very well that he would eat his weight in gummies if he could get away with it. She looked at Riley, who had turned on her laptop. She knew a lot about these kids now. Could she, in a distant future, be a mother to them? She smiled a little, imagining them as one happy little family, then happened to glance up. Her gaze fell on the portrait of Susanna.

Jane's little smile faded.

She quickly sat down next to Levi, and while Levi looked at the pictures in his book and Riley talked about her latest earth-shattering conversation with Tracy, Jane tried to picture what life had been like at Summer's End before Susanna had died. Levi had only been a toddler, but Riley must have noticed the changes in her mother. Jane had studied bipolar disorder for a class, so she knew a little what this family might have endured, and it was sobering. She glanced at the portrait of Susanna again. That portrait was eerie to her now, even a little creepy. It almost felt as if Susanna was looking at Jane, telling her that she knew what she was doing with her husband.

Jane shuddered and looked down. Yes, very surreal.

When at last Riley's convoluted story about Tracy had come to its glorious end, and the kids had settled down to watch TV, Jane stepped into the office off the kitchen and called information, asking for Debbie Carpenter in or around Fredericksburg. The operator came back with two numbers. "Do you have an address?" she asked in that harried voice of someone who was counting the minutes until her shift ended.

"Unfortunately, no. May I have both?"

The operator gave her the first number for a Deborah Carpenter. The second was D. Carpenter. "I'll connect you with the second," she said. "Hold for the number."

The phone rang twice. Jane worried the eraser of the pencil with her teeth, frantically thinking what she would say when someone answered. On the third ring, a man answered. "Hi!" she said. "I am trying to find Debbie Carpenter of Fredericksburg. She lives on a ranch outside of town, and I was wondering, could this be her number?"

"No, ma'am, you've got the wrong Carpenter. This is Dan Carpenter."

Jane could feel her body sag with disappointment. "Sorry to have bothered you," she said and hung up. She was phoning the second number when she heard the mudroom door open and Asher's footsteps.

Grinning, Jane stepped out. Lord, but he was handsome in his suit and tie, his face illuminated with his warm smile. He slipped one arm around her waist and pushed her back into the office to kiss her. Jane made a halfhearted attempt to resist him, whispering something about the kids.

"Right," he murmured. His hand fell to her hip, skimming down her skirt, finding her skin beneath. "God, I missed you today," he said and kissed her neck.

"Me, too," Jane whispered.

"Daddy!"

Levi's voice came from the kitchen. Asher instantly broke away from Jane, but his eyes were locked on her. "Yeah, buddy?" he called.

"I have a new book!" Levi called, and Jane could hear him padding across the kitchen, coming toward them.

"Great!" Asher said, and with a wink for Jane, he stepped out of the office before Levi reached it. "Dinosaurs, cool! I love me some tyrannosaurus rex. Come on upstairs with me and we'll look at it."

A moment later, with the feel of Asher's hands still warm on her skin, Jane walked out of the office. The late afternoon sun was slanting in the windows, and it cut across the portrait of Susanna.

Jane shivered.

She returned to the guesthouse and called the second number she had for Debbie Carpenter. It rang four times before voice mail picked up. *"You have reached the Carpenter residence. We can't take your call at this time, but if you—"*

Jane hung up. She didn't know what sort of message to leave; she'd try again later.

The days that followed looked normal, but for Jane and Asher, they consisted of stolen moments where they could manage it. Mostly, they had to make do with an exchange of looks across the heads of the kids.

It was great for Riley and Levi—Asher and Jane's desire to be together meant they spent the week playing games or watching movies together after dinner. Or Jane and Riley sat together flipping through magazines, planning Riley's fall wardrobe, while Asher and Levi wrestled on the floor or looked at his book of dinosaurs.

Jane tried to imagine living her life like this with Asher. With the kids. On the one hand, it felt natural. She loved the time she spent with them, even when Levi was acting out or Riley was in a mood. She felt part of them. On the other hand, she still had the same questions and doubts about herself and what she was doing with her life. She called the Carpenter number twice more, finally leaving a bit of a rambling message on the third attempt. She made a list from the phone book of all the Carpenters in and around Cedar Springs—five in all—and began to call them, hoping against hope that someone knew Debbie Carpenter. She had no luck.

Nevertheless, for the most part, Jane was very happy in this new relationship. At night, when the Scrabble or Monopoly board was put away, Jane and Asher always went their separate ways. But when Asher was sure the kids were asleep, he'd sneak into the guesthouse and he and Jane would make love. Afterward, they would talk about anything and everything. The more Jane knew Asher, the deeper her feelings went.

Asher was wonderfully attentive to her in a way Jonathan had never been. It was different somehow, as if he needed her happiness to feed his own. They discovered many things they had in common: they both loved burgers and disliked sushi. They both liked to read thrillers and watch foreign films. Jane discovered that Asher's cousin,

Jack Price, was married to the international pop singer Audrey, which she thought was very impressive. Asher discovered that Jane's cousin Vicki had won her bowling league, which he found equally impressive.

They started running together in the mornings. Asher went to work late. Carla was particularly suspicious of this sudden change in him, but Asher explained that it was the heat of summer and most people straggled into work late. He told Jane later that Carla hadn't seemed to accept that explanation.

From the things he told her, Jane had a picture of Asher as a man who tried to do the right thing but who was torn between a career and his kids, torn between Susanna's memory and the need to move on. She'd sensed he was a loner from the beginning, but for the first time, she began to see how lonely he had been in his life. She understood it all too well.

Her feelings for Asher were growing. She didn't know if it was love, but it was something very powerful. He was the only thing she was entirely certain of, and oh, how he moved her. She discovered in him a tender heart in a strong and capable man. A sexy, handsome man. And he made her laugh! This man, whom she had thought was the devil incarnate, made her laugh; deep, belly, tear-producing laughs.

Time flew. The days grew hotter and longer. The Fourth of July fell on a Sunday, and Asher and Jane started that day with a run. Later, Asher was taking the kids to Helen and Bill's for fireworks and a barbeque. He'd invited Jane along. When Asher had mentioned it to the kids the previous day, Riley had said, a bit incredulously, "She's going to Grandma Helen's?"

"Yes," Asher said. "It will be fun."

When Asher and Jane returned from their run, they

walked into the kitchen for water. Riley was sitting at the kitchen island, eating cereal.

"I was thinking we could all go to brunch," Asher said as he filled two glasses of water from the fridge. "Jane, are you up for that?"

"Sure!"

Riley's spoon clanked against her bowl. She looked at Asher. "She's going to brunch with us, too? I thought she had weekends off. Why is she hanging out with us?"

"Riley!" Asher said sternly. "Don't be rude. What's the matter with you? It's a holiday—do you expect Jane to sit in the guesthouse alone?"

"Why didn't she go to Houston? I thought people went home for holidays," Riley said, looking at Jane.

"That's a long drive for a day," Jane said. Her cell phone rang; she picked it up off the kitchen desk. "And besides, I don't want to miss the fireworks."

"I don't understand your attitude," Asher said to Riley as Jane answered her phone.

"Ah . . . hello. I am trying to reach Jane Aaron, please?"

"Speaking."

"Dad, are you kidding me?" Riley said loudly at the same time the woman on the other end of the line spoke. "What about *your* attitude?"

"I'm sorry," Jane said and stepped outside. "Could you repeat that?"

"I said, I'm sorry I didn't get back to you sooner, but I went to Indiana to see my sister, and I don't get up there as much as I'd like, so we decided to make a little vacation of it and took a few weeks off."

"I'm not sure who I'm speaking to," Jane said, confused.

"Debbie Carpenter," the woman replied politely.

31

*J*ane's heart began to pound. "Hello, Mrs. Carpenter! Thank you so much for calling me back."

"I hope I didn't call at a bad time."

"No, no, not at all," Jane assured her. "I'll try not to take too much of your time. The reason I am calling is because Dr. White gave me your name. I was looking for nurses at Cedar Springs Memorial in nineteen eighty, nurses who might have worked in the maternity ward."

Debbie Carpenter chuckled. "I was a nurse in that maternity ward for thirty-five years. Did Dr. White tell you that? He is such a good doctor, especially with the babies."

"Yes, he told me. He was trying to help me and gave me your name as someone to talk to."

"Well, that's all you needed to say. What can I do for you, Jane?" Debbie asked cheerfully.

Jane took another deep breath and expelled it along with, "I am trying to find my birth mother. The only thing I know is that I was born in Cedar Springs on April twenty-fifth, nineteen eighty. The hospital won't give me any records, and the *Cedar Springs Standard* only had some vague mention that three girls and one boy were born in that week. That's all I have. So I thought that perhaps someone might remember something—"

"Oh my goodness, Jane, that was a long time ago," Debbie said. "Excuse me—*I'll be right there!*" she called out to someone. "What was I going to say? Oh yes. I worked at Memorial all those years and retired three years ago. I can't possibly remember all the babies that came through there."

"Yes, right, I know it's a stretch," Jane said a little desperately. "But I thought maybe the fact that it was an adoption might jog your memory. It was a private adoption, and I think only a lawyer was involved."

"Hmm," she said thoughtfully. Jane heard a male voice in the background. "Honey, I said I'd be right there," Debbie said. "Don't they have an adoption registry or something?" she asked Jane, sounding reluctant. "Isn't that a better way to go about it?"

"I've tried that, but both parties have to sign up. And the lawyer passed away a few years ago. The court records are sealed. I am running out of options."

"Well, you know, sometimes there's a good reason for that."

Jane bit her tongue to keep from telling Debbie there could be no *good* reason that she shouldn't be allowed to know who'd brought her into this world. What possible *good* reason could there be that most humans knew their parentage, and she knew nothing?

"Oh, Lord, my husband is about to drive me batty. We're going to a family picnic today. Are you free to come out to the house late this afternoon? We ought to be back around four or so. I've got some things I can look at to see if it will jog my memory."

"Yes!" Jane said. "Yes, thank you, Mrs. Carpenter. Are you sure? I know this is asking a lot—"

"You sound like a nice girl, Jane. Come on out and we'll see if we can't dredge up something. But I can't promise you anything. I want to be really clear—the chances of me remembering anything to help you are probably pretty slim. But I'm willing to try for Dr. White's sake."

Jane closed her eyes. "I know it's a long shot, Mrs. Carpenter. I know that you probably cannot help me. But I have to try, and I can't tell you how much I appreciate your effort."

"Well then, come on out," Mrs. Carpenter said. "Do you know where Highway two eighty-one intersects with two ninety?"

"Yes," Jane said and listened attentively to the directions.

After they'd agreed on a time, Jane walked back into the kitchen. Her head and heart were spinning with hope and anxiety at once. Debbie Carpenter seemed pretty sure she wouldn't remember anything . . . but what if she did?

"I just don't see why she has to do everything with us," Riley was saying as Jane walked in.

"Why is it suddenly a big deal?" Asher asked irritably. "I thought you liked Jane." To Jane, he said, "Sorry, Jane."

"Daddy, can we go water my garden?" Levi asked.

"In a moment."

"I like her as a nanny, but not glued to our side," Riley said.

"I am hardly glued to your side," Jane said calmly.

"You didn't seem to have any problem with her being around last night when you needed her for Scrabble, did you?" Asher reminded Riley.

"Why do *you* want her around?" Riley shot back. "What's the matter, did Tara get tired of you?"

"Tara?" he said, looking confused a moment. "Oh, my—Riley, did you think I was seeing Tara? No, honey. Tara is my assistant. That's all."

Riley colored—she clearly had believed that. "I don't

care what she is," she said flippantly. "I just don't want her hanging around. Or Jane. She's supposed to be here when you're at work, not all the other times."

"She can be around whenever she likes," Asher said tightly. "We're not running a prison camp here, so let's get a few things straight. I am allowed to have friendships besides you and Levi. That means with Tara, or Jane, or anyone else. I don't see any reason that Jane can't participate in the things our family does. Why would we exclude her?"

"Maybe because she's not our family?" Riley asked sarcastically.

"Watch your tone, young lady," Asher said sternly.

"I don't want to go to brunch," Riley said and abruptly stood and flounced from the kitchen.

"Come back here and clean up your mess!" Asher called after her, but it was pointless—she was already halfway to her room. He looked at Jane.

Jane shrugged a little. It didn't surprise her, really—Riley had a very strong sense of how the world should be ordered.

"So much for brunch," Asher muttered.

"Daddy, can we go water the garden now?" Levi asked.

"Yeah, come on, kid," he said. He looked at Jane. "Everything okay?" he asked.

"Yes. Really good. That was Debbie Carpenter, the nurse."

Asher's eyes widened. "No kidding?"

"Daddy, come on," Levi said, already at the door.

"No kidding," Jane said. "She wants me to come and meet her this afternoon. I have to go—I'm sorry, but I'll miss today's fun. Can I take a rain check?"

"Yes, of course," Asher said as Levi grabbed his hand and pulled. "And given the scene we just had, it's probably not a bad idea for your sake."

"That will blow over," Jane said confidently, gesturing toward the stairs, but she noticed that Asher didn't look so sure of it.

Levi opened the door. Jane smiled down at him. "Asher, you'd better go before Levi tugs your arm off. I'll see you guys later, okay?"

"Good luck," Asher said as Levi dragged him out. "I'll keep my fingers crossed for you."

Debbie Carpenter lived at the end of a narrow two-lane road, bordered on both sides by Hill Country vineyards. Her house was a split-level, with a wide bottom floor and a square addition up top. Dr. White had been right about her hobby—her yard was planted with azaleas and hollies, black-eyed Susans, columbines, lantanas, and sage.

Debbie looked much like her house, with wide hips and a sturdy torso on top of them, and a short crop of graying curls. She'd said she'd retired from nursing three years ago, but when Jane drove up, Debbie walked out to greet her wearing a scrub top that had little stick figure children all over it.

"You must be Jane!" she said cheerfully as Jane climbed out of her car.

"Thank you so much for taking the time," Jane said, shaking her hand.

"Oh, think nothing of it! It's nice to get a little company out this way. Come on around to the back. I thought we'd have coffee on the patio."

Debbie's patio was a redbrick semicircle attached to the house, shaded by a pergola. The backyard, like the front, was planted with something on every square inch, including a vegetable garden. The view beyond her yard was a pasture where cows were grazing.

"Those belong to my husband, Yank. He has about fifteen cows that he tinkers with so he can call himself a rancher. But he wouldn't sell a one of 'em." Her laugh was warm and deep.

The coffee service was set up on a tempered glass patio table. The chairs were covered in a loud, floral-print vinyl. There was a plate of home-baked cookies, too, which Jane found terribly endearing. Personally, she'd never understood the appeal of drinking coffee outside when it was hot and humid, but they were fortunate this afternoon— there was a bit of a breeze in the shade to keep them from melting.

"Do you have children?" Jane asked as Debbie handed her a cup.

"Oh my, too many. I have six," she said proudly. "All grown, all doing their thing." She pointed to a prefab shed that sat in the corner of the yard. "See that? Full of riding toys. I've got three grandchildren and two more on the way." She beamed at Jane.

"Congratulations," Jane said. "This seems like the perfect grandma house."

"We try," Debbie said. "And Lord knows they come around often enough. Tell me about yourself, Jane. Are you happy with your adoptive family?"

"Yes, very happy." Jane gave her the quick description of her family. Debbie laughed when Jane explained to her she was hopeless in a pool of natural-born chefs.

"Well, it's good to hear that you were taken in by such a loving family," Debbie said. "God was looking out for you."

"I think so," Jane agreed. "I've had a great life, but I would like to know where I come from. Unfortunately, the only thing I have to go on is that I was born here on April twenty-fifth, nineteen eighty."

Debbie squinted out at the pasture. She shook her head. "That's not much to go on, is it?"

Jane's spirits began to flag. She'd guessed this would lead nowhere, just like all her ideas. It almost seemed as if the universe was conspiring against her.

"But I've thought about it," Debbie added. "I don't know if what I am going to tell you has anything to do with you or not, but I thought I'd tell you anyway. I mean, you've come all this way. I'd sure like to help you if I could."

"Oh . . . thank you," Jane said, sitting up a little straighter. "What things?"

"Well, for years there was another nurse who worked maternity with me. Gwen Wright was her name. Anyway, I remember when I went out on maternity leave with my youngest, I had lunch with Gwen one day so she could see the baby. I remember her telling me she had a family friend who had gotten into trouble and was going to give her baby up for adoption. But the family wanted to keep it all very hush-hush. I don't know if she told me they were very wealthy or I just assumed it, but that's what I think. This wealthy family wanted to keep this girl's baby a big secret."

Jane's pulse began to quicken.

"Anyway, they'd arranged for a private adoption and I think Gwen told me that it was a lawyer who took care of it all. Didn't you say it was a lawyer who handled your adoption? I am almost certain Gwen told me some slick lawyer came over from Austin and handled it all."

Now Jane's breath was shortening and her palms were damp. She was going to have an anxiety attack. "Did she say any more than that?" she asked quickly. "Did she say the baby's name?"

"Not that I recall. But I remember clear as a bell that Gwen was sitting there holding my little Bruce, and she was very upset that the poor mother only had about an hour with the baby before it was taken away."

Jane's heart stopped beating altogether. "That's it? An hour?"

"Now Jane," Debbie said, reaching across the table and patting Jane's arm, "I don't know if that was you. I only thought of it because I had Bruce at the end of March, and I think it was about a month or so before I saw Gwen. It could have been any baby born in that hospital, and I may even have my timing off. But I thought it was worth mentioning to you."

"And the family?" Jane asked, rubbing her palms on her shorts. "Were they from around here?"

"Well that I don't know. Gwen was Cedar Springs born and raised, and I think she said the girl was a family friend."

"That means she could possibly be here," Jane said, her mind rushing ahead. "I mean, even if she's not, there's bound to be someone who might know. Is Gwen here? Do you think I could call her?"

"Oh, Jane," Debbie said, her face falling. "I should have said that right up front. Gwen lost her battle with breast cancer about a year ago."

Jane didn't even realize she'd spilled her coffee until Debbie jumped up and said, "Don't you worry about that. I'll get something to wipe it up."

She hoped Debbie would bring a very big rag with her, because Jane would need it to wipe up all the disappointment she felt pouring out of her. She was one year too late. One lousy year.

32

*I*t was after eleven when Asher and the kids arrived home. He put Levi to bed straightaway, turned off the light, and stepped into the hallway.

The door to Riley's room was closed, but Asher could see light under her door.

He retreated to his room, walked out onto the balcony, and looked down at the guesthouse. Lights were still on. He could call Jane and ask if he could come down, but he decided to surprise her. He needed to see her in the flesh to satisfy his sense of unease.

Jane opened promptly when he knocked and grinned when she saw him. "Hey, you."

"Hey, yourself," he said and reached for her as he stepped inside, pulling her to him to kiss her.

"Where are the kids?"

"In bed."

"How were the fireworks?" she asked, brushing her fingers over the shadow of his beard.

"Boring." He smiled and kissed her again. "How was your meeting? Did you learn anything?"

"She had a great story to tell me," Jane said. "Not the story I wanted to hear, but a story." She recounted her visit with Debbie as she retrieved a couple of beers from her fridge. She handed one to him. "But when she had finished telling me about this friend of a friend, she said, 'Oh, sorry, Jane, I should have told you earlier. Gwen died of breast cancer about a year ago.'"

"No way," Asher said, stunned.

"That's what I said. But it's true." Jane gave him a tremulous smile. She opened her mouth as if she meant to say something, but then suddenly sank down to her haunches.

"Jane!" Asher exclaimed. She had her arms around her legs, her face in her knees. *"Jane."* He squatted next to her, embracing her, helping her stand.

"I can't believe it," she said tearfully. "Every clue I find is a dead end." She laid her head against his chest and let Asher hold her. "I don't understand why I don't get to know where I come from."

He certainly couldn't answer that.

She sniffed and leaned back, rubbed her hand under her nose. "I'm sorry. But it's been a very frustrating journey for me." With a weary sigh, she slipped out of his embrace, picked up her beer, and took a seat on the couch. Asher joined her. "I don't know what else to do," she said. "I'm at the end of my rope, and I am so disappointed. I have needed this for so long now."

"Well . . . maybe Gwen Wright had family in town," Asher said. "If she knew about it, her family probably did, too."

"I thought of that," Jane said, nodding thoughtfully.

"You know who might know?" he said. "Laru."

"Do you really think so?"

"I do. And if she doesn't know, she would know who to ask."

Jane grabbed his arm; her eyes fired with hope. "Asher, that's a *great* idea!"

He loved the shine in her eyes. He loved the way she

lit up his life. He loved everything about her. He put his beer aside, playfully pushed her back on the couch, and kissed her. "Hey, Levi and I got you a present today."

"You did?" She smiled with pleasure. "What is it?"

He grinned, reached in his pocket, and pulled out a cheap, bright pink plastic ring.

Jane gasped. She covered her mouth with her hand, then said, "It's *beautiful*. You must have spent a fortune!" She slipped it on her finger. It was a gaudy, monstrous thing, but she wiggled her fingers like it was a diamond.

Asher laughed and kissed her again. And again. Yet as much as he would have liked to remove her clothes and put his hand and mouth on every inch of her skin, he still felt a little uneasy. Even though everything seemed fine, he couldn't shake the feeling. Perhaps it had been that light from Riley's room that had done it. He wondered what his daughter was doing while he was here, kissing Jane. He lifted his head. "Is the monitor on?"

"No. Let me get that," Jane said and scrambled out from beneath him to turn it on.

He despised all the hiding they were doing. He didn't want to continue this way, as if he were ashamed of Jane. He'd announce it to the world when he told his kids, but that was the rub. He didn't know how to tell his kids, and especially Riley, who was acting so strange all of a sudden. She'd been so testy earlier, almost as if she suspected something was going on between him and Jane.

The sense of foreboding began to creep back in, and Asher stood up.

Jane looked surprised. "Are you leaving?"

"I think I should. The kids," he said.

"I understand." Jane looked disappointed, but she didn't argue. "We're running tomorrow, right? At seven?"

"We're running. And we're doing four miles," he said with a wink.

"Slave driver! You really are trying to train me for a race, aren't you?" she laughingly accused him. He grabbed her up and kissed her, playfully dragging her along as he walked to the door. As he reached to open the door, Jane grabbed his head in both hands and rose up on her toes to kiss him. Asher couldn't resist her; he held her up with one arm around her waist and kissed her back as he opened the door. Jane's hand slid up his chest, to his neck—

"Dad."

Riley's voice, full of revulsion, startled them both. Jane gasped and shoved against him, but Asher stood there dumbly, his arm still around Jane. Standing just beyond the door, gaping at them, was his daughter. "Riley—"

Riley shot a dark look at Jane as she whirled around and ran back to the house.

"Oh *shit*," Jane whispered.

That was the very least of what Asher was thinking. "Riley!" he called and went after her.

He found her sitting at her desk in front of her laptop as if she'd never left this room. She didn't look at him as he walked in and stood there with his hands on his hips. Slowly, he noticed the room itself. There were drawings tacked up on one wall, and his heart climbed to his throat. Riley was drawing again. Thank God, she was drawing. It was enough to make a father want to weep.

"I can't believe you," she said. "That is so gross, Dad. The *nanny*? Are you seriously hooking up with the nanny?" She turned to look at him, expecting an answer.

"Her name is Jane," he said calmly.

"*Are* you?"

He clenched his jaw; he couldn't lie to her. "We are seeing each other, yes."

"Oh *God*," she said with disgust and twisted around in her chair, her back to him.

"Listen to me, baby girl," he said, walking deeper into the room. "There is something really cool between me and Jane, something very real. I will always love Mom, but she's been gone a long time." He stopped short of telling her he was a man and he couldn't live like this, without a woman, for the rest of his life. "People need companionship and love."

Riley twisted around to face him again, her mouth gaping open in disbelief. "What are you saying?" she cried. "You *love* her?"

"I'm saying—"

"It's your fault Mom is dead, you know. If you hadn't been so mean to her, she never would have left that day. Did you do it on purpose, Dad? Did you do it so you could hook up with *nannies* and *secretaries* and *whores*?"

"Don't," he said, pointing at her, his anger barely controlled.

"You don't care about me or Levi—all you care about is *sex*." She ran into the bathroom and slammed the door behind her, locking it.

Thirteen years old or not, her accusation stung Asher. He could hardly wrap his mind around the fact that those words were coming out of his daughter's mouth, much less that she believed them. He braced his arms against the bathroom doorjamb. "Come out, Riley!" he demanded. "Let's talk about this."

"I don't want to talk to you!" she shouted.

"Riley, come—"

The sound of the shower reached him. She had turned it on full blast to drown him out. Asher stared at the door.

He had never intended for this to happen, not like this. He didn't want to hurt his daughter, he didn't want to reopen old wounds. But neither could he live like he'd been living for the rest of his life.

He had no idea what to do, at least in the moment. But he would not allow his thirteen-year-old daughter to dictate the course of his life.

Jane was pacing in front of the big bay windows, waiting for Asher to come down. Her heart leaped when she heard his footfalls; as he walked into the kitchen, he looked tired. "So?" she asked.

He sighed, pushing a hand through his hair. "It's not good," he said and recounted his conversation with Riley.

"Oh, no," Jane said. "What are we going to do?"

"I don't know." Asher tucked a strand of hair behind her ear. "When I finally coaxed her out of the bathroom, she let me know in no uncertain terms she did not approve of me making out in the guesthouse. She said it was gross. She said we were gross. I tried to explain to her how attraction works, that I have a life outside of her and Levi, but it didn't do much good. I think she fears I am replacing her mother."

Jane winced. "Understandable. How are you doing, Asher?"

He gave her a wry smile. "I am conflicted," he admitted. "I want to protect my kids like any father. I want them to be happy. But at the same time, I can't forget that I have a life in there somewhere. There has to be a middle ground for us, but I'll be damned if I know where it is tonight."

Jane bit her lip. She felt responsible for his conflict and Riley's unhappiness. "Maybe I should move."

"No," he said instantly, and touched his fingers to her

chin, forcing her to look up at him. "No. Let's ride it out a couple of days. Give me some time to think about it. Don't worry, Jane. This will all work out."

She wished she could be as confident as he was about it.

"I'm beat," he said, pushing a hand through his hair. "We better call it a night. I'll see you in the morning. Four miles," he reminded her.

"I am *so* looking forward to it," she said with playful sarcasm. She kissed him good night, but as she went out, she couldn't help noticing just how tense and conflicted he looked.

His expression hadn't changed much when they ran the next morning. More telling, perhaps, was that Asher talked about everything but Riley.

As for Riley—she had not come down for breakfast when Jane arrived at work later, but Levi was up and dressed in his favorite camo shorts for camp. "We're making whirly birds today," he said. Jane had no idea what that meant, but Levi was anxious to get there.

When she returned, she walked past the garbage cans on her way inside, and something caught her eye. Jane paused and looked again. There were several pieces of thick sketch paper tossed carelessly onto the top of the trash can. She picked one up. It was a drawing of the lake. More specifically, it was a drawing of the lake at night, from the vantage point of one of the balconies. A moonlit lake drawn from Riley's balcony. No wonder Riley had appeared when she had. She'd probably been on her balcony and had seen Asher come into the guesthouse.

Carla met Jane when she walked into the house. "What is wrong with Riley?" she asked, eyeing Jane suspiciously. "She refuses to come out of her room."

"She's being thirteen," Jane said. "I'll go talk to her."

Jane marched upstairs to Riley's room and knocked on

the door. "Riley, it's Jane. I want to talk to you." A moment later, the door opened. Riley tried to walk past Jane without looking at her, but Jane put her hand on the girl's arm. "Hey, come on, Ri, I'm standing right here."

"Yeah, I can see that," Riley said.

"I know what you saw and you must—"

"I don't care," Riley interrupted. "Really, Jane, I don't care. You and Dad can do whatever you want to do."

"I think you *do* care."

"Oh, great, the counselor has returned," Riley said with a roll of her eyes.

"I'm an adult, Riley. There are things I know that you don't know. For example, sometimes men and women can't help their attractions," Jane said.

"Oh, God." Riley turned around and walked into her room.

Jane followed her. "Sometimes, the heart just knows what it knows and you can't fight it."

"I already heard the 'people have needs' speech," she said in a mocking voice. "And I don't care. I don't want to hear about it; it grosses me out. I really just want you to leave me alone." She sat down at her desk with her back to Jane.

"Okay," Jane said. "If that's what you want, I'll leave you alone. But when you're ready to have a mature conversation about this, let me know."

Riley suddenly exploded. "A mature conversation? You *lied* to me!"

"What? What did I ever say that was a lie? I have never lied to you. I have been very honest with you."

"How can you even say that?" Riley said with a cold laugh. "The only reason you are here is because you want my dad. You're poor and he's rich, and you want to get in on that."

"Oh, Riley," Jane said wearily. "There is so much you don't understand—"

"I am *thirteen*, Jane, and I understand things way better than you know," she said, her features turning hard. "You made me believe that you were here for me and Levi. You said we could be friends, that you would always be there for me. But you were here to get laid."

Jane's pulse jumped. "You're really wrong about that, Riley, and I will be more than happy to discuss it with you if you can speak like a young lady and not someone who crawled out of the gutter."

"Oh, yeah, that's telling me," Riley scoffed.

Jane bristled. "You think you're so mature? Does a mature young woman destroy her art because she's mad at me? That hurt only you, not me. That was the act of a little girl throwing a tantrum, not a mature thirteen-year-old expressing her concerns."

"Hey!" Riley said angrily. "You're the one who crawled out of the gutter if you're going through the trash—"

"I didn't go through the trash," Jane snapped. "You left it lying on top, in clear view, so it was impossible to miss. You wanted me to see it and know that you were mad."

Riley's cheeks colored. "I really want you to leave now," she said coolly.

"Look, I know you hate me right now. But I will tell you honestly that neither your father nor I ever intended for this to happen. I took this job for you and Levi, and I wasn't lying when I said I would always be there for you. I will be. But Riley, something changed between me and your father. The sooner you accept that it happened, the sooner we can figure out how we're going to deal with it."

"You are, like, epically stupid," Riley said calmly. "I don't have to deal with anything."

"No, of course not. Little girls dig their heels in and refuse to talk to anyone. Young women learn to stand up for themselves in a way that other people will respect."

"God, will you please just leave?" Riley cried.

Jane walked out of Riley's room and closed the door behind her. She found herself questioning everything, not the least of which was whether or not she should be here at all.

"Well? Is she coming down?" Carla asked when Jane came downstairs.

"Probably not," Jane said and continued on to the guesthouse. She wouldn't allow the drama with Riley to derail her. Jane called Laru.

"I know exactly who Gwen Wright was," Laru said unequivocally when Jane reached her. "That was so sad. She was only fifty-eight. Her mother died of it, too. Why are you asking?"

"It's a long shot," Jane admitted. "But Debbie Carpenter thought Gwen might have known something about a private adoption that happened about the time I was born. She said Gwen had indicated it was a family friend. I thought maybe some of her family might know."

"Gwen doesn't have much family to speak of," Laru said. "Her father has Alzheimer's and her son is in Iraq. But her husband still lives on Elm Street as far as I know."

"He does?"

"Ken Wright," Laru said. "It's on the corner of Elm and Loquat. I don't know the exact street address, but it's a green house with black shutters and a yard full of azaleas. Ken does like his azaleas. They all do in that part of town."

"Thanks. Thanks so much, Laru."

Jane found the house after she picked Levi up from camp.

"Who lives here?" Levi asked.

"Just a man. Stay here, I'll be right back," Jane said. She walked up on the big wraparound porch and knocked on the door, then stood back, waiting for an answer.

"Hell-oooh!"

Jane turned around and saw a woman standing across the street in the middle of another yard full of azaleas. She had a large brimmed gardening hat and was holding a spade. "If you are you looking for Ken, he's been working that swing shift. He gets home every day around two," the woman offered.

Jane groaned. She couldn't come back at two today— she had to take Levi for a dental checkup.

"I can tell him you came by . . ."

"Thank you, but that's okay," Jane said with a wave. "He doesn't know me. I'll stop by another time."

At the end of that stellar day, Jane couldn't wait to see Asher. She was a little surprised by how much she needed to see him. Fortunately, Riley had given them a reprieve— she'd hastily arranged a sleepover with Tracy.

When Levi was soundly asleep, Asher came to her in the guesthouse.

"Hey," Jane said when he opened the door. Asher responded by striding across the room to her, grabbing her up, kissing her madly as if he hadn't seen her in days or weeks instead of a couple of hours. Jane reacted ardently; she needed his strength to surround her, his touch to reassure her.

"I thought this hour would never come, either," he whispered roughly into her ear, as if she had spoken those thoughts aloud.

Their connection ran deep, Jane realized. Their desire was entirely mutual, and Jane knew as she submerged herself in him—really knew—that she loved Asher. They made love like it was the last time, as if they would never see each other again, as if there was nothing more important, more demanding than sharing that intimacy.

Afterward, they lay in bed, their bodies entwined, talking softly about the last twenty-four hours. Jane told Asher about her phone call with Laru. "I'm going back tomorrow," she said. "I'll go back every day until I can talk to him."

Asher told Jane about the trouble with the BMW account as he lazily brushed his cheek with the ends of her hair. "I don't want to go to Germany again," he said. "But I may be forced to go if things don't turn around."

"What is Germany like?" she asked.

"Cold," he said. "But the beer is excellent."

"Aha, I thought so. I always envied those guys in lederhosen with giant steins of beer. They always look like they are having so much fun."

"Do the Germans sparkle?"

"Oh no," Jane said, and teasingly bit his earlobe. "Germans are industrious. Big workers over there. It's more of a haze."

He laughed. "I didn't know you were so familiar with the work habits of Deutschlanders."

"Yes." Jane stretched long. "Ask me any nationality, and I will tell you."

They played the game of nations, as Asher called it, and then Jane listened as he told her about ending up in a German pub where the steins had indeed kept flowing in his direction, courtesy of some jovial Germans he'd met. They talked about Jorge's work on a retaining wall, and how prices had gone up at the pump. It seemed to Jane that they talked about everything, but talked over and around what had happened with Riley.

It was almost as if Asher had forgotten. But as the hour grew late, Jane finally broached the subject. She had to. Riley knew. Their secret was no longer a secret. "I was thinking . . . maybe we should sit down with Riley and try and explain things to her. You know, have a meeting of the minds."

Asher immediately shook his head. "She won't listen."

"She might."

He sat up. "I don't want to talk to her about it. I don't want to deal with it."

Surprised, Jane watched him as he pulled on his shorts. "But we have to deal with it, Asher. I think Carla already suspects, and Riley will surely tell her. Then everyone will know."

He put his hands on his hips and stared at the floor a moment. "I know we have to deal with it. And I know I'm being selfish about it, but Jane, I want this." He looked up at her. "I want *you*. I want what we have right now, and I don't want Riley to ruin it. I can't live my life by her rules."

Jane certainly understood that. "Everything is so blasted hard, isn't it?" she asked, pulling a T-shirt over her head. "What we have is so wonderful, Asher. I can lie here with you and think, *This is meant to be.* But then the sun comes up, and Riley is so angry and hurt, and I keep butting my head against the wall in my search. I haven't even *touched* that damn thesis, which makes me wonder if I ever will, and to top it all off, I got an email from my principal today. She has to know by next week if I want my job or not."

"Wait—what?"

Jane got off the bed and walked to the French doors,

where she looked out at the pool. "She has to know by next week if I am coming back so she can make class assignments." She risked a look at Asher then. He was staring at her, his expression incredulous. She smiled a little self-consciously. "I guess sooner or later, one of us is going to have to fish or cut bait, right?"

"Excuse me?"

"I mean that sooner or later, we're going to have to decide where this thing between us is going, especially now that Riley knows."

"Are you trying to tell me something, baby?"

Jane looked at the gorgeous man standing before her, full of honor and integrity and all those things women yearned for. She wanted him to tell *her* something, to assure her that this could work, that she'd find her birth mother, that Riley would be happy, and everything would be okay. "No. I'm just thinking ahead. We can't keep our affair a secret anymore, and I think we should talk about where this is going. Where it could possibly go. Where we *want* it to go."

"God," he said. "I don't know what to say."

Her heart fluttered madly; she looked down. He was going to tell her he couldn't commit, that he loved her, but not like that. That he had his kids to consider, and so on.

"I have felt things for you that I have never felt for another woman," he said, his voice low. "I'll be totally honest, Jane. I am in love with you."

Jane gasped.

"What?" he asked, frowning a little. "Is that a surprise? Can you not see that I do? Don't you know it? Yes, I have fallen in love with you," he said, moving to her. "And I don't want to lose you. But . . ." He took her hand, rubbed his thumb over her knuckles. "I can't tell you where this is headed. Not yet. I know where I think I'd like it to go, but it's too soon to be so definitive, isn't it? I have two other people to think of. The only thing I know with any certainty is that I do not want to lose you. So I want you to stay." He kissed the corner of her mouth. "Please stay." He kissed the other corner and whispered, "Tell me you will stay."

Jane's heart swelled with love and despair. As mad as it made her seem, as crazy as she believed herself to be . . .

He took her arms, put them around his neck, then pressed his body against hers. *"Tell me."*

"I can't tell you that," she said softly.

Asher slowly lifted his head.

"I have fallen in love with you, too, Asher. And I'm selfish because I want you to want me to stay. I want to stay here with you, but honestly? I don't know if I *can* stay."

His arms began to slide away from her. He sank back on his heels. "What the hell does that mean?"

"Look . . . we obviously have some issues here. Your daughter is not ready for you to have someone else in your life. I am focused on finding my birth mother. There are a lot of variables in our relationship right now, and I need to be sure of some things before I can decide if I will stay. We both need to be sure of some things."

"Those sorts of issues can bring people together, you know. They don't have to push us apart."

"Maybe in the land of wishful thinking they bring people together, but come on, Asher, we both know that's not always true. I need to think about it all. Don't you? Shouldn't we be able to tell Riley what this all means?"

Asher frowned. "How long will it take you to think all this through?"

Here she was again, telling a man she loved that she

didn't know how long it would take her to figure things out. But this time, Jane felt a pressing weight on her chest. This time, she had a great deal more to lose. She sighed, tired of herself, and shook her head. "I don't know," she answered honestly.

33

*A*t least one thing was going right at Summer's End. When Jane picked up Levi from camp the next day, Charlotte told her his behavior had improved. "I don't know what you did," she said, "but he's been a model citizen all week."

Jane had no idea, either.

Levi sat in his booster with two Transformers in hand. "Where are we going?" he asked as Jane pulled away from the park and headed north instead of south.

"We are going to the library," Jane said cheerfully.

"Can I get another dinosaur book?"

"Yes, you may. And when we are through there, I have to stop by and see a man about something, and *then* we'll go and pick up Riley from Tracy's house."

At the library, Jane stared out at the parking lot, her mind spinning around her conversation with Asher while Levi looked through several books. At two o'clock, she put Levi in the car and drove past the town square, then turned into the older part of town with the old Victorian homes. She made a right onto Elm Street and pulled up in front of the green house with black shutters.

"We've already been here," Levi said, as if she'd forgotten.

"I know. But this time, I think the man will be home."

She unbuckled her seat belt. "I have to speak to this gentleman, Levi, so I want you to be on your best behavior."

"Okay," he said agreeably, unbuckled his belt, and got out with his Transformers.

Jane put her hand on his back and led him up the walk. They hadn't even reached the steps of the porch when the door swung open and a gentleman who looked to be sixty or so stepped outside, wiping his hands on a dish towel. He wore glasses and Dockers, and his gray hair had been slicked down and combed neatly back. "Hey there," he said. "You must be the lady that come 'round yesterday."

"Ah . . . yes, sir," she said. How did people in this town always *know* things?

The man smiled a little at her apparent confusion. "Got a pretty observant neighbor across the way. What can I do for you?"

"I am sorry to bother you. My name is Jane Aaron, and this is Levi."

"I have Transformers," Levi said, holding them up.

"Mm-hmm," the man said, without sparing Levi much of a glance. "I've got to be downtown in about fifteen minutes. What can I do for you?"

"Mr. Wright?" she asked. He nodded. Jane smiled. "Debbie Carpenter gave me your name, sir. I'll say this as quickly as I can. I'm adopted."

"What does 'dopted mean?" Levi asked.

"I'll tell you later," she said, clamping down on his shoulder. To Mr. Wright, she said, "The only thing I know is that I was born in Cedar Springs on April twenty-fifth, nineteen eighty. I have tried everything I know to find out who my mother was, but with no luck. Debbie Carpenter remembers your late wife had a friend who came to Cedar Springs to have a baby, and she gave it up to private adoption. It fits the time that I was born, and I think it could have been me."

Her voice broke when she said it; she quickly cleared her throat.

Mr. Wright didn't say anything.

"I am probably going down another rabbit hole, Mr. Wright," she said desperately. "It was thirty years ago, and I don't expect you to remember. But it's my last shot and I thought it was worth asking. Did your wife ever mention a friend who gave a baby up for adoption? Do you know who it was?"

Mr. Wright tossed his towel onto a chair on the porch and adjusted his glasses. "I remember it. Upset Gwen something awful. She didn't think she needed to give up her baby, but the gal wouldn't listen to her. Gwen had a soft heart that way," he said.

Jane gasped. "Do you . . . do you remember the woman's name?"

"Now, that I can't tell you," he said. "I'm sorry, but I don't recall her name. She was a friend of Gwen's family, not anyone I ever knew."

"Oh, no." Jane felt her knees weaken.

"I hate to be the bearer of bad news here," Mr. Wright said. "But it wouldn't do you much good if I could recall her name because she died a couple of years ago in a bad car accident."

That statement was so startling that Jane couldn't respond at first.

"So did my mommy," Levi said. "It was a *big* crash."

"She hit another car just square on out there on the highway. Tore Gwen up something awful. Sorry to have to tell you that, ma'am. I'm real sorry."

"No, thank you," Jane said, trying to find her bearings. "Thanks for the information, sir."

"You bet. Good luck, ma'am."

"Thanks."

He opened the door of his house and walked back inside. Jane heard the turn of the lock.

"It's hot," Levi said. "Can we go?"

Still, Jane couldn't move. She was rooted to that sidewalk, her hand on Levi's shoulder. It wasn't possible. It *couldn't* be possible. She looked at Levi, at his almost black hair, his blue eyes, and suddenly removed her hand as if he'd burned her.

"Can I get in the car?" he asked.

"Yes," she said, and followed him down the walk to her car, her legs shaking, her gut churning to the point she thought she would be sick.

Something felt wrong when Asher came home from work Thursday evening. The house seemed too silent. Too dark. He walked to the kitchen, but there was nothing out of the ordinary, no smell of recently cooked food. He continued on to his office to put away his things. He couldn't hear any stirring of life upstairs, either. He returned to the living room, carelessly discarding his coat and tie. As he pulled his tie free of his collar, his eye caught a flash of blue outside. He moved to the French doors and looked out. Levi was splashing around in the water; Jane was sitting in a lounger, looking out over the lake.

"Hey, Daddy!" Levi said when Asher stepped out. "Watch me, watch me!" He climbed up onto the grotto to the first level, where Asher expected him to stop and jump. But Levi climbed up to the next rock, and the next.

"*Levi!*"

Levi grinned and leaped. Asher's heart stopped; he watched in horror as Levi landed in the pool. A moment later, Levi's head popped up. "Did you see me?" he asked excitedly and swam to the side.

"I saw you, buddy, but I don't want you to do that again. It's too high." He looked back at Jane. She was gazing at him strangely, as if he were a stranger. "Jane? I don't think it's a good idea that Levi is jumping off the top level."

"Can I jump here?" Levi asked, pointing to the second level.

"*No.*" Asher pointed to the shallow end. Levi very cheerfully jumped into the shallow end and began paddling around, heading for the zero edge, where he could create little waterfalls with some of his toys.

"Jane," Asher said, taking a seat on the lounger beside her. "Where is Riley?"

"In her room, avoiding me."

She seemed distant. She looked sick. "What is the matter with you?" he asked softly. "Are you okay? Are you unwell?"

She made a sound as if she was trying to catch her breath and couldn't.

Her demeanor alarmed Asher. "Jesus, Jane, what is the matter?"

She looked at Levi, who was on the far side of the pool. "You knew my birth mother better than anyone," she said.

"*What?*" he said, recoiling. He had that slightly queasy feeling he used to get when Susanna would begin to cycle, that sixth sense that all hell was about to break loose and there was nothing he could do to prevent it. "What the hell are you talking about?"

"It was Susanna," Jane said, her eyes filling with tears. "She gave birth to me."

The queasy feeling got stronger, and he suddenly stood

up. "I don't know what you think you are saying, but you aren't making any sense—"

"I went to see Mr. Wright today," she said, sitting up. "He remembered the woman Gwen Wright knew. He remembered her because his wife was so upset about the adoption. But he couldn't recall her name. And then he told me it wouldn't have mattered, because she died a couple of years ago in a head-on wreck out on the highway. I looked it up, Asher. I went to the paper and looked it up. Emma helped me. We looked it up and do you know how many people died on the highway out here in the last couple of years? Five. And do you know of those five, they were all the wrong sex or the wrong age except for one? It *had* to be Susanna."

It was a kick to the groin, a right hook from nowhere. Asher looked at his son, who was diving under for rings and bringing them up, one by one, stacking them on the edge. "That's insane, Jane," Asher said gruffly. "It's bullshit."

"She would be what, forty-four, forty-five now?" she asked frantically. "That means she would have been about fifteen in nineteen eighty. She obviously got pregnant when she was a teenager and gave me away. A wealthy family, Debbie said! Don't you get it? I *look* like her!"

"You don't look anything like her!" he said angrily, standing up.

"Then tell me what other woman died on a highway out here, head-on, in the last couple of years?" Jane said. "Tell me! I went to the police headquarters after the paper and looked at *their* records. Who else could it have been?" She suddenly jumped up and strode to the guesthouse.

Asher followed her. He threw open the door and stood on the threshold so he could watch Levi. "Jane, you're being ridiculous. This is crazy! I am certain Susanna did not have a baby when she was fifteen years old! Did Mr. Wright have any more information than that?"

"No. That was it," she said. She was pacing, her hand on her forehead. "But it all makes sense, Asher, think about it! I can't believe this! I fell in love with a man who was married to my *mother*. It's almost . . . incestuous."

"Jesus Christ, stop saying that!" he snapped. "This is cleared up in one phone call. I will call Helen and ask her."

"Yes! Yes, call her, please call her and ask her!"

He took his cell phone off his belt and punched in Helen's number. He got Bill. "Bill, I have something very serious to ask you," he said. "Is it possible that Susanna had a baby when she was fifteen?"

"What?" Bill exploded. "What the hell kind of question is that?"

"Did she?" Asher demanded and held out the phone so Jane could hear.

"Hell, no! I don't know what you're talking about, Asher, but you better not be saying something like that in front of my grandkids! What kind of girl do you think we raised? Hell *no* she didn't have a goddam baby when she was fifteen. Where the hell did that come from?"

"Thanks, Bill. I didn't think so. I'll talk to you later," Asher said. He clicked off and stared at Jane.

"I don't know what to think," Jane said. "Who else could it be? If my birth mother died in a traffic accident in the last two years out here, it had to be Susanna, because it couldn't have been anyone else."

"Then your mother didn't die on a highway out here in the last two years! It was some other highway, it was some other woman. My wife was not your mother!"

Jane said nothing. Her eyes teared up, and she folded her arms. "I'm going back to Houston."

His heart sank. *"Why?"*

"Because it's just too much, Asher," she said tearfully. "This has really freaked me out. I hear what you are saying, but I can't get the possibility out of my head, no matter how remote it is. I have to go home. I have to go to work or lose my job. I have to finish my thesis, I have to get on with my life and stop playing like I am lady of this house. I'm not. I should never have come here; I should never have left everything behind. They all warned me, but I wouldn't listen."

"Warned you about what?" Asher asked angrily. "That you might fall in love?"

"No! That I might find out things I don't want to know, and trust me, this is not something I wanted to know. Falling in love was . . . it was something that happened along the way."

Asher took a step backward, physically repelled by that. "Wow," he said. "And here I thought you were the best thing to have happened to me in a long time."

"Don't do that," she said angrily.

"Me? What about us, Jane? What about the kids?"

"What about us, Asher? We are seeing each other in secret. Your kids obviously aren't ready for you to move on. Riley won't even speak to us. Levi misses his mother. You know they aren't ready—you admitted as much this morning. *You* aren't ready to broach it with them. There are just too many issues, and now *this.*"

"But *this* isn't true, Jane. You are freaking out, you are blowing this way out of proportion."

Jane gazed sadly at him. "Am I really? I am living in Susanna's shadow here, one way or another. She is everywhere. She is in your children's hearts; she is in your every memory. Her art and her pictures fill this house. Even this house is her creation. That alone would be enough to deal with under any circumstance, but now that there is even a shadow of an ugly doubt, no matter how improbable, I can't just let it go. Add that to the fact that your kids aren't ready for you to move on, and that I have all these questions about myself . . . Asher, I have to leave. I have to get centered before I can be part of us."

Asher felt panicked. She was too important to lose this way. If he did lose her, he couldn't imagine what would happen to him. "I am begging you, Jane," he said quietly. "Don't do this. We can take her pictures down—"

"It's not that," she said, exasperated now. "Okay, what if you did take them down. What would you tell Riley and Levi?"

He hesitated, picturing that scene with his kids.

Jane choked on a sob and dropped the things she was holding. She slipped her arms around his waist, pressed her check against his chest. "I'm sorry. I'm so sorry. I would give the world to be what you need, Asher. I would."

"But you *are* what I need."

"You've already been through so much. I can't put you through more."

Asher's arms hung limply at his side. He couldn't think, he couldn't feel. He was suddenly numb. He thought of the day they'd buried Susanna. He'd held Levi in his arms, the boy's head on his shoulder, asleep, exhausted from the long day's events. Riley had stood beside him like a little statue. He remembered thinking how odd it was that the sun had been shining and people around the world had been going on about their business when something so profound and jarring had interrupted their lives.

He felt that same way now. He could hear Levi splashing in the water, and all he could think was that the world was spinning on as he was silently imploding. "Do what you have to do," he said shortly, separated from Jane, and walked out of the guesthouse.

He fished Levi out of the pool and suggested that he, Levi, and Riley go to town for a burger. He had to get out of Summer's End.

They ended up at Whataburger, where Riley sat with her head down, texting, and Levi talked and talked about something he'd seen on television. Asher smiled. He nodded. He said things like, "Really?" and "Wow," but he never heard a word his son said. All he could think was that Jane was leaving them. Not just him, but Riley and Levi. Levi had been a self-destructive, bedwetting little mess when Jane had come. Now he was a happy boy and the proud owner of a very large vegetable garden. Riley had blossomed right before his eyes since Jane had stepped into their lives. She was turning into a young woman, was growing up and out and had an infectious laugh and a beautiful smile that Asher had once feared he'd never see again.

Jane was leaving. The earth was tilting too far on its axis.

At home, Riley went to her room and locked the door. Asher set Levi up with a *SpongeBob SquarePants* marathon and walked out to the guesthouse.

Jane's hair was wet and pulled back into a knot. Behind her he could see an open suitcase stuffed full and a couple of boxes. "You're running away. You know that, don't you?"

"I'm being smart," she said quietly. "I don't see how I can be with you when I can't really *be* with you. I want us to be the best, Asher, and I would hope you want that, too. But until things settle for us both, this is the only thing I can do in good conscience."

"And then what? You'll come dancing back here? I'm not sure we'll be up for that," he said angrily.

Her face fell. "I hope that's not true."

"You're not the only person to ever have been adopted, Jane."

"Don't," she said. "Don't lecture me about being adopted. I have thirty years of living with it. You've had, what, a few weeks of knowing about it? You have no idea what it feels like."

"Maybe I don't," he said. "But I do know what it's like to twist in the wind, and that's no life."

She sighed, ran her hand over her hair. "Did you come out here to fight?"

"No. I came to see that you are really leaving. I don't understand why you can't stay and work this out. I don't understand what you are going back to."

"Oh, Asher," Jane said, tears filling her eyes. She pressed her hand to his heart. "I am so sorry."

"Stop saying you're sorry," he said angrily and pulled her hand from his chest.

"I don't know what else there is to say," she said tearfully. "I've tried to explain it, but I am obviously doing a poor job."

"You've said enough, Jane, trust me. Let me say something now. Don't pass up this chance at true happiness, because God knows you will regret it. I know what it's like to be held back by the unknown. I know what it's like to be chained by the expectations of others, and to give up everything you are to meet them. It makes for a very long life, Jane. No one gets many chances for happiness in this world, and you are a fool to squander yours."

He didn't know what he thought she would say to that, but as she said nothing, and looked at him with tears in her eyes, he walked out. He couldn't look at her another moment without crumbling.

The Price family assembled on the drive Saturday morning to see Jane off. Riley said a stiff good-bye, only because Asher made her, and promptly returned to the house. Jane had expected that, but she hadn't expected it to hurt quite like it did.

Levi, on the other hand, had taken Jane's leaving very hard. He'd cried when Jane had told him she had to go back to Houston. She'd tried to soothe him, but poor Levi hadn't understood why and had fled outside, where he'd proceeded to destroy his garden, save one tomato plant. Yet Saturday morning, he presented her with a painted rock as a gift. "I made it in camp."

It was painted orange, Levi's favorite color. There were white spots on it, which Levi explained was snow. Tears blinded her, and Jane could feel her heart breaking. She hugged Levi, kissed his cheek, and told him she loved him.

But the worst was Asher. He stood in the drive, his hands shoved in the pockets of his jeans, his jaw clenched. "Safe trip," he said woodenly.

"Thank you. I guess this is it," she said solemnly. For someone who hadn't dated that much in her life, Jane had done a lot of breaking up this summer, and it sucked. "Thanks for everything, Asher."

He snorted and looked away.

"You can't know how sorry I am things have turned out like they have, but I . . . I'm sorry."

"So you've said. On several occasions."

She debated telling him how much she loved him, but thought that would add salt to the very open wound between them.

She meant to get in her car, but she leaned down to kiss Levi once more, and when she straightened, she impulsively grabbed Asher and hugged him tight. He looked so forlorn, like he needed someone to hug him, and she couldn't bear to see him like that. When she put her arms around him, he stood like a wooden soldier.

For a moment.

But then he sagged against her, one arm going around her back. He pressed his face to her hair and whispered, *"Don't go."*

Oh yeah, she'd done a number on the whole family in her search for herself. She should have driven off the edge of the earth and ended all their agony, including her own. It was beyond her ability to understand how she could love someone like she loved Asher and walk away from him.

Maybe because she did love him so much.

34

*T*he summer heat was oppressive. Most days were over-cast in the mornings and hazy and humid in the after-noons. Asher quit running the lake trail and used the treadmill at work instead. Everyone assumed it was the heat. No one knew it was that he couldn't bear to set foot on that trail after Jane had left. Every step, every breath, reminded him of her.

She'd been gone two weeks, two miserable weeks, and Asher had spent every single day missing her in a way he could never have missed Susanna. He was angry with himself for missing Jane. He was angry with her for leaving.

Levi moped about in her absence, too. He'd wet the bed the night she'd left and complained that Mommy was stomping around in the attic. If summer camp hadn't ended when it had, Levi would have been kicked out. His behavior there went from good to horrible in the course of a week. There was nothing Asher could say to Levi to help ease the loss of Jane.

Fortunately for Asher, as kids have a way of doing, Levi bounced back after a few days and seemed, at least on the surface, to be okay.

As for Riley, if she missed Jane, Asher would be the last to know it. She'd suddenly developed friendships and managed to stay gone from the house. Asher didn't like it—she'd been such a loner the last two years that it seemed unnatural to him that Riley would suddenly be the social butterfly. But his temporary nanny, Tiffany—a glorified high school babysitter—knew nothing about thirteen-year-olds and allowed Riley to do whatever she liked.

"I'm working on it," Tara assured him when he asked about the search for a new nanny. "They are hard to come by out there in the hinterland."

And then there was him. Asher had been dealt an invisible blow, although no one could see the bruises. He existed in his own little world. He knew every stripe, every curve, every tree on the road between Cedar Springs and Austin. He knew how many steps there were from his room to his office. He knew all the bumps in the ceiling, all the places the carpet needed to be tacked down or replaced. He knew the exact figures on the BMW account, that Levi hated peas and Riley liked yogurt and how much detergent to put in the washing machine. But he didn't know how he was going to get over Jane Aaron.

The days slid one into the other, and with them, Asher felt himself sliding back into his black hole. When work took him to New York, he was glad to go, to get away from Summer's End, where he missed Jane the most.

The kids stayed with Helen. When he came back, he drove out to Helen and Bill's lakefront home to pick them up. He found Helen outside, sitting beneath a fan on her covered deck. Levi and Bill were down at the water's edge, fishing.

"Where's Riley?" he asked when he'd greeted them all and settled in for iced tea with Helen.

"She's at the movies with her friend Tracy."

"Again?" Asher said wearily.

"Linda Gail said she'd bring them home."

"Daddy, look!" Levi said, running up to the deck. He held out a colorful fishing lure. Tiny beads of perspiration formed on Levi's brow, but the kid didn't notice; he was having too much fun.

"Very cool," Asher said.

"We're fishing!" Levi shouted happily, pointing at the lake.

"Nice to see you, Ash," Bill said, walking up behind Levi. "You don't get out here much anymore."

"No," Asher said. "I've been swamped." Honestly, he couldn't remember the last time he'd been out here, other than to pick the kids up or drop them off.

"Ever take that boat out on the lake?" Bill asked, referring to the boat Susanna had insisted Asher purchase a few years ago.

"No," he said. "I ought to sell it." He ought to sell Summer's End and move to Austin.

"Well I guess that was always Susie's fun anyway, wasn't it?" Bill said, and took Levi's lure to attach it to a fishing pole.

When Susanna had been alive, they'd gone out every weekend, usually with friends. *Her* friends. Friends who had drifted in and out of their lives, friends who'd never seemed to make it past one manic episode. Susanna would just find more.

"What time will Linda Gail have Riley home?"

"By seven," Helen said. "Ash, we need to talk. I'm worried about Riley. She doesn't seem to feel well lately."

"That's because Daddy and Riley *fight*," Levi said, then punched the air. *"Pow!"*

Asher smiled ruefully. "We don't fight, buddy. We have disagreements."

"Come on, Levi, let's catch some fish," Bill said.

"Well, she's thirteen, Ash," Helen said as Bill and Levi walked down to the water. "You have to allow for the fact that thirteen-year-old girls will not agree with you on most things. Oh, how I wish Susanna were here, don't you? She had such a way with Riley, didn't she?"

"Yes," Asher said, looking at Helen curiously. "She certainly did." Susanna and Riley had been close, but Helen also knew that no one could antagonize Riley quite like Susanna had been able to.

"She was an angel," Helen said with a sigh. "My beautiful angel girl."

"Watch!" Levi shouted to Asher, and cast his line with Bill's help.

"Do you know what I was thinking about the other day?" Helen asked pleasantly. "I was thinking about the winter we all met in Rio for Carnival."

Asher could not begin to guess where Helen was going with this.

"Do you remember how beautiful Susanna looked that night we attended the Golden Ball?"

He remembered all too clearly. "You're making yourself sad, Helen," he said shortly and leaned forward in his seat.

"It doesn't make *me* sad. My memories give me some peace. Remember, she wore that deep red dress that fit her like a glove. And that elaborate black mask, as black as her hair," she said, wiggling her fingers at her face. "Remember how the heads turned as she walked through that crowd?" Helen laughed. "You must have been so jealous that night."

Asher peered at her. "What are you doing, Helen?"

She looked surprised. "What do you mean?"

"You know what I mean. This little trip down memory lane. What's it all about?"

Helen's gaze was shrewd. "Well, I guess I thought perhaps you might need a gentle reminder of how beautiful and lovely your wife was."

"I don't know why you think so, but perhaps you need a gentle reminder that she's dead," he said curtly.

Helen gasped.

"She's dead, Helen. She was beautiful and lovely, but she was also very sick. Do you know what I remember when I think about that ball? I remember how much she drank."

"All right, Ash, you don't need to—"

"I think about how she danced provocatively with men she didn't know until I had to pull her away. And how subdued she was the next day, so vulnerable and lost in herself, because she was beginning to cycle, and there we were, away from her doctors in a goddamn foreign country. I remember how beautiful she was, Helen, but I remember everything else, too."

Helen glared at him. "Susanna was my only child! I want to remember her how she was in the best of times, just like any mother would. I don't want you to ruin that memory for my grandchildren by getting involved with the *help*."

Riley. Asher's pulse began to pound in his neck. He sucked down a breath to keep himself from erupting. "Jane was not the *help*. And you have no right, no say in who I see or don't see."

"Grandpa, I have a bite!" Levi shouted gleefully.

Asher stood up and glared down at Helen. "I will move on with my life, and so will my kids. We are not going to spend our lives idealizing a woman who was as brutal as she was loving—and neither should you, Helen."

He walked away, down to the water, ignoring Helen's gasp of indignation.

35

*J*ane had been back in Houston a couple of weeks when she ran into Jonathan. "Yes, I'm back home," she confirmed when he asked. "Still teaching, still working part-time at The Garden."

"That's great, Jane," he said. "What about your thesis?"

"I have three weeks left, but I am making progress. I've written the intro and edited what I had. Things are really coming together!" She probably said that a little too enthusiastically.

"Sounds like it," he said, nodding approvingly. "So . . . have you given up looking?"

"I haven't given up. I've just run out of ideas." She laughed.

So did Jonathan. "Well, at the very least, maybe you'll be reasonable about it now."

Jane gulped down her laughter. Be *reasonable* about it? She realized then what had been in the back of her mind for a long time. Jonathan thought the hunt for her birth mother was a whim. He'd indulged it; he'd been indulging her all along, thinking she'd been playing at things that meant quite a lot to her. "I haven't given up hope yet," she said coolly. Maybe she'd finally come to terms with the fact that, in spite of a few lingering doubts she had about Susanna having given birth to her, she would probably never know if she was Spanish or Italian or whatever, or if she was predisposed to any illness or to longevity. She hadn't really analyzed it, she only knew that a tiny door had opened in her heart and somehow she'd made herself step through it. She still didn't know exactly where she belonged, but she had hope she would learn to adapt.

She thought about Asher and the kids every day. When she and Nicole had gone shopping for supplies for their classrooms, she'd wondered if anyone had thought to take Levi to get his school supplies. One night at the restaurant, when a couple had come in with a sullen teenager with a cell phone, she'd pictured Riley's blonde head bent over her phone.

Asher weighed most heavily on her mind. She thought about him so much that she ached with memories that bent her back, stooped her shoulders. She relived their lovemaking a million times over, remembered the way he'd looked at her when he'd been inside her. She thought of his smile, so startlingly warm, of his hand, light but possessive, on her back. Or how he would push her unruly hair from her face. She thought of their conversations, especially those they'd had in bed, when they'd been listening to the night air rustle the leaves of a cottonwood outside her window. They'd talked about everything. *Everything*.

Jane thought of Asher all day, every day.

She denied anything was wrong to Nicole, although she confessed something had happened. "Summer fling," she said airily one afternoon when she and Nicole took Sage to the park.

Nicole was dumbstruck. For a moment. "You had a *summer fling* and you didn't tell me?" she cried, punching Jane in the arm.

"Yep. But it's over," Jane said, focusing on the monkey bars.

"Really? Because you've seemed really preoccupied lately."

"With my thesis," Jane said. *Yes, deny it. That keeps tears at bay.* "I am so close, did I tell you?"

"Who cares about your thesis? Are you going to tell me about the fling?" Nicole asked excitedly.

Jane smiled and shook her head. "Another day, okay, Nic?"

Jane denied it to her mother, too. "I'm just bummed, Mom. I really wanted to know more about my birth mother." She had told her family that her birth mother had been killed in a car wreck and had left it at that.

Jane also denied it to her family at dinner when Eric asked bluntly why she was so down.

"I've just been through a lot this summer," Jane said patiently.

"I guess so," Eric said. "I mean, a, you went to look for a mom who really means nothing to you," he said, holding up her index finger. "And b, you didn't find her, go figure, and c, now you're home with a family who loves you. So lighten up, sis."

"Eric!" her mother said.

"Mom, I don't know why we have to tiptoe around it," Eric said with a shrug. "Janey was adopted. So what?" He pushed back from the table and looked at Jane. "I say get over it."

Terri's gaze flew to Jane. "Oh, honey—"

"No, it's okay," Jane said. "He's right."

All heads turned toward Jane.

Jane shrugged and stood up, picking up her plate. "He *is* right. We all know he is. I do need to get over it. It's dominated my life for the last couple of years and honestly, it's not worth another moment. I am so lucky to have one of the best families on the planet, aren't I? You guys are the best." She smiled at their surprised faces, their sighs of relief, and walked out of the dining room.

But I'm not blonde like you. I'm not tall like you. I can't cook like you.

On the Thursday before Jane was due to start back to work in the classroom, her mom called her and told her to stop by the restaurant. "You have a letter here."

"From who?"

"I don't recognize the handwriting," her mother said. "But I think you should come and get it."

Curious, Jane drove down after the lunch rush. Her mother was in the office, a pencil stuck behind her ear, her reading glasses on the tip of her nose as she pored over the books. "There it is," she said, pointing to her father's desk across the room without looking up from her task.

Jane walked to her dad's desk and spotted it almost immediately, because the envelope had been colored. "Oh, my goodness," she murmured.

Inside the envelope was a crude drawing on orange paper of Levi and, Jane presumed, Riley, standing by a tree. Snow was falling all around them. Levi had carefully scrawled his name across the bottom of the picture.

There was more.

Levi wants you to know that he didn't wet the bed last night and he has four new tomatoes on his plant and that Jorge built a fort so the coyotes can't get them.

That was all Riley had written, but it was enough. Jane sank into a chair and read the letter again. And again.

"The suspense is killing me."

She'd almost forgotten her mother was in the room. "It's from Levi and Riley." To Jane's horror, tears suddenly sprang to her eyes. She held the picture up.

Her mother got up out of her chair and walked across the room to have a look. She smiled. "Snow in August sounds wonderful." She pushed her glasses to the top of her head. "Are you going to tell me, sweetie?"

"Huh? Tell you what?" Jane asked as she wiped her eyes.

"Tell me what's really bothering you."

"Mom, honestly, nothing is bothering me. I'm fine."

"Don't tell me that. I know you like I know myself, Jane Aaron, and I know when something is bothering you." She ran her hand over Jane's dark head. "Was it him?"

"Jonathan?"

Her mother frowned. "No, not Jonathan. Mr. Price."

Jane's cheeks bloomed. "What makes you say that?"

Her mother chuckled and pulled up a chair. "Maybe because you blush every time I mention him. Or because of things you've said, like 'Asher says this, and Asher says that.' Or maybe it's because once you broke up with Jonathan, you never looked back, and I know how hard that is to do once you've loved someone—unless you love someone else even more."

"Wow," Jane said. "I'm impressed."

Her mother laughed. "It comes from fifty-three years of solid living. So are you going to tell me?"

Jane looked at Levi's letter. "Are you sure you want to hear it?"

"Every word," her mother assured her.

So Jane told her mother about her extraordinary three months in Cedar Springs.

She told her how she hadn't liked Asher at all at first,

but how she'd begun to see a different side of him, and he of her. She told her about how hard it had been to befriend Riley, who had seemed so lost, and how Levi had been a little boy in desperate need of attention. She told her mother about Cedar Springs, and the cactus and the old trucks that drove up from the valley to sell farm produce on the side of the road, and a big Victorian house in the old part of town with the carvings on the little spires. She told her about Carla, and Laru, and Linda Gail, and Emma, and all the people she'd met during her search.

She also told her that Susanna had been everywhere, and how she'd slowly learned something had been wrong with Susanna, and what Asher had finally confessed to her about his late wife, and all that the family had been through. And how, in the end, everything had come full circle back to Susanna. Jane told her mother that as much as she loved Asher, she couldn't live in Susanna's shadow, especially if there was any hint that she might have been connected to Jane somehow.

Jane told her mother how deep she thought her love ran for Asher, and how it hurt her that there probably wasn't a future with him.

Her mother listened, asked a few questions, and then stared at Jane thoughtfully. "What?" Jane said, smoothing her hair back self-consciously.

"What did Asher say about your leaving?"

"He wasn't happy. But the kids weren't ready for him to be in a relationship, and I had my thesis and my job . . . and, you know, I felt like I had to get my life back on track."

"It seems to me your life is on track, Jane. You've almost finished your thesis. You can teach anywhere. And as disappointing as it is, you have a pretty good clue that your birth mother is gone. What other issues are there for you to resolve?"

"What about that tiny doubt about Susanna that stays in my head?" she asked, fluttering her fingers at her head. "I don't see who else it could have been."

Her mother smiled a little. "Look, I know it's possible that a girl could get pregnant and have a baby by the time she was fifteen, but that is awfully young. Susanna came from good stock. I don't think it was her, either."

"Mom, Emma and I went through the traffic deaths on the highway for three years. I even went to the police station and looked at their records. Those I found were either too young, or the wrong sex, or died in a rollover and not a head-on crash. There were only two women who died in a head-on collision by Cedar Springs in that time frame, and that was Susanna and the older lady she hit."

"How old?"

Jane shrugged. "Sixty something, mid-sixties. I don't remember."

"Why are you so convinced that your birth mother was young?"

Jane snorted. "Well she wasn't *old*."

Her mother's eyes narrowed slightly. "Think about it, Janey. The woman in her midsixties would have been in her midthirties when you were born. Last I checked, those are some prime child-bearing years."

"Yes, I know, Mom, I thought about that, too, but a woman in her thirties would not have to sneak around to give a child up for adoption. That makes no sense."

"Really? I can think of any number of reasons," her mother said. "Maybe she was unmarried and couldn't give you a life. Maybe she was married and they had more mouths than she could feed. I think there are a million reasons a woman in her thirties might give up a child."

Something suddenly sparked in Jane. She'd never truly considered it, had always dismissed it as highly improbable. She'd assumed her birth mother had been a young girl who had gotten into trouble. She stared at her mother as thoughts began to rumble through her head. "Oh, my God," she said. "Oh, my *God*." She suddenly looked at her watch. "I have to call Emma. She'll be there another hour." Jane dug her cell phone from her purse, phoned the *Cedar Springs Standard,* and almost rejoiced when Emma answered the phone. "Emma! It's Jane—Jane Aaron."

"Jane! Hey, how are you? Are you back in Cedar Springs? I was so sorry I didn't get to say good-bye before you left."

"No, I'm in Houston. Hey, listen, could you do me a favor?" Jane asked anxiously.

"Yes, please give me something to do," Emma laughed. "I am so bored."

Jane's leg started to bounce. "Could you look up the traffic accident report for Susanna Price again?"

"Sure! Give me about fifteen minutes to pull it up. I'll call you back."

Those fifteen minutes stretched into the longest thirty minutes of Jane's life. Her mother blithely went about her business as Jane paced. "Please don't wear a hole in my carpet," she said primly.

When her phone finally rang, Jane jumped a foot.

"Sorry that took so long," Emma said when Jane answered. "Ed decided he'd come out and look at the files again, and of course he can't do that without talking his way through it. Anyway, I've got it," Emma said. "I can fax it—"

"Can you read it?" Jane asked, picking up a pencil.

"Okay." Emma read the article to Jane, landing on the one item she needed: *Sandra Fallon, 64, of Fredericksburg.*

"Thank you, Emma," Jane said. Her hand was shaking and her heart was beating so hard that she was beginning to feel a little dizzy. "Thank you."

"You bet. So when are you coming back to Cedar Springs?"

"Ah . . . I'm not sure," Jane said. "Maybe sooner than I thought."

It was Eric's idea to call the funeral home in Cedar Springs and see what records they had for Sandra Fallon. "They'll have the name of whoever it was who made the funeral arrangements."

The gentleman at Felix and Sons—Mr. Fernando Felix—was more than happy to help Jane. He got back to her within a couple of hours with the information. "I remember that one," he said. "Very small service. Just a few people. Cremation." He gave her a phone number and a name: Rhonda Robertson. "I think she was the sister or cousin," Mr. Felix said.

Armed with a name and a phone number, Jane packed a bag for the second time that summer and headed for Cedar Springs.

Marilee, Jane's principal, was very upset about her abrupt departure. "You are leaving me in an awful bind, Jane," she said. "You won't be able to get a job with the school district this late in the game."

"Then substitute teach until you do," Nicole advised when Jane told her about it. "You know as well as I do something will open up." She hugged Jane and wished her good luck.

Her family gave her a big send-off one night at supper, and the mother of all surprises was a gift from Vicki.

It was a silver picture frame for the picture of her birth mother Vicki was certain she would get. "You better scan it and send it when you get it," she said.

"But I don't even know if she is really the one," Jane said.

"Well, if she is, we all want to see her. Just hurry up and go and get it over with, will you? I can't be in the ping-pong of your life anymore without losing my mind," Vicki said and hugged her tightly.

She was set. On a very hot and humid August day, Jane cranked up Green Day on her MP3 and headed west.

36

The week school started, a hurricane hit the central Texas coast and moved inland, spreading dark clouds and rain across central Texas. It was a gloomy, wet week, and Asher felt just as gloomy and dark as the skies above his head.

He hated Summer's End now. Maybe Jane was right. Maybe he and the kids were living with Susanna's ghost here . . . although since the exterminator had come and rid the house of the raccoons that had taken up residence, Levi had stopped talking about hearing his mother in the attic at night. He had a new ghost: this week, he'd claimed to have seen Jane driving around town.

Asher mentioned the possibility of moving to Levi first. "What would you say to a new house somewhere, buddy?" he asked.

Levi looked at him curiously. "Can we have a dog?"

"Yes, we can," Asher said resolutely.

Riley, however, was horrified at the suggestion. "I'm not moving," she said. "You and Levi can go if you want, but I won't go. I'm not leaving my friends, Dad. They're all I have left."

Nevertheless, Asher put in a call to Wyatt Clark about selling Summer's End and maybe finding some ranch land. Wyatt was a hard guy to get hold of these days. He was still recovering from the shock of losing Macy to her first husband, Asher figured, and he understood what that could do to a man better than he'd ever wanted to understand.

As Asher drove through the gates of his house on that gloomy afternoon, the place looked so monstrous and empty that he made a mental note to call Wyatt again.

How strange that this place had actually felt like home for a couple of months. How funny that things could change so drastically in the space of a heartbeat.

The rain was picking up; Asher dashed inside, hung up his raincoat, and dropped his briefcase. The new nanny, Yolanda, was standing in the foyer with her raincoat on. "*Hola*," she said cheerfully. "The kids are fed and Riley and Tracy are supposed to be doing their homework."

"Tracy is here again, huh?"

"Her mother said she'd be back in a couple of hours to pick her up."

"Anybody give you any trouble today?" he asked absently.

"No, sir. Levi, he's very excited about kindergarten. His teacher sent a letter home today about the supplies he needs by Monday."

"Got it," Asher said and opened the door. "Have a good weekend, Yolanda. Be careful out there." Yolanda hurried out to her car.

After his experience with Jane, Asher had decided it wasn't a good idea to have the nanny live at the house. Not only could he not walk into that guesthouse but he also couldn't begin to imagine someone else at Jane's place at the kitchen table, or wandering around the garden in the early evening with Levi.

Speaking of which, his son had grown some monster tomatoes. Levi had wanted Asher to send the pictures to Jane, and Asher . . . God help him, but he'd lied to his son and told him he didn't have Jane's address. He couldn't stand knowing Jane was out there when he couldn't touch her or talk to her. He couldn't bear to address a letter to her.

"Carla has it, Daddy," Levi had said. "She sent my picture."

Asher had stared at his son. "What picture?"

"The one I drew of me and Riley in the snow. Jane likes snow."

Levi dashed out of the kitchen as Asher shut the door behind Yolanda, almost colliding with Asher. "Daddy, can we get my supplies today?" he asked eagerly as Asher picked him up to give him a hug.

"You bet," Asher said. Anything to get out of this house. "We'll go in a minute. Let me go speak to Riley."

"She and Tracy are talking to *boys*," Levi said and jumped up on the stairs, then off.

Not what Asher wanted to hear.

When he knocked on Riley's door, Tracy answered it. She smiled broadly. "Hi, Mr. P," she said cheerfully.

"Hello, Tracy. I'm taking Levi to the store. I'll give you a ride home so your mom doesn't have to get out in this weather. Can you let her know?"

"Sure," Tracy said and whipped out her cell phone.

He looked over Tracy's head. Riley's gaze was glued to her laptop. "Riley, you want to come with us? We can go get Italian food if you want."

"No."

He sighed. That was the way it was between them of late. "You have to eat."

"I'll find something," she said.

Tracy's smile looked like a bit of a smirk to Asher. "Can Riley spend the night tomorrow night?" she asked. "My dad is making barbeque."

"I don't know," Asher said. "You two are practically living together these days. Don't you need a break?"

"Told you," Riley muttered.

He was in no mood for Riley's attitude. "I'll meet you downstairs, Tracy," he said and walked out.

After he and Levi dropped Tracy off to a very appreciative Linda Gail, they drove across town to get Levi's school supplies. The rain was coming down in sheets, and traffic was snarled. They were stopped at a light when Asher thought he saw a red Honda like Jane's turn onto a street ahead. Fantastic. Now he thought *he* was seeing her drive around town.

"That was Jane," Levi said from his booster seat behind him.

"I don't think so, buddy. There are a lot of cars that look like hers." Did that one have the little peace symbol on the right rear bumper? He tried to see it again in his mind's eye, turning right. There *had* been something there. Yes, maybe, but no way was it Jane. She wouldn't come back to Cedar Springs and not tell him . . . would she?

Jane was very grateful to Samantha Delaney for letting her crash on her couch for a few days, although she was curious about why Jane wasn't at Summer's End. "Well, I quit to go back home to teach," she said carefully. "But I had to come back and finish up some last details on my research." *Don't ask what, please don't ask.*

"I never see him anymore," Sam said, thankfully uninterested in Jane's research. "Since you left, he hasn't been in. Kids either."

Jane was sorry to hear that. She was dying to know how Levi was doing in kindergarten, and if Riley had found anyone to take her to the mall to buy the outfits she had meticulously planned from catalogues all summer. She wondered if Levi was eating gummies instead of supper and if Riley was letting her hair grow. Jane supposed she would find out herself eventually, but first, she was on a mission.

In spite of the horrible weather, she paid one last visit to Mr. Ken Wright, who said the name Sandra Fallon was familiar, but he couldn't be certain.

Another visit to Debbie Carpenter—who was thrilled Jane had made some headway—finally gave Jane the answer she'd been seeking for so long. Debbie was kind enough to call the hospital and persuade Brenda to look in the records of the recorded births for April 25, 1980. Brenda hadn't liked it, but she'd called Debbie back a day or two later and said, yes, Sandra Fallon had been admitted and had given birth on that day.

"Congratulations!" Debbie said.

"Thanks," Jane said. She was stunned. She couldn't believe that she had actually succeeded, that Sandra Fallon was truly her birth mother. A mysterious name, a mysterious death . . . and one woman who might hold the key to Jane's past.

Jane screwed up her courage and called Rhonda Robertson.

When the woman answered the phone, all of Jane's carefully rehearsed speech flew out of her head and she said, "I am sorry to bother you, but I . . . I think Sandra Fallon might have given birth to me."

Her blunt opening was met with silence on the other end. Cold, hard, deep silence. And then a release of breath. Followed by a small gasp. "Lucy? *Sandy's* Lucy?"

Jane melted onto the floor, her phone pressed against her ear. "Lucy? My name was Lucy?"

And now, on this windy, overcast Saturday, Jane was

seated across a kitchen table with a plastic covering and bouquet of paper bluebonnets between them, as Rhonda stared at her, shaking her head in disbelief. "You look so much like her, you know?"

Jane looked down at one of two pictures Rhonda had given her of a dark-haired woman with wide brown eyes and a warm smile. In one photo, she was much younger. Rhonda said that it was taken about the time she'd gotten pregnant with Jane. The other photo had been taken a few days before she'd died. She was on a boat, holding a glass of champagne. "We'd just bought it," Rhonda said.

Rhonda, as it turned out, was Sandy's half sister. "Our mother," she said with a sad sigh, "wasn't exactly the sticking-around, nurturing type. My dad raised me. Sandy was raised by her grandmother. I don't remember much except that she was from Greece and she was really hard on Sandy."

"Then I'm Greek?" Jane said aloud, her voice full of wonder.

"Greek-Italian. Your father was about a quarter Greek. Our mom was Italian. My goodness, you're a pretty thing, Jane. Sandy would have been so proud."

"Would she?" Jane asked, looking again at the woman smiling at her in the photo. "Why . . ." Her breath caught. It was too difficult to ask aloud the one question she had to have answered.

"Why did she give you up?" Rhonda asked.

Jane nodded.

Rhonda sighed. "That Sandy," she said sadly. "She was never really settled, you know? She bounced from man to man, and let me tell you, it seemed to me she had the pick of the crop. Oh, I used to look up to her. She was eight years older than me and I thought she was a goddess. She was smart, and educated, and so stylish. She put herself through law school and worked at some big downtown law firm. She never wanted to settle down and have kids or that sort of thing. She wanted a career, and to travel and see the world."

"Is that why?" Jane asked, surprised by how much the idea hurt her. Sandy hadn't thought her own child had been worth settling down for?

"Goodness, no," Rhonda said. "She'd gotten involved with one of the partners of the firm. But he was married, Jane. He had three little kids. And Sandy loved him, oh how she loved him . . . but she wasn't going to ruin his life, or the life of those three children. That was the way she saw things; if she kept you, it would ruin other lives. He'd made it clear from the outset he would never leave his family, and if she couldn't be with him, she decided adoption was the way to go. She didn't want anyone to know, so I told her to come out here. Gwen and I were friends, and I knew I could trust her. So Sandy took a leave of absence, said it was a family emergency, and she came out here, and had you. She got some friend to handle the adoption."

"Did she see me? Did she hold me?"

Rhonda's eyes suddenly filled with tears. "Oh, sweetie, yes, she held you. She *loved* you. And she cried and cried when the man took you from her arms."

Jane's eyes filled with tears, too.

"Sandy heard a couple of years later that you were doing really well with your family, and she was happy about that." Rhonda looked down, shook her head, and looked up again. "Let me be perfectly honest with you, Jane. Sandy was like our mom—she wasn't cut out to be a mother herself. She always wanted her freedom. My guess is that God was looking out for you. You ended up where you were supposed to be."

Jane had never had any question of that. "What about my dad?"

"I know who he is if you want to know. He's still in Austin. He's a judge now. Sandy, she quit that job in the firm when the affair ended, and she moved out here. She married Bud Fallon, and I think she was truly happy. Then Bud died of cancer, and not six months after that that drunk driver killed Sandy. And then Gwen went . . . *Lord*." Rhonda's eyes took on a distant look for a moment. But she quickly recovered. "You know she told me once that she'd never felt peaceful after giving you up. She could never get past the pain of her choice. Right or wrong, it left her drifting for a long time, like she didn't know where she belonged."

Those words, which Jane had said so often, gave her a preternatural shiver.

She stayed for a couple of hours, and Rhonda told her everything she could remember about Sandy and what Sandy had said about Jane's father, Raymond Hilliard.

When Jane finally left, with a promise to see Rhonda again, she drove one block before she pulled over and called her mother. "Mom," she said, and suddenly burst into tears. "I found her. *I found her!*" she cried. "I look like her! She was a lawyer. But Mom . . . *Mom*. I love you. I am so glad you are my mother, and I am so sorry for putting you through this, but I had to know, and now I know, and I love you and I am so, so thankful that you are my mother."

She told her mother everything that Rhonda had told her, clutching the picture of her birth mother in her hand as she talked. And when she finally hung up with a promise to call and tell her father later, Jane felt something come over her. It was a calm. A sense of peace.

She knew. At last, she *knew*. All of the questions were

flittering away, scattering like tiny pieces of paper, because
Jane had the basic answers of who she was, of where she'd
come from. Her search hadn't ended like she had hoped,
obviously—she would never know her birth mother,
would never be able to ask her what her favorite color
was, or what she'd done all those years, or anything else.
But it was okay, because Jane knew, at last, who she was.

And with stunning clarity, she knew exactly where she
was going.

Where she belonged.

The worst of the storm passed overnight, and by early
afternoon Saturday, there was nothing left but wind, over-
cast skies, and the occasional light rain. Asher had to get
out of the house, away from a moody teen and the sounds
of *SpongeBob SquarePants* laughter. He decided to go for a
run. He asked Riley to keep an eye on Levi and started out.

He ran, his mind cleared by his breathing and the
music pumping from his iPod, following Arbolago Drive,
which looped around the subdivision, then winding back
up through the neighborhood, his rhythm slow but steady
as he took the last hill. But as he neared the gates of his
house, his pace slowed.

He stopped and stared.

Jane's red car was parked there, and Jane was standing
beside it. She was wearing a red skirt and a denim jacket,
and the hem of her skirt kept lifting in the breeze, along
with the tail of her ponytail. Her hands clasped behind
her back, she stood watching him.

Asher couldn't believe what he was seeing. He was so
taken aback that he couldn't think of what to say.

She glanced at the gate, then took a few steps toward
him. "I, ah . . . I saw you running and decided to wait
here."

Asher put his hands on his waist, catching his breath, staring at Jane. Words failed him.

"I had a little speech rehearsed, but I can't remember a word of it now," she said sheepishly. "It was really witty and sophisticated. I was hoping you would laugh. I thought it best to go with something like that, because as we both know, I'm not very good at expressing myself, but now that I'm standing here in the middle of the road, I can't think of a word of my grand little speech. Just so you know, I spent a lot of time on it." She smiled a little.

Asher was afraid to ask why she was here.

"You're supposed to be up there," she said, pointing toward the house. "You're supposed to listen to my speech and then say, Oh, Jane, I forgive you, and we fall into bed before the kids get up, and then Levi sees me and he applauds, and Riley . . . well, I'll be honest, I hadn't quite worked that one out, but then we'd make pancakes for breakfast, and then . . . then maybe the director yells cut, I don't know." She nervously brushed her hair back. "It's all ruined now, but here goes." She took a breath, planted her hands on her hips. "I am . . . I can't stop thinking about you."

Asher's heart skipped.

"I can't stop, and I don't want to stop. Before you say anything—not that there seems to be any danger of that, but just in case—I know that I left, that I said I couldn't live in her shadow and I didn't know where I was supposed to be. But I . . . things have changed, Asher. I found my birth mother, and it wasn't Susanna. My mother was the woman Susanna hit, which means, instead of the freaky thing of Susanna being my mother, it's a freaky thing of Susanna bringing us together in a . . . well, in a very tragic way for us both, but still, no matter how you slice it, Susanna brought us together. And in a weird way, that has opened up a new door, and there is sunshine and laughter and flowers and love through that door, and *you* are through that door. I hope. My God, how I hope. And even if you aren't through that door, I still had to come and say I love you," she said, pressing her hand to her heart. "I *love* you. I can't stop missing you. I can't stop wanting you. And I am here to beg you for another chance."

His heart was still pounding. "How long have you been back?"

"Four days. I've been sleeping on Samantha Delaney's couch."

He wanted to touch her. Heaven help him, he wanted to touch her. "How do I know you won't take off again?"

"Good question," she said shakily. "Well, trust would seem to be a poor choice of words given the last time I was here, but . . . I am giving you my word. I have settled all of my issues. I'm serious when I say that blue skies have opened in me and sunshine is streaming in. I know who I am. More important, I know where I belong." She took another step closer. "Asher, nothing ever felt as right as it did with you. Nothing. I believe with all my heart I belong with you."

He wanted to believe that, too. "And if I don't believe it?"

The hope in her face dissolved and tears began to shimmer in her eyes. "Then I'll be heartbroken and spend the rest of my life regretting how I left things."

"Heartbroken. Like me," he said flatly.

A tear slipped from her eye and ran down her cheek. "Like me, too. It's true. I have been so empty without you. I would have come sooner, but I really thought I should work out all the things that made me leave in the first place. But maybe I shouldn't have come here." She turned toward her car.

"You were right," Asher said.

She glanced over her shoulder at him. "About?"

"To go and work it out first," he said.

Jane's eyes widened. Hope shone in them again. "So? . . . "

Asher didn't speak—he just reached for her, held her in his arms and against his body, his face in her hair, his lips on her cheek. "What took you so damn long to figure it all out, girl?" he asked gruffly.

"I know, I *know*," she moaned.

"I've missed you. I have missed you more than I thought I could actually miss another person. I can't tell you how happy I am that you've come back."

She lifted her face to him and kissed him. Rain started to fall. A car drove by and honked at them. And still they stood locked in a tight embrace and a tender kiss.

But when the rain started to come in sheets, Asher lifted his head. "I think the director is yelling cut," he said. "Let's go tell Riley and Levi you're back."

"Let's," she said, her eyes shining brightly. He opened the car door for Jane and thought, *God, what a beautiful day.*

꧁

37

*J*ane!" Levi shouted the moment he saw her. "Jane, look!" he cried, and held up his new library book about a pair of monster trucks that go on adventures, as if she had merely gone to the store instead of leaving them for two weeks.

"Wow, Levi, that is sweet," she said and grabbed him up, holding him so tightly that he began to complain. She didn't care; she'd missed him so much. She kissed his cheeks and let him go.

"Did you come to babysit?" he asked curiously.

"No, buddy," Asher said. "Jane came back so that we could tell you something."

"*Jane?*"

Asher and Jane both turned toward the sound of Riley's voice.

She was standing on the stairs in her pajama bottoms and My Chemical Romance T-shirt, gaping at Jane. "What are you doing here?"

"Hi, Riley," Jane said.

"Why are you here? Did you forget something?"

"In a way," Jane said, smiling.

"Come down, Riley. Jane and I want to talk to you both."

"About what?" Riley asked suspiciously.

Asher took Jane's hand in his. "About us. All of us. Jane and I love each other. We are going to see each other. And we are hoping that the four of us can give it a go."

"Go where?" Levi asked.

"He means, be a family," Jane said.

"Does that mean you're going to stay here again?" Levi asked. "Are you going to take me to kindergarten?"

Jane smiled. "Maybe."

"You're kidding," Riley said. She folded her arms. "You can't be serious, Dad."

"I am, baby girl," Asher said quietly.

She looked from him to Jane. "This is unbelievable," she said coldly and ran upstairs.

"Oh, no," Jane whispered, but Asher squeezed her hand and kissed her forehead.

"It's okay. I'll talk to her." He let go of her hand and walked upstairs.

"Jane, look, I got a robot book, too," Levi said eagerly.

"Come show me," Jane said, and sat with Levi on the couch. Levi pressed against her, and Jane looked around the living room. She could see the family portrait in the dining room, and from where she sat, it looked as if Susanna was actually looking at her. And she was smiling.

Or maybe it was the light, who knew? Jane looked down at the robot book and hugged Levi tightly to her. "Let's see some robots," she said.

Asher trudged up the stairs. He was happy, very happy, and the last thing he wanted to deal with was Riley's anger. But he geared up for the fight.

Riley's door was open and she was sprawled on her belly across her bed, her feet crisscrossing in the air, her hands on her cell phone, texting away. "Riley, we need to talk," Asher said.

"Fine," she said without looking up from her cell phone.

"Can you put the phone down?"

She tossed it aside like it was trash and began to examine her fingernail polish instead.

"I am going to explain this the best way I know how," he said calmly. "I will have a life. So will you. There will be changes in both of our lives, but that's part of the deal. Everything changes. Things rarely remain the same. And if they did, we would be very bored."

"Whatever," Riley said and rolled off the bed.

"*Sit.*" He said it in a voice that suggested she not argue. Riley sat on the chair at her desk. "We can face the changes that are going to come together. That is what I'd prefer, but it's up to you. But we will face them, Riley. We're not going backward. We are going forward."

She suddenly looked up. "Face them together?" She looked wildly about. "Jane was my friend, Dad. You ruined it. You ruin everything."

That surprised Asher, but something clicked. He suddenly understood her unrelenting anger. She blamed him for Susanna's death, and now she blamed him for taking Jane from her. "Oh, baby girl . . ."

"I am not your baby girl," she said angrily. "I am thirteen. I don't care what you do anymore. I have my own life and my own friends. I am going forward."

"Riley," he said softly, "I love you all the way to the moon and back, remember? I will always be here for you, no matter what. And now we have Jane in our lives, and she'll always be there for you, too."

"So then why did she leave in the first place? Because of you. Because you couldn't stay away from her."

"That's not true, honey," he said. "She left because she

had to work some things out with her family and her job. But now she's back and she and I want to try and make us a family. Is that okay with you?"

"Does it matter?"

He didn't know how to answer that. "There is nothing I want more in this world than for you to be happy. But Mom isn't coming back, honey. I can't make you happy. Only you can do that. The only thing I can do is be here to help you."

She tossed her head and looked away from him. "Can you just leave me alone now?"

Asher stood up. He walked to where Riley sat and ran his hand over her head. Riley flinched. "You will always be my baby girl. You will always come first and you always have."

"Whatever," she muttered and dipped her head away from his hand.

Asher left her alone. He walked back downstairs and looked at Jane sitting with Levi on the couch. It would take time with Riley—the girl had been through so much. But she would come around; he had faith in her.

He could feel the darkness lifting already.

When the doorbell rang an hour or so later, Asher was in the kitchen, preparing his world-famous pizza. He walked into the foyer and saw Helen standing there, looking very disapprovingly at Jane. "I guess it's true. Your nanny is back," she said to Asher.

He didn't like the tone of her voice. "I wasn't expecting you tonight, Helen."

"That's obvious."

"I'm ready, Grandma."

Riley came running down the stairs, dressed in shorts and a camisole.

"Wait—ready for what?" Asher demanded.

"Grandma is taking me to the movies," Riley said. She avoided looking at him and Jane.

"Really? You forgot to ask permission, Riley Ann," he said curtly. "When did this come up?"

"Today," Helen said. Her cool blue gaze was fixed on Jane. "I want to take her and Tracy. I think she could use some breathing room, given everything that's happened. Don't you, Ash?"

Helen had manipulated her fair share of situations with Asher and Susanna through the years, but this was way out of line. "I think she could use some family time," Asher said and looked at Riley.

"We're just going to have a little girl time first," Helen said. "She'll be home after the movie."

"When is that?" Asher asked.

"Eight," Riley said, her gaze still on the floor.

Asher looked at Helen, then at Jane. He didn't want Riley to go, but neither did he want to force the issue with Jane. His instincts told him that would be worse. "I'd really appreciate it if you would check with me next time," he said to Helen. "We've got a lot of rebuilding to do, and I need your cooperation."

"Whatever you want, Ash. But given the circumstances . . ." She smiled.

Asher looked at Riley. "*Eight,*" he said.

"Fine," she muttered and walked out the door.

"Good night," Helen said crisply.

Asher watched them walk out to Helen's car, then slowly shut the door. He looked at Jane. "What do you think?"

"I think it's going to take some time with Riley."

"I think you're dead right," he said and put his arm around her shoulders. "I hope you brought your armor. Thirteen-year-old girls have some pretty sharp claws."

Jane smiled. "Tell me about it. But I have hope that

Riley will get used to the idea. It's your mother-in-law I'm worried about."

Asher looked out the sidelight as Helen's car drove out the gate.

"Hey," Jane said. "Where's that world-famous pizza?"

38

Asher and Jane's reunion felt magical to Asher. He couldn't believe she was back in his house, laughing at the things he said, reading books with Levi, tossing out suggestions for desserts that had him doing all the preparation and her all the eating. He was happy, truly happy. They could make this work. Love would conquer all this time. . . .

But he really wished Riley was with them tonight.

He was anxious for her to come home and was relieved when eight o'clock rolled around. By 8:30, she still hadn't come home, and he agreed with Jane that perhaps the movie had run long. He looked it up on the Internet. It had ended at 7:30.

"Maybe they stopped to get a burger or something," Jane said. "I am sure Helen wouldn't be too late."

He called Helen. "Oh . . . Linda Gail is bringing them," Helen said airily. "Didn't I tell you?"

"No, you didn't tell me," Asher said angrily. "I thought you were taking them to the movie."

"Honestly, Asher, I just dropped her off. She was so distraught about your affair—"

"Helen—"

"She just wanted out of the house!"

"Fine. Thanks. Don't show up here again to take my

daughter without clearing it through me first," he said. He hung up and called Riley's cell again. No answer.

"I'm worried," he said when Jane came down from putting Levi to bed. "I'm calling Linda Gail."

"Hello, Asher," Linda Gail said cheerfully when he got her on the phone. "The girls giving you trouble already?"

Asher's heart stopped. "What do you mean? I thought you were bringing them home from the movies."

"No," Linda Gail said slowly. "Tracy said she was spending the night with Riley. Oh, my God," Linda Gail said angrily. "I am going to kill her! Let me call her—I'll get right back to you."

But Linda Gail couldn't reach her daughter, either.

"This is my fault," Asher said after Linda Gail called back.

"It's no one's fault but Riley's," Jane said and squeezed his hand. "Don't worry. She's fine."

"Yeah, well, she won't be when I get my hands on her. I may just strangle some sense into her." That was if his fear didn't strangle him first. He pulled on a windbreaker. "I have to go look for her."

"Where are you going to look?" Jane asked.

"I don't know. But I can't sit here and wait."

"Try the Saddle-brew. I've seen kids around there at night," she said and kissed him quickly. "I'll stay with Levi. Go. Go find her, Asher."

Asher tried. He drove the streets of Cedar Springs, panicked and angry and uncertain what to do. He drove past the movie theater, down near the middle school, and up Main Street, to the square. He went into the Saddle-brew. No Riley. Fear was beginning to choke him when Jane called him to tell him the sheriff's office had Riley in a holding cell.

Fortunately, Cedar Springs didn't have a lot of crime,

and when Asher strode through the small entrance of the sheriff's office, he saw Riley on the other side of a glass wall, sitting on a bench. She seemed so small and so young. She was dirty and disheveled, her hair had leaves or something in it, and she was missing a shoe.

Asher almost broke the glass trying to get to her. When they at last let him through, Riley burst into tears. His anger bled out of him, and relief washed over him. He gathered her up and held her tight. "Jesus, Riley, you scared the life out of me," he said. He cupped her face with his hands and looked at her. "Are you all right?"

"Sort of," she said shakily, but another torrent of tears had begun to flow. "I'm so sorry, Dad. I'm so sorry."

"It's okay," he said, hugging her tightly to him again. "It's okay. I'm here, baby girl. It's okay."

He didn't ask her much on the way home; he was so grateful that she was unhurt for the most part. The deputy told him what had happened: she and Tracy and a couple of boys had used the movies as an excuse to go down to the lake. Things had apparently gotten out of hand between Riley and the boy she'd been with, and she'd tried to walk out of the woods and walk home. They'd picked her up walking along the side of the road.

Asher's heart sank to his toes when he heard that. He could only imagine what might have happened to his daughter if a patrol car hadn't happened by. He wanted to shake her for being so foolish, to rant at her for being so reckless, but he couldn't. He could only hold her hand. Tightly.

Jane was waiting when they walked into the house. "Oh, Riley," she said, touching her fingers to the leaves in Riley's hair. "Are you all right?"

Riley burst into tears again and threw her arms around Jane.

Jane hugged her tightly for a moment. "Come here," she said, leading Riley into the living room. The two of them sat on the couch. Asher remained standing, too worked up to sit. "Can you tell us what happened?" Jane asked softly.

Riley sniffed. She rubbed her fingers under her nose. "It was Tracy's idea," she said. "She really likes Jason, but she can't date yet, and so . . . so she had this idea."

She told them how Mike Howser's big brother Wade picked up the four young teens from the theater and drove them down to the public access ramp on the lake and set them free.

"It was really dark," she said. "So Mike and Jason built a fire. They had a bottle of schnapps, and Mike and Jason and Tracy were drinking it, but I didn't, because I remembered all those times Mom would get drunk and pass out, and I hate the smell of it."

Asher clenched his fist to keep from hitting something. "Didn't you know I was calling you?" he demanded. "Why didn't you answer the phone?"

"Because," she said tearfully, "I didn't want to talk to you. I wanted to be bad. I wanted to hurt you for everything you've done, for Mom dying and taking Jane—"

"Oh, sweetie," Jane said, putting her arm around Riley and hugging her. "He didn't take me from you."

"Riley, honey," Asher said as he crouched down before her. "Jane is here now. She's here for all of us. We want to be a family."

"We can't be a family!" Riley said. "What about Mom?"

"I'm not your mom, Riley, and I will never try to be your mom. But I'd at least like to be someone you can talk to. You don't have to do anything bad to get our attention."

Riley looked at her lap. "I just wanted to do something really bad, and then . . . then Mike wanted me to do something, and I didn't want to do it. I didn't want to be like them."

Asher could feel the blood drain from his face. He would kill that punk. "What happened?" he asked tightly. "What did he do to you?"

Riley seemed to shrink into Jane's side.

"Asher," Jane said quietly and put her hand on his arm. Asher looked down at her hand. "Do you mind if Riley and I go upstairs to her room and talk?" Jane asked.

He didn't want to leave Riley.

"I think she might be more comfortable up there," Jane said pointedly, and Riley nodded.

He was afraid to let her out of his sight, but he clenched his jaw and put his hand on his daughter's head. "Are you going to be okay, Ri?"

"Yes," she said meekly. She stood when Jane stood, leaning limply into Jane's side, allowing Jane to lead her upstairs.

Asher realized he was shaking, he was so angry. He walked outside to get control of himself.

Upstairs, Jane put Riley's clothes in the laundry while Riley showered. She emerged a few minutes later looking like her old self in girly pajamas, then crawled on top of her bed and lay on her side.

"Feeling better?" Jane asked.

Riley nodded.

"Do you want to talk?" Jane asked.

"No."

Jane turned to go, but Riley said, "Mike wanted me to put my mouth on him," she said. "You know . . . on his thing. Because I told him I'd done it loads of times."

"Oh," Jane said, feeling a little sick. "Did you?" *Say no. No, no . . .*

"No," Riley said to Jane's great relief. "That's when I left.

I didn't know what I was supposed to do with it, and it felt really weird."

Thank God for that, Jane thought silently. "You know you never have to do that, right? Boys who respect you won't ask you to do that if you're not comfortable."

Riley frowned. "I don't know. Everyone talks about it, and I think everyone does it. Tracy and Jason were making out, and I just had to get out of there. But that made Mike really mad and I thought he was going to hurt me," she said, tearing up again.

Jane drew a steadying breath and sat on the edge of the bed. "Did he?"

Riley shook her head. "He tried, but I ran away, and I lost my shoe and my iPhone, and it was so dark and wet and I didn't know where I was, and then I heard a car and I thought I was going to be murdered and Dad and Levi would see my face on an episode of *America's Most Wanted*." Tears were cascading down her face now. "And Dad would be so sad, because he would have lost his wife and his daughter, and I just wanted to go home, but red and blue lights were everywhere and I was going to jail!"

Jane's heart ached for Riley. She loved her. She loved both of these motherless children, and it was painful to see Riley hurt and scared and so vulnerable. She wanted to wrap her arms around Riley and keep her safe. Yes, she belonged here with these kids. She belonged with Riley now, and she moved, stretching out next to Riley on the bed. "Wow. That was a pretty bad night."

"I feel like Janis Joplin," Riley said. "I did all night. I kept thinking about what you said, how she didn't fit in with the other kids."

"I know. I feel that way sometimes, too. Like no one gets me, you know?"

"Yes," Riley said tearfully. "I don't know how guys and girls get together," Riley said. "It doesn't make sense."

"It's weird," Jane agreed. "Sometimes it seems like there is no reason for it. But sometimes, it feels like you've known that person all your life and it feels really natural."

Riley didn't say anything.

"Are you okay?" Jane whispered.

"Yes. I'm just mad. Tracy is a liar. And Mike Howser is just . . . *gross*."

Jane agreed.

"I want to move from here," Riley said. "I can't go back to school now. Do you think we can move?"

Riley said "*we*," Jane couldn't help noticing. "I don't know," she said honestly. "Maybe. Where would you want to move to?"

Riley shrugged. "Maybe Houston. We could all work in your restaurant. I mean, except Levi."

Jane smiled at the ceiling. "Maybe."

"But I'm not washing dishes. I'll be the girl out front who gives you the menus."

"Okay," Jane said. "I'll wash dishes. I'm pretty good at that."

"Just don't cook. Let Dad cook."

Jane grinned and laced her fingers with Riley's. "Deal," she said.

It was, Jane thought, a start. A fragile start, but a start nonetheless.

Jane stayed with Riley until she fell asleep. She made her way downstairs then.

The back door was open; Asher was on the patio, a beer bottle dangling from his fingers, his head tilted back as he looked up at the night sky.

It was a brilliant night sky Jane noticed as she walked out; the clouds had finally broken and there was nothing but the majesty of billions of stars twinkling above them. She slipped her arm around Asher's waist and rested her cheek against his shoulder. She could feel the tension in his body.

"How is she?"

There was anxiety in his voice. "Tired," she said. "Scared. Bewildered, disappointed, you name it."

"Is she hurt? Did that kid—"

"No, no," Jane said. "She's okay, Asher. She was smart—she got out of that situation before it got out of hand." She smiled. "Your little girl is a survivor. She's going to be okay. She's going to be great. She actually talked about all of us moving to Houston to work in the restaurant."

"Do what?" he asked incredulously.

Jane laughed softly. "At least she was talking about the four of us. I thought it was a small step in the right direction." She looked up at the stars.

"She's grounded," Asher said. "And there will be no new cell phone, at least not for a while. And I'll be paying a visit to the sheriff tomorrow to talk about this Mike Howser kid."

"I knew you would," Jane said.

Asher looked up and released a long breath. "Are the stars making you hungry tonight?" he asked, harking back to the night he'd found her floating in the pool.

"No, tonight I feel very glittery," Jane said. "Like a constellation." She used to know the constellations and where to find them, but the details had faded from her mind. "Andromeda," she said, recalling one. "Yeah, I feel like Andromeda. I'm not alone in that big vast sky, because I have my stars around me." She looked up at him. "We're a cluster, the four of us."

"We're a cluster, huh?" Asher said thoughtfully. He

smiled down at her and caught a wisp of her hair, tucking it behind her ear. "We're going to make it, aren't we?"

"We're going to make it," Jane affirmed, and looked up at what she thought, perhaps, was Andromeda—a small but glittery cluster of stars, standing out in a sea of billions.

ONE SEASON
of SUNSHINE

READERS GROUP GUIDE

INTRODUCTION

Determined to find a missing piece of her past and her own identity, elementary school teacher Jane Aaron cancels her summer vacation plans and goes to Cedar Springs, Texas, to find her birth mother. Asher Price, a wealthy advertising executive whose wife was killed in a car accident two years ago, hires Jane to look after his thirteen-year-old daughter, Riley, and five-year-old son, Levi. Around town, Jane learns that Asher's late wife had a drinking problem and suffered from bipolar disorder, making life for those around her difficult.

As June turns into July, Jane finds herself growing attached to Riley and Levi and discovers how a woman can come to love children she didn't give birth to, just as her adoptive mother must have done. She and Asher are falling in love with each other, but he refuses to talk about his late wife, whose presence still fills the house. At summer's end, Jane goes back home to her teaching job in Houston broken-hearted. But when her mother remembers a clue that takes her back to Cedar Springs, Jane learns more about her birth mother and why she gave Jane up.

DISCUSSION QUESTIONS

1. The book opens with Susanna's wild ride and her devastating car crash. Discuss the author's choice of this scene for the prologue. How does Susanna's rather glorious death inform the rest of the book?

2. Jane is intent on finding her birth mother. Do you agree with her cousin Vicki, that some things are best left unknown?

3. Why does Jane feel the need to uproot her whole life and move to Cedar Springs? What does she feel she needs that can't be accomplished in phone calls and weekend trips?

4. Jane's decisions impact those around her, but she doesn't consider anyone else when she makes her abrupt departures and returns. She also refuses to consider that her birth mother might want to retain her privacy and not be found. Is Jane selfish or just driven?

5. Jane has a fantastic, supportive family, a job, friends, and a great boyfriend. Why does she still feel incomplete? How would you feel in her situation—would you be content with the life you'd built, or would you need to know more about your past to inform your future?

6. Jane puts her life on hold to move to Cedar Springs, but once there, she is very slow to get started on researching her birth mother, and puts off her thesis entirely. Why is she stalling?

7. Do you see anything symbolic about the name of Asher's house, "Summer's End"?

8. *One Season of Sunshine* has a great cast of supporting characters, such as Laru, the small-town busybody who knows everyone; Vicki, Jane's outspoken cousin; Riley, Asher's difficult but sweet preteen daughter; and Levi, Asher's precocious five-year-old son. Who was your favorite, and why?

9. Why does Jane feel such a sense of peace from knowing her birth mother's name and a tiny amount of her history? Did she find what she was looking for?

10. Jane and Asher both discuss traveling abroad in attempts to "find themselves." Why do you think it was necessary for them to strike out to an unknown place to do so?

11. Jane says that Susanna helped bring her and Asher together. Do you believe in fate, or was that just a coincidence?

12. Why do you think the author chose the title *One Season of Sunshine*? What does it mean to you?

ENHANCE YOUR BOOK CLUB

1. Jane's family bonds over their kitchen table, sharing a family-style meal of Italian dishes. Spend an evening in the kitchen with your book club, then discuss the novel over eggplant parmesan or lasagna.
2. Jane's adopted family and her search for her birth family are both important parts of her life. Do you know much about your ancestry? Talk to some older relatives and share stories of your heritage with your book club. How does your past impact your present?
3. Susanna suffered from bipolar disorder. Learn more about this devastating illness to better understand what she, Asher, and their family went through. Check out a website such as http://www.mayoclinic .com/health/bipolar-disorder/DS00356.
4. Both Susanna and Riley are talented artists. Even if you didn't "inherit the artistic gene," bring a sketchbook along to your meeting and have fun trying to draw a still life. Or share a talent that does run in your family.

1983